JUMPNAUtS

JUMPNAUTS

Book 1 of the Folding Universe

HAO JINGFANG,
translated by Ken Liu

SAGA PRESS

LONDON SYDNEY **NEW YORK** TORONTO NEW DELHI

SAGA PRESS

AN IMPRINT OF SIMON & SCHUSTER, LLC

1230 AVENUE OF THE AMERICAS, NEW YORK, NEW YORK 10020

First Saga Press trade paperback edition March 2024

SAGA PRESS and colophon are trademarks of Simon & Schuster, LLC

Simon & Schuster: Celebrating 100 Years of Publishing in 2024

For information about special discounts for bulk purchases, please contact Simon & Schuster Special Sales at 1-866-506-1949 or business@simonandschuster.com.

The Simon & Schuster Speakers Bureau can bring authors to your live event. For more information or to book an event, contact the Simon & Schuster Speakers Bureau at 1-866-248-3049 or visit our website at www.simonspeakers.com.

Interior design by Kathryn A. Kenney-Peterson

Manufactured in the United States of America

1 3 5 7 9 10 8 6 4 2

Library of Congress Cataloging-in-Publication Data is available.

ISBN 978-1-5344-2211-7
ISBN 978-1-5344-2213-1 (ebook)

Translator's Note

As I depart from some practices commonly seen in translations of contemporary Chinese fiction (including practices that I myself followed in the past), a brief note of explanation feels appropriate.

Names

Chinese names always have the family name come before the given name (e.g., in a name like Jiang Liu, *Jiang* is the family name, *Liu* the given name—which, by the way, is not the same *Liu* as my family name). I follow that order in this text for all Chinese names. (American names like "Chris Zhao," on the other hand, are written in the "Given-name Family-name" order familiar to readers of this text.)

The practice of addressing or referring to someone only by their given name, common in Anglo-American contexts, is much rarer in Chinese culture, and practically unheard of for monosyllabic given names. Translations into English often ignore this and refer to Chinese characters by their given names only, which is awkward. That is why in this text you'll see Jiang Liu, Qi Fei, Yun Fan, and so on, instead of Liu, Fei, or Fan.

Contemporary Chinese cultural practice incorporates a complex system of honorifics, titles, nicknames, diminutives, and so on when speakers address one another (instead of simply using the given name or full name). These help speakers express a variety of social information, such as the relative statuses of speaker and addressee, feelings of respect or intimacy, mockery, empathy, exclusion or inclusion, and so forth. The nuances of the system are impossible to directly translate into English, for contemporary American society (as one example) generally does not have an exactly analogous system. I've tried to convey the social information encoded in these forms of address in other ways. However, some aspects of the system survive in the translation, such as reduplications for intimates or "adorables" (*Fanfan* and *Huhu*) and diminutives formed by adding to the family name or given name various prefixes: *Ah*, *Da* (literally "big"), *Xiao* (literally "small" or "young"), *Lao* (literally "old"), etc. Context is usually enough to tell readers what's going on—and if not, a little confusion is not always a bad thing.

Much more can be said about the use of names. (For instance, a treatise could be written on Tong Yueying's absurd insistence on calling her son, Jiang Liu, by the English name "Eric" that literally no one else in the novel uses. It is very much in line with her character, however.) But as we're all impatient to get on to the novel, I think I'll stop here.

Imported Words

Next, a comment on my decision to leave many specifically Chinese concepts such as *loong*, *fenghuang*, *qilin*, *shixiong*, *ren*, *yuanfen*, and so on untranslated. When a word has no exact equivalent in English, often the best way to translate it is to import it into English rather than come up with an awkward, approximate periphrastic construction. (I've always found the practice of translating *loong* as "Chinese dragon" or *fenghuang* as "Chinese phoenix" strange and more than a little insulting to all of us English speakers—as though we require even other cultures' mythical creatures domesticized and reframed into our own context, as though we cannot be bothered to learn a new and interesting word.) English has always been incredibly welcoming to new words, and I've often wished we could add a word like *shixiong* or *shijie* to our vocabulary. Years of standardized testing have honed the contemporary Anglophone reader's skill in inferring the meaning of unfamiliar words from context, and should that prove insufficient, the search engine is waiting right there on the personal tracking devices we've all agreed to carry with us 24/7. In the age of Google and Wikipedia, there's simply no reason to avoid the importation of new words.

A translation that reads as though it had been originally written in the target language is a bad translation—it doesn't try to challenge the reader, to show them that there are things that can't be said with the existing vocabulary and idioms and grammatical forms and familiar tropes of the target language; good translations must strive to enlarge and grow the target language to encompass a greater variety of the human experience.

However, I haven't insisted on importing Chinese words into English in every instance. For example, I adopted the (flawed) translation of the Mohist concept of *jianai* into "universal love." Likewise, instead of the much better Ruism, I've stuck with Confucianism. There are many other instances where I simply acquiesced to less-than-ideal but "standard" translations. Translators can only push so far before readers are too tired to follow them, like tour guides who venture too far from the beaten trail. I can only hope that future translators, building on my work, can import more words into English and grow our language into an even more comprehensive and beautiful instrument.

Footnotes

Some readers don't like footnotes in fiction. I won't bother trying to change their minds except to note that it's very easy to skip over them: just don't look at the bottom of the page.

As a rule, I only added footnotes where I thought it would be difficult for the reader to use a search engine to find their own answer (or where I found the answers returned by search engines to be inadequate or wrong). Thus, I didn't footnote most of the imported Chinese words or proper names from myth and history: taotie, ding, Yu the Great, Nezha, the Eight Masters of the Tang and Song, and so on. Enjoy looking them up at your own leisure (or don't bother and rely on context alone, a perfectly fine approach).

On the other hand, most readers of this text will not recognize the allusions to, and quotations from, classical Chinese texts that form such an integral part of the novel. Googling will not help because (1) the reader may not even recognize that there is an allusion or quotation, and (2) many of these texts didn't have translations that I liked, forcing me to come up with my own original translations, which cannot be found on the internet. Rather than leaving the reader puzzled, I inserted footnotes in these places to help them (and so that they now have the words to do more googling with, if they wish). The Chinese classics may not be a part of most Anglophone readers' education, but that doesn't mean they can't or shouldn't enjoy this novel.

JUMPNAUTS

Prologue

Exploding shells shook the lights in the bar.

The glass on the bar jumped, swishing the liquid inside without spilling any over the rim. Through the window, the glow of distant fire bursts could be glimpsed, which limned the angular houses stacked against the mountainside. Along the coast, a crescent of seawater sparkled, bright orange, a dab of paint where the sand met the waves.

The ocean farther toward the horizon was still steeped in darkness, like the inside of some monstrous beast. A young man sitting at the bar almost picked up the glass in front of him before restraining himself. This was already the third attack of the night.

The young man's name was Jiang Liu: about twenty-six or -seven, graceful, pale, slender jaw, neat hair that curled a bit at the tip, an aloha shirt with three buttons undone, a pair of star-shaped studs in his ears, and a smile that seemed to play hide-and-seek with the corners of his mouth—the very image of youth to break many hearts.

If he weren't forced to be on this holo-call, he would really like to drain the contents of the glass in a single gulp. But he held himself back, his Adam's apple tightening and then relaxing.

A blue glow haloed his left lower arm. A closer look revealed that it was coming from the vine-like tattoos that encircled his wrist like a thick bracelet. The blue glow projected a three-dimensional image on the bar top: an imposing middle-aged woman, hair neatly pinned up, eyebrows slightly lifted; clearly someone used to being obeyed.

Jiang Liu had a hard time understanding his mother's words. It was partly because of the noise: the bombing in the distance as well as the music and crowd in the bar. But it was also because he had developed the habit of tuning her out whenever they conversed, as though he were wearing glass cups over his ears so that he could swim through the stream of her language without letting a drop through. Listening to Mom, he felt as peaceful as being in a vacuum.

He adjusted his earpiece. From afar it looked rather ostentatious, like an ear clip attached to a stud. But despite the enhanced voice profile, he still couldn't stand listening to her.

Life is so short. How much time have we all wasted in futile efforts at communicating with one another?

Another explosion. The dark floor-to-ceiling windows glowed bright orange.

"All right," Jiang Liu said. "I understand."

"You have to do as I say this time," Mom said. "You're getting on that plane at six in the morning. This isn't a joke. I had to call in all kinds of favors to get your second uncle the Brussels flight pass through the restricted zone. All for you! You cannot slip away this time, no matter what. Do you understand?"

"Yes. Yes."

"The target for the next bombing raid is practically right next to you. You'll die if you don't get out." Mom's eyes bored into him. "I'm not kidding around."

"Of course. Not kidding."

"Also, Dad is very angry with you. You know that he doesn't like it when you get involved in disreputable situations. Be careful."

"Understood."

Talking with his parents turned him into a voice-activated answering machine. He kept on speaking without saying anything. He couldn't remember when this pattern started. When he was twelve? Ten? Even earlier? Maybe it was because his older brother and sister were always so eager to answer the parental queries at the breakfast table.

"How should one avoid losses from shifts in the exchange rate?"

"Rebalancing. Buy assets that move out of sync, to hedge."

"Better modeling and optimizing through big data."

"*Jiang Liu, your turn. What do you think?*"

"*Ah? Oh . . . what they said.*"

It was always like that. Whenever these "family exams" occurred, he never wanted to say anything; instead, he just wanted to play on his phone. His older brother and sister would give the model answers anyway.

His own mechanical answers sounded like the product of an AI. Jiang Liu wanted to grab that glass again. Just one sip. Ice-cold bourbon.

"One more thing." Mom's dark eyes locked onto him, as though trying to see through him, the same way she stared at rebellious directors at board meetings. "Don't think for a minute I don't know what you've been up to. Stay away from the riffraff. If I catch you with the wrong crowd, you're going to rue the day—"

"All right, Mother. Stop hovering." Jiang Liu disconnected the holo-call.

+ + + + +

Noticing that Jiang Liu was done with his call, the bartender strolled over. Hapa, fifty-something in age, he exuded a kindness that put the patrons at ease.

"Another?" The smiling bartender slid his fifth shot in front of him.

"Forget it." Jiang Liu waved the tumbler away. But a deep sense of regret seized him as the whiskey disappeared. He called the bartender back. "What's one more drink, right?" *Who knows how many more shots I'll get to enjoy?*

Jiang Liu believed his mother's news. His parents had a web of connections throughout Europe, the US, and Southeast Asia, updating them with the latest intelligence to protect the family wealth and business from the raging war. The looming attack Mom spoke of was probably the result of political maneuvering by the Atlantic Alliance. He was sure that the crowd around him, trying to lose themselves in alcohol and pleasure-seeking, were completely unaware of such top-secret information. Yet he couldn't dispel the feeling that these people also knew, at some level, of their impending doom. By choosing to stay on these islands, the nexus of three separate front lines, they surely knew such a fate was only a matter of time.

Jiang Liu had been in Hawaii for about thirty-two months. He had visited the islands in childhood while on vacation with his family. His only lasting impressions of the place were of the pools at the five-star hotels and the photogenic beaches. As a child, he had no sense of the strategic value of these islands, which were like a juicy piece of steak for all the major alliances.

"David," Jiang Liu said to the bartender, "can you do me a favor? Put a message on the Tianshang chain. Just say that the Pacific conflict is about to escalate, and everyone should focus on protecting their friends and families and do their best to move underground."

"Sure. Who should I designate as the source of the intelligence?"

"Don't put my name on it." Jiang Liu hesitated. "Say it's from the General Council of the World Trade Organization."

The bartender nodded. Then, casually, he asked, "Why don't you want to go home?"

Jiang Liu realized that David had heard the conversation between himself and his mother. "I don't have a home. What is home anyway? My parents' place isn't my place." He looked thoughtful. "But where could my home be in this world? For a while I thought about settling down somewhere, but now I don't think I'll ever find the right place. Even this sack of flesh and bones is nothing more than a temporary shelter. In the end, we're all vagabonds who have to move on when we die, am I right?"

David took the glass out of Jiang Liu's hand. "You've had enough." His voice was kind. "Go dance it off."

Jiang Liu reached for the drink again, but David blocked his hand with his arm. "Go dance."

Jiang Liu's hand paused in the air for about three seconds before he finally gave up. *Fine, I'll dance. If there are only hours of peace left in these islands, then I'll be merry for these hours.*

+ + + + +

The bar's separate dance room had thick, sound-absorbing walls so that all the music was held inside and no noise from the outside world could disturb the revelers. But once through the door, one immediately plunged into waves of deafening music. Immersed here, even if bombs were falling on the other side of the walls, the dancer would be completely unaware.

Swelling currents of electronic dance music swept up everyone like tornadoes, like dark clouds. The music surged around the writhing bodies, entangling itself with the mixed-reality scenes and projections, tumbling awareness and upending reality. For a time, the projected virtual background became the endless vacuum of space, and all the dancers experienced the illusion of weightlessness. Jiang Liu felt as though he had been taken to the edge of the universe. That was why he didn't notice the new message blinking on his collar for a long time.

By the time the flashing blue glow finally caught his attention, he was having trouble staying on his feet. Still swaying to the music, he brought up the message. He couldn't quite read the words with his blurred vision, but he could just make out the time stamp: August 24, 2080, 21:38.

He ignored it to dance some more.

Eventually he stumbled out of the room, his arm over the shoulder of a redhead—as though she were one of his football buddies. In heels, she was almost his height, her long legs bare under the revealing shorts. As they stumbled along, she kissed him. Jiang Liu laughed, another bottle dangling from one hand.

The blue glow in his collar lit up again. This time, Jiang Liu decided to accept the call. It was his family's chief steward, Du Yibo—Jiang Liu had always called him "Uncle Bo."

"Numbskull, why didn't you pick up earlier?"

"Uncle Bo!" Jiang Liu smiled sweetly. "I'm with a girl here. Try not to embarrass me."

"Are you really that stupid? You're about to die!" Uncle Bo grew even angrier. "I'm on the plane right now, touching down in Hawaii two hours from now. You better be packed and ready to go when I arrive."

"Two hours?" Jiang Liu smiled at the redhead. "That's not enough time at all. What's the rush? We agreed on six in the morning."

"There's new information: The bombing raid has been moved forward to dawn. You must get out now!" Uncle Bo was fairly screaming. "Also, do you remember asking me to keep an eye on that astronomical data for you? There's been a new signal the last couple days—very unusual. You should check it out."

"Wait wait wait." Jiang Liu sobered as a thrilling sensation filled every pore in his body. "Say that again, please."

"You asked me to keep tabs on that girl named Something Fan, remember? And to follow up on the data you gave me. All of a sudden, there's been a new signal; some sort of flying object—"

"Got it." Gently, Jiang Liu separated himself from the woman. "I need you to access and download the latest observations—from the solar system, as well as those white dwarves. Also, don't just focus on our family's data; get NASA's as well. And oh, don't forget—never mind, I can't wait that long. I must get back to my place and check it myself right now. Can you send over everything?"

Jiang Liu disconnected the call. The woman was staring at him in disbelief. "I'm so sorry. There is . . . some new scientific data that I have to process. I'll call a car for you, all right? I'll take a rain check on our date until the next time I'm in Hawaii. I bet you don't believe I'm an astronomer, but I really am."

Back at his apartment, the smart walls were already filled with the super low frequency radio emissions observed by the satellite network. *It's really here.* His heart pounded and his throat convulsed, suddenly thirsty.

He waved his hands through the air, a conductor of numbers and computations on the walls. It had been a long time since he was so excited by data. Observing him, a stranger might think he was practicing some exotic form of martial arts. After mobilizing all the distributed computation resources from around the world he had authorization for and deploying his long-neglected skills for filtering, he finally got the result he wanted. With a long sigh, he fell onto a sofa.

He was thinking of Yun Fan—long hair, little makeup, a cute nose, eyes that he wanted to kiss on the lids, and that determined, calm expression, cool and collected, like a drop of dew at dawn. The first time he saw her, he had no idea that she would ask him about astronomy, much less that one day he would be so excited to pursue the answer to her question. *It must be fate.*

Two hours later, the Jiang family hoverjet pulled up outside his window, right on time. A short, collapsible airway extended from the plane to anchor against his lanai. Jiang Liu took a single glance at the jet and understood immediately that Mom had likely dispatched such an outdated vehicle to pick him up because she was worried that he would commandeer something new and shiny and run away.

He smiled to himself. *Do you really think this will stop me?*

He got on with his overnight bag. The inside was furnished the way he was used to: cabin walls showing projected scenes of untouched forests and pristine beaches, a full auto-bar, and a snack drawer stocked with truffles and foie gras. Uncle Bo took the overnight bag from him and reproached him for not calling home more.

Jiang Liu waved his hand and adjusted the emissions inside the cabin to resonate with alpha waves; likewise, he changed the music to repetitive bass chords. It didn't take long before both Luka, the pilot, and Uncle Bo had fallen asleep. Chuckling to himself, Jiang Liu directed the autopilot to change the destination from Zurich to Xi'an.

That was the address Yun Fan left him four months ago.

1 | Signal

Jiang Liu tried to tiptoe his way off the plane without waking Uncle Bo, but the plan failed miserably. As soon as he opened the cabin door, a frigid blast of air forced its way in and woke the steward. The blast also made him realize that his body was definitely not ready for the sudden shift from a tropical island in the Pacific to a wintry city in north China.

Du Yibo rubbed his eyes, sat up with half his muscles still asleep, and realized that he was at the wrong airport. The sight of Jiang Liu trying to sneak away on the tarmac enraged him. He was out of his own seat in seconds and chased after Jiang Liu, who gave up the attempt at stealth and began to run like a gazelle.

"If I don't bring you home, your father is going to skin me alive! Get back here!"

"I'm sorry, Uncle Bo! I'm afraid you'll have to take my father's wrath again for me. That's what good friends do for each other, right?"

"Who's your friend? Who? What did I ever do in my previous life to deserve this? Get back here! I'm not taking the fall for you again."

"I'll be sure to make it up to you next time!"

Du Yibo chased Jiang Liu through half the airport. However, despite the encumbrance of his bag, Jiang Liu was able to disappear into the crowd. He was sorry for Uncle Bo—Dad had a way of making those who failed him feel utterly worthless. But what else could he do? He certainly didn't want to face the old man himself. Mom had already hinted that he wasn't entirely ignorant of Jiang Liu's recent doings—well, there was no way to hide everything since the blockchain was transparent and there were cameras everywhere. He shuddered at the thought of what Dad would do if he went home. Luckily, he had already shut off all communication channels before he got off the plane. This should buy him a few days of peace.

The self-driving taxi took him through kilometers of abandoned farmland outside Xi'an toward the Mausoleum of the First Qin Emperor. Jiang Liu found the scenery along the way rather shocking, like a forlorn fantasy land forgotten by time. He imagined the landscape outside the car looking pretty much the same way for thousands of years: a rectilinear grid of farm fields, squat houses made of red bricks, and a few copses here and there. The fields, left uncultivated for years, were now overgrown with weeds. He didn't know if the former inhabitants had been driven away by war or had been forcibly relocated to the mechanized fortresses nearby.

The taxi dropped him off at a complex of buildings in the middle of nowhere. The gate to the compound was Chinese Classical in style, and next to the gate were the remnants of turnstiles and other old equipment that had once guided thronging visitors. He stepped through the gate and saw the elegant form of the museum. One corner of the museum had been destroyed by war, but most of the building was still intact, dignified and immaculate. A few oversized hanzi on one side of the building proclaimed: Museum of the Mausoleum of Qin Shi Huang.

A young woman exited the museum and headed Jiang Liu's way.

It was Yun Fan. Looking the same as she did in his memory, efficient and graceful, her cheeks dimpled as she smiled, like the glow of the sun after a shower. She was in a classic white dress, with a ruffled, off-the-shoulder neckline that showed off her collarbones.

"Welcome, Dr. Jiang."

"Always a pleasure to visit a beautiful woman."

Yun Fan pretended not to hear this. "I understand you brought the data with you? Please come to my office."

"Why is it so deserted? Are you the only one here?"

"That's correct. Because of the war, the museum is not open to visitors."

"Not so good to be alone in such a desolate place. Good thing I'm here to protect you."

Yun Fan didn't change her tone. "There's no danger here."

She kept walking, forcing him to keep up. Jiang Liu found that with each step, the projected image underfoot changed. Sometimes it looked like packed earth, sometimes flagstones, and the ground was even marked with the names of different locations. Intrigued, he began to hop around, trying to see what else the ground would show.

"You're walking through a model of ancient Xianyang, Qin Shi Huang's capital," Yun Fan explained. "This was designed as a full holographic display, but since we have no visitors, most of the projections have been turned off. Only the interactive floor is left on. If you're interested, I can turn on the whole thing for you later this evening."

They kept going until they entered the museum proper. The floor in the main exhibit hall was made entirely of glass, and under the glass could be seen a replica of the underground palace of the mausoleum. As Jiang Liu looked down, he saw models of the mountains and rivers of the Qin Empire's territory, with stars reflected in the curves of the streams. There were only a few buildings here and there, sort of like observatories in the mountains and among the stars.

Yun Fan clapped her hands together, and bright lights came on to illuminate the underground palace. The flowing mercury in the river channels caught the lights, as though the Milky Way had fallen into the sublunary sphere. To realize that engineers and builders from more than two millennia ago had constructed something so magnificent and complex, a model of the entire empire to accompany Qin Shi Huang in the afterlife, was awe-inducing.

"This is only a 1:100 scale replica." Yun Fan seemed to guess what he was thinking. "The real underground palace is 168 meters by 141 meters. If you add in the tumulus over the mausoleum, the entire complex is about 78 times the size of the Forbidden City in Beijing. Also, no one really knows what the underground palace looks like because it remains unexcavated. We made this model based on the best available data."

"To build something like this more than two thousand years ago . . ." Jiang Liu was at a loss for words.

"That's how I know Qin Shi Huang himself didn't build it."

"What do you mean?" Jiang Liu was confused.

Yun Fan kept walking toward one wall of the exhibit hall. Suddenly, the floor opened in front of her, leaving a rectangular hole. Startled, Jiang Liu ran after Yun Fan before realizing that it was the entrance to an underground elevator. He followed Yun Fan into the elevator, and the cab began to descend quietly. After what Jiang Liu estimated was three or four stories, the elevator stopped, and the door opened to reveal a neatly appointed study. One wall was filled with bookshelves, while a desk in antique Chinese style was placed near the opposite wall. Behind the desk hung a delicate brush painting of plum blossoms.

"What an elegant office," exclaimed Jiang Liu. "But why do you have it in such a secretive location?"

"Guess."

"To . . . ward off people you don't want to see." Jiang Liu quirked a brow. "Or . . . to guard treasure!"

"Both correct. Tea? Green or Pu'er?"

"Whatever you have. I'm more of a whiskey man."

Yun Fan nodded. "I'm well aware. Look, let me be frank. I have a small temple here, not suitable for a powerful bodhisattva like yourself. I'd like to get started on the real business right away to give you more time to get back to your whiskey."

"No rush!" Jiang Liu chuckled. "In your company, I'm not sure I need any more intoxicants."

Yun Fan's face showed no expression as she brewed green tea. She used the first two infusions to rinse the teacups and to feed the unglazed tea pet.[1] Only after brewing the third infusion, which had the requisite restrained scent and the refined flavor, did she pour the tea into a cup and present it to Jiang Liu.

"Go ahead," she said. "You contacted me at an ungodly hour last night. What did you discover?"

"It's related to the question you asked my mentor last time." Jiang Liu took a sip of tea. It was unexpectedly scalding, and he had to smack his lips to cool down. "Aren't you even a little bit moved that I care so much about what you're interested in?"

"What did you discover?" Yun Fan asked again, looking directly into his eyes.

---

1   A "tea pet," or *chachong*, is a small clay figurine kept by a tea lover. It's "fed" with fresh-brewed tea (the unglazed clay absorbs some of the tea), and then changes color in response.

+ + + + +

He saw Yun Fan for the first time about four months ago.

It was at an international academic conference in Hawaii where Dr. Johnson, Jiang Liu's mentor and a renowned astronomy professor at the University of Hawaii, was one of the big-name speakers. After graduating from Harvard College, Jiang Liu had taken a gap year before joining the University of Hawaii's graduate astronomy program, largely based on his mentor's reputation as a leading researcher in the frontiers of human knowledge.

Yun Fan had come to his mentor's talk early and then approached him immediately afterward. Jiang Liu noticed her because she stood out from the crowd like a glowing unicorn in the woods. Yun Fan had put up her hair in a high ponytail and worn a black high-necked dress. Though she was the first to approach the lectern, she wasn't the first to ask a question. His mentor was surrounded by students, researchers, and science reporters—all peppering the academic star with queries.

Finally, it was Yun Fan's turn. "Dr. Johnson, I've noticed that in the past year, several pulsars closest to us have exhibited regular changes in their emission patterns. I believe this may be the result of manipulation by extraterrestrial intelligence."

Johnson hesitated before responding. "My research is mainly in extremely energetic electromagnetic events, such as fast radio bursts and gamma ray bursts. I can't claim to be an expert on common pulsars."

Yun Fan, however, wouldn't give up. "But you also suggested one time that some of these high-energy electromagnetic events may be the work of extraterrestrial civilizations."

Johnson was about to explain further when he was interrupted with an urgent summons to be elsewhere. But before he left, he asked Jiang Liu to follow up with Yun Fan.

Thus, Jiang Liu had the perfect excuse to ask Yun Fan out to dinner. However, it was the most boring could-be date in his memory. Yun Fan kept the conversation focused on astronomy. FSRs, next-generation occultation survey techniques, cosmic microwave background, dark matter . . . she lobbed question after question at him. He was amazed by the breadth of her knowledge. Although she lacked the specialist's grasp of the technical details, he could tell by her questions that she had devoted considerable effort into understanding these subjects. Time and again, he tried to redirect the conversation to her personal life, but she never gave an inch: either skillfully stepping around his attempts at flirting, or even openly mocking him when he vexed her.

He couldn't remember the last time he had failed so miserably with a girl.

+ + + + +

Jiang Liu pulled out of his reverie to focus on the present, determined to find out just what Yun Fan was after.

"Last time, you told me you were using the raw data from LAHEO, right?"

"That's correct," she said. "Although I did use the built-in software to do some basic filtering and smoothing, I performed no advanced analysis."

"I must confess that I'm very curious. How did an archaeologist end up being so comfortable with astronomy data and software?"

"Dr. Jiang . . . there is a human behavior known as 'learning' or 'skill acquisition.' Have you heard of it?"

"All right, then what made you decide to study astronomy?"

Yun Fan smiled. "I can't imagine why a man with a PhD in astronomy would find it odd that someone should be interested in astronomy. Surely you can answer that better than I can."

Jiang Liu could see that he would never get anywhere like this. Telling himself that he was ready to take the long road to his goal, he decided to first show her the data he brought.

The Large Area High Energy Observatory (LAHEO) was the last astronomy satellite launched by the European Space Agency before the war, with an emphasis on observing high-energy celestial bodies. The culmination of years of effort by some of the world's best astrophysicists and aerospace engineers, it represented a quantum leap over previous-generation instruments. There was virtually no possibility for an error in its data.

After Yun Fan's visit to Hawaii, Jiang Liu began to pay attention to nearby pulsars. Soon, he found that she was right. Five pulsars showed changes in their emissions, more than 10 percent in magnitude. The dips and rises in the spectrum were plain to see, and all five followed the same pattern. This was impossible to explain as an error or a mere coincidence.

Yun Fan had proposed a theory in Hawaii that the altered pulsars were serving as beacons for extraterrestrial navigators. But Jiang Liu didn't see why the functions of a lighthouse required such large-magnitude alterations to the pulsar's emissions. His guess was that the alien spaceships were using the pulsars for energy, not navigation. But such a possibility made the hairs on his back stand up. A pulsar's energy was a million times greater than the sun's, and if the amount of energy a pulsar output during a single second could be converted to usable electricity, it would satisfy Earth's current needs for several billion years. If a single alien ship could cause a 10 percent dip in a pulsar's radiation magnitude, then it was equivalent to absorbing a hundred thousand times the sun's energy output. Even if the absorption efficiency was only 0.01 percent, that would still translate to ten times the sun's energy output. A civilization capable of such a feat was unimaginably ahead of humanity, technologically.

But something else sent an even greater chill down Jiang Liu's spine. While attempting to calculate the trajectory of the alien ship based on the changes in the pulsars, he realized that the first pulsar was about 300 light-years from Earth, the second 220 light-years, the third 160, the fourth 120, and the fifth 89, but all the changes were observed within the last few months. This meant that the ship itself was approaching Earth at nearly the speed of light—the realm of science fiction.

If the aliens were hostile, Earth could not possibly come out ahead in such a conflict. Jiang Liu didn't dare to work out the full implications. Only half believing his own conclusions, he went to the satellite networks that his family could access and concentrated on data involving pulsars within fifty light-years. In addition, he directed the family's private probes near Jupiter and Saturn to scan for unidentified flying objects in the solar system.

"I've correlated the data between multiple astronomy satellite networks, space stations, and multiband radio telescopes to be sure of my conclusions." Jiang Liu used his bracelet to project the results onto the wall of Yun Fan's office, highlighting the key points in the dense cloud of data. "Look here. This pulsar is about twenty-five light-years away, and it's located on the same trajectory projected from the previous pulsars—possibly an elliptic arc. Two-and-a-half months ago, this pulsar showed the same change in its emission as the other pulsars. After that, about two months ago, a Saturn-orbiting probe detected an object entering the solar system. This object has been decelerating the whole time, and as of half a month ago, it finally passed the orbit of Saturn and is now approaching Earth. My family's own satellites only go as far as Saturn, and the rest of the data I had to get from international networks—I'm just trying to explain to you why it took me so long to put it all together and come to you. It's due to lack of data, not because I didn't care about your question."

Yun Fan bit her bottom lip thoughtfully. She didn't seem surprised by any of this. "How long until the ship reaches Earth?"

"I can't say exactly. The deceleration is not constant and hard to project. My best guess is about two weeks."

Yun Fan nodded. Jiang Liu couldn't tell from her complicated facial expression what she was thinking.

"Can you locate the ship?"

"That's not easy. The object only shows up in super low frequency radio wave data. There's nothing in any of the other bands, including visible light. That's how it was able to evade the probes from multiple countries near Jupiter and Saturn. But there's not much precision if we rely on super low frequency radio waves for location. I couldn't even be sure there was a ship until I did the calculations myself—see that red circle? That's the best I can do for a trajectory."

"Can you give me authorization to access the data you're using?"

"Sure! This is from my family's own satellite network. I don't think many networks in the world will be able to get you better data. I can get you an account. No problem."

"Thank you very much. I really appreciate the data. I won't take up any more of your time today. After I get my account, if I have any more questions, I'll be sure to reach out."

"Come on!" Jiang Liu put on an aggrieved expression. "I gave you such good data, and you won't even ask me to dinner? That's so cold. Look, my plane has already left, and I've got nowhere to go. Are you really going to toss me out on the street, hungry and exhausted?"

"I'd love to feed you, but I don't have the resources. This place is right next to a military restricted zone, so none of the delivery services would accept orders from here. I get my meals from home—Mei, my family's helper, sends them to me using a drone. But it's just enough for me, and the food is all very plain, not suitable for a princeling like Dr. Jiang."

"I eat very little, and I love plain fare. This is perfect."

"Um . . ." Yun Fan's face was on the verge of breaking into laughter. "That doesn't fit the data I have on you. My understanding is that you never eat at any place that doesn't have a Michelin star."

"Oh?" Jiang Liu was very happy. "Do I understand that you've been looking up interesting info on me?"

"You don't think you're the only one who knows how to use the web, do you?" She smiled sardonically. "Please, I think it's best that you go home. I'm sure it takes but a few minutes for you to summon a hoverjet to pick you up. I really do appreciate the help you've given me. As soon as I'm done with my project, I'll be sure to pay you a return visit and thank you properly."

"No worries. Even if you don't have food here, we can go out," Jiang Liu persisted.

"That's actually not possible. As I mentioned, this is next to a military restricted zone. No ride service would dispatch here. I usually have to call Mei to come and pick me up if I need to run an errand. But unfortunately, Mei is visiting her daughter right now in Yunnan."

"That's no problem." Jiang Liu smiled. "I'll take care of it. If I can get us a ride, then you'll come to dinner with me. Deal?"

Yun Fan finally laughed in exasperation. "I've never met anyone so shameless. What I really want to say is that I have no interest in going to dinner with you. I was trying to turn you down politely, but you leave me no choice except to come out and say it."

"Well, you didn't deny that we have a deal. *That* is the same as agreeing. So when the ride comes later, you have to keep your promise."

A few minutes later, an ancient car stopped outside the compound. It was so outdated that it required a human driver, probably one of the last manual models from the 2050s. Yun Fan couldn't remember the last time she had ridden in such a vehicle. *Where in the world did he find such a thing?*

In any event, since Jiang Liu did find a ride for them, she felt that she couldn't turn him down again. So she took a few minutes to groom herself before getting in the car with Jiang Liu.

Having spent so many months all by herself at the museum, she was starting to feel like a tree rooted in the museum grounds: alone, carefree, needing no one, sustained by the glow of the morning sun under a blue sky. She found no need for human company, nor the need to return to the bustling world. The only time she left the museum was when she needed help from the outside world, but as the signal she was seeking grew stronger, she had even less need to go away. More and more, she wanted to turn away from the entanglements of society.

Yet somehow, Jiang Liu had gotten her out. There was something . . . interesting about him.

+ + + + +

The driver was an old man—not surprising since anyone who still knew how to drive a fully manual car these days had to be quite aged. As he drove, he chatted with Jiang Liu and Yun Fan. He told them that his life was pretty good—see, he was making enough to buy a new car, and he was hoping to do something meaningful with his life, even at his age.

Yun Fan was puzzled why a stranger would tell them such personal details. Was he talking to her, or to Jiang Liu? She had a feeling that the old man knew Jiang Liu—at least the tone he was using suggested old acquaintances. But then again, the old man's questions for Jiang Liu seemed to imply that he knew nothing about the young man at all: Where was he from? How many people were in his family? And so on. Yun Fan could make no sense of it.

They had been driving through the desolate countryside for about ten minutes when a sudden strong gust of wind caught them out of nowhere. The trees on the right side of the road leaned over, the leaves flapping violently, and even through the windows those inside the car could sense the power of the buffeting air. Yun Fan looked out and was surprised to see in front of the car, on the right, a silver unibody low-altitude aircraft. Polyhedral in shape, but with aerodynamic surfaces, the aircraft made little noise despite the swirling vortices it threw up. On one side, painted discreetly, was the logo of Jiang Lang Trading Limited Company.

Ah, that explains it, Yun Fan thought.

"What the . . ." Jiang Liu muttered. "Uncle Bo is persistent, isn't he? Uncle Wang, do you mind taking a left up ahead and going down the dirt path in the woods?"

"You sure about that?" asked the old man. "With all the fields abandoned, that dirt path is full of weeds and deep ruts. We could get stuck."

A stream of bullets shot out of the silvery aircraft and struck near their tires, throwing up clods of earth. The old man swore. "What's wrong with these people?!" He stepped on the gas and turned the wheel hard to the left, plunging the car into the copse. The dense trees shielded them from further strafing.

"Isn't this your family's plane?" Yun Fan asked. "Why is it shooting at you?"

"Who knows?" Jiang Liu said, rather peeved. "Uncle Bo has gone crazy."

"Who's Uncle Bo? A family enemy who wants you dead?"

"No. He just . . . wants me to go home."

"Aha!" Yun Fan laughed. "What did you do to make you run away from home?"

"It's a very long story . . . which I may tell you some other time." Jiang Liu rubbed the ring on his left hand, and the tattoos on his wrist lit up again. This time, the projected images appeared directly on the skin of his arm. He tapped the images a few times, scrolled around, zoomed out with a finger pinch, until a red dot blinked on his arm.

"Uncle Wang, take the second right and enter the village. Once you are in the village, take the second alley on the left and stop at the entrance to the next home."

The driver followed his directions. As he parked, the silver plane caught up to them and shot again. One bullet struck a tire, but fortunately the car was no longer in motion. The three of them exited the car and leaped through the open door in front of them. As soon as they were safely inside, the door shut behind them silently.

Yun Fan was still recovering from the narrow escape when a shabbily dressed, middle-aged man came into the front room, leaning on a cane. He gestured for them to sit at the few stools around the room, then sat down himself and greeted them with an old-fashioned fist-and-palm salute. In response, Jiang Liu held out both hands and made a strange pose with each: the middle finger and pinkie extended, the other fingers pinched together. The middle-aged man and the driver made the same gesture. Then, as he stacked the right and left hands together, alternately placing the fingers of one atop the other, he whispered, "Universal love, mutual benefit."

The middle-aged man began to move his fingers in the same way, and responded, "Divisive hate, mutual harm."

All satisfied now, the three sat back down.

"Who are the people chasing you?" the man with the cane asked in a hoarse voice.

"They're not bad people," Jiang Liu said. "It's . . . my family. I don't want to go home, so they're overreacting a bit. I'm so embarrassed."

"Why don't you want to go home?" the man asked.

Jiang Liu could feel the tension in the question. He noticed the man's eyes focusing on somewhere near the door. Turning around, he saw a photograph of a boy, about seventeen or eighteen years of age, a goofy smile on his face. The photo frame was black, with a white flower of mourning atop. Jiang Liu understood that he had unwittingly stepped into a private regret.

"How are things going lately?" he asked, trying to change the subject.

"All right," said the middle-aged man, his voice placid. "Just trying to live out the rest of my years."

"Don't put it like that," said Wang, the driver. "If you think you're old, then I must be halfway in the ground already. But I think I'm still young. I can still be useful; I can still make a difference."

"I suppose if you think that way, then I ought to strive to make an even bigger difference."

Jiang Liu chuckled and broke in, "I think what would make the biggest difference right now is dinner."

The middle-aged man got up and asked the driver to help him slaughter a chicken in the yard. This left Yun Fan and Jiang Liu alone together; the silence stretched awkwardly.

"Am I going to hear the explanation now?" Yun Fan finally asked.

"That almost sounds like a girl asking why her boyfriend is flirting with another girl," Jiang Liu said, laughing.

Yun Fan refused to take the bait. "You told me that you were going to explain why your family is after you."

"You care about me that much?"

"Stop it." Yun Fan's voice was cold. "I'm trying to determine whether it's dangerous for me to allow you to stay at the museum tonight. If you don't want to tell me, that's fine. I'm leaving right now, and we can be strangers in the future."

"All right!" Jiang Liu held up his hands. "I'll tell you." He hesitated for a moment. "My father is angry at me because I carelessly leaked some details about his business dealings."

"What kind of business dealings?"

"They involve uranium."

"Oh . . ." Yun Fan looked thoughtful. Then she asked, "How do you know so many people around here? I understand that you spent your childhood in Beijing, and then went abroad for high school. How can you possibly have so many acquaintances near Xi'an?"

"The metaverse is flat, as you well know. I know you, don't I?"

"Then why did you—"

"Wait!" Jiang Liu interrupted. "You've asked me many questions. I think it's only fair that I ask a few. Why do you live by yourself at the mausoleum museum?"

"I'm an archaeologist. It's my job."

"Then how do you know about alien spaceships?"

"Because of my academic work, I'm familiar with all kinds of ancient legends and myths passed down through the ages. I simply put two and two together."

"What sort of legends and myths?"

"The Diagram of Hetu and the Magic Square of Luoshu, Egyptian pyramids, Shang bronze technology explosion, King Wu's righteous war on Zhou of Shang, Qin Shi Huang's Mausoleum, Maya pyramids . . . all the evidence of extraterrestrial intervention in human affairs is right there for anyone to see."

Jiang Liu couldn't stifle a laugh. "As a kid, I devoured books about ancient alien space visitors, too. But I never imagined anyone would take this sort of thing seriously. Come on! You can't have so little respect for me. Please make up a better story."

Yun Fan sat up, her expression completely serious. "I don't care if you don't believe me. But if you don't believe me, stop following me around. I've never lacked people who want to profess their love for me, but few would believe me."

Jiang Liu stared at Yun Fan. Sensing the melancholy behind the words, he wiped all flippancy from his face and tried to think of something to say that would comfort her. The two other men returned just then with a few simple dishes. A collapsible table slid out from one of the walls, and the rough wall turned into a screen, showing the daily news broadcast. Apparently, this was how the middle-aged man who lived here took all his meals. The dishes were plain and common—Chang'an hulu chicken, Chinese-style omelette, braised pork, stir-fried choy sum—but the preparation and flavors were top-notch.

"I guess you really are doing all right." Jiang Liu caressed the smooth wood of the table as he spoke to their host. "When we first came in, and I saw you . . . I was worried that—"

The man with the cane chuckled, looking at his own shabby clothes. "Since my son and spouse are both gone, I don't bother dressing up anymore."

"I have to compliment the chef," Yun Fan said. "Our little prince here never eats anywhere without a Michelin star. But just now, you saw how quickly he finished everything and went back for another bowl of rice. I'm guessing the sun is going to rise in the west next."

Jiang Liu gave Yun Fan a gentle kick under the table and indicated with his eyes that she should stop joking this way. Yun Fan noticed that the driver and the man with the cane looked at each other and then pretended that she hadn't said anything. The meal continued after that in this manner, with the conversation drifting from one harmless topic to another, as though everyone around the table were relatives sharing a meal, all with an unspoken understanding to never get too personal. Yun Fan and Jiang Liu both felt a sense of unreality. They each tended to come and go as they pleased, to spend most time alone, and it had been years since they had experienced these scenes of ordinary life. It felt like they had stumbled into someone else's life.

After dark, Wang first got into the car to lure the Jiang family plane away on a fruitless chase. The man with the cane then took Jiang Liu and Yun Fan back to the museum with his motorcycle. On the way, Jiang Liu gently put his arms around Yun Fan to keep her secure.

+ + + + +

Earlier that day, in a secure compound about five kilometers from the mausoleum museum, a young military researcher was being summoned to the office of General Yuan, the Pacific League's Supreme Commander of the Northwest and Central Asia Theater of Operations.

The researcher, Qi Fei, was not a military officer; instead, he was the director of a top-secret research institute operated by the military. Although he was only twenty-eight, everyone who knew him was impressed by his maturity and commanding presence. When he spoke, he was insightful and logical, authoritative and composed; when he distributed tasks and recognized contributions, he was fair and thoughtful. That was why more than a hundred researchers—including some experts far older—all supported and followed their young leader gladly. To be sure, everyone also understood that Qi Fei had the full support of his patron: General Yuan. Tall, handsome, with especially piercing eyes, Qi Fei was the sort of man that drew extra looks from women—and there were rumors that General Yuan intended him to become his son-in-law.

As soon as Qi Fei stepped through the door to the office, he noticed the overflowing ashtray on the desk: a sure sign that the general was troubled. In the seven or eight years he had known the general, he could remember only three occasions where the old man smoked so much. The general sat facing the large window, his back to the door, his view dominated by the flat expanse of the tarmac and the row of advanced fighters next to the runway. Qi Fei knew that the general had picked the office precisely because he wanted the comfort of seeing his cherished fighters anytime he wanted.

"General."

General Yuan turn around in his chair. "Ah, Xiao Fei. Please sit."

"Something troubling you?"

"Let me start by congratulating you," said the general. He tapped the surface of his desk to wake it up and summoned a new chart. "The intercept operation near Hawaii last night was a complete success. Our missile-defense system responded quickly to the Atlantic Alliance's sneak attack, and although they managed to destroy one tower and part of one runway, most of the air base survived intact. A few stray bombs damaged some nearby civilian buildings, but our strike force was unharmed. Your AI work was instrumental in this success. I'll make sure that the brass knows what you did."

"The credit should be shared by the intelligence staff. They told us a day earlier that the Alliance was redirecting its attention to the islands."

"Speaking of intelligence . . ." General Yuan sighed. "We've suffered multiple intelligence leaks in recent days, including three instances where hackers breached our network. We still don't know who's responsible."

"It's not the AIA?"

"No. We're familiar with the techniques used by the AIA. Even though they disguise their tracks with quantum encryption, there are still telltale signs we can use to identify their work."

"Then . . . maybe it's from our friends near the Red Sea?"

"I don't think so. The techniques are far more advanced than what they've shown themselves to be capable of so far."

"That's odd. General, let me look into it. I should have something for you in a week."

"Thank you." The general nodded appreciatively. "However, that's not why I asked to see you today. Last week, I sent the report you gave me about the unusual signals emanating from the mausoleum up to Central Command. They took some time to analyze it, and today they gave me the order to send someone onsite to investigate immediately."

"Why does Central Command care so much about this?"

"The signals you picked up are simply too odd. They can't decipher it, but the persistence of the signals suggests communicative intent. The super low frequency signals also aren't used in the communication bands of any of the major powers. Moreover, there appears to be some noise in the transmission that is of unknown origin." The general brought up the details in the analysis to show Qi Fei. "The most important point is this: Why is the mausoleum sending signals into space? What equipment is used to generate such signals and who installed it? The mausoleum is too close to our base, and we can't afford to have an adversary or saboteur there. You have to find the source as soon as possible."

"As far as I know . . ." Qi Fei hesitated. "The area around the mausoleum is virtually uninhabited. Only a few archaeologists—"

"That is exactly why we must be extra vigilant. The darkest shadow is at the base of the lamp. I won't feel comfortable until you investigate it thoroughly. I'm asking you to do this personally for two reasons. First, since your institute detected the signals initially, the credit should be yours. Second, the archaeologist stationed at the mausoleum is someone named Yun Fan, an old friend of yours, if I'm not mistaken. I want you to find out if she has been compromised."

Qi Fei froze for a few seconds before he recovered. "I understand."

"Qi Fei," the general said, looking at him meaningfully, "I don't think it's helpful for me to be too direct. But I believe you have good judgment. When it's a matter of duty versus personal loyalty, I hope you understand which you must uphold. After you complete this mission, we should also get the acknowledgment for your meritorious service last night. I'll host a celebratory banquet for you, which may be a good opportunity to announce the wedding plans for you and Bailu. Do you approve?"

Qi Fei lowered his eyes. "I'm sure you've thought of the best plan, General."

As night fell, Qi Fei stood atop the main building of the research institute and gazed silently in the direction of the mausoleum. For a long time, he didn't move or make any noise. In the darkness, no one could see the expressions on his face, much less what was in his heart.

2 | Mausoleum

Jiang Liu spent the night in the museum guesthouse. Although no one had used the facilities in some time, the robots had done a good job of maintaining it. An insomniac, Jiang Liu was used to the uneasy rest forced on himself with the aid of alcohol. But he was surprised at how well he slept in this deserted place away from his usual haunts.

It rained the next morning. In northwestern China, autumn was marked by chilly storms. Having flown here with a single bag from the tropics, Jiang Liu had nothing appropriate for the climate. As soon as he opened the door, the frigid air forced him back into the guesthouse. But he didn't come back in alone; a meal-delivery robot took the opportunity to scoot in right after him. The robot was about knee-height and took the form of a small replica of one of the bronze chariots from the mausoleum. On top of the chariot was a black lacquer box.

Lifting the lid off the box, Jiang Liu discovered a piping-hot bowl of soup, a few steamed buns, and a plate of fruit. The arrangement and preparation clearly took care. Jiang Liu smiled to himself.

+ + + + +

After breakfast, he found his way back to the main exhibit hall and pressed a tiny bronze-colored button on the wall. Yun Fan had told him this was the button to the intercom to her office.

Just then, the heavy footsteps of a man echoed behind him. Instinctively, Jiang Liu turned and tilted slightly to the side, subconsciously adopting a defensive pose.

A slender, very tall man ascended the museum steps. With his gold-rimmed glasses, black shirt, and black pants, he looked serious and trustworthy.

After a few tense seconds during which the two men took measure of each other, the pair said simultaneously, "Who are you?"

"I'm here to see Yun Fan," Qi Fei said.

"Why do you want to see her?" Jiang Liu asked.

"Who are you?" Qi Fei asked. "Are you here to see her too?"

"I'm her . . . agent. Whatever business you have with her, you need to tell me first."

Qi Fei frowned as he looked Jiang Liu up and down; Jiang Liu treated Qi Fei to a similar probing gaze, except with a flippant smile. The two were staring daggers at each other when the light tapping of heels on floor sounded behind them. They turned at once.

"Stop spouting nonsense, Jiang Liu." Yun Fan stopped before both men. "If you keep it up, I'll have to ask you to leave."

Jiang Liu grinned at her. "Fine, I won't pretend to be your agent anymore. Since we're living together, what difference does it make what name we give to our relationship."

Yun Fan gave him another severe look. "I've located your family's plane at the airport. I can ask my friend at the airport to contact your Uncle Bo if you'd like."

"All right! I'll stop," Jiang Liu said.

He had noticed how the man in black's facial expression had flickered through a range of emotions during the last few seconds. It was obvious that he and Yun Fan knew each other—and more than that, they had a history. Surreptitiously, he raised his hand and snapped a picture of the other man with the camera in his ring and then twisted the ring to send the AI agent within it on a search for information about the man.

At the same time, Qi Fei had done the exact same thing to him, except in his case it was by casually tapping the right temple of his glasses with two fingers. Unbeknownst to Qi Fei, Jiang Liu caught the gesture (and Jiang Liu was also aware that Qi Fei had seen his own attempt).

"How can I help you?" Yun Fan asked Qi Fei.

"I have to ask you something," Qi Fei said. He took a glance at Jiang Liu and then added, "But it has to be just you."

Jiang Liu laughed. "What a coincidence! Fanfan, I also have something I can only tell you when we're alone."

Qi Fei tsked scornfully. "Has no one taught you that it's rude to insert yourself into a conversation that has nothing to do with you?"

Jiang Liu kept on smiling. "Has no one taught you that it's rude to criticize and judge others when you know nothing about them?"

Yun Fan broke in. "Enough! Both of you, follow me to my office." She turned and walked away.

Jiang Liu rushed after her. But he had taken barely two steps before he felt a heavy weight on his shoulder pulling him back. Instinctively, Jiang Liu's left arm shot up to block, and Qi Fei let go of Jiang Liu's shoulder and switched to a grappling hold to seize his left wrist. Jiang Liu slid his left hand forward to escape the hold and turned it into a palm strike at Qi Fei's waist—a strike that Qi Fei dodged with a quick sidestep.

Yun Fan looked back and saw that the two men, though looking at each other warily, were following her without complaint. Reassured, she turned back around—having missed their fight altogether. Although the entire sequence had taken no more than a second, each man had ascertained the other to be a skilled opponent in close combat.

Once in the office, Yun Fan poured tea for both in identical teacups; she scrupulously made sure that even the amount of tea in each was the same.

"Who wants to talk first?" Yun Fan asked.

Neither said anything.

"I'm not going to be alone with either one of you. If you have something to say, say it right now."

Jiang Liu and Qi Fei looked at each other.

"I'll go first," Jiang Liu said. "Last night, I did some more processing on the SLF signals. The trace is a lot clearer now. The time estimate I gave you before was basically right. What do you want to do next?"

Yun Fan pondered this. "Do you have a way of contacting them?"

"I'm not sure. But if you agree, I can take you to a place where we can try something that may work."

"Where?"

"I can't tell you yet. But it's worth trying."

"Let me think about it." Yun Fan bit her bottom lip. "If—"

"I won't allow it," Qi Fei interrupted.

Yun Fan stared at him. She had maintained an unusually serious expression from the second she saw him. Although she never directly met his eyes, she seemed to pay attention to every move from the man, even when she was walking or scanning through some document. When she turned so that one of her sides faced Qi Fei, the muscles on that side seemed especially stiff. The tension between them was like an invisible wall. Even Jiang Liu sensed it.

Yet, as Qi Fei spoke for the first time in the office, Yun Fan also looked directly at him for the first time, astonished. The wall in the air seemed to develop an invisible crack, behind which loomed a flood of emotions. It was the last moment of calm before a storm.

Qi Fei seemed to regret his rash outburst. Adopting a calmer tone, he said, "I'm here to investigate unusual signals being transmitted from the mausoleum pursuant to a warrant from the Alliance. No one is allowed to leave the museum campus without my authorization."

"What signals do you mean?" Jiang Liu asked.

Qi Fei kept his face expressionless as he intoned, "Recently, we discovered that some source within this compound has been sending out SLF signals, and the signal has been getting stronger over time. We have grounds to suspect unauthorized transmission equipment being used for espionage communications."

"You have SLF transmission equipment here?" Jiang Liu was amazed.

"I have no idea what you're talking about," Yun Fan said.

"Did you install a new transmitter recently?" Qi Fei asked.

"Do I look like someone who can install radio equipment?"

"I didn't think it could be you," Qi Fei said. "I suspect some other organization with nefarious purposes is taking advantage of your semi-deserted compound." He glanced meaningfully at Jiang Liu. "Have you been away from the museum for extended periods during the last half year? Do you have a log of visitors? Did you tell anyone else how to gain entry to this place?"

"You don't need to dig anymore," Yun Fan said. She didn't seem fazed by the barrage of questions. "Although I know nothing about SLF transmitters, I think I have an idea about the communication attempts you're referring to. I didn't install the equipment responsible, but I assure you it's not any nefarious organization."

Qi Fei frowned. "I don't understand."

Yun Fan's eyes briefly met the eyes of each man, as though probing how trustworthy they were.

"I know that each of you have your own agenda," Yun Fan said. "I'll be frank: there is a secret in this compound; the secret that brought you here. I don't want to know about your goals in detail. In a time of turmoil and conflict like now, everyone has their own master to obey, their own ideals to follow. I don't care. But I need someone to help me. I can bring the two of you to a certain place right now, where you'll get many answers to your questions. However, after that, I'll only trust and cooperate with whoever can really help me achieve *my* goal."

She walked over to the wall opposite the tea table and swept her hand gently across. Only now did Jiang Liu realize that the plum flower painting hanging there was nothing more than a well-crafted mixed-reality holographic projection.

The vanished painting revealed a narrow vertical seam on the wall. Yun Fan stood in front of it, and a beam of light scanned her face. The block of wall in front of her retracted and then parted at the seam like a pair of doors, revealing a dark passageway.

"This must lead into . . ." Jiang Liu's voice trailed off.

"Yes, you guessed it: the interior of the Mausoleum of Qin Shi Huang, the very first emperor." Yun Fan was already inside the tunnel as she finished, her voice echoing and her celadon-hued dress glowing enigmatically in the darkness.

+ + + + +

Jiang Liu's curiosity grew with each step they took through the long, dark tunnel. A thousand thoughts flitted through his mind, visions of magnificent wonders to be found inside the famous tomb. He had never imagined that he would one day be inside the mausoleum. Anxiously, he expected to find a rammed-earth barrier at the end of the tunnel, the entrance to the burial chamber, perhaps protected by hundreds of mechanical crossbows and deadly spring-loaded swords.

But as they came to the end of the modern excavation tunnel and entered the tomb proper, he was disappointed to find neither wondrous treasures nor deadly traps. The tomb passage they were in, constructed thousands of years ago, was wide, long, and completely dark. As the beams from their flashlights roamed about, they revealed doors and pottery figurines of people and animals—perhaps guardians for the emperor. If Jiang Liu hadn't seen the Terracotta Army, he might have been impressed with the lifelike appearance of these figurines, but now he didn't even bother to look at them for long, his gaze drawn instead to the darkness deeper down in the tomb and the imaginary monsters to be found there.

The passage sloped down the entire way, though not too steeply. After a few hundred meters, the passage turned left and continued. None of the three spoke, and the only sound accompanying their progress was their footsteps.

Jiang Liu felt his admiration for Yun Fan grow. He imagined her exploring these passages in darkness by herself, and he wondered at her determination and courage. Now she led them through the murk, never hesitating, never fearful, her inner strength on display like a protective glow around them.

At the same time, he also felt the constant presence of the man in black walking next to him. Qi Fei's footsteps, steady and even, were almost silent, a sign of years of professional training. The brief exchange earlier wasn't enough for him to identify Qi Fei's style of martial art, maybe sanda boxing, or maybe a new kind of military fighting technique, but it clearly emphasized simple, direct strikes at close range.

With the two tall men walking side by side, the passage no longer seemed so spacious. But the two avoided any contact with each other. From time to time, Jiang Liu would lean toward Qi Fei as a test, but every time, the latter nimbly slid out of the way almost instinctively, further confirming Jiang Liu's hunch that Qi Fei had extensive combat training.

Jiang Liu pondered the relationship between Qi Fei and Yun Fan. A day earlier, Yun Fan's facial expressions had often belied her cold words as she sometimes smiled at his attempts at flirting. But today, she seemed to have turned into a stone statue in Qi Fei's presence. Such an ostentatious coldness, he suspected, hinted as a very complicated story.

"This is it." Yun Fan stopped in front of a wall and began to feel around the surface.

"Where are we, exactly?" Jiang Liu was baffled. The flashlights revealed little.

"There's an elevator here. Please watch your step." Yun Fan pushed open a door and stepped in. She turned on a single dim yellow bulb, illuminating the crude lift car she was in. "Oh, don't look so surprised. This part was obviously built during modern times—by my grandfather, to be specific."

Recovering from their shock, Jiang Liu and Qi Fei stepped in. The cramped space pressed the three together, and all strove to look away from one another to minimize the awkwardness.

The elevator descended slowly, stopping after a few seemingly interminable seconds. The three exited to find themselves in an even deeper and darker tunnel. Far in the distance, a few flickering red lights could be discerned, like the eyes of some giant beast. Jiang Liu felt his spine tingle.

"Right here." Yun Fan crouched down and began to brush away the earth at the foot of the rammed-earth wall.

Jiang Liu could tell that the ground near where Yun Fan was digging had been disturbed multiple times, such that there was a clear border around the area. As Yun Fan continued to remove loose earth, a red glow appeared under her brush, and the deeper she dug, the brighter and bigger the glow grew. Soon, silvery twinkles appeared around the red glow under her.

Jiang Liu's heart raced. This was the wonder he had been anticipating.

The flashing signal was coming from something deep within the earth—not a modern instrument, but something that was part of the earth itself.

"What is it?" Jiang Liu asked, his voice hoarse.

"A detector," Yun Fan said. "My father thought it might be a neutrino detector. It was part of the original construction of the mausoleum."

"Huh?" Jiang Liu's eyes widened.

In his experience, neutrino detectors were gigantic apparatuses of pure Nobelworthy science, usually involving huge tanks of water deep under mountains. In the twenty-first century, only a handful of countries had built neutrino observatories, and the only operational ones were under Mount Ikeno in Japan, the Jinping Mountains in China, and the Rocky Mountains of the United States. But now Yun Fan was telling him that the first emperor's tomb contained a neutrino detector from more than two millennia ago?

"How is that possible?" Jiang Liu crouched down to get a closer look at the glowing rammed-earth wall. "How does it work?"

"I can't tell you that for sure," Yun Fan said, gazing down at the flashing red light. "All I know is that in the underground palace of the tomb of the first emperor, buried below our feet, there is some device for capturing neutrinos. The captured neutrinos then cause certain particle reactions that result in radiation, which is detected and shows up as these flashing signals. I suspect there are conduits between the underground palace and here that transmit the signal from the detectors to the 'display' here. However, the core of the mausoleum remains unexcavated, so I'm only speculating."

"Is that why historians recorded the extensive use of mercury in the construction of the mausoleum?" Qi Fei broke in. "So it wasn't just to model the rivers and lakes of the Qin Empire, but to capture neutrinos . . . but why mercury?"

Jiang Liu looked puzzled as well. "Most of the detectors I know rely on pure water and Cherenkov radiation; I'm not aware of any that use mercury."

"Wait." Qi Fei held up a hand. "I could have sworn that Oak Ridge National Laboratory experimented with neutrinos using mercury. Didn't it involve smashing protons into mercury and creating unstable nuclei? I can't remember the details."[2]

"Now that you mention it, I have a vague memory of it too. I need to look up the reference."

"I may be able to access it quicker. Let's—"

Abruptly, both realized that they sounded too much like two colleagues or lab mates collaborating on a project. Working together was not something either wanted. An awkward silence followed.

Qi Fei finally remembered the *real* mystery. "How can there be any neutrino detectors in the Mausoleum of Qin Shi Huang? That makes no sense."

Yun Fan's voice was soft but sure. "They left it as a sign for the descendants of those who built the mausoleum. When they are about to return, the signal gets stronger. It's a beacon."

"They?" Qi Fei's expression stiffened.

"Extraterrestrials." Yun Fan's tone was calm, as though talking about the weather. "I'm guessing that the transmissions you asked me about were from here as well. Hailing their spaceship."

---

2 Readers who are so inclined can read about the experiment referenced here in D. Akimov et al., "Observation of Coherent Elastic Neutrino–Nucleus Scattering," *Science* 357, no. 6356 (August 2017): 1123–6.

"Hold on," Jiang Liu said. "How do you know it's a neutrino detector at all? All we see are some flashing red lights. How did you conclude that this has anything to do with neutrinos?"

"I don't understand the technical details," Yun Fan said. "I'm just telling you what my father told me. I remember seeing these flashes when I was a little girl, but back then the lights were far dimmer."

"How did your father figure this out?" Jiang Liu pursued.

"My grandfather told him."

"How did your grandfather learn it?"

"He had an . . . encounter. Forget it. You wouldn't believe me if I told you anyway."

"You haven't told me, so you can't know that I won't believe you," Jiang Liu said. "Please tell me."

"She doesn't want to tell you," Qi Fei said. "Don't you have ears? She said no."

"She's afraid that I won't believe her." Jiang Liu refused to back down from the other man. "I promise to believe you. Yun Fan, please tell me your grandfather's story."

Yun Fan kept her gaze on the dark depths of the tunnel, her voice soft. "The first time my father brought me here, I was only ten. I loved to read as a child, especially history. So my father thought I would be interested in ancient ruins. But he was wrong. The first time I came here, I was frozen with terror. It was too dark. He dug into the earth so that I could see the faint red lights, but I didn't want to see them; they were like the glowing eyes of some monster in the darkness waiting to devour me. I screamed and ran away and refused to ever come back with him.

"Eight years passed. I was eighteen, on the verge of my gaokao examination, when I came here a second time. My father and I, we weren't speaking back then, like two sides in a cold war. Somehow he managed to drag me, kicking and screaming, here, and showed me the flashing red lights again. I could see that the lights were brighter. Ten years earlier, the lights had been so faint that you had to look away a bit to see them. But this time, they reminded me of a heartbeat. Even so, I refused to believe the story my father told me."

She turned to the men. "I can't ever forget that scene . . . when I failed him. I don't want to ever have to go through that again, this time as the one doing the telling. So this is all I'm going to say on the subject today. If you believe me, great. If you don't, that's fine too. I don't care."

She opened the door to the crude elevator and went in. "I'm heading up."

+ + + + +

As they ascended the sloping tunnel, Jiang Liu was the first to speak.

"I suppose the need to house neutrino detectors can explain why the mausoleum must be so large. Neutrinos only participate in the weak interaction, and so you need a very large surface to detect a significant number of them. And you have to do it deep underground to filter out other radiation. It's not too different from detecting cold dark matter."

"You're right about the size of the mausoleum," Yun Fan said. "Even as a little girl, I knew that the big mound out there is the tallest hill for kilometers around. In elementary school I learned that the hill is no natural formation, but the burial mound atop the tomb of the first emperor, entirely artificial. I couldn't imagine how humans could build such a thing within a few years, or why. But the project makes sense if it was meant to house a neutrino detector."

"But most ancient Chinese tombs have tumuli above them," Qi Fei said, "especially emperors and kings. I don't think that's unusual."

"The mausoleum is different," Yun Fan said. "Many facts about it are very hard to explain without some power outside of human agency. For instance, how many people had to labor to construct the tumulus as well as the underground palace? To the best of our knowledge, we think the whole complex was completed during the five years of Prime Minister Li Si's regency—let's give them a little more time and say they had a full decade. How can humans with no modern construction equipment accomplish such a thing without a miracle? Moreover, the Terracotta Soldiers and the bronze chariots, mere grave goods not even deemed good enough to be inside the tomb proper, are already considered wonders of the world. Can you imagine the treasure that must be inside the unexcavated tomb itself? How is it possible to complete such a complicated, multilayered engineering project, requiring unprecedented scale as well as skill, in a mere few years?"

"But they drew on the resources of an entire empire," Qi Fei said. "Everyone in subsequent ages denounced Qin Shi Huang for exhausting the people and wasting resources."

"It's not that simple." Yun Fan shook her head impatiently. "You can't just throw people at a project like this. For example, in the 2160s, outside the tomb proper but still in a part of the mausoleum complex, we discovered a burial pit even bigger than Pit 1, which housed the Terracotta Soldiers. From this pit we excavated more than ten thousand sets of stone armor. Each set of armor is made from bronze wires stringing together hundreds of stone plates, each no thicker than three millimeters. Archaeologists tried an experiment: with modern power tools, a skilled operator could cut, polish, and drill no more than six such plates in a day. But each set of stone armor contains more than six hundred such plates. Can you imagine how long it would have taken artisans in the ancient world, wielding only hand tools, to accomplish such a feat?"

"It does seem rather incredible," Jiang Liu said. "But you still can't rule out the possibility that they managed it by working really hard."

"No, you still don't get it. Yes, the accepted theory is that the mausoleum was built by about 720,000 laborers. But this is nonsense. As I explained with the stone armor example, the construction required skilled artisans, not just unskilled laborers. Where could you find so many skilled artisans back then? Moreover, our best estimate of the population of Qin China is about 15 to 20 million. If you exclude women, the elderly, and children, you are down to a pool of about 5 million. If 720,000 were working on the mausoleum, then you needed about four to five times that number working to support and supply them—meaning the vast majority of the entire country's available labor force would be devoted to this single project. If you were alive then, it would mean you and virtually everyone you knew were working on it.

"Yet, when we examine the biography of Liu Bang, the future founder of the Han Dynasty who grew up during this time, there is no evidence that he or anyone he knew worked on the mausoleum. That tells us that the hypothesis is flawed."

"I see what you're saying," Jiang Liu said. "But I still can't quite accept the jump to aliens as an explanation."

As their footsteps echoed in the empty passage, Jiang Liu felt the solemnity in this space. Recalling everything he had seen so far and Yun Fan's explanations, he felt a sense of unreality. *Aliens were here more than two thousand years ago? Why did they come to Earth? What did they do here? If aliens had visited the Qin court, why was there no record of it?* He kept all the questions to himself, unwilling to show Yun Fan his skepticism.

"All right, I know you still can't accept it," Yun Fan said. "I know you have tons of questions in your mind. Let me show you something else."

They were now at the point where the passage turned. On the way down, they had passed two stone doors in the rammed-earth wall without stopping. Yun Fan now approached one of the doors and pushed it hard. The door retracted a few centimeters, revealing two vertical grooves in the doorframe packed with wooden and stone levers of different lengths. Yun Fan manipulated these "keys" with practiced ease, and soon, with a loud crack, the stone door slid back over a set of rollers.

Yun Fan stepped inside the new passage that opened up. Jiang Liu and Qi Fei, sensing an enigmatic whiff of danger, hesitated for the briefest of moments before following.

Abruptly, something erupted from the darkness inside the passage and swooped through the air, heading straight for Yun Fan.

Instinctively, Jiang Liu wrapped an arm protectively around Yun Fan and tumbled down with her. As they struck the ground, he supported himself on one arm so that Yun Fan was completely shielded. At the same time, Qi Fei had extracted a short baton, flicked it to extend it like a collapsible telescope, and then struck the flying object in one smooth motion. The struck object fell to the earth but continued to flop around. Qi Fei chased after it with his baton.

"No!" Yun Fan yelled. "Stop!"

Carefully, Qi Fei approached the unknown object and held it down with the baton. "What is it?"

Yun Fan flicked on her flashlight. "A bronze fenghuang. Be careful. It's more than two thousand years old."

Qi Fei and Jiang Liu both exclaimed in shock.

"From the Qin dynasty?" Jiang Liu said. "How can it be moving?"

Yun Fan sat up and fixed her hair. "It's powered by a wind-up mechanism. The door I just opened serves as a trigger. Even after so many years, the mechanism still functions perfectly—that should give you a sense of the craftsmanship. There are many more like it deeper inside." Carefully, she picked up the flapping mechanical creature and cradled it in her hands. "It's not trying to harm anyone. The automaton is designed to surprise whoever opens the door and try to escape. If it got out there, it would follow the tunnel up and out and head straight to a preprogrammed location to send a message."

"You are obviously familiar with it," Qi Fei said.

"I am." Gently, Yun Fan set the bird down on the ground. "We should leave it here. Once exposed to sunlight and fresh air, it's easily corroded. I can show you one that's in the exhibit hall."

The two men stood up and brushed off the dirt on their clothes. "Um . . ." Jiang Liu cleared his throat. "Just now, when I . . . you . . . sorry about that."

"It's all right," Yun Fan said. "Thank you both."

She took out some towelettes from her purse so that the men could clean themselves. The ice had cracked.

+ + + + +

They exited the tunnel from a different opening than the one they had used on the way in. Yun Fan took them through a long and narrow corridor until they emerged into a grand hall. The space was suffused with sunlight from a lightwell that pierced the ceiling. In the middle of the hall, a replica of a bronze chariot excavated from the mausoleum sat atop a tall mound, imposing and magnificent. They had apparently reentered the museum from a side door.

Yun Fan took them through the hall and made a right turn. Here, inside the main exhibit hall, the original pair of bronze chariots, excavated in 1980, occupied the most prominent display case. Jiang Liu had seen these treasures from countless photos, including 3D captures, but there was nothing like coming face-to-face with the real thing. The horses and the charioteers had such vivid expressions, every detail so meticulous and realistic, that it seemed as if they had been alive just seconds ago, and the bronze had merely replaced their bodies atom by atom.

"These chariots are the pinnacle of classical Chinese bronze casting," Yun Fan said reverently. "There are more than six thousand components making up the sculptures, and every component displays painstaking craftsmanship. Even more incredibly, there's a high level of standardization among the components, almost at the level required for modern assembly line production. Look here: Do you see the collar around the horses, each made from forty-two golden tubes and forty-two silver tubes? We still have no idea how they connect. Oh, one more thing."

She led the men to the side of the display case so that they could see the umbrella-shaped chariot roof better. "The roof is almost two meters across, but its thickest point is only four millimeters and the thinnest point less than one millimeter. There are no signs of welding or forging, so it must have been cast as a single piece. With no hydraulic forging press, no modern machinery, how did they do it? We have spent more than half a century working on this puzzle and still have no answers. For this kind of result to be achievable using only hand tools requires, again, a miracle."

"It really is wondrous." Jiang Liu admired the intricate components.

"There's even more." Yun Fan pointed to the hoofs of the horses. "We've found that these were cast using the lost-wax method. However, traditionally, the main technique used to produce Chinese bronzeware was piece-mold casting. To be sure, during the Spring and Autumn period, there were a few pieces done by lost-wax casting, but those were very different from the technique used on the chariots, as you can see from the supports inside the horses' legs and the patchwork. So where did the craftsmen working on the mausoleum learn such advanced lost-wax techniques? It's a complete mystery."

"Maybe there was more international trade and exchange than we thought," Qi Fei said. "The ancient Near East was very advanced in metal casting. Some scholars speculate that metallurgical techniques traveled east from West Asia."

"Yes, there was transcontinental exchange and trade," Yun Fan said. "However, the spread of technologies is generally gradual and piecemeal, and one would expect to find plenty of archaeological evidence for intermediate stages along the route of transmission and over time as the target culture mastered the new technologies. But the maturity of the lost-wax method used on the bronze chariots defies that explanation. Before the mausoleum, there's nothing remotely similar, and yet here we see a phenomenal masterwork."

Yun Fan walked toward another exhibit hall and gestured for the men to follow. "Come. Let me show you yet more mysteries."

She pointed to a display case of swords. Jiang Liu examined them carefully. The edges glinted sharply, and the patterns along the blades seemed untouched by the passage of millennia.

"Chemical analysis revealed these swords to be plated with a 10-micron layer of chromium oxide. But such corrosion-resistant techniques would not be developed by scientists until the 1930s." Through the case, she caressed the blades from afar. "Without modern chemistry, without any advanced equipment, how could they have done this more than 2200 years ago?"

"So . . . you think these are also from aliens?" Jiang Liu asked.

"I can't claim that definitively," Yun Fan said. "I'm just saying that even if you don't believe my grandfather's story, you can draw your own conclusions from the evidence."

Yun Fan led them into the next exhibit hall. In the center was a platform shaped like a truncated pyramid. At the top perched a bronze fenghuang about a meter tall.

Jiang Liu and Qi Fei gasped. The bird was incredibly intricate. The craftmanship exceeded the bronze sacred tree from Sanxingdui a hundredfold. The torso was covered by hundreds of individually-cast bronze feathers, each distinct in shape and texture, some even curling up at the edges. The fenghuang's pose was graceful and vivid, the wings slightly raised, the long neck arched, as though captured at the moment it was about to take off. The movable joints were complex and refined, the mechanism so sophisticated that it was almost impossible to see the individual components. It didn't look like something cast, but 3D-printed.

"Is this the same kind of fenghuang we saw earlier?" Jiang Liu asked.

"Yes." Yun Fan led them to the side so that they could see the mechanism at the bottom of the bird's neck better. "In 2032, when my grandfather led a team to open up the first tunnel into the tomb proper, this bird burst from the opening—not unlike what just happened to us earlier. In fact, during the Chu–Han Contention, graverobbers tried to break into the mausoleum, and they saw birds flying out as well. We'd always treated these records as mere legends, but now we know they were true. My grandfather's encounter was even caught on video; I can show you the recording later if you like. The fenghuang at the time almost got away, but my grandfather was able to catch it with a drone and bring it down to the ground."

"Where was it trying to escape to?" Qi Fei asked.

Yun Fan shook her head. "Nobody knows. After it landed, it never moved again. My grandfather thought it was trying to fly somewhere to deliver a message—the opening of the tomb was the trigger. Later, using X-rays and quantum grating analysis, we were able to determine that the alloy used in its construction is unique; there's nothing like it in any of the artifacts excavated all over China. Moreover, the body of the fenghuang is filled with tiny gears, chains, and complex clockwork mechanisms that rival the greatest feats of modern master watchmakers."

Jiang Liu stared at the fenghuang for some time. "Incredible."

Yun Fan lifted her head, as though gazing at somewhere among the stars. "I learned these stories in childhood. I saw these chariots, the fenghuang, and everything else in elementary school. I knew that they are much too sophisticated to be achievable with the level of technology at that time. But I still couldn't believe, not really, that aliens had visited Qin Shi Huang. It's just too ridiculous. I needed extraordinary proof, proof that my family couldn't give me."

Jiang Liu nodded. He could well understand Yun Fan's skepticism.

"That lack of faith led to the greatest regret of my life," Yun Fan said. With her tilted head and determined look, she seemed another elegant bronze fenghuang perched atop a parasol tree. "I will not make the same mistake again. I'm going to finish my task, no matter what."

Qi Fei and Jiang Liu both felt the heat and chill in her determined words, like burning ice.

+ + + + +

After dinner, Yun Fan returned to her office to do more work. Qi Fei asked Jiang Liu to meet him outside the museum.

The bright moon dimmed the stars. Jiang Liu, strolling ahead with his hands in his pockets, admired the moon as though he were a college student on a moon-gazing date. For a few minutes, the two men walked without talking. A stranger might have thought the two were good friends who no longer needed to fill the silence with chatter.

"Director Qi," a smirking Jiang Liu said, having read over the publicly available information on Qi Fei earlier, "how can I be of service?"

"What are you up to, exactly?" Qi Fei said, making no effort to disguise his sneer. "Why is the little prince of the Jiang family, the head of the world's largest nongovernmental intelligence network, here in the middle of nowhere?"

"I'm here for Yun Fan," Jiang Liu said, his eyes probing Qi Fei's face for a reaction. "She's so smart, accomplished, beautiful—don't you agree? I can't possibly miss the chance to get to know her."

Qi Fei's face was stony. "As a graduate of Harvard and . . . I'm told that you could be described as handsome, surely you already know plenty of beautiful and smart women."

"No no no!" Jiang Liu laughed. "Surely you know that what matters the most in relationships is yuanfen. It's that kind of fateful affinity that brings about unbreakable bonds. I, unfortunately, lack yuanfen with other girls. But with Yun Fan, I feel a deep sense of yuanfen. Oh, Director Qi, you seem to disagree?"

"I don't care who you want to chase after or how you want to make a fool of yourself," Qi Fei said. He waved his hands as if emphasizing how little he cared. "But I do care a great deal about your actions as a hacker. Please come with me to the institute so that I can interrogate you."

Qi Fei's gestures had been a signal. About two dozen men, dressed completely in black and their faces masked, leapt out of the darkness pervading the museum grounds. Each tossed out a thin strand of artificial spider silk tipped with a spherical anchor. The anchors, AI-enhanced, scanned for a preprogrammed target. Once the target had been identified, the anchors would stick to them and, no matter how much the target struggled, would never let go. Since the nanomaterial-reinforced spider-silk strands couldn't be cut with ordinary tools and tended to entangle with one another, the more the target struggled, the more trapped they became. However, since the spider formation required so many skilled operators, it was rarely deployed.

"Wow! I had no idea I was so valued!" Jiang Liu laughed even harder as the spider-silk strands cocooned him. "I thought I was a useless nobody, but clearly Director Qi thinks of me as a very important individual. But Director Qi, this is all so unnecessary. I've long admired your reputation. What a lovely night this is! Such a beautiful moon must be shared with a worthy friend. We should drink together, admire the moon, and compose poems. If you had simply asked me to join you for such a charming conversation atop your institute, I would have raced you to your place. We could have saved you all this trouble."

Qi Fei said nothing, his penetrating gaze trying to discern the true character of the man under that mocking smile. After a few seconds, he turned and walked away, tossing behind only an order for his men, "Bring him."

3 | A Night Fight

Inside his detention cell, Jiang Liu sang to himself. He had seen the hidden camera strips overhead as soon as he was brought in, and so he sang and made faces and posed for the camera, making the operators on duty laugh. Qi Fei was annoyed, but there was little he could do.

He felt rising waves of anxiety. By regulation, the general was supposed to lay out the interrogation strategy and procedure for an important suspect such as Jiang Liu. But tonight, even though he had sent in the report on Jiang Liu more than an hour earlier, there was still no response.

Qi Fei couldn't explain *why* he felt so anxious; he hadn't felt so emotional in carrying out a mission in a long time. He tried to breathe and focus his mind the way he did when he played bridge, but it did no good. He followed up with the general's staff; the response: The general was in a meeting at Pacific League Headquarters. There was no way to reach him and no estimate for when the meeting would be over.

Qi Fei got up and walked into Jiang Liu's cell. He couldn't wait any longer.

"How did you and Yun Fan meet?" Qi Fei loomed over the other man, not even bothering to take a seat at the table.

"Oh, she came to an academic conference and asked me about pulsars." Jiang Liu smiled again. "What about you two? How do you know each other?"

"I'm asking the questions here," Qi Fei said. "It's none of your business anyway; she and I are old friends."

"Hmm, but when she saw you, there was no 'How have you been' and so forth. Maybe . . . not old friends, but old enemies?"

"My only enemy here is you." Qi Fei's tone was icy.

"Director Qi," Jiang Liu said, lacing his hands behind his head and leaning back in his chair, "you really must learn not to be so hostile all the time. If you have questions for me, let's sit down together and share a bottle. I promise to tell you everything. But if you keep on yelling at me, I may become so scared that I forget all the valuable information I possess."

"Fine, we'll have a friendly chat," Qi Fei said, but there was nothing friendly in his tone. "Are you the founder of Tianshang?"

"Yes."

"Why did you name it that?"

"It's derived from Mozi's writings: 'Those who follow the will of heaven love all and mutually benefit, their reward certain; those who oppose heaven's will divide themselves and harm one another, their punishment certain.' Since we only do good deeds that follow the will of heaven, we'll surely mutually benefit and receive the reward of heaven." [3]

"Good deeds?" Qi Fei leaned into Jiang Liu's face. "Tianshang is the world's largest hacking collective, and it's devoted to the leaking and selling of intelligence, sowing destruction everywhere. How dare you claim to be doing good?"

"Please! Don't slander us." Jiang Liu looked unfazed. "We're not the world's largest hacking collective, and we certainly don't go about spreading destruction. Tianshang tries to help the poorest of the poor find a way to make a living. If I had done something, I'd certainly own up to it. But if I hadn't, I'd never agree to take the credit or the blame."

Qi Fei leaned closer and kept his tone just on the verge of contempt, the way

---

3   Mozi (circa 470–391 BCE) was the founder of a school of philosophy. Mohism, in contrast with Confucianism, which (in some interpretations) justifies prioritizing some people above others based on one's attachment to them, and Daoism, which prizes the absolute freedom of the individual, tends to emphasize the notion of jianai, sometimes (imperfectly) translated as "universal love." Only by embracing and empathizing with all humanity, without distinction of family, clan, class, nation, state, can a truly just world be achieved. The quote recited by Jiang Liu is from Mozi's *Heaven's Will*.

an experienced interrogator was supposed to do, as he asked, "Is that right? I'm very interested in the good deeds Tianshang is responsible for."

"No problem," Jiang Liu said, looking up to meet Qi Fei's gaze directly. "I'll be glad to give you a comprehensive report. But before I do that, let me assure you that although Tianshang is not nearly as clever as CloudMind, our desire to do good is just as strong."

Qi Fei's pupils contracted slightly. CloudMind was a top-secret military project. Cutting-edge AI would analyze all available data and compute the optimal deployment plan as well as provide ongoing coordination and control as the situation developed. Although initially limited to the battlefield, it soon grew to encompass energy allocation, productivity calculation, logistics, transportation, personnel, and even the aggregation and analysis of real-time intelligence and monitoring data. As the project's scope grew, more computing resources were devoted to it, more parameters were placed under its control, and the hardware-software integration evolved to be deeper. Although the project had been born in the 2120s, it was Qi Fei, the new director, who managed to take it to the next level.

Very few people actually knew that Qi Fei was in charge of it. Even the name of the project had changed over time from CloudNet to CloudBrain, then Cloud-Wise, before finally settling on CloudMind. The fact that Jiang Liu could tell him the current name as well as the fact that Qi Fei was in charge . . . it implied that Jiang Liu's intelligence-gathering operations had penetrated the heart of the Pacific League.

The more he thought about it, the more concerned Qi Fei grew. "Jiang Liu, I'm warning you. If you don't answer my questions completely honestly, there will be severe consequences."

Jiang Liu wiped the smile off his face. "Ask away."

Qi Fei pulled over a chair and sat down facing Jiang Liu across the table.

"Does Tianshang use blockchain technology?"

"Yes."

"Do the members use it to sell intelligence?"

"Yes."

"Who are the buyers and sellers?"

"All anonymous."

"You understand that trading military intelligence is a crime, don't you?"

"I know nothing of the sort," Jiang Liu said. "I have no control over what kind of intelligence is posted to the chain. Buyers and sellers negotiate their own deals."

"Then how do you ensure that the intelligence on the Tianshang market is accurate?"

"I provide no editorial function," Jiang Liu said. "Whoever has provided good intelligence—meaning buyers found their info valuable—will be given more weight in the future by the system. The better your information, the more money you make. The more you benefit others, the more others benefit you. The system is self-correcting."

"What if someone doesn't care about income but only spreads disinformation?"

"The information will still be part of the chain." Jiang Liu shrugged. "Who can say definitively what is disinformation and what isn't in this world? The truth can sound like lies, and lies can also sound like the truth."

"Don't try to hide behind koans," Qi Fei said, his tone once again growing heated. "You must know who's buying intelligence on the chain. Who pays *you*?"

"Anyone can participate in the chain," Jiang Liu said, leaning forward, "including you. But let me be clear. Tianshang is an easygoing place, however we do have one ironclad rule: Never reveal your sources. If anyone buys intelligence and then unmasks the seller, then that person will be the confirmed enemy of all members of Tianshang. We'll aggregate all intelligence and go after the traitor. If your intent is to use Tianshang to root out sources, then you'd better be ready to spend the rest of your life running from all of Tianshang. We're never going to be the aggressors, but if someone treads on us . . . I think I've said enough."

The contempt fairly dripped from Qi Fei's voice as he said, "Oh, I see you're models of ethics. Let me ask you: Is it doing good when you, for private gain, undermine the plans of the League?"

Jiang Liu regarded Qi Fei coolly. "We've never gotten in the way of any of your plans. Your strategic advances and retreats, your tactical surprises, your ruses and tricks—we've never interfered with them."

"Hackers have breached the Pacific League's core network defenses multiple times. Are you telling me that you aren't responsible?"

"Tianshang facilitates the buying and selling of intelligence, but we don't organize any hacking."

"Recently, the Pacific League conducted an operation in the Strait of Malacca. However, the planned routes for our fleet were leaked ahead of time, and the enemy was able to intercept. The spies responsible were caught and confessed that they got their information from Tianshang. How do you explain this?"

"I have to repeat the same point I've already made: Tianshang is just a marketplace; it doesn't arrange any deals. If someone in possession of intelligence wishes to sell it, and someone else not in possession of it wishes to buy it, they'll make it happen. We didn't fire a single shot at your ships, and we didn't sell the intelligence to your enemy. Tianshang is not responsible for the failure of your operation.

"We did nothing more than warn those who had the misfortune of being caught in the clash of great powers; we helped them from becoming cannon fodder. Do you know what kind of people buy intelligence on Tianshang? I'll tell you. It's not as complicated as you think. The buyers are all ordinary people. The intelligence they buy allows them to go hide in the basement before the bombs fall, to conceal their goods before the riots start, to find a safe way home before borders are sealed. When you design and plan your grand military plans, did you even give a second's thought to the lives of these people? You won't warn them to get out of the way before the missiles start to fly, and now you're telling me that they aren't allowed to save themselves? Helping people save themselves is the point of Tianshang."

Qi Fei stared at Jiang Liu and said nothing more for three seconds. When he spoke again, his voice was low and steady. "So you think of yourself as some sort of bodhisattva, a savior of the suffering people, do you? Tell me, little princeling, how exactly do you benefit from this? I don't believe for a second that Tianshang is nothing more than a common marketplace."

Jiang Liu stood up slowly. "I'm done, Director Qi. Yun Fan was right. 'If you believe me, great. If you don't, that's fine too. I don't care.' There's never been any way to prove what's in someone's heart. You must judge me based on what's in your heart, and I care not how you view me." He walked toward the door of the detention cell.

"Where do you think you're going?" Qi Fei said, getting up after him.

"It's late. I'm going back to sleep," Jiang Liu said.

"Stop!" Qi Fei reached out for him.

Jiang Liu spun to the right, dropping his left shoulder out of the way of Qi Fei's grabbing hand. His left arm shot out to block Qi Fei's grappling hold while his right arm extended forward, the dancing fingers tapping out the unlock code on the security pad. Qi Fei grabbed Jiang Liu's left arm, but Jiang Liu, leading with his right shoulder, had already pushed open the door and was halfway out. Qi Fei braced his feet and tried to pull Jiang Liu back in, but Jiang Liu anchored himself by grabbing the doorframe with the right hand as he twisted and slid his left arm, taiji-style, in order to free himself. Parry, strike, deflect, lunge . . . the two put on a masterful display of close-range combat in the space of two minutes.

Abruptly, the tattooed lines on Jiang Liu's left wrist glowed blue. Qi Fei felt a tingling numbness in his fingers, which were wrapped around the other man's wrist. Stunned for the briefest of moments, Qi Fei let go, and Jiang Liu exited the room with a long leaping stride.

As Qi Fei ran after him, he realized that Jiang Liu's brisk gait, covering meters with every stride, couldn't be explained by natural ability. The man's shoes were surely augmented: possibly with some kind of pneumatic mechanism, or microjets, or even electromagnetic boosters. Within a few seconds, Jiang Liu had pulled away from his pursuers and bounced his way to the end of the corridor.

Qi Fei took out his collapsible baton and extended it—this was in fact a gesture-based input device that he used to communicate with his personal AI, Qiankun.[4] He waved it about and directed Qiankun to lock the main door to the building. The door wasn't controlled by a security code, so there was no way for Jiang Liu to get out even if there was a mole in the organization helping him, as had likely happened with the code to the detention cell. He could leap about like an excited rabbit all he wanted, but Qi Fei was going to recapture him shortly.

But Qi Fei had celebrated too early. Jiang Liu reached the door and gave it an effortless push. The door opened, and Jiang Liu shot out.

Qi Fei, though stunned, had no time to figure out what had happened. He raced outside the building and jumped on his hoverbike to continue the pursuit. A few subordinates rushed up for orders.

"Sir, should we try to head him off?" one of them asked.

---

4   Literally "Heaven and Earth." The name is derived from Daoist cosmology, being the names of two of the eight fundamental aspects of the universe: heaven, marsh, fire, thunder, wind, water, mountain, and earth. The eight aspects are represented by eight trigrams (a symbol written as three lines, each of which may be broken or unbroken), collectively known as the bagua.

"No. I have to take care of him myself," Qi Fei said.

He gunned the throttle, pushing the sixteen thrusters to their max. As this style of hoverbike was never meant for pursuing fleeing suspects, but for scouting in uneven terrain, it couldn't fly too fast without becoming aerodynamically unstable. However, it should have easily outclassed someone escaping on foot.

Yet, despite pushing the hoverbike to its limit, Qi Fei was only slowly catching up to Jiang Liu. He could now see a blue glow at the bottom of the fleeing man's shoes—clearly some form of electromagnetic boosters, but he was too far away to discern the exact mechanism. Leaping and bounding, Jiang Liu seemed a graceful gazelle; Qi Fei himself, on the other hand, was a hunter on horseback.

Jiang Liu was approaching the gate to the military compound. Qi Fei pulled out his baton and drew a complex pattern of arcs in the air. All the lights along the paths suddenly shut off, plunging the area into a terrifying darkness. In the deep silence, the only sound was the clang of heavy locks bolting into place in the distance. Qiankun had secured all possible exits from the compound.

For a brief moment, Qi Fei could see Jiang Liu standing still, perhaps adjusting to the darkness. But then, as his eyes grew used to the moonlight, he leapt to the side and followed a narrow footpath through the dense wood on the grounds. Qi Fei had to admire the man's judgment. Given enough time, Jiang Liu was sure to lose to the hoverbike in open space. Initially, Jiang Liu had followed the paved road because he was gambling that he could reach the gate in time. Now that the compound gates were locked, Jiang Liu's best choice was surely to stick to narrow footpaths and dense woods, trading agility for speed. Moreover, by now Jiang Liu had probably figured out that Qi Fei's baton allowed him to control all equipment in the compound, so the further away he stayed from any kind of machinery, the better.

Qi Fei turned the hoverbike and plunged into the wood as well.

The footpath that Jiang Liu chose led to a flower garden. General Yuan liked to fill all the offices with fresh flowers, and that was why the military compound set aside some land for a flower garden. The place was also crisscrossed with synthetic rubber jogging paths for the enjoyment of the staff. Once inside the garden, Jiang Liu headed for narrow hairpin turns among bushes and trees, apparently hoping to force Qi Fei to get off his bike.

A few turns later, Jiang Liu had disappeared from sight. Qi Fei chuckled to himself. If Jiang Liu thought it was that easy to get away, he was going to be very surprised. The director waved his baton about, ordering Qiankun to tap into the automation system in the garden.

The sprinklers came on; Qi Fei heard muttered curses.

Jiang Liu emerged from the bushes, his hair and clothes soaked. Qi Fei smirked. Soon, he began to laugh heartily as a cloud of microdrones, no bigger than bees, swarmed around the flustered figure of Jiang Liu. These microdrones were typically charged with spraying pesticides, monitoring the health of the plants, gathering fruits, and similar tasks. Apprehending an escapee was probably the most exciting thing in their electronic lives. Qi Fei had no intention of seriously injuring Jiang Liu, so he waved his baton gently through the air, trying to get the drones to spray pesticide all over Jiang Liu.

Jiang Liu retreated to a clearing at the center of the garden and stopped, moonlight cascading off his figure.

Qi Fei could see that Jiang Liu was waving his hands about. On his left wrist was a chain bracelet, while three bangles adorned his right wrist. He also wore three rings on his right hand. Earlier that day, when they first met, Qi Fei had been surprised by what seemed an excessive amount of jewelry on Jiang Liu—adding to his contempt for the rich princeling. But now he realized that the pieces of jewelry were wearable tech devices, far more advanced than what was commercially available. The bracelet, bangles, rings, and tattooed lines all glowed various shades of blue, turning Jiang Liu into a veritable one-person rave.

As the swarm of bee-drones approached Jiang Liu, the man intensified his dance-like movements. Abruptly, the microdrones dropped out of their orderly formation and behaved more like erratic, confused flies. Not only did they stop attacking Jiang Liu, but they also began to collide with one another, dropping to the earth immobilized.

Qi Fei frowned. Gesturing with his baton, he indicated to Qiankun that it should redeploy the microdrones in a new assault. He was surprised, however, to find that Qiankun gave him no acknowledgment over the wireless link with his cranial implant.

"He's jamming the radio link!" Qi Fei blurted.

The night was so quiet that his exclamation, not intended to be heard by anyone else, nonetheless was carried across the air.

"That's right," Jiang Liu said. "I was going to leave you and your AI pet alone, but you were too naughty and sent these bugs after me. I had no choice but to interrupt your loving whispers."

Qi Fei swore under his breath. Qiankun was his most powerful weapon, capable of directing anything placed under the control of CloudMind. But the AI couldn't do anything without a reliable wireless link. All systems that relied on wireless communications suffered from this weakness. That was why military installations and deployments all prioritized anti-interference technologies and interference-resistant equipment. But right now, as he and Jiang Liu engaged in one-on-one close combat, there was virtually nothing that he could do against the high-intensity electromagnetic interference coming from Jiang Liu's jewelry. Somehow, the powerful wearables, perhaps enhanced by stealth technologies, had fooled the compound's security scanners into not raising an alarm when he was brought in. Qiankun had been rendered deaf, blind, and mute.

Qi Fei tried to adjust by modulating the signal used by Qiankun, but there was no effect. The microdrones continue to fall at Jiang Liu's feet.

"Not a bad move," Qi Fei reluctantly conceded.

"Thank you." Jiang Liu chuckled. "I'm pretty useless when it comes to attacking, but I do know a few tricks for protecting myself and others."

"Feigong." Qi Fei nodded. "Defense only. I suppose you haven't forgotten the precepts of your heroes."[5]

"Director Qi, may I finally leave now?" Jiang Liu asked. "Or are you going to send more of your little friends after me?"

"It's still too early to speak of leaving." Qi Fei jumped off the hoverbike. "My steed would like to test you first."

Qi Fei grabbed the handlebars of the hoverbike and began to pull. Instantly, the bike split down the middle into two pieces. A bystander might have thought Qi Fei a superhero, capable of tearing apart a vehicle as though it were a piece of fried chicken. But a closer examination revealed that the hoverbike was built to

---

5   Mohism developed during the Warring States period, when the various Sinitic states engaged in unceasing warfare that brought a great deal of suffering to the people. Mohists denounced war, but they were not strict pacifists in the modern sense; rather, they believed that peoples and states had the right to defend themselves against aggressors, and many Mohists became specialists in defensive warfare. Feigong, a core Mohist concept, can be literally translated as "no aggression."

disassemble itself in this manner, and each half now writhed to fit around Qi Fei's body like living armor.

The skeleton of the partitioned hoverbike flexed and buckled, extending, bending, folding, twisting. The handlebars and shocks molded themselves around Qi Fei's arms to become vambraces and gauntlets, with sharp blades extending forth. The frame split apart and reshaped around Qi Fei's legs as greaves, with one wheel under each foot—turning him into a mechanical version of the peerless Nezha. The bike-mecha, its transformation now complete, seemed a perfect extension of Qi Fei's body.

His torso, joints, and head remained unencumbered by armor. Far from making him vulnerable, this design left him with a nimbleness impossible to achieve in a full suit of armor. He continued to leap, spin, strike, parry with all his martial arts techniques unaffected, but the armor on his lower arms and legs enhanced the power of every move by orders of magnitude. The armor also gave him a whole suite of new weapons, from projectiles to blades.

Qi Fei examined his cyborg hands with satisfaction before looking at Jiang Liu. "You can't interfere with signals passed through my nervous system, can you?"

The wheels under his feet spun, sending him after Jiang Liu. No matter how Jiang Liu advanced, backed up, turned, or leaped, the wheels recognized his movements and calculated the best intercept course, sealing off every retreat. At the same time, the armor over Qi Fei's arms began to spit out the same spider-silk lines that had entangled Jiang Liu earlier tonight. AI-enhanced cameras followed Jiang Liu no matter how he feinted and dodged, and the highly elastic silk lines extended and retracted like nimble tentacles, gradually tightening into a web around Jiang Liu.

Qi Fei moved so fast that he was a blur. It was no longer possible to say whether he was directing his armor or if the armor was directing him. In fact, he had trained with the armor for months to achieve this state of perfect melding of man and machine. The armor, directly tapping into his nervous system, had formed procedural motor memories in his cerebellum, the kind of "muscle memory" that enabled fluid and semi-autonomous movement unachievable by the forebrain alone. The actual implementation of the man-machine interface was extremely complex, the result of dedicated research by the CloudMind group.

As the two men continued their close combat dance in the tightening web of silk strands, Qi Fei could feel Jiang Liu's movements slowing. The wheels and the spider-silk strands were too good. Jiang Liu's shoes allowed him to leap much higher than unaugmented muscle, but no matter how high he jumped, he must eventually come back down. The web was going to seize him sooner or later.

Suddenly, Jiang Liu seemed to vanish. But moments later, the wheels and the spider strands found him again: he was running toward the wall of the compound, just a few long strides away.

Qi Fei harrumphed scornfully. It was common knowledge that AI systems performed best in open spaces. Had Jiang Liu tried to run deeper into the woods, it would have given Qi Fei more trouble, and he had been careful to position himself so as to prevent the other man from escaping in that direction. But Jiang Liu was now running the other way, in the open space between Qi Fei and the wall. Either he was too arrogant or too desperate, but regardless, Qi Fei was going to bring him down in seconds.

The wheels carried Qi Fei closer and closer; silk strands arced through the space in-between, the capturing grapplers aiming for Jiang Liu's back. Abruptly, Jiang Liu bent his knees and leaped up and forward, his unprotected head aimed at the stone wall itself.

Before Qi Fei could exclaim in shock, Jiang Liu had turned in the air so that his feet, not head, touched the wall. Kicking off the vertical surface, he leaped even higher, tumbling backward over the spider-silk strands that passed harmlessly under him, before landing right next to Qi Fei, greeting him with a wink.

Qi Fei pulled the strands back, and Jiang Liu leaped toward the wall again. Bouncing back and forth, the two repeated the same sequence a couple of times. Qi Fei sneered. Jiang Liu's antics didn't concern him. The wall around the compound was three stories tall. Even with those shoes, there was no way for Jiang Liu to jump over it. Despite Jiang Liu's best efforts to play the part of an oversized flea, he was doomed.

For the third time, Jiang Liu jumped at the wall. By now, the AI directing the spider-silk strands had learned the fugitive's pattern and come up with a counter: While three of the strands chased after Jiang Liu, the other three were held in reserve, shooting out only when Jiang Liu was on his way bouncing back from the wall. With three strands behind him and three strands ahead of him, Jiang Liu was helpless.

Jiang Liu fell to the ground; Qi Fei fully expected the strands to wrap themselves around him. But to his utter surprise, Jiang Liu managed to shrug out of his coat and tossed it at the wall. The coat, equipped with electromagnetically stiffening fibers and thrusters, held the shape of a man as it drifted toward the wall on its own. The AI, mistaking the coat-shell for Jiang Liu, shot three spider-silk strands from Qi Fei's right arm after it, but held the other three in reserve.

That was the moment when Jiang Liu, shorn of his coat, jumped at Qi Fei. Instinctively, Qi Fei raised his left arm to block the assault. Just as Jiang Liu's feet touched Qi Fei's left arm, the AI launched the other three spider-silk strands from Qi Fei's left arm to go after the drifting coat-shell.

The timing was perfect. Jiang Liu's shoes glowed a bright blue. The combined force from the shooting spider-silk strands and the shoe's electromagnetic boosters sent Jiang Liu flying straight up eight meters, just enough for him to grab the top of the compound wall with ease. Jiang Liu pulled himself up onto the wall and looked back down at Qi Fei, his face full of playful joy, like a child who had climbed to the top of the highest slide.

"You can keep my coat," Jiang Liu shouted down. As he swayed gently atop the tall wall in the moonlight, he laughed as though he really were drinking and moon-gazing with Qi Fei.

Qi Fei clapped softly. "The golden cicada escapes by casting off its old skin; you borrow my strength to augment yours. Impressive. Very impressive."

"I told you: I'm no good at attacking. But when it comes to protecting myself and running away, I daresay I know a thing or two."

"Don't think this is over." Qi Fei's voice was cold. "Qiankun now has you in its sights. Even if you run to the ends of the earth, Qiankun will find you and catch you."

"Ha! Director Qi is quite a joker. I have no interest in running to the ends of the earth. I would like to be right next to you; the darkest shadow is at the base of the lamp, right?"

Qi Fei's face reddened at this jab. "Don't be too overconfident. I won't be so careless next time."

"I look forward to it. There's nothing better than sparring with a skilled partner. But . . . forgive me, my friend, I have a parting word of advice. Do you know what is the biggest weakness of AI?"

"I told you: I don't do koans. Say what you have to say."

Jiang Liu smiled. "The biggest problem with AI is too much attachment.

Buddhists speak of ātma-grāha and dharma-grāha, attachment to the self and attachment to dharma. You know about the problems of attachment to the self, obviously. But AIs are weak because of attachment to dharma.

"I'm going back to Yun Fan's place. See you tomorrow."

Jiang Liu leaped off the wall and disappeared.

For a long time, Qi Fei stood under the wall, looking up at the empty spot where Jiang Liu had stood. He couldn't remember the last time he had been so curious about someone, or the last time he had felt so much desire to win.

+ + + + +

Qi Fei told all his subordinates that unless the brass asked about it directly, no one was to volunteer any information about the failed attempt to capture and interrogate Jiang Liu. It was simply too embarrassing for CloudMind to fail in a such a spectacular way. The fewer people who knew about it, the fewer complications.

"What should we put in the report for General Yuan?" his assistant asked.

"Limit your report to three things," Qi Fei said. "First, Tianshang is a big deal, probably involved in many dark web deals. Second, Tianshang is not responsible for recent hacking attempts. Third, we have a mole working with Tianshang, but I haven't figured out who yet."

"Should we report on what we've found out about Jiang Liu's background?"

Qi Fei hesitated for a moment. "No."

The assistant nodded and left.

Qi Fei was troubled. "Self-attachment" and "dharma-attachment" kept swirling around his mind. Jiang Liu had managed to hit upon one of his insecurities. He had always strived to maximize the chances of success, to minimize all likely risks, to optimize for the greatest probability with the most advanced algorithms—could it be that this obsession with calculation was a form of attachment, a blind spot?

But how else was one supposed to face the cold patterns found in war? And yet, the calculations couldn't explain Jiang Liu's escape. Was the answer to everything more computing power, more data? Qi Fei knew that he shouldn't be so disturbed by a throwaway comment from Jiang Liu, but the man had managed to put a finger on the most vulnerable part of his psyche.

Qiankun broke into his reverie, alerting him to an incoming call.

It was so late that Qi Fei was hoping to have a glass of wine and go to bed. But he readied himself just in time as General Yuan appeared on the wall. The high-resolution display revealed every pore on the general's face, as well as the old man's exhaustion and unhappiness. He was calling from Okinawa, where it was already past two a.m., and he had been in high-level meetings for the Pacific League all day.

"I'm sorry to call so late," the general said. "I couldn't step away until now."

"No problem at all, sir."

"I saw your report. You captured the head of Tianshang, did you?"

"Uh . . ." Qi Fei tried to find the best way to phrase this. "He's not yet completely under control."

"You mean he escaped?"

"No, no! He's still at the mausoleum. He's here for the mysterious signals as well."

General Yuan nodded. "Keep after him. I don't care if Tianshang isn't behind the hacking attempts. They're a threat. They don't care who sells or buys intelligence on their chain, and that's a problem. The terrorists near the Red Sea pay a lot of attention to them, but the Atlantic Alliance is also getting interested. The best course is to eliminate Tianshang altogether."

"I understand."

"Oh, there's one more thing," the general said.

"How can I help?"

General Yuan looked thoughtful for a moment. "Our friends in Melbourne said that they also detected unusual VLF signals . . . but coming from somewhere near Mars. You should investigate whether they are connected to the ones coming out of the mausoleum." The general paused before continuing. "Some analysts believe that the Atlantic Alliance also detected the signals, which was the cause for their latest retreat. We don't know what sort of opportunity this affords us; you need to get to the bottom of it to give us the initiative."

Qi Fei nodded. "Absolutely."

Instead of hanging up, the general remained on the screen, looking like he still had more to say. Qi Fei waited patiently. He wondered if he should ask about the discussions during the day's meetings, but in the end decided against it. Finally, General Yuan sighed and said, "There's a storm coming . . ."

Qi Fei probed carefully, "I'm not entirely sure I understand . . ."

"Until we put our own house in order, we won't have success against our enemies."

After the call, Qi Fei pondered the general's cryptic comment for a long time. He suspected that the escalating war, with its constantly shifting crises and threats, was making the general feel helpless. Qi Fei hoped to help relieve some of the general's burdens. There was no problem that Qiankun couldn't solve, if given sufficient data. With enough data, anything could be controlled—Qi Fei put his faith in that.

There was no doubt that Jiang Liu had more data about the League than the League had data about him. Those in the shadows always had an advantage over those in the light. Qi Fei hated the man. Hated, *hated* him. *Why is he here bothering Yun Fan? Of all the women in the world, he picks Yun Fan! He's doing this on purpose, to torment me.*

He didn't get much sleep that night.

+ + + + +

The next morning, as Qi Fei entered the museum again, the first person to greet him was Jiang Liu, a half smirk on his face.

"I've missed you so much, Director Qi!"

Qi Fei glared at him. Yun Fan rolled her eyes.

"Did you sleep well last night?" Qi Fei's tone was cold.

"I slept *extremely* well. Thank you for asking. It is *so* quiet in the countryside. I haven't enjoyed such a wonderful rest in ages." Jiang Liu beamed as though he really was enjoying a life of rural simplicity. "Even in my dreams, I was striving to find a way to make our dear Fanfan happy, and so, as soon as I woke up, I came to tell her about my new idea! And"—Jiang Liu paused dramatically to quirk his eyebrow at Qi Fei—"she loved it!"

Qi Fei tamped his anger down. Expressionlessly, he said, "I'm intrigued."

"I think we should fly up into the sky to meet them!" Jiang Liu laughed. "Why should we wait for them to land?"

"You have no idea if they're hostile or friendly. How is it prudent to take such risks?"

"It's all about yuanfen, my over-attached friend. If we don't go, we'll never know."

Yun Fan broke in. "They're friendly."

Qi Fei frowned. "How can you possibly know that? We can't even be sure we know the ship's trajectory. We know nothing about them."

"Historically, they've helped humanity again and again."

"What?"

Yun Fan swept her hand over her desk. The imitation-antique patterns faded, and the surface displayed a long scroll showing a civilization timeline, densely annotated with images.

"Look here," she said, pointing to the scroll, "Ancient Egypt, Atlantis, the Maya . . . each alien visit coincided with a sudden leap in a civilization's advancement. I'll use China as a typical example. Take a look at the dates for all the major inflection points in Chinese civilization: twenty-sixth century BCE, Liangzhu culture, Yan Di and Huang Di; eighteenth century BCE, Erlitou culture and bronze ritual vessels; eleventh century BCE, the fall of Shang and the rise of Zhou; third century BCE, Qin Shi Huang. Do you see a pattern?"

Qi Fei pondered. "I see . . . about seven to eight hundred years between each."

"That's right. The period is just under eight hundred years. Each visit from them brought a sudden burst of innovation and advancement, pushing civilization into a new age. The discontinuity in technology across each leap is obvious. I don't think this is a coincidence. There's no explanation that fits all the data except friendly, helpful aliens."

Qi Fei tried to work it out. "So if you start with Qin Shi Huang and add eight hundred years—"

"You get to the fifth century CE and Maya civilization," Yun Fan said. "And then the thirteenth century, and after that, the twenty-first century."

"So you think they've returned," Qi Fei said.

"Yes." Yun Fan nodded emphatically. "They're our friends."

Better than just about anyone, Qi Fei knew how much pressure Yun Fan had faced in the pursuit of her ideas, and how much she needed something to prove herself. Her work was the engine that drove her life. She couldn't possibly be objective. Yun Fan was single-mindedly pursuing contact with what she deemed a friendly alien civilization, but Qi Fei was deeply skeptical. There was no such thing as true altruism. All instances of human kindness were, ultimately, derived evolutionarily from the drive to procreate. Different sentient species in the cosmos were completely unrelated, so how could any species help another species solely out of unprofitable kindness? The very idea was absurd. In the dark forest of the universe, there was only competition and exploitation. Imagining rainbows and unicorns would do nothing but make sure you were slaughtered quicker and suffered more. If Qi Fei were in charge, he would rather make the mistake of killing the innocent than becoming the victim. It was better to be paranoid against the aliens than to be a trusting fool who would make all humanity pay the price for his own ideas about universal kindness.

Qi Fei gave Jiang Liu a meaningful glance, trying to convey the idea that he should dissuade Yun Fan. But Jiang Liu paid him no mind.

"I believe you." Jiang Liu filled his voice with tenderness. "I will help you fly into space and make contact. My family owns a space transportation company. I can easily find a spaceship to take you to them."

He met Qi Fei's glare with a smile. Qi Fei was biting down so hard that he thought his teeth would crack.

"This is not a game," Qi Fei said gravely. "By making contact with an alien species, you're altering the fates of billions. If you insist on going, I must come as well." He paused before adding, "Also, without military authorization, you can't fly through restricted space at all."

Yun Fan smiled. For the first time in ten years, she was smiling at him. But she did so only because of the aliens. The realization convulsed Qi Fei's heart with a sharp pang.

"Thank you. We'll all go together."

"Oh, I don't think we need to trouble Director Qi," Jiang Liu said, deliberately provoking. "My family can get us the authorization from the Atlantic Alliance."

"You can't!" Qi Fei forced himself to calm down. "Also, Yun Fan is a citizen of the Pacific League; she can't go through restricted space only with the Atlantic Alliance's authorization. The only choice is for me to get us a Pacific League authorization."

"All right." Jiang Liu continued to smile. "I've long wished for more opportunities to learn from Director Qi. This will be perfect."

Later, as he thought back on this moment, Qi Fei couldn't understand just how he had ended up on that fateful, secret journey with Jiang Liu and Yun Fan. He was compelled by some mysterious force: a force that pushed him toward the pair, but also drove him to try to stop them. Qi Fei had lived for years in an environment governed by data: Everything was based on plans, computations, algorithms, optimizations. All his colleagues analyzed the pros and cons before taking each step, discussed and reasoned to come to every decision. But Jiang Liu and Yun Fan were impulsive, carefree. If they wanted to do something, they just did it. Qi Fei almost didn't know how to react to them. All he could rely on was an instinctive feeling that he couldn't allow them to go without him.

He had no idea that Yun Fan and Jiang Liu were just as plagued by doubt as he was.

4 | Kidnapping

To make the first part of their journey easier, Qi Fei called his personal autonomous off-road military vehicle for the group.

A fight followed over the seating arrangement. Yun Fan wanted to sit in the front of the ORV, but Qi Fei and Jiang Liu refused to sit together. Jiang Liu then suggested that he sit in the back with Yun Fan, leaving Qi Fei alone in the front. Qi Fei said he would rather cancel the car than agree to that plan. In the end, a compromise was reached: Jiang Liu sat in the front; Qi Fei and Yun Fan sat in the back seat—each chose to sit pressed against the door on their side, leaving an invisible wall between them.

Jiang Liu was amused by the gap. "It seems there's plenty of room back there. Maybe I should sit between the two of you so we can really have a heart-to-heart."

Yun Fan and Qi Fei shouted "No!" together.

Jiang Liu turned in his seat, and, still wearing that flippant smile, tried to engage Yun Fan.

"Fanfan, after we get into space, I'll take you to a really pretty place. Most space tours can't take you there because it's on the far side of the moon. From there, you can see the Earth peeking out—breathtaking, I tell you."

Qi Fei ignored him. "I want to reiterate that meeting the aliens like this is a bad idea. If they turn out to be hostile, we'll basically be lambs sent to the slaughter. It's safer to remain on Earth and scout them from here."

"How can we possibly scout them from here?" Jiang Liu asked. "The alien spaceship is equipped with such superior stealth capabilities that we can only detect it via VLF emissions. We're practically blind if we stay on the Earth. They could land within the next ten minutes, and we'd still never know."

"I didn't say we shouldn't try to observe them from space," Qi Fei said. "I just meant we don't need to risk ourselves. A drone would do just as well. The enemy is in the dark, but we're in the light. Going in like this is foolhardy."

Jiang Liu snorted scornfully. "Drones? You're always overestimating the capability of machines. How is an AI supposed to know how to react to an alien? What past data can it call on? How will it make decisions?"

"You think I overestimate machines? I think it's more accurate to say that you're always overestimating yourself. Maybe machines won't know what to do, but I can guarantee you that an AI isn't going to make a fool of himself just to show off in front of a girl."

Jiang Liu laughed. "If you are irked because I'm making a fool of myself, maybe it's best that you stay behind. Fanfan and I can go into space ourselves. It will be fantastic!"

"What makes you think she'll want to go with you?"

"Enough!" Yun Fan didn't even bother looking at the two of them but kept her eyes on the scenery sweeping by the car window. "I want to go into space."

Jiang Liu smiled smugly. Qi Fei took a deep breath. "Do you understand that this is extremely dangerous?"

Yun Fan's voice was so soft that it could barely be heard. "I don't want to miss them. I can't. The last time they came to Earth, they seemed not to have landed. If they choose not to land again, I can't wait eight hundred years."

"Do you know for sure that they've ever landed?" Jiang Liu asked.

"Yes. In their earliest visits, they would stay for a long time," Yun Fan said. "The mythological classics speak of Mount Kunlun, a wonder that connected earth to heaven and thrummed with power. In reality, it was most likely a spaceship that had landed. This happened in about the eighteenth century BCE, when Chinese civilization was still in its earliest stages. For subsequent visits, there were also records of landings, but they grew rarer over time. I suspect aliens didn't want to be 'discovered' once we had reached a certain stage of development."

"How . . . did you come to the conclusion that Kunlun was a spaceship?"

"You can ask my mentor when you meet him."

"Fanfan, I'll be honest: Even now I find the idea of aliens rather implausible. I believe it only because you're the one telling me. If anyone else presented me such theories, I'd probably tell them to go jump in a lake."

"There's nothing stopping you from telling me to go jump in a lake."

"Fanfan, don't be mad," Jiang Liu pleaded. "I'm sorry I said that. Look, if we pass a lake, you can push me in to feel better."

"What an idiot," Qi Fei muttered. "You know nothing."

"Oh, I see," Jiang Liu said. "You know everything, do you?"

"I know more than you—"

"Why can't the two of you just shut up?" Yun Fan broke in. "You're both heads of globe-spanning intelligence organizations, with secret identities that would terrify people. Yet here you are, bickering like five-year-olds. Just stay quiet if you can't be civil."

At last, silence prevailed in the car.

Jiang Liu was more than a little astonished that Yun Fan had figured out his role in Tianshang. He had always taken pride in the way he had built Tianshang: decentralized, nonhierarchical, known only to those who deserved to know it. The Tianshang blockchain was completely distributed and anonymous; every Tianshang member knew the taboo against attempts to discover any other member's identity. It was the key to the un-organization's rapid expansion as well as its secrecy. Sure, someone like Qi Fei could figure out his relationship to Tianshang, but how did Yun Fan even know about the decentralized autonomous collective, much less his own role within it? Jiang Liu realized that he had underestimated the girl. A quick glance at Qi Fei assured him that the other man was similarly puzzled.

Qi Fei was indeed nonplussed. More than ten years had passed since the last time he and Yun Fan had talked. They had seen each other at certain functions, but neither had spoken to the other. He hadn't even known what Yun Fan was working on after college. Although the mausoleum was practically next door to his military research institute, he knew nothing about her life. He had tried to keep up with her through the social media feeds of mutual friends, but Yun Fan seemed to have vanished from the lives of all their classmates, never showing up in anyone's photo stream.

Seeing Yun Fan again, he realized that although she looked pretty much the same as she had more than a decade earlier, the air she gave off had changed dramatically. Back then, she had been agreeable and sweet, but now she was like a gleaming, cold blade, her every look and movement sending the message: *I know what you're thinking, but I will carry out my chosen task. No one can stop me.* Qi Fei had sensed a similar determination in someone else . . . The thought sent chills down his spine.

Qi Fei also couldn't figure out how Yun Fan had figured out his real job. The institute's official mission involved hardware and software development, and its role as an intelligence agency was a state secret. It was no surprise that someone like Jiang Liu would figure it out, but how did Yun Fan do it? He felt like he didn't know her anymore after so many years.

The car stopped. Before getting out, Yun Fan addressed the two men. "I don't know what's going to happen once we're in space. I can't rule out the possibility of danger, and I don't have plans for every contingency. However, I'm prepared for the worst, to give my all. I'm going to say it again: you don't have to come with me. In fact, if you were rational and cared about safety, you should stay away from me. I'm going whether you come or not. Don't try to talk me out of it. Just don't."

Jiang Liu and Qi Fei had nothing to say in response. She gave them the feeling of someone marching toward the edge of a cliff; they knew there was no chance that either of them could stop her.

+ + + + +

For their first stop, Yun Fan directed the car to take them to the office of Professor Huang Langyi, Yun Fan's mentor.

Now in his seventies, Professor Huang had long retired from active teaching. But despite his white hair and slow movements, his mind was as sharp as ever. Before entering his office, Yun Fan had told the two men that Professor Huang, a pioneering authority in the field, had not only been her teacher but had also taught her father. The two men were to be on their best behavior and accord the professor the great respect an elder in his position deserved.

Professor Huang seemed to know right away why his visitors had shown up. As soon as they sat down, the old man said, "Let me retrieve the box from the study."

"Please don't rush on our behalf," Yun Fan said. "I'd love it if you would stay and chat with us first. I haven't seen you in ages."

Pleased, Professor Huang sat down and lit a cigarette. The old man and Yun Fan asked after each other's health, and then the professor filled Yun Fan in on his postretirement research projects. Soon, the conversation turned to the subject of their visit. The old man advised Yun Fan to be mindful of the larger environment. "If one is too stubborn," he said in a kind voice, "and makes enemies of everyone around them, it can be self-defeating."

"I know you're referring to my father," Yun Fan said. "To be honest, a decade ago, I shared that view. But now I no longer think so. I feel that a person determined to do something must be prepared to press ahead regardless of the views of everyone around them. I regret that I failed to stick with my father and to be stubborn with him; instead, I tried to tell him to be smart and give in to protect himself. He ended up with two voices fighting in his head: one telling him to push forward, another telling him to retreat. The two voices never left him alone until they drove him mad. If I had stood by him and supported him on the path he had chosen, he would have succeeded. Often, what we need is just someone to stand by us. Even just one person."

Professor Huang exhaled a flavorless smoke ring; the thickening smoke concealed the expressions of everyone present. In a strained voice, he responded, "I suppose you're right. When all those people were attacking him for his ideas on the net, if I had stood up and spoken in support of him, maybe things would have turned out differently."

In an emotionless voice, Yun Fan said, "I meant no criticism at all. You had good reasons to stay silent."

Professor Huang sighed. "Your father was, without any doubt, my most talented student. What a waste!"

Jiang Liu broke in. "Pardon me . . . but do I understand correctly that Dr. Yun had proposed some unpopular idea back then and became the target of vicious attacks by colleagues?"

Yun Fan said nothing. After a moment, the professor nodded.

"May I ask what Dr. Yun's ideas were?"

Professor Huang glanced at Yun Fan to be sure she had no objection. Then he got up and went over to a shelf filled with classical texts and artifacts and took down a bronze ding about the size of a book. Given the detailed decorative patterns and signs of wear, Jiang Liu would have sworn that it was a real, priceless artifact. Yet the way Professor Huang so casually handled it cast doubt on that conclusion.

"It's a 3D-printed model based on a scan of the original, which was found in one of the pits outside the underground palace," Professor Huang answered Jiang Liu's unspoken question. "We've dated it to the middle of the Shang, contemporaneous with Erlitou culture, possibly part of the collection the Qin amassed from all over the empire after unification. Take a closer look at the decorative patterns on the sides."

Jiang Liu leaned closer. The ding was rectangular, and the sides were decorated with two bands. The top band was narrow, like a belt, and made of repeated swirling motifs; the bottom band was broader, filled with images of the heads of birds or beasts—also constructed from swirling motifs.

"It's common knowledge that ritual vessels produced during the height of China's bronze age were primarily decorated with two types of patterns. One is the cloud-thunder pattern, consisting of stylized representations of swirling clouds; the other is the taotie pattern, which doesn't necessarily depict taotie, but beasts that were likely tribal totems. While we don't really understand the significance of the motifs, we know both evolved from earlier antecedents." He brought the ding closer to Jiang Liu. "Take a really good look at the patterns. What do they remind you of?"

Jiang Liu focused on the bands. The patterns were constructed from tight spirals and symmetrical whirls. They did remind him of something . . . "I can't really say."

Professor Huang swept a hand over the tea table, turning the surface into a display. "Bring up the bronze vessel decorative pattern database," he said to the AI assistant. The table responded with a dense grid of images. Professor Huang selected a few images and enlarged them for Jiang Liu.

"Yun Yi—that's Yun Fan's father—curated this database. He sorted through more than seven hundred years of bronzeware and organized everything by date of production and location. The earliest entries were from the eighteenth century BCE, and the latest ones were from the twelfth century BCE. Ah, you probably don't know enough about archaeology to understand the significance. Let me explain: The earliest large bronze vessels in China were from the third period of Erlitou culture, which dates the origin of sophisticated bronze techniques to around seventeen hundred BCE. But even the earliest bronzeware we've found so far are incredibly sophisticated, as though the people learned their craft in a single bound. For decades we've continued to excavate and analyze, but we are no closer to an answer. In any event, look over the images I've selected, which show the evolution of the decorative patterns over time. What do you notice?"

"The earlier patterns seem simpler and less fussy," Jiang Liu said.

"Correct. In fact, the very earliest pattern consists of a double spiral spinning out from a common center. Yun Yi believed that this was a stylized depiction of the Milky Way."

"What?" Jiang Liu couldn't quite believe his ears.

"Yun Yi's hypothesis was that the serpentine spiraling arms, a common motif in later decorations that most people thought represented two loong, were derived from the shape of the galaxy. The further back you go in time, the clearer this correspondence becomes. Look here: It's a fragment from one of the earliest vessels excavated from Erlitou. The whirling pattern on it is clearly the basis of the cloud-thunder pattern, and it looks just like our galaxy. Yun Yi made the bold claim that the pattern was derived from the even-earlier Liangzhu culture and depicted our galaxy. Over centuries of refinement, it eventually evolved into cloud-thunder pattern, taotie pattern, and even bagua."

"And he suggested that the only way people could know the shape of the galaxy was because of aliens," Jiang Liu guessed. "Was that why people attacked him?"

"Exactly," Professor Huang said. "He suggested that aliens showed the people images of our galaxy, and these images then became worshipped as divine revelations. The aliens also taught the people metallurgy and casting techniques, and the people then decorated their ritual vessels with patterns that symbolized the extraterrestrials. His theory also explains a mystery that we've never been able to satisfactorily resolve: Why did the people of Shang and Zhou make bronze ritual vessels at all? Producing bronzeware was incredibly energy- and resource-intensive, and an agricultural society barely surviving should devote the new technology to productive uses such as farming and hunting implements; yet the vast majority of bronzeware turned out to be ritual vessels, and large, heavy vessels at that. If the very technology came from aliens, then this imbalance wouldn't be as surprising."

Jiang Liu pondered the professor's explanation. He frowned. "I can see that's a plausible story, but I don't think there's enough evidence to stand up as scholarship."

Professor Huang sighed. "How right you are. After Yun Yi published his paper, he was roundly ridiculed. But matters escalated when a coalescing mob began to attack his character, and then turned to question the integrity of our department and university. Yun Yi had done extensive scholarship on other topics as well: the nature of Mount Kunlun, the legends around Hetu and Luoshu, the historical reality of Fuxi and Chang'e, and so on. However, all his research then became the subject of mob scrutiny. As you well know, a net mob has neither the patience nor the training to evaluate specialist research, but they're very good at picking a few sentences out of context and manufacturing controversy. Yun Yi's personality was unsuited to dealing with this sort of troll-storm. He fed them by confronting them and arguing with them, as if they cared about evidence and reasoning. The controversy escalated until the school administration, under pressure, dismissed Yun Yi. Even now, I regret my own cowardice at the time. I failed to stand up for him, to—"

"I think we've talked enough about the past," Yun Fan interrupted. "It's getting late. Let's take what we came for and leave Professor Huang in peace."

The professor got up and went into a room in the back. After a few minutes, he emerged with an octagonal box. He was so reverential in the way he held the box that Jiang Liu thought he was carrying out the ashes of Yun Fan's father. But as the professor approached, he saw that the box was not for holding ashes, but a strange object on its own. The professor set the box down and dusted it with a lens cloth. The box was smooth all over, perfectly black, devoid of any decorative patterns, seams, or buttons.

"I've kept it safe all this time," the professor said.

"Thank you." Yun Fan picked it up and set it down on her knees. "It's the only thing my father left behind. I had no idea where else to keep it, which is why I had to trouble you."

"I understand," the professor said. "Don't worry. No one else knows of its existence."

Yun Fan looked up at him. "Thank you. I really appreciate it." Her eyes misted over, but in the end, no tears spilled.

The three got up to say good-bye. Before leaving, Yun Fan gave the professor a hug. "Don't linger too much on the past. I don't blame you, and I know my father didn't blame you. Take care of yourself."

+ + + + +

As they descended the stairs, Yun Fan told Jiang Liu and Qi Fei to wait for her while she went back to her old office to retrieve something. Jiang Liu and Qi Fei stood in front of the anthropology building gazing at the young undergrads rushing about the campus. For a moment they seemed to have traveled through time, glimpsing again their own youth.

"You seem unusually quiet today," Jiang Liu said to Qi Fei.

"I've never liked useless chatter."

"I seem to recall a lot of words lobbed my way when you were chasing me." Jiang Liu smirked.

"You don't know me at all."

Jiang Liu turned serious. "Just now, when we were talking with Professor Huang, you were quiet because you didn't want to talk about any of those things, am I right?"

Qi Fei said nothing.

"You knew about what happened to Yun Fan's father, didn't you?"

Qi Fei nodded.

"Let's see . . ." Jiang Liu did the math in his head. "This would be . . . back when Yun Fan was in high school?"

"She was a third-year in junior high."[6]

"What happened, exactly?" Jiang Liu asked. "I still don't understand the details. Yun Fan said she regretted what she did back then, but what could she have done as a junior high student? Why the regret?"

"She didn't do anything wrong," Qi Fei said. "She shouldn't blame herself."

"Then who should she blame?"

Qi Fei glared at him. "You are both too smart and too stupid. You're clever enough to see that I clearly don't want to talk about it, but you're also just enough of an idiot to keep on pestering me. You're like some bored old lady with nothing to occupy herself but gossip, you know that?"

---

6   China's education system has three years of junior high (equivalent to seventh, eighth, and ninth grades in the US) and three years of senior high school (equivalent to tenth, eleventh, and twelfth grades in the US).

Jiang Liu laughed. "Oho! That sounds like misogyny. I think I'm going to report you—"

"All right, then, you are a bored old man with nothing to do but gossip. Anyway, I don't want to talk to you. Go sit in the shade of that tree over there."

Just then, music started to blast from Qi Fei's shirt pocket. He took out his phone and flipped it open. As soon as he saw the name of the caller, he frowned awkwardly and flipped the phone closed. But it started to ring again. He opened it and closed it again. For a third time, the insistent ringtone blared out.

A sweet feminine voice sounded behind the men. "Qi Fei! I found you!"

They turned and saw a tall woman in a form-fitting skirt and a black, high-collared, short-sleeve top. As she approached, Jiang Liu could think of only one word to describe her: elegant. Every step, every gesture seemed just right; just looking at her made one feel like spring had arrived.

"Hi, Bailu." Qi Fei's voice was subdued.

"I was right!" Yuan Bailu said, smiling. "As soon as I saw the ORV parked near the campus gate, I thought you might be visiting. To be sure, I called my dad, but he said he didn't think you had any errands that would take you here. I had to get your license plate number to be sure that it really was your car. So then I tried to call you, but you didn't pick up. However, I could hear the ring from where I was, so I just followed it. Oh, I'm sorry, I don't believe I've met your friend."

"This is Jiang Liu." Qi Fei made the introduction reluctantly. "He's . . . from Hawaii."

"Oh, Hawaii is so lovely," Yuan Bailu said. "I bet you're regretting it already, given the climate here."

"I'm adjusting." Jiang Liu smiled back. "Besides, seeing so many beautiful women is a good compensation."

"You should come to my home for dinner with Qi Fei!" Bailu said. Turning to Qi Fei, she added, "My mom is finally back from vacation. She brought a ton of Yunnan matsutake, and she wants to cook a feast tonight. Both of you should come!"

"Oh, I can't make it," Qi Fei said. "I have work."

Jiang Liu broke in. "Nonsense! Don't worry about work, buddy. I'll take care of it for you. You should totally go!"

Yun Fan emerged from the anthropology building holding a box full of books and file folders. She saw Bailu and stopped about three meters away. Jiang Liu went up to help Yun Fan carry the box, and only then did Qi Fei notice Yun Fan.

For about five seconds, none of the four said anything. Yun Fan looked from Qi Fei to Yuan Bailu, and then back to Qi Fei. Bailu gazed at Yun Fan with curiosity. She clearly didn't know her and glanced at Qi Fei, waiting for an introduction. But Qi Fei looked away. Bailu sensed the awkwardness between the two. Everyone was waiting for someone else to break the uncomfortable silence first.

"Fanfan, I think the two of us should go," Jiang Liu said, seizing the moment. "Qi Fei has plans for tonight."

Yun Fan nodded and walked away with Jiang Liu. As Jiang Liu carried the large box, Yun Fan reached out to steady it. From a distance, it looked as though the two were holding hands. Although the pair never looked back, the whole way they could feel two pairs of eyes staring at them from behind.

"I should thank that Bailu." Jiang Liu glanced at Yun Fan walking next to him. "Without her, you wouldn't be holding my arm right now."

Yun Fan glared at him. "That box is full of books I care about. I don't trust you not to drop it."

"Qi Fei and you have no yuanfen, Fanfan. But you and I are all about yuanfen." Jiang Liu's tone was as irreverent as ever. "Tell me, what do you want to eat tonight? My treat. Though I've never been to Xi'an, I have my places."

+ + + + +

Yun Fan called a car to bring the black box and the cardboard box of books and papers back to the mausoleum before following Jiang Liu into the city. She hoped that they could settle on the itinerary for going into space. Jiang Liu told her that he needed to contact his family to figure it out, and so the two went together to one of Jiang Liu's so-called "places."

Yun Fan balked when she found out that Jiang Liu was taking her to a nightclub. "I'm not here to party," she said.

Jiang Liu insisted that he wasn't here to party either. The club was managed by a subsidiary of Jiang Lang Trading, he explained, and it offered a secure and convenient place for him to marshal his resources. Reluctantly, Yun Fan followed him in.

The club entrance used a gimmick called the "cloud corridor." Each group of guests stepped onto a separate "cloud," a small moving platform engulfed in mist and fog. The platforms then dispatched guests into different passages bathed in moody lighting: up, down, spiraling . . . Even the walls were a mix of real and virtual. Sometimes a group would be sent careening toward a wall, only to find out at the last minute that it was a projection. Sometimes a group would see a new passageway approach only to find out that it was a trompe l'oeil painting. Every group of guests was sent on their own separate journey, and in the end, no one knew how they ended up at their destination.

"A bit disorienting, right?" Jiang Liu said to her. "This is how we keep everyone safe."

"Safe? What do you mean?" Yun Fan asked.

"Think about it." Jiang Liu smiled enigmatically.

Yun Fan was about to ask for more clarification when she suddenly had an inkling of what he meant.

Although Yun Fan didn't know the exact nature of Jiang Lang Trading, she was aware of rumors that the family had built its wealth through cryptocurrency— not speculation in the coins themselves, but anonymous cryptocurrency transactions on early global blockchains. Jiang Liu had mentioned earlier that his father was angry with him for leaking business data about "uranium." Obviously, business deals involving ordinary nuclear power plants would not require the sort of secrecy and anonymity suggested by the cloud corridor; even her toes had enough awareness and intelligence to figure out what other sorts of deals involving uranium *would* require such elaborate "safety" measures. Furthermore, for Jiang Liu, a mere graduate student, to turn Tianshang into the world's largest intelligence exchange within a few years, he had to have drawn on his family's vast infrastructure and resources.

Jiang Liu took Yun Fan into a private suite whose walls were covered in mirrors. The endless reflections made her feel as though she had fallen into a spacetime abyss. Jiang Liu waved his hands and put calming scenes of nature on all the walls except one, which he left open for a video call.

Soon, Uncle Bo's face, red with rage, appeared on the wall.

"You bastard! After everything you put me through, you still have the gall to call me? Your father—oh, wait till I get my hands on you, I'll—"

"I'm so glad you got home safely!" Jiang Liu said, grinning innocently.

"Did you really think I was going to wait for you in Xi'an the rest of my life after you escaped?" Uncle Bo panted. "Don't you dare come home, ever. If you do, I'll make the spankings you got as a kid seem—"

"Uncle Bo!" Jiang Liu pleaded with puppy eyes. "I am sooooo sorry. I'll bear any punishment you see fit to impose, and I'll give you a relaxing shoulder massage in thanks! The only thing I ask is that you help me get a ride on a spaceship for a little tour. As soon as you do, I'll come over and offer my bottom for a spanking. And with every strike, I'll shout, 'Uncle Bo is the best! May I have another?'"

Uncle Bo was so mad that he lost his voice momentarily. "You . . . you think I'm going to do you a favor after all that? Do you really take me for a fool? I raised you—"

"Uncle Bo really is the best! I know that you may sound mad, but no one else cares about me as much as you—"

"You can't always get your way just by sweet-talking me! Look, kid, even if I wanted to help you, I can't. The corporate spaceships are scheduled months in advance, and your father has to personally sign off on any deviation."

"You're talking about commercial spaceships, but I'm asking just for a small private ship. I know that our company owns four—my father takes VIPs and people he's trying to impress on space tours. I remember one Christmas when he took the British prime minister and her family . . . oh, my sister went too! Also, two of the ships are equipped with high-capacity engines and can fly all the way to Mars. I know those are available any time."

Uncle Bo snorted. "I see you aren't nearly as ignorant of the family business as you act. Surely then you also know that these private ships are even more directly under your father's control."

"Well . . . yes, but people with real power in the family"—he winked at Uncle Bo—"always have ways of deploying resources. I mean, it's a time of war, right? There are lots of unforeseen circumstances needing snap decisions. What if some VIP suddenly needed one of our ships? My father can't possibly oversee everything. Come on, Uncle Bo, I know you have ways. I'll be sooooo grateful!"

"What good is your gratitude? No!"

"What about two bottles of your favorite whiskey? Three?"

"Do you think I can't get all the whiskey I want myself?"

"Oh, I know! I'll take you skiing for a whole month. Just you and me."

Finally, Uncle Bo's tone softened. "A whole month?"

"Yes, even one with thirty-one days! I promise."

Uncle Bo sighed. "I must have done something wrong in my last life to end up taking care of you. From the time you were a boy, how many times have you gotten me in trouble? I always have to clean up after your messes. Fine . . . Just tell me, which girl are you trying to impress this time?"

Jiang Liu blinked frantically, trying to silently stop Uncle Bo from this line of inquiry. The older man looked around the room, finally noticing Yun Fan in the corner.

"Oh! Uh . . ." Uncle Bo swallowed. "I forgot that you're in Xi'an to pursue your academic research. So this must also be for research. Research."

Jiang Liu continued his conversation with Uncle Bo another minute, admonishing the older man to make contact as soon as he had secured a spaceship. Then he hung up, and the screen went blank.

He turned around to find Yun Fan glaring at him contemptuously. He blushed. From Uncle Bo's question, she must have guessed that he had often asked the steward to misuse his family's assets to help him impress women. He wanted to explain, but he couldn't.

In his private life, he knew he was hardly a model of responsible behavior. His high school and college years were all spent abroad, and much of that time was devoted to drinking and chasing girls. He had countless one-night stands and multiple girlfriends—the girlfriends were distinguished largely by the fact that he could recall their names when sober. None of his relationships had ever lasted longer than three months.

He had pursued such a hedonistic lifestyle because it allowed him to avoid thinking about the unpleasant aspects of his own life. He couldn't stop his own inner Socrates from demanding a deeper examination, from asking questions for which he had no answers. Sober, he felt depressed, alone, incapable of connecting and forming deep attachments, out of place, the world layers of emptiness piled on meaninglessness. At those moments, he could find refuge only in the oblivion of alcohol and the momentary pleasures of the flesh; otherwise, he would drown in his own questions.

But how could he explain all that to Yun Fan?

So he pretended that nothing had happened and threw himself into planning. Even if Uncle Bo could get them a spaceship, there was still so much more to do to prepare for their trip. He brought up his private chain space, sent out some queries, and then dispatched two AI agents to look for what he needed on the network. The manager of the club then came in to discuss something with him in a corner. Finally, two women in tight dresses came in and sat on either side of him to get their orders—although professionalism pervaded all their interactions, the sight still would have struck an observer as sensual.

Finally, he was done making arrangements, but when he looked up, Yun Fan was gone.

She must have found the whole nightclub atmosphere too distracting and left, he thought. But since she didn't know her way around the place, he wasn't sure she could find her way out. He dashed out of the suite to find her.

The cloud corridor platform moved too slowly for his taste. For the first time, he found the design annoying rather than clever. The interior of the club was like a three-dimensional labyrinth, full of twists and turns, dead ends and false doors. There were numerous private suites like the one he had just left, as well as several cavernous AR dance halls, pulse karaoke galleries, and brainwave deep-dream massage parlors. Even Jiang Liu himself wasn't familiar with all the services on offer, though he knew clubs like this were one of the most profitable lines of business owned by his family. In an increasingly technologically fragmented, postindustrial age, more than half of the annual profit reported by the Jiang Lang conglomerate was from its global network of nightclubs.

As he shuttled among the strobe-lit rooms, surfing from one wave of deafening music to another, he grew disoriented and dizzy. But Yun Fan was nowhere to be found.

Finally, he exited the front door and stepped onto the sidewalk. His phone beeped with a message from Yun Fan.

"Come to the Old City Wall. Changle Gate."

Jiang Liu grabbed a self-driving taxi and headed for the Old City Wall. Something about the whole situation felt off. The taxi was caught in a traffic jam, and he got out, continuing his way to the wall on foot. The ongoing war had devastated the economy. Most of the shops were shuttered, and many people sat on stools on the sidewalks, idle, looking lost. As Jiang Liu ran past them, the memory of the nightclub still fresh, he felt as though he had entered a parallel world.

Finally, he arrived at Changle Gate. Panting, he looked around for Yun Fan but didn't find her. Unexpectedly, Qi Fei had arrived as well. He had also received the same message.

"Oh no," they said simultaneously.

+ + + + +

Every time the navigation AI on the cloud corridor platform asked for her input, Yun Fan requested to be taken to the exit. After many twists and turns, a completely disoriented Yun Fan finally found herself outside the nightclub—but she had exited from a different entrance than the one she had used on the way in. She was in an alleyway, surrounded by warehouses and empty lots piled with trash. No taxi would be able to make its way through this mess, so she started walking, hoping to find a big street soon.

She found a major road, but her phone couldn't hold a steady signal for her to hail a taxi. The barely there connection allowed her to text, at least. She tried several times before a car finally stopped next to her. Sighing with relief, she got in, telling the AI to take her back to the mausoleum.

Yun Fan's mind was all confusion: Qi Fei, Jiang Liu, the women around each . . . She didn't want to think about them, and so she closed her eyes and tried to control her breathing, trying to return to the tranquility she achieved during yoga or meditation. Emotions were unwanted; she needed now, more than ever, rational planning and a steady list of tasks to be completed.

Thus, she was too distracted to pay attention to where the car was going. Instead of heading toward the mausoleum, it was circuitously taking her closer and closer to downtown.

The car stopped; the door opened. A man in a suit got in.

Before Yun Fan could react, the man struck her in her head. She felt a sting, followed by a tingling near her temples, and then lost consciousness.

"To the Old City Wall," the man said to the car's navigation AI. "Changle Gate."

He held a finger under Yun Fan's nostrils to be sure she was okay. The car began to move, and the man smiled with satisfaction. His plan had worked far better than he expected, and thinking of the conversation to come, he rubbed his hands together in anticipation. A few days ago, his spies had brought him the news that Jiang Liu and Qi Fei both had been found in the company of the same woman. He knew he had to meet her. What sort of woman could entice both of these men? What secrets did she harbor?

Changle Gate was just a few minutes away.

5 | A Party of Four

Jiang Liu and Qi Fei climbed onto the Old City Wall and saw Yun Fan right away.

Since it wasn't a holiday, and the war had cast a pall over everything, there were very few tourists atop the wall. A few local parents were there to take pictures with their children, and a few couples took walks or rode bikes. The ancient battlements, having weathered centuries, were in ill repair but nonetheless bore witness to the weight of history.

The setting sun lit up the watchtowers, casting a red glow against the wispy clouds in the sky.

Yun Fan sat on a bench on the scenic view platform next to one of the watchtowers. A man sat next to her, his arm wrapped intimately around her. Yun Fan's head rested on his shoulder, her eyes closed, and to all the passersby they appeared as a couple taking a break from a lovers' stroll.

Right away, Jiang Liu and Qi Fei noticed Yun Fan's slack facial expression, a sign that she had been drugged. The man's arm around her waist likely meant that he was holding a concealed weapon against her.

Yun Fan was a hostage.

Jiang Liu and Qi Fei locked eyes for a second before carefully approaching the bench. Jiang Liu twisted his ring; Qi Fei touched the right temple of his glasses. Their personal AI agents began to search for information on the kidnapper.

The man greeted the approaching pair with a smug smile.

"The youngest son of the famous Jiang family and the head of a top-secret

Chinese military research institute!" The man spoke Chinese with a foreign accent. "I've been waiting for you for a while now. In fact, I was getting worried you might miss the appointment."

He held up his right hand to indicate that Qi Fei and Jiang Liu should stop before getting too close. He continued to hold Yun Fan with his left arm, even pulling her closer to him. Qi Fei and Jiang Liu stopped about two or three meters away.

"Ah, Chris Zhao," Qi Fei said. Qiankun continued to stream data about the kidnapper into his cranial implant. "Graduate of West Point, executive director of the International New Energy Consortium, investment advisor for the Global Technology Territory Fund, and on top of all that, an investigative reporter. To what do we owe the pleasure of a visit from such a notable personage?"

Chris nodded and grinned in acknowledgment. "Since you already know so much about me, I imagine there's no need to conceal my other identity either?"

"Of course," Jiang Liu said. "It's not every day that you get to meet a high-level operative from the AIA."

"Normally, I'd have to kill you just for that," Chris said. "But you two are special. We have no secrets before one another, do we?"

Jiang Liu was also listening to his AI whispering to him everything about Chris Zhao via his ear clip. He had to figure out what the man wanted. "Is Mr. Zhao, perhaps like me, also here to admire the beauty of this ancient Chinese capital?"

Chris laughed. "Mr. Jiang, like you, I'm here for this girl."

"How do you know Yun Fan?" Qi Fei asked, an edge coming into his voice.

"I didn't. Not at first. But I got to know her through the two of you! I've long been impressed by both of your exploits, and so I wanted to know what sort of extraordinary woman could bring two masters of the intelligence game together." As Chris spoke, he was also observing Qi Fei and Jiang Liu closely, noting every reaction. "I thought that the two of you would start fighting over her, but unexpectedly, you began to cooperate. Very strange, no? I'm intrigued by strange things."

Qi Fei and Jiang Liu looked at each other. Assuming Chris was telling the truth, then Qi Fei and Jiang Liu had both been under heavy surveillance. Their recent movements and actions, deviating from their habits, must have triggered some sort of alert that brought Chris Zhao to investigate Yun Fan. As for who was tracking them and analyzing their data, they quickly sorted through the possibilities in their heads and settled on one answer: Quantum Fog.

"Let's not beat around the bush any further," Qi Fei said. "What do you want?"

"I just want to get to know the two of your better. The setting sun is so lovely. Perfect for a heart-to-heart with new friends, don't you think? How about we start by discussing your travel plans?"

"What . . . travel plans?" Qi Fei asked, probing to see how much the AIA agent already knew.

"You came to find Yun Fan in order to go on a trip. Tell me, where are you all going?"

Jiang Liu laughed. "Oh, so that's what you have in mind. Let's find a good restaurant and talk about it over dinner. Oh!" He took a few steps toward Chris, eyes on Yun Fan. "I think she's really tired. Why don't we send her home to rest, and we'll meet over lunch tomorrow for a good chat? My treat."

Chris's pupils contracted slightly as he watched Jiang Liu move closer. "You better stop where you are. I asked the two of you here because I'm interested in making a deal with you. My proposal is very simple: Whatever your plans are, make me a part of them. If you agree, then we're all friends and Yun Fan can go home tonight. But if you don't want to be friends, that's also no problem. I'll just have to talk to Yun Fan and take her on her trip all by myself."

Qi Fei and Jiang Liu didn't even bother looking at each other; they already knew the decision the other had come to. The two of them were already locked in a rivalry to help Yun Fan. To involve Chris Zhao, a representative of the Atlantic Alliance, their common adversary, would only make the situation even more complicated. In a free-for-all, neither Qi Fei nor Jiang Liu was sure to come out on top; therefore, it was advantageous for both to work together to prevent Chris from becoming involved.

The pair took a step forward simultaneously, blocking the left and right sides of the long bench. They figured that Chris would now have no choice but to fight for a way out, and the two of them could subdue him together and rescue Yun Fan.

But as they got within one meter of Chris, the bench suddenly lifted off, hovered a few centimeters above the brick floor, and slid away along the top of the wall. The unexpected movement caught Qi Fei and Jiang Liu off guard, and by the time they recovered, the bench had carried Chris and Yun Fan more than ten meters away.

Only now did the two realize that there were no other benches atop the city wall save this one. Their attention had been so focused on Yun Fan and her kidnapper that they failed to notice this unusual fact. Jiang Liu examined the spot where the bench had been and saw faint metallic tracks. Instantly, he understood the principles behind the moving bench. It sprayed metal to form instantaneous tracks, and then hovered over them with electromagnetism. The advances in high-temperature maglev technology by the Atlantic Alliance were truly extraordinary.

"We can't catch him on foot," Jiang Liu whispered to Qi Fei.

Chris stopped the bench. Apparently, he wanted to try to elicit more information out of them.

"You know, you shouldn't resort to violence so quickly," Chris shouted at them. His loud voice caused a few passersby to glance their way. "Tell you what: I'll ask you questions, and you just have to answer yes or no. First question: Does your plan involve space?"

Qi Fei leaned toward Jiang Liu and whispered, "I'll stop him; you save Yun Fan at the first opportunity."

"You think you can stop him?"

"Ha! You've seen nothing of what I'm capable of." Qi Fei pulled out his collapsible baton and ran at the bench.

Instinctively, Chris drove the hovering bench back, away from Qi Fei, but behind the bench, a giant metal frame suddenly rose up and fell toward the top of the wall like a collapsing mountain. It was the support framework for a stage inside the city wall. Ordinarily, the framework raised and lowered the stage on performance days, but somehow, it had come alive like a giant's forearm. The falling framework struck the city wall just behind the retreating bench, and Chris had to brake hard to avoid colliding with it.

Jiang Liu was also running toward the bench, right next to Qi Fei. As the bench came to a stop, he reached out for the unconscious Yun Fan.

But Chris was too skilled and experienced to be so easily overcome. Just as Jiang Liu's fingers came within inches of Yun Fan, he pulled her back and tilted hard to the right, his hand slamming down on the right arm of the bench. Instantly, panels in the bench unfolded, twisted, extended, separated—until the bench had transformed into a mini hovercar. Though the vehicle had neither wheels nor a traditional engine, it was equipped with powerful maglev motors, which allowed it to hover easily above the top of the wall.

The hovercar was only about the size of a motorcycle, extremely nimble and maneuverable. With nozzles under the car spraying some unknown liquid metal that instantly hardened into highly conductive temporary tracks, Chris easily drove the car away from Qi Fei and Jiang Liu.

Chris stopped the car, once he was a safe distance away. Using his left arm to secure Yun Fan so that her head leaned on his shoulder, the AIA operative held up a small transparent sphere in his right hand. Around the sphere wound a band filled with electronics and twinkling lights.

"Stop," Chris warned. "This is a miniature tactical nuclear device. It's more than enough to incinerate this watchtower and everything within it."

Qi Fei and Jiang Liu skidded to a stop. "Don't do this."

"I told you," Chris said, "I just want some answers. Let me ask you one last time: Are you planning to go to space? I began to pay attention to you when Mr. Jiang downloaded large amounts of classified data from NASA without authorization. Now, I was responsible for the quantum encryption on the data, so I was very curious who had the skills and the temerity to break into my house. I'm sure you thought you left no traces, but my design had multiple anti-intrusion measures that, even when the system was breached, would tag and track the intruder. I followed the trackers and found out that Mr. Jiang was the responsible party. But lo and behold! Who did I find with Mr. Jiang? Director Qi, who also recently seemed to have developed an interest in astronomy, redirecting satellites to observe space.

"Obviously, this is no mere coincidence. We're all in the same line of work, so don't try to give me some silly story about stargazing with a pretty girl. I want to know what you've discovered."

He held up the mini nuke threateningly and raised the hovercar another few inches off the ground, as though getting ready to depart for good.

"If the two of you don't want to make a new friend and share the discovery, that's fine. I'll just take Yun Fan with me so that we can stargaze together tonight. When you've changed your mind, you can come to my hotel. So what will it be? Do you want to talk now or later?"

For a couple of seconds, neither Qi Fei nor Jiang Liu moved, their minds racing to find a way out of the impasse. But Yun Fan saved them the trouble.

Suddenly, her eyes snapped open, and she slammed her left hand down on Chris Zhao's left wrist, a row of spikes popping out of the bracelet she wore to enhance her strike. The struck man grunted from the pain and pulled back his left hand instinctively. Yun Fan used the opportunity to throw off his left arm, jump off the hovercar, and aim a series of precise kicks at her captor. Her heel struck Chris in the chest, knocking him back, and a second kick tipped the mini nuke out of his hand, the sphere tumbling harmlessly to the ground.

She turned and ran toward the edge of the city wall, leaping off into the air beyond with no hesitation. "Jump with me!"

Jiang Liu and Qi Fei followed behind and leapt as well. As they did so, Jiang Liu questioned his own sanity. *What am I doing? I have no idea what her plan is—if she even has one. I hope this is not it for us.*

He looked down and saw an autonomous flying car hovering in place, its twenty-four propellers keeping it trimmed in midair. Yun Fan and Jiang Liu tumbled into the seats perfectly, as though they had meant to get in this way. Qi Fei had overshot the car slightly, but he was able to grab on to the car's fins. Jiang Liu and Yun Fan pulled him in easily.

"Wow!" Jiang Liu exclaimed. "Let's do that again." The car, meant for only two, was a bit cramped with all three of them in it.

"How did you know there would be a car waiting here?" Qi Fei asked.

"I knew Chris's nuke was unarmed," Yun Fan said. "It's just for show. His plan was to throw it and force you to take cover, and as soon as you did, he would activate this car and jump into it from atop the wall."

"So that was why you kicked the mini nuke with no fear," Jiang Liu said. "Were you just pretending to be unconscious?"

"No, he did manage to drug me. But I woke up as soon as he began to move the bench. I was biding my time."

Jiang Liu had more questions. "So how did you—"

"Now is not the time. We must get out of here. Remember: this is Chris's car, and he can summon us back at any moment."

Indeed, the flying car was already slowing. It stopped and began to reverse, slowly backing up toward the watchtower. They twisted around in their seats and saw Chris peering at them from on top of the wall. Qi Fei waved his baton to make one of the streetlamps lean over, close enough that they could jump out and grab the lamppost. They scrambled down the post and disappeared into the busy streets.

Before they turned down a narrow alley, Jiang Liu looked back and saw that the lamppost had unbent itself, and Chris was nowhere to be seen on the watchtower. He sighed in relief.

"I'm impressed, Qi Fei," he said. "I had no idea Qiankun could do so much. Is the whole city all networked like this?"

Qi Fei grinned with pride. "All that infrastructure to build a smart city has its advantages."

"Where do we go now?" Yun Fan asked.

Qi Fei thought about it. "I don't think it's a good idea to go back to the mausoleum. Chris is sure to be waiting for us there. I have a friend nearby who owns a bistro; we can stay with him for a bit."

Since they were in a tourist area filled with pedestrian lanes, they went down one winding lane after another, making their way undetected through the metropolis. Qi Fei purposefully doubled back a few times and took them on the most circuitous route possible to shake off any tails. Even Yun Fan had trouble keeping up with him. Finally, they ended up in front of a building constructed in classical Chinese wooden architecture. Qi Fei looked around one more time, taking care to check for miniature drones before pushing open the yard gate and leading everyone in.

The bistro was designed to evoke the ancient past. The building's frames and swooping roof copied Tang dynasty originals. The paths inside the yard were covered in white pebbles and bluestone. Two palace lanterns, glowing a warm and welcoming orange, stood on each side of the main entrance to the building.

Just as they were about to go in, Qi Fei abruptly stopped. Yun Fan and Jiang Liu almost ran into him, and Jiang Liu muttered a complaint.

Qi Fei ignored him. Looking only at Yun Fan, he said, "I should have told you earlier; my friend . . . you know him too."

+ + + + +

Chang Tian, the proprietor, greeted Qi Fei right away. By the way he showed no surprise, it was clear that Qi Fei often patronized this place. He asked Qi Fei whether he wanted his usual table before turning to greet the rest of the party. As soon as he saw Yun Fan, he stopped awkwardly. It was as if the very air froze.

"Is that really you?" Chang Tian muttered. "Yun Fan. I can't believe it."

Yun Fan nodded almost imperceptibly. "Why don't we sit down somewhere private first?"

Chang Tian took them to a private suite in the back. The low table, Tang-style, was designed for everyone to kneel or sit around it on the floor, as was the custom of that time. However, the material in the flooring had been modernized to improve comfort. The table was covered in small sancai pottery dishes, timeless and refined. The small suite, even with four people packed into it, didn't feel cramped but exuded comfort and hospitality. Finally, the food in the dishes, though simple, was elevated in preparation and presentation: sashimi, raw oysters, sour plum pork ribs, lychee shrimp . . . interesting twists on traditional combinations. Chang Tian warmed a few sancai flasks of house-distilled baijiu and placed one in front of each person as though they were at a classical poetry party.

"How's Qianqian doing?" Qi Fei asked.

"She's visiting her parents back home," Chang Tian said. "Her mom is dealing with some health issues; she wants to be there for her."

"And is business good?" Qi Fei asked.

"It's all right. Better than a few months ago, for sure. Now that the war isn't as heated as before, people want to go out and have fun again." Chang Tian shrugged. "But I can't say I'm making a lot of money."

"See? I told you not to leave the air force," Qi Fei said. "If you had stayed, I bet you'd be a major now, maybe a group commander."

Chang Tian grinned and took a sip of baijiu. "Let's not talk about me. Too boring. Yun Fan, I haven't seen you in ages. How've you been?"

"I'm still the same." Yun Fan's answer brought different images to the three men, each with a different idea about what she used to be like. "I didn't realize you had enlisted."

Chang Tian nodded. "I did. Was in the air force for a few years."

"He's being modest," Qi Fei said. "You're looking at a real hero. Three years ago, in an encounter in the South China Sea, he led a flight of ten pilots to take on an entire wing from an enemy aircraft carrier. Somehow, his small group disrupted the enemy and prevented them from taking off and launching an attack. Later, he fought in the defense of Qinghai and made a name for himself as an ace dogfighter. He shot down two Grantz K-82s, the best fighter from the other side. The Atlantic

Alliance had planned to switch entirely to drone fighters, but Chang Tian's record changed their minds. Now they send their own aces to take on ours."

Yun Fan exclaimed in admiration, "Then why did you leave the air force?"

"I got tired of it," Chang Tian said. "One day, I woke up and realized that I was afraid. I don't have the mental makeup to be a hero. Better for me to live an ordinary life: run a bistro and cook for my customers."

"I know the real reason you quit," Qi Fei teased. "It's that girlfriend of yours. You want to stay home and make babies."

"Nah, don't put this on Qianqian. Even if I hadn't met her, I would have quit."

"What were you afraid of?" Yun Fan asked. "I don't believe you were scared of fighting."

Chang Tian refilled everyone's cup. "I was afraid that I would never get a chance to open my bistro."

Yun Fan and Qi Fei were both silent, pondering what Chang Tian really meant by that.

Jiang Liu broke the silence. "Since you're an ace fighter pilot, do you think you can fly a spaceship?" Seeing Chang Tian's guarded expression, he held out a hand to introduce himself. "I'm Jiang Liu, an astronomer. I'm Qi Fei's . . . friend from Hawaii. I'm organizing a really important trip and need a good spaceship pilot."

"It depends on what kind of spaceship—"

"Excellent! So you *do* know how to fly some spaceships, at least. What about a small Zeta-class? Can you operate those?"

"I think they're similar to the Betas, if I remember—"

"Exactly. They're simplified and upgraded versions of Betas."

"I did fly Betas a few times," Chang Tian said, "but I can't claim to be an expert. I don't know anything about the Alphas; those have different propulsion systems and handle nothing like the Betas."

"Perfect!" Jiang Liu rubbed his hands excitedly. "I feel fortune is smiling on us. My family's spaceship is a Zeta-plus, which should handle much like the Betas. Why don't you come with us tonight and take us into space?"

"What?" All three stared at Jiang Liu as though at a madman.

Jiang Liu drained his cup of baijiu. "Think about it! We can't afford any delays. Chris Zhao found us because he noticed the data I downloaded and the orbital adjustments you made. Do you think he's the only one to connect the dots? Quantum Fog is only one of the more covert intelligence networks operated by the Atlantic Alliance. But if the AIA proper starts to pay attention, we're going to be in real trouble. They have the best VLF data gathering capability in the whole world, and the only reason they haven't detected the alien ship is probably because their observatories on the far side of the moon haven't been optimally positioned. But given a few more days, they'll surely notice the anomaly and detect the ship. By then, we'll have no chance to make first contact ourselves."

Qi Fei harrumphed. "What makes you think the Atlantic Alliance will discover it first? We in the Pacific League are just as technically skilled. Once everyone knows about the alien ship, in a fair race I'm confident we'll win."

"You fool!" Jiang Liu said. "If matters develop to the point where the great powers race to meet the aliens, I guarantee you there will be missiles and lasers and a war in space. By the time either side gets to the aliens, I'm pretty sure the trigger-happy humans will start to fight the aliens. Most likely, the aliens will just kill all the humans, but even if humans managed to somehow defeat the aliens and kill them all, Yun Fan's mission will have failed. Yun Fan wants to deliver something to the aliens; we need to get to them before anyone else."

Yun Fan and Jiang Liu looked at each other. A warm feeling filled Yun Fan's heart. She had never said outright that she was trying to deliver something to the aliens, but Jiang Liu had figured it out. And now he was making plans to help her accomplish her mission to the exclusion of all other considerations. This was the kind of support she had never had.

Yun Fan nodded emphatically. "We must do everything we can to prevent a war. The aliens don't mean us harm, and it's best we make contact with them covertly, before any governments are involved."

Jiang Liu turned to Qi Fei, "Also, if the aliens really could help humanity advance in technology, as Yun Fan theorizes, don't you wish the Pacific League would get first dibs on the technology? You lose nothing by going along with this plan, but you have the potential to win the jackpot. Surely you don't want Chris Zhao to be first, do you?"

Qi Fei seemed convinced, but he still replied in his habitual cool manner, "I'd like to make a report tonight to my superiors. If the League supports our mission, we may even go into space on a military spaceship."

"You want to go into space on a League spaceship?" Jiang Liu's voice dripped with disdain. "I see, so your plan is to have us be shot out of the sky by Atlantic Alliance missiles at the first opportunity."

Qi Fei stared suspiciously at Jiang Liu, trying to discern a trap. "I just don't understand why you're so enthusiastic about meeting the aliens."

"I'm doing it for Yun Fan, obviously," Jiang Liu said.

"I have to think through all the angles," insisted Qi Fei.

"There's no time." Jiang Liu twisted the bracelet on his left wrist and the tattooed lines glowed blue. The light projected onto the wall to form a map, on which a red dot was approaching their present location rapidly. "That's our friend Chris. I sprayed him with a tracking powder this afternoon during our little sparring session. He'll be here in ten minutes."

"Who's Chris?" Chang Tian asked.

"Someone who wants to kill us," replied Jiang Liu. "Chang Tian, I suggest that you pack up and leave with us right now. Once he's here, he'll destroy everything you've built."

Chang Tian looked over at Qi Fei, his face full of disbelief. Qi Fei pondered the situation for a few seconds and nodded. "Jiang Liu is right. You need to come with us. If Chris Zhao takes you as a hostage, we won't be able to complete the mission."

Qi Fei knew Chang Tian well. The former ace pilot was not afraid to die and cared little for glory or riches, but he valued friendship and sentiment. Telling him that staying behind was dangerous was useless; he would just stay and take his chances. But telling him that staying behind would compromise his friend's mission was sure to rouse him to action. In the twenty years Qi Fei had been Chang Tian's friend, he'd had to threaten him multiple times in this manner to get him to do things that would have benefited him anyway.

Chang Tian went away to grab some communications and survival equipment and then led everyone to the bistro's back door.

"We'd better split up," Jiang Liu said. "Since Chris followed us here, he must have put some tracking device on one of us. We don't have the time to figure out who it is right now."

Someone began knocking on the front door of the bistro. After no one answered, the knocks became much more insistent and urgent.

"Yun Fan can't be alone," Qi Fei said.

"I'll go with her," Jiang Liu said. "You go with Chang Tian. We'll make preparations separately and meet up at a designated spot. Let's all shower and change to get rid of any tracking devices."

Qi Fei nodded in agreement. "We'll meet up in front of the college gate at eleven tonight—where we were this afternoon. We have two and a half hours."

The knocks on the front door became even louder, followed by the sound of splintering wood. They quickly exited the back door into a quiet, dark alleyway.

"Don't be late," Jiang Liu said. "If you don't show up on time, I'm taking Yun Fan all by myself."

Qi Fei glared at him. "Less talking, more doing. Don't be late yourself."

They parted ways just as the front door broke open with a loud crash.

+ + + + +

Qi Fei and Chang Tian rode in the ORV toward Qi Fei's home.

"How did you and Yun Fan get together again?" Chang Tian asked. "Don't try to dodge the question. Tell me the truth."

Qi Fei roughly outlined the events. "The mausoleum is too close to the military compound. The suspicious signals had to be investigated." He kept his tone businesslike and unemotional.

"Were you monitoring the mausoleum the whole time, then?" Chang Tian asked. "Why?"

"Because . . ." Qi Fei swallowed. "Because it was nearby. I told you."

"Hmmm." Chang Tian waited a beat. "Why were you so riled up by Jiang Liu?"

"You saw the guy! He's arrogant, brazen, always picking a fight. I hate people like that."

"You've known plenty of arrogant and brazen people in life. We had so many of them in college. But you've never lost your cool with them. In fact, I can't ever remember seeing you so irate with anyone."

Qi Fei felt something roiling in his chest. He couldn't tamp it down; he couldn't let it out. The only thing he could do was bite down hard and say nothing. His ears burned.

"Do you think Jiang Liu really has feelings for Yun Fan?" Chang Tian asked.

"Would you stop talking about those two?"

"Come on, Qi Fei. It's clear that you still care for her. Don't pretend."

Qi Fei harrumphed. "I have no idea how he feels. And I don't care."

"How do they know each other?"

"Jiang Liu claims that Yun Fan went to him to ask about astronomy. But I think it's more likely that Jiang Liu went after her . . . for his own reasons. The man is the founder of the world's largest intelligence blockchain, with millions of users buying and selling information on it. The Jiang family gained their wealth through criminal means. His grandfather dealt in cryptocurrency trades for arms and smuggling, and even issued his own coins to make massive profit. His father tried to get away from those roots and go legit, but after all the laundering, that family is still embroiled in a ton of transactions involving potentially dirty money. Every major financial institution and watchdog keeps an eye on them. A while ago, we had a report that our uranium suppliers in Southeast Asia had trouble with underground forces aligned with the Jiang family. Jiang Liu may talk like an innocent little rich boy, but who knows what he's really after? I have to watch him closely."

"Seems like you've been really digging into his background," Chang Tian said. "Has he done the same to you?"

"Definitely."

"Then . . . does he know about your past with Yun Fan?"

"How am I supposed to know what he knows?" muttered Qi Fei.

Chang Tian rolled down the window. The whooshing cold night wind cooled their faces and also muted their voices. "Qi Fei, tell me the truth: Do you think you two will get back together?"

After a beat, Qi Fei coughed. "No. It will never happen."

"Why? I wouldn't have even thought of asking you this a few years back. But just now . . . I could see that you still—"

"Stop! Never bring this up again. Especially not in front of my mother."

The car decelerated. The navigation AI told them they were about to arrive at Qi Fei's mother's home.

"Don't say a word about Yun Fan," Qi Fei said, emphasizing every word. "Don't say anything about the mission, either; just claim everything is classified."

+ + + + +

Qi Fei was shocked to find his mother's apartment filled with people. The whole Yuan family was there: General Yuan, Mrs. Yuan, and Bailu. The elders sat around the dining table, chatting casually, while Bailu, in a ponytail and apron, looked the very image of domestic bliss as she served soup. Steam from the soup made her face flush prettily. As Qi Fei opened the door, everyone turned to look at him, their expressions a bit awkward.

"Auntie," Chang Tian said to Qi Fei's mother, "how are you?"

"Oh, it's Ah Tian!" She got up and smiled. "It's been so long since you visited."

Bailu quickly set out bowls and chopsticks for Qi Fei and Chang Tian at the table. "I didn't realize you'd be back to early! Earlier this afternoon you said you were on an urgent mission, so I figured you'd be gone till midnight. That's why I didn't call you earlier."

"How . . . how come you're all here?" Qi Fei asked.

"I asked you to come to my home for matsutake, remember?" Bailu glanced at Mrs. Yuan. "My mother said that since you were busy with work, that meant Auntie would be all alone here. So we decided to come over and bring the food; it's always better to enjoy food with more people, right? My dad also landed this afternoon. When he heard about our dinner plans, he decided to come over as well."

Bailu made everything sound like the most natural thing in the world, just a home-cooked dinner to be shared between two families about to become one. But General Yuan, overhearing, frowned. "What urgent mission are you talking about, Qi Fei? I know nothing about it."

"Ah . . ." Qi Fei leaned down to whisper into the general's ear, "I'll give you a full report later. There was an Atlantic Alliance operative creating a disturbance at the Old City Wall this afternoon."

The general wiped his mouth and got up. "Come with me to the study."

Chang Tian sat down at the table, and the dinner continued as General Yuan and Qi Fei left the dining room and went into the study. Qi Fei closed the door behind them.

"Did you return ahead of schedule, General?" Qi Fei asked.

"There are some strategic redeployments the brass wants to make. I came back early to get a head start."

"What sort of redeployments?"

"There are indications that the Atlantic Alliance wants to refocus on the Indian Ocean and reclaim control of the Arabian Sea."

"Why?" Qi Fei was surprised. "Are they going to intervene in the mess of the Red Sea Pact?"

"No, nothing like that." The general shook his head worriedly. "An independent biotech research institute in the Maldives has made a breakthrough in genetic engineering; the Atlantic Alliance desperately wants to claim it. But the intelligence on all this is hazy. I want you to look into it. If true, we need to accelerate our super AI deployment."

"That is a troublesome development," Qi Fei said.

The general wasn't interested in discussing the topic any further. "So, tell me what happened this afternoon."

Qi Fei gave a quick summary. Throughout the report, General Yuan's brows remained knitted, apparently disturbed by Quantum Fog's all-encompassing surveillance capabilities as well as the brazenness of its creator, Chris Zhao, openly disrupting public life in a metropolis. He was unsure what to make of this unexpected development.

The general was under unprecedented pressure: rumors of new biotech breakthroughs, intelligence leaks, hackers breaching network defenses, constant naval engagements, disruptions to the uranium supply, delays in the development of next-gen AI, loss of space superiority, falling behind in the development of new particle weapons . . . War was a matter of total competition across every domain of science and technology, and everything was careening out of control. He didn't know where to bet their resources, and where to find that one breakthrough that would lead to certain victory. Given enough time, he knew he could figure it out, but there was never enough time. The situation changed a thousand times every day, and defeat could come from any direction.

It was the first time the old man had felt so hopeless in his long military career. Years of fighting had conditioned his spirit to be as unshakeable as steel. Throughout the decades, his courage and faith in himself had always carried him through every crisis, allowed him to conquer every obstacle. But now, science and technology had transformed warfare; it was conducted under the surface, like two giant icebergs clashing out of view. A transformative technology could erupt at any second. The general was exhausted and confused.

He knew that the battlefield no longer belonged to those like him, but to younger men and women. He gripped Qi Fei's arms and tried to let him feel his own faith.

"It's all up to you now," the general said. "You have my full support."

"General Yuan." Qi Fei's tone was hesitant. "Jiang Liu suggested that we depart right away tonight to try to make contact with the alien ship, just the four of us. What do you think?"

"Why are you in such a rush?"

Qi Fei explained Jiang Liu's reasoning, emphasizing in particular Yun Fan's theory that the aliens had interfered in the development of humanity multiple times. Any civilization that received advanced technology from the aliens had the potential to achieve hegemony: ancient Egypt, Shang and Zhou, the Qin Empire . . .

"Do you believe her?" General Yuan asked.

"Oh . . ." Qi Fei hesitated. "I can't be sure. There's a chance she's right."

"If there's even a one-percent chance she's right, we should try to seize it and not let the opportunity fall into our adversary's hands," the general said. "It's worth the gamble. You and Chang Tian should definitely go. If there is anything that would allow us to achieve technological superiority, bring it back! It's our job to find possibilities among impossibilities."

Qi Fei nodded in agreement.

"Oh, when an opportunity arises, eliminate Jiang Liu," the general said. "He's a dangerous man. We found that he was responsible for several acts of sabotage and destruction of munitions stores. His loyalty is also questionable: we can't be sure which side he's on. Safer to just get rid of him."

Qi Fei did not like this at all, but he nodded reluctantly.

As everyone else continued at dinner, Qi Fei went to his room to pack. Chang Tian knew Qi Fei's mother well, so there was plenty to talk about, and Mrs. Yuan and Bailu also added to the good cheer. After a while, Qi Fei's mother's gaunt face finally softened into genuine laughter, and even the general felt his taut nerves relax.

Having packed, Qi Fei said goodbye to his mother. He told her that he was going on an important mission, and he didn't know when he'd be back. He wanted her to remember to take her medication and visit the doctor regularly. General Yuan told his family that it was time for them to leave as well.

While Bailu helped to clear the table and do the dishes, Qi Fei and the general waited near the front door.

"Qi Fei, you should ask Yun Fan what other unexpected technology achievements are in the mausoleum. If there are any, we should ask the League to authorize excavation and research. Also, try to probe what's in that black box carried by Yun Fan and how she plans on making contact with the aliens."

The general kept his voice low, but the name he mentioned nonetheless managed to waft across the room and land in Qi Fei's mother's alert ears.

"Qi Fei," she said in a trembling voice, her face drained of blood, "what did the general just say?"

"Nothing. I'll tell you more after I get back." Qi Fei rushed to put on his shoes. He looked at Chang Tian, telling him with his eyes to get out as soon as possible.

"Qi Fei, don't you dare lie to me!" Her voice rose. "I heard 'Yun Fan'! I told you, you are never, ever to have any contact with that woman. How dare you? Come back now!"

Qi Fei ran out the door like a rabbit fleeing the hound, leaving his mother's shrill voice echoing in the corridors of the apartment building. He knew that General Yuan would stay behind to comfort Mom, but still, his chest ached as though her words were needles stabbing into his heart.

+ + + + +

The group flew on a military plane from Xi'an to Gansu, where they switched to the Jiang family's superconducting train. The train traversed the Gobi and the deserts of Central Asia, arriving at the spaceport near dawn. No one spoke much throughout the night, their minds heavy with aimless thoughts.

The sky was dark and studded with brilliant stars; the Milky Way glowed overhead, brighter than any city. The four looked up together, their thoughts miles apart.

They strode toward the towers of the spaceport.

6 | Departure

Jiang Lang Trading's spaceport was on the shores of Lake Balkhash, Kazakhstan. The Belt and Road superconducting train, speeding along at 800 kph, traversed the more than two thousand kilometers between Lanzhou and Lake Balkhash in three hours. Qi Fei, who had been to the spaceports in Wenchang, Xichang, and Jiuquan, found the Lake Balkhash site to be much more commercially developed. Although it wasn't near any major city, the place was designed for the comfort of tourists. Next to the lake were multiple vacation resorts, all of them luxurious and new. Qi Fei sensed that this was a playground for the rich and powerful, probably also a place where the Jiang family cultivated relationships and built influence.

They entered the welcome center of the spaceport. Though the facilities here most likely paled in comparison to the nearby resorts, they were still impressive. There were restaurants, bars, an AR gym, a nightclub, and a casino. The flooring was made of some trendy polymer material that felt good against their feet. Overhead, massive abstract sculptures dangled from the ceiling, the polymer material glowing in every shade of the rainbow, their entangled curves and lines sensual and mesmerizing. Paintings on the walls portrayed scenes of explosion and eruption, with placards in the corners unobtrusively noting the artists and the costs. It was so early in the morning that most of the facilities remained closed, and the empty hall, bathed in dawn light, seemed to be there just for the four of them.

"Look at this place." Chang Tian whistled in appreciation. "I'd love to redecorate my bistro the same way."

Jiang Liu laughed. "Which interests you more: decorating restaurants or making money? Let me tell you, this place is a hole in the ground into which my family throws money. You see that sculpture next to the sofa? Can you even tell what it's supposed to be? What my family paid for that is enough for you to open several restaurants. Trust me, if you want to run a good business, don't waste money on these useless vanity knickknacks. You'll never make it back."

"Then how does your family make their money back?" Chang Tian asked.

Jiang Liu grinned. "Did you know that Disney theme parks don't make any money?"

"Really?"

"Really," Jiang Liu said. "Disney's films are advertising, the theme parks draw customers in, but the real money is made from all the merchandise sold in the theme parks. Business always involves the same game with the same steps: advertise, channel, merchandize. Capitalism works so long you make enough money in one step to make up for the rest."

Chang Tian looked thoughtful. "I take it that your family makes money here from space tourists, then?"

"Not quite."

"Then what step do they make money from?"

"Guess." Jiang Liu grinned like the Cheshire cat.

Qi Fei interrupted them. "We don't have a lot of time. Let's get to our mission."

"The spaceship is right there." Jiang Liu pointed to the small ship on the launchpad, looking like an advanced airplane. "I already told my steward to rush here overnight with the launch authorization codes. He couldn't make the arrangements earlier because getting us a pilot and slotting us into ground control requires my parents' authority. But since we have our own pilot and navigator, we can take off anytime we want."

"We have our own navigator?" Qi Fei quirked a brow.

"Director Qi, you told me that I've seen nothing of your boundless capabilities." Jiang Liu moved his hand as though waving a conductor's baton. "Now here's a grand stage for you to really show off."

"This is the kingdom of Prince Jiang." Qi Fei's voice was cold. "How could I, a mere no-name outsider, dare to overstep my welcome?"

Jiang Liu said, "The sages of old tell us that a person of virtue should not shirk their responsibility. Director Qi, you are a man of virtue; please take up your duty."

Qi Fei shook his head. "Not at all, Prince Jiang. You're a follower of the great Mozi, practitioner of the universal love of jianai. In front of you, how dare I claim to be a man of virtue? Clearly this duty is yours."

"I'm like the man who drifts along on a raft because he cannot achieve his ideals.[7] How can I possibly be compared to Director Qi?"

Chang Tian stared at the two men, completely bewildered. He turned to Yun Fan. "What's wrong with these two?"

Yun Fan, looking away, didn't turn around. "Neither of them wants to be the navigator."

Chang Tian finally understood. "I see. It's much harder to navigate from space than from the ground. The calculations are much more complex. Even in the military, we relied on ground control as much as possible. Also, the navigator must get us into orbit first before plotting an intercept course—it's a really tough job."

"Exactly." Yun Fan strolled away from the bickering men. "If it were an easy and pleasant task, do you think they'd work so hard to get the other to do it?"

"Fanfan, where are you going?" Jiang Liu ran after her.

"I heard some voices," Yun Fan said.

"What are you talking about?"

"I'm not sure." Yun Fan held up a hand to silence the others as she found her way next to a column. She leaned over and listened intently. "Right around here. I think the conversation happened last night, but I can't make out the exact words."

The other three stared at her, dumbfounded. Qi Fei and Chang Tian looked at each other, but neither could recall ever hearing Yun Fan saying anything like this. Jiang Liu examined the area around Yun Fan, trying to see if there was some way to interpret Yun Fan's words that wouldn't sound so irrational. But before they could ask her for clarification, everyone heard approaching footsteps, the loudest from a pair of crisp, confident high heels.

They turned around and saw two men and two women striding toward them. The middle-aged man in the lead—dark suit, slicked-back hair, lean face with a

---

7   The two men are quoting Confucian classics at each other—their allusions are purposefully off the mark.

disproportionately wide forehead—looked serious and used to being obeyed. The middle-aged woman next to him was perfectly put together in a dark blue dress with pearl-trimmed cuffs and collar, the features of her beautifully made-up face reminding observers of Jiang Liu—except she looked even more energetic. The pair moved with an air of authority that could be felt a dozen meters away.

Yun Fan heard Jiang Liu mutter to himself, "Uncle Bo, you sold me out!"

The middle-aged pair stopped in front of them.

"Mom, Dad." Jiang Liu's voice was barely above a whisper.

"Oho! I'm amazed!" The woman's voice dripped with sarcasm. "Such an honor to be recognized by our son! I thought you'd forgotten about us."

"Uh . . . well, you know you've been in the news a lot," Jiang Liu said, being deliberately provocative. "The AI alerted me."

Mom raised her eyebrows. "How dare you! Since you seem hell-bent on cutting off all ties with your parents, why do you still want to ride our spaceship? If you're so high-and-mighty, why don't you go make your own way in the world?"

"Fine. We'll leave." Jiang Liu turned around and began to stride away.

"Stop right there!" Jiang Liu's mother flushed with rage. "Do you really think I have no way to bring you to heel? Go wait in that conference room over there. Your father will talk some sense into you."

Jiang Liu glanced at his father, and then looked at Qi Fei and Yun Fan. After a moment of hesitation, he decided to see what his parents had to say. As he walked toward the conference room, he turned and asked, "How long should I expect to wait?"

"We'll be right there," she said. "We just want to have a few words with your little friends."

Only when Jiang Liu had entered the conference room and closed the door behind him did the middle-aged man extend a hand toward Qi Fei. "I'm Jiang Ruoqin. Pleased to meet you."

"Pleased to meet you, Mr. Jiang. I'm Qi Fei."

"I know you," Jiang Ruoqin said. "I hosted a banquet in Beijing once in honor of General Yuan Jinjia. You accompanied him."

"Ah." Qi Fei was startled. "I . . . hadn't realized that you were the host. What a small world."

"Is the world really small?" Jiang Ruoqin spread his hands. "I don't think the world is small at all. But there are very few truly capable individuals, and sooner or later, they always manage to end up together. When you go back and see General Yuan, please give him my regards and tell him that I'm ready to be of service to him whenever he needs me, and that I hope he and I can support each other for a long time to come."

Qi Fei pondered Jiang Ruoqin's speech but couldn't figure out what hidden message he was trying to send to the general. He thought of the general's orders to him and felt even more anxious. "I will make sure to deliver your message."

Jiang Liu's mother held out a hand to Yun Fan. "Hello, I'm Tong Yueying. Jiang Liu is my son."

Yun Fan bowed slightly but didn't shake hands with her. "Pleased to meet you, Ms. Tong."

Tong Yueying casually withdrew her hand. "Du Yibo, our steward, told me that Jiang Liu went to Xi'an to visit you instead of coming home. I was confused at first . . . but now that I've met you, I can see why. You're indeed a girl of extraordinary qualities."

Yun Fan gave her another slight bow without saying anything. Qi Fei could sense the tension in her guarded pose.

"I'd like to tell you something, woman to woman," Tong Yueying said. "My Jiang Liu is not a good child. He has brought many girls home. At first, I was so excited about each, and I always made sure to make her feel welcome, to get to know her. But before I could even get a sense of her, Jiang Liu had already moved on to the next. After a while, I didn't even bother to learn their names, knowing that a new one was just around the corner.

"I tell you these . . . embarrassing facts because I care about you. I think girls your age don't always know how to protect yourselves. You lack experience. You don't yet know that you won't find happiness just because he seems to be interested in you. Now, I fully accept that I didn't do a good job bringing up my son, and I need to reflect on my own errors. As soon as Jiang Liu comes home this time, I'm going to lock him in the bedroom and force him to study the books of the ancient sages. He's such a disappointment.

"Once Jiang Liu is safely locked away, if you like, I'd love to invite you as my guest. It's almost Christmas, perfect time to go skiing in Davos."

Yun Fan kept her voice polite and cold. "Ms. Tong, I think you have the wrong idea about me. I have two rules in life. First, I'll never let two men fight over me. Second, I'll never fight another woman over some man. I've never broken these two rules so far, and I don't see myself breaking them in the future. You don't need to invite me to go skiing with you. I'm busy with my own research. Thank you for trying to warn me—though it's entirely unnecessary."

Qi Fei admired Yun Fan's answer, but he couldn't help feeling a trace of bitterness at hearing her "rules." He knew that Chang Tian's eyes were on him, so he deliberately turned to look outside the window, pretending to have heard nothing.

Tong Yueying nodded and turned to her husband, whispering to him that they should go talk to their son. Ever the gracious hostess, she directed her staff to set out a western-style breakfast for Yun Fan, Chang Tian, and Qi Fei: coffee, fruit, cereal, and omelet.

Even after Tong Yueying and Jiang Ruoqin had disappeared into the small conference room, Yun Fan stood rooted in the same spot. Chang Tian finally dragged her next to the breakfast table, but even sitting down, her mind seemed miles away. Qi Fei felt his heart convulse seeing Yun Fan so lost. Both ate their breakfast without speaking.

As for Chang Tian, eating along and in silence, this breakfast ranked as the most flavorless meal of his life.

+ + + + +

In the small conference room, Jiang Liu waited with trepidation.

His parents entered the room, and for a minute or two, no one spoke. They glared at him. He, on the other hand, rehearsed in his mind all the possible accusations they could lob and all the responses he could toss back, unable to settle on any course.

"I haven't seen you in a while," intoned Jiang Ruoqin. "You seem to have gained a lot of skills in the interim."

"For that I have to thank my father, an excellent teacher." Jiang Liu just couldn't stop himself.

Jiang Ruoqin slammed the table. "If I were such a good teacher, how did I end up with a son who willingly surrounds himself with riffraff?"

Jiang Liu's face reddened. "Let's all choose our words with more care, shall we? Who, exactly, are you calling 'riffraff'?"

"Do you think I'm blind?" Jiang Ruoqin shouted. "Take Southeast Asia. Our caravan there was hit by a bunch of bandits—drug dealers, addicts, wastes of human flesh. When I figured out that you were behind the hit, I couldn't believe it. Even back in the old days, when our family business wasn't yet respectable, your grandfather made sure to partner only with the biggest bosses of the underground world to make our first pot of gold. But you! You don't seem to pick or choose at all. Whether they're petty thieves or beggars, you take everyone! You gathered a bunch of no-name dregs of society and attacked your own family's caravan! What the hell is wrong with you? Do you crave the feeling of being worshipped by your useless minions? Or are you so dumb that you think the petty profit of robbing your own family is worth it? I just don't get it. Why? Why???"

"Father," Jiang Liu spoke with a seriousness that was rare for him, "since you ask, I'll give it to you straight. Our family business, sprawling as it is, has certain rules. There are some things that we cannot sell to terrorists—you know exactly what I'm talking about. How could you bend the rules and sell to him just because he has the money?"

Jiang Ruoqin's expression turned stony. "I negotiated the deal with an Afghan prince! That was perfectly legal. I know nothing about any organization behind him, *if* there is even an organization."

"You know nothing?" Jiang Liu asked, his voice rising with indignation. "That prince . . . Ha, are you telling me that all those spies you pay are so useless that you don't know how he became a prince? Do you expect me to believe that you had no inkling what would have happened if those people got their hands on the uranium? Have you forgotten what happened the Night of Tears in Jerusalem, 2054? If I hadn't stopped your caravan . . . how would you face your conscience if five million people vaporized in a mushroom cloud?"

"What do you know about conscience?" demanded Jiang Ruoqin. "A trader's only duty is to deliver the goods when paid. That is the beginning and the end of business. You cannot worry about matters beyond your domain. Remember that! So long as I do my duty, my conscience is clear."

"You don't even believe what you just said," Jiang Liu said. "Shameful."

Tong Yueying stepped between the two men. "Enough! That's all in the past. I hate to see father and son arguing like this." Her tone suddenly turning maternal, she grabbed Jiang Liu's hand and said, "My little Eric, come on, it's been so long since you've been home. Things have changed a lot! Actually, after you intercepted that shipment of uranium, your father ended up realizing that it actually helped him and kept him out of trouble. So he's not really mad at you. It's just that you should be a bit more careful about who you associate with. We're just worried that you may be taken advantage of by those around you."

Jiang Liu snorted. "I've yet to meet the man who can cheat me."

"Are you going to be home for Christmas?" Tong Yueying tried to change the subject.

"I don't know," Jiang Liu said.

"Your sister misses you." Tong Yueying patted his head. "How long has it been since you last saw her?"

Jiang Liu leaned away from her. "Mom, do you have anything else we have to discuss? I'm on a schedule."

"There is something we should discuss." Tong Yueying sat down across from Jiang Liu. "We know what you're planning to do with that spaceship—you know perfectly well that your Uncle Bo can't keep a secret. We can help you! But we should be on the same page as far as what happens afterward."

"What do you mean, exactly?" Jiang Liu was on guard.

Tong Yueying sighed as if getting ready to tell a long story. "Eric, you know how hard it's been for our family. We have to pick up crumbs in the little gaps and seams in the regulations of the great powers, and there's always risk. Your grandfather and father are idealists, hoping to legitimize blockchain and other technologies—"

"Mom," Jiang Liu broke in, "get to the point, please."

"All right." Tong Yueying's face turned serious. "Your grandfather was hated and despised as much as he was admired. Your father has spent much of his life trying to change that legacy, and after much effort, has finally rebuilt the family business on a stable foundation of international blockchain transactions. But it's not enough; we're barely seen as legitimate. He's worried that you and your siblings can't sustain the business, and so he's hoping that he can do a little more and help the three of you secure your futures."

"Whatever you and Dad plan to do, just do it," Jiang Liu said, frowning. "Don't bring me into it. Children have to make their own luck."

"Why do you always have to sound so coldhearted!" Tong Yueying's tone turned sorrowful. "We really just want the best for you three. You never come home, and I don't know what's on your mind. But every mother in the world just wants the best for her children!"

Jiang Liu said nothing. Mom's speech seemed to have softened him.

"Dad is thinking of doing something for the UN," she said. "Geneva is in a bad state. Neither the Atlantic Alliance nor the Pacific League thinks much of it, and it has little influence on global affairs. The whole institution has been taken over by bureaucrats, whose inefficiency is only matched by their arrogance. These days, the UN pretty much survives on its past prestige and glory, accomplishing absolutely nothing—which country in the world even cares about what the UN thinks or says? But the UN's decline also presents it with a perfect opportunity for reform and revitalization. Your father has been working for the General Council of the WTO for a while now, which has legitimized our business to some degree. Now he wants to lead the reform of the UN, possibly even the Security Council."

Jiang Liu was confused. "What does this have to do with me?"

Mom looked to Dad. "Why don't you explain this part?"

Jiang Ruoqin gently tapped the table with the fingers of one hand as he explained, "I've thought long and hard about the influence of blockchain technology. As you know, although the total global economic activity on blockchains has exceeded the off-chain economic activity for at least the last decade, most people still think of the blockchain purely as a tool of commerce and finance; they don't understand its full potential. I've long believed that the true purpose of blockchain technology is to enhance democracy, to facilitate the aggregation of preferences, to decentralize authority, to put democratic will beyond manipulation. I want blockchain technology to replace the outdated decision-making mechanism at the UN.

"I believe my ideals are compatible with Tianshang, don't you?"

Jiang Liu sucked in a breath. Even though he knew that he couldn't keep Tianshang a secret from Dad forever—after all, he was using the technology and infrastructure developed by the Jiang family—it was still shocking to hear the elder Jiang say it out loud.

"Your father thinks it would be wonderful for the two of you, father and son, to transform the world together using blockchain technology," Mom said. "Imagine that! Tianshang would greatly benefit all humanity—and only then will all the effort you've put into building it be worthwhile."

Only now did Jiang Liu finally understand why his parents wanted to talk to him instead of simply dragging him home. In the end, he had something they wanted: Tianshang could be an asset in Dad's bid for political influence and power. It should have been obvious from the start. On a blockchain, the most important resource was the number of participants. Tianshang had gathered many, many users, and that made it valuable to Dad. Jiang Liu could never have imagined such a consequence for his invention.

"I see . . . you don't mind the 'riffraff' now, do you?" Jiang Liu, smirking, asked Dad.

"It's to the benefit of the poor and powerless users of Tianshang to become part of the global democratic process," Tong Yueling declared piously.

"Right," Jiang Liu said. "Maybe you could also tell me which of your rich and powerful friends will benefit from their participation?"

"Eric, don't always be so cynical!" Tong Yueling gently put her hands on Jiang Liu's shoulder. "Your father means well. He's happy to lend you a spaceship for your trip and can even allocate ground control resources to help you navigate. You go on your fun ride, and when you come back, you can help your father, as we discussed. Sound good?"

Jiang Liu was silent. His heart ached. For the briefest of moments, he had indeed felt sorry about his own estrangement from the family, regretted not fulfilling the duties of a good child. But now, he found the whole situation ridiculous. He was ridiculous, his parents even more so. His parents could have saved everyone a lot of time and brain cells by simply coming out and speaking plainly: *Hey kid, we'll offer you a deal. We help you; you help us. Do you accept?* But instead, they had to resort to innuendos, emotional blackmail, threats, enticements, a whole pile of schemes and plots disguised as attempts at forging an emotional connection with their son. It was all nonsense.

He stood rooted to the spot, as though twenty-plus years of hypocrisy and unreality had all fallen on him at once.

He had always known Dad to be a cautious man, unwilling to take chances as his grandfather had. Jiang Ruoqin loved numbers; he loved to reduce everything to numbers, to see numbers grow, to use them to ward off risk. One time, he hired a group of math and physics majors out of top colleges to help him deploy conics and cubics to reduce the uncertainty in hedging transactions. Even in the notoriously unstable business of crypto trading, he was famous for deploying models that minimized risk at the cost of reduced profits. He didn't care about unlimited upside, only that each step brought him closer to the goal. Even as a child, Jiang Liu had known that he could make deals with Dad. Jiang Ruoqin never wasted any time on things that couldn't be justified by the numbers; so, from the moment he saw Dad, he should have known that he didn't fly to the middle of nowhere just to reconnect with his son.

As for Mom, she was a master of language. She talked and talked but said little. Ever so skillfully, she drew you into her plans while leaving behind no evidence, giving you nothing to hold on to. Her meaning was buried in feints and deflections, requiring you to carefully parse through a thousand layers of verbal frills before arriving at the hard kernel of intention. A goal-oriented executive, she was the absolute master of the subsidiaries she managed. Yet her favorite move was to deploy words like a chess master laying out the pieces: First, she cut off your retreat with a well-placed invitation; then, she trapped you with a hidden offer, pressed you with a disguised threat, and finally sealed your fate with an emotional appeal declaring how much she had been worrying herself for *you*, how everything had been planned for *your* benefit. In the end, you did exactly what she wanted, *and* you believed that it was your own idea to do so. As a child, every time Jiang Liu got to see Mom practicing her art on the guests at a dinner party, he experienced a sensation of emptiness. Mom managed to erase the world from the awareness of her guest, leaving behind only one thing: the task that she wanted her guest to perform for her.

Jiang Liu was certain that if he continued to resist her, she would start to play verbal chess with him.

"Speaking of the family spaceship," Mom said, her tone so casual that it sounded unreal, "you know it's very desirable. A lot of people want to ride it. Let me see . . . oh, there's this sheik who was just asking about it. I was about to rent it to him when your father found out that you were interested in it. So he told me, 'No! We should save it for Eric. We'll have a nice talk with him first.' Since you're so hesitant, this talk is taking a lot longer—"

"I'm not hesitant," Jiang Liu said. "What's there to be hesitant about? You got yourself a deal. I will borrow the spaceship to fly with my friends; when I get back, I'll deploy Tianshang to help Dad."

"Well, let's not put it so bluntly. A 'deal' sounds so businesslike. We're family, after all. I think the right way to think about it is as a win-win collaboration, when the two hearts of father and son beat as one! Family means everything."

"Please keep your expectations realistic." Jiang Liu's tone continued to be businesslike. "The riffraff are poor and powerless, but that also makes them free. I can't guarantee they'll do what you want."

"Of course. We're not putting pressure on you to deliver the impossible. Who knows, maybe when given the chance, the people on Tianshang will see the benefits of cooperation and greatly improve themselves." Tong Yueying patted her son's shoulders, satisfied. "Don't make your friends wait. Go. Go."

Jiang Liu looked at Mom. *Do you even hear yourself?*

Or maybe this is the way the world is, and I'm the fool who can't be "normal."

As Jiang Liu headed for the door of the conference room, Jiang Ruoqin stopped him. "Be careful of that boy from the Pacific League. He's not your friend. If you get the chance, get rid of him. Don't always think the best of others—you'll end up the one hurt."

Jiang Liu forced himself to not respond.

+ + + + +

True to his word, Jiang Ruoqin made available to his son the best ground control team. With their help, there was no need for any piloting throughout the entire process of launch, parking orbit, transfer burn, and initial intercept vector. The real challenge would come only after leaving Earth's orbit. Since the best projected position for the alien ship was between Earth and Mars, but closer to Earth, the estimated total flight time was about four days. Chang Tian wouldn't need to do anything until the third day, when they'd have to locate and intercept the alien ship.

For two whole days after boarding the spaceship, the four of them would have nothing to do.

The Zeta-plus was a fairly new model, capable of reaching a geosynchronous orbit within ten minutes. Once the spaceship was in orbit, passengers were free to roam about the cabin. Although microgravity conditions prevailed, magnetized surfaces and metal weights allowed everyone to move around the ship with little difficulty.

The first thing Jiang Liu did after he got out of the straps was open up all the cabinets and fridges in search of alcohol. Since the Jiang family spaceship was meant for wealthy families on vacation, the ship's stores were enough to keep the four of them fed for a month. Most of the food was in the form of vacuum-sealed convenience packages. Depositing them into special heaters was enough to leave one with a cooked, prepackaged dish. However, for those willing to go to the trouble, the packs could also be unsealed so that the ingredients could be combined and cooked in the traditional manner with electric appliances. Jiang Liu immediately thought of Chang Tian.

"We were just looking for a pilot," Jiang Liu said, "but we got a chef for free too! You want to open a fancy bistro, right? Why don't you show me what you can do? Once we land, I'll partner with you."

"Let me take a look at what we have first," Chang Tian said. "Don't get your hopes up."

He returned after a few minutes in the galley, holding up packages in both hands. "I can't believe it!"

He was holding up Hokkaido snow beef and raw foie gras, among other delicacies. A chef given good ingredients experienced the same joy as a martial artist who found a well-balanced weapon. Chang Tian's pleasure infected the other three, and the air, slightly awkward at first, seemed to relax, as did everyone's expressions.

Qi Fei turned to Chang Tian. "You know, I wasn't sure you wanted to come. Last night I almost told you to stay home."

"How many years have we been friends?" Chang Tian asked. "You've rarely asked me for help. I had to come."

Qi Fei laughed. "I had no idea that you were so obliging. But why didn't you listen to me when I asked you to stay in the air force?"

"That was a totally different situation. I can tell that this time your mission is your own, something you care about. Trying to keep me in the military was your job, and I could tell it wasn't something you really wanted to do."

"Ridiculous," Qi Fei said. "I love my work, all right?"

"Oh please." Chang Tian laughed. "After knowing you so many years, do you think I can't tell what you really want to do and what you don't? You may be able to fool others by looking so serious all the time, but I know it's just a mask. Yes, you enjoy working with Qiankun, but you despise all the bureaucratic politics, and you don't want to be the institute director at all. Am I wrong? Ha, I left the military early so I could do what I wanted, and you envy my freedom. That's why you spend so much time at my bistro, isn't it?"

"I go to your place for the free food and alcohol. You're reading too much into it."

Qi Fei didn't want to admit that Chang Tian was right. He needed to tell himself over and over that he loved his job, to convince himself that he loved not just the technical aspects, but also the position and all the entanglements that came with it. He needed that kind of assurance to get through the day, to accomplish what he needed to do. He was different from Chang Tian.

"All right, I'm going to cook. Prepare your tastebuds." Chang Tian went to the galley.

Jiang Liu started on a bottle of whiskey. He offered some to Qi Fei, who declined (claiming it was too strong) and went for a burgundy instead. Jiang Liu tried to get Yun Fan to join him, but she only wanted to read a book with a cup of tea.

"Oh, I remember now," Jiang Liu said, sitting up. "Fanfan, earlier, at the welcome center, what did you say you heard next to the pillar?"

Yun Fan didn't look up from her book. "I heard the remnants of a conversation from last night. The gist was that they discovered something underwater, but I couldn't make out the details."

Jiang Liu and Qi Fei stopped drinking. "What are you talking about?" Jiang Liu asked. "How could you hear 'remnants' of a conversation from last night?"

Yun Fan finally put her book down on her knees and put her right hand against her necklace. "With this, I can hear conversations that took place within the last twenty-four hours."

Jiang Liu looked closer at the necklace. It was black and formed a wavy pattern against Yun Fan's skin, right above her collar bones. He had admired the piece of jewelry and its effects on the beauty of the wearer, but he hadn't, until now, paid attention to its construction. The material was unusual, stiff, thin, neither leather nor fabric, and certainly not metal—it reminded him of the octagonal black box that Yun Fan had retrieved from Professor Huang.

"Is that from the mausoleum?" he asked.

Yun Fan nodded. "It's one of three artifacts left by my grandfather."

"What are the other two?"

"One is the octagonal box, which you've seen. The other . . . you'll see in a few days."

"Aha, Fanfan has learned not to give everything away," Jiang Liu said. "So tell us more about the necklace."

"I don't know how it works, to be honest. Its operation is as mystifying to me as the neutrino detectors in the underground palace. But I know I can use it to catch traces that words leave behind in the air. It's like . . . when you speak, you leave behind echoes. Some of the echoes stay in the place where the conversation took place, but you also carry some with you. If you wait long enough, the echoes dissipate. But within a day, the necklace can help me hear them."

"I don't see how," Qi Fei said. "There's no scientific basis for any of this. How can the energy of sound waves stay around—"

"I told you, I don't know how it works," Yun Fan said. "But I really can hear the words people spoke earlier. That was how I knew Chris Zhao hid his car below the Old City Wall. After I awakened, I kept my eyes closed and listened to everything he had said earlier that day. He gave a bunch of verbal commands to his car and the bomb he used to scare you."

"Oh . . ." Jiang Liu suddenly remembered something else that puzzled him. "That day, after I returned from Qi Fei's office . . ."

Yun Fan nodded. "Yes, you carried with you the remnants of the conversation between you two. I could hear it, just like right now I can hear everything you said to your parents earlier today." Turning to Qi Fei, she added, "And I can hear everything you said to General Yuan last night."

"Stop!" "Don't say anything!"

Jiang Liu and Qi Fei looked at each other awkwardly. Now they both knew that the other had had an important private conversation within the last twenty-four hours, conversations that they didn't want the other person to know about. Also, they both knew that Yun Fan knew everything—and yet, she didn't seem to care. This last point was puzzling to both of them.

"Your necklace is very odd," Qi Fei said.

"Can I take a look at it?" Jiang Liu asked.

Yun Fan took off the necklace and handed it over. Jiang Liu and Qi Fei took turns examining it but found nothing remarkable. The necklace was entirely black, showing no seams or cracks, as though it had been cast into its final shape. They returned the necklace. She didn't put it back on right away.

"My father always kept this with him," she said, holding up the necklace. "He gave it to me only on his deathbed. If he had given it to me earlier, I would have believed him. It's different when you've experienced what it's capable of."

Jiang Liu didn't know what to say when Yun Fan brought up her father. He was no good at comforting anyone. Whenever he felt troubled himself, the only way he could find peace was to find some external release: sports, alcohol, dancing, adventuring around the world. But Yun Fan was the complete opposite. She was the type to sit still and stuff all the troubles and sorrows into herself, like a bottomless pit. Keeping everything in was her way of coping. In her stillness was a power, like a Daoist charm that could seal away all demons and monsters. But Jiang Liu felt there was a danger in her superficial tranquility.

Jiang Liu placed his hand gently on her shoulder. "Don't blame yourself. An anonymous mob went after your father on the web. You can't be responsible for that."

"It *was* my fault," Yun Fan said. "I moved out of the house when I was in high school. But if I had stayed by my father's side, he wouldn't have ended up like that."

Chang Tian chose to return at that moment with the product of his labors in the galley: medium-rare snow beef steaks and penne in a foie gras and mushroom sauce. "Perfect with either whiskey or red wine," he said as he laid out the place settings and dishes, his expression full of delight. But as no one responded, he finally noticed the awkward air around the room.

"I'm sorry." Yun Fan got up. "I'm going to eat in my cabin."

"Come on," Chang Tian said. "It's always better to share a meal together."

"I don't feel well," Yun Fan said, picking up her plate. "You guys enjoy."

"Let me help you carry that to your cabin." Qi Fei got up and took the plate from Yun Fan.

Jiang Liu picked up his plate and stood up as well. "Fanfan, I know you are annoyed. I'll go eat with you so we can chat."

"Can't you tell she doesn't want to be with you at all?" Qi Fei said. "Leave her alone."

"It's better to talk to someone rather than holding everything in," Jiang Liu said. "Fanfan, I'll keep you company."

"She doesn't need your company," Qi Fei said. "I'll go."

"Why don't you both stay right here?" Yun Fan took her plate back from Qi Fei. "I don't need either of you."

She took a few steps away before pausing. "I told Mrs. Jiang earlier today: I will never let two men fight over me, and I'll never fight with another woman over some man. I meant it. One of you has innumerable girlfriends, and the other has a fiancée. I really want you two to stop acting so ridiculously in front of me. You each have your own master, your own agenda, your own reason for coming on this mission. If you want to fight, just fight. Don't use me as an excuse."

The three men watched silently as Yun Fan departed.

Qi Fei picked up his own plate, and, without saying a word, left the room.

Chang Tian was depressed. He had worked so hard to put together a meal for everyone to enjoy. How did it end up like this?

Jiang Liu patted him on the shoulder. "Forget about them. Let's take our food and drinks to the observation deck up front. Who knows, maybe yuanfen brought us together."

That did cheer Chang Tian up. The two took their plates and glasses and went to the bow.

The back of the spaceship was devoted to the sleeping quarters, consisting of six private cabins. In the middle was the common social space and the galley. Up front was the cockpit, study, and a small conference room. In the tip of the bow was a small observation deck, just enough space for three or four people.

The observation deck was a glass bubble, allowing unimpeded views of space. At the moment, they were in Earth's orbit, so half of their view was dominated by the planet, while the other half showed the brilliant stars. It was impossible to be in the presence of such grandeur and not be moved. Even though Chang Tian and Jiang Liu had been in space before, the sight still filled them with awe.

They sat down, clinked their glasses, and began to eat and drink.

"You've known Qi Fei for a while, haven't you?" Jiang Liu asked.

"Twenty-five years," Chang Tian said. "I first met him when I was two and he was three. We played together every day. Later, we went to the same kindergarten, the same elementary school, the same junior high, the same senior high. He was a class ahead of me, but we spent a lot of time together after school. Our homes were in the same apartment complex."

"What about Yun Fan?" Jiang Liu asked, his tone casual.

"Her?" Chang Tian thought for a while. "Hmmm, she moved into the same complex when she was nine. I was eleven then, and Qi Fei twelve. Her mother worked in the same company as Qi Fei's father, and many employees of that company bought apartments in our complex. I knew Yun Fan from school even before she moved, and after that we became good friends. Our school went from first grade through the end of junior high, so the three of us would walk home together after school."

"So, Qi Fei and Yun Fan, were they—"

"Yes, they were each other's first boyfriend/girlfriend. You can tell right away, can't you? They are so awkward with each other, not like old classmates at all. Yun Fan was pretty, even as a teen, and Qi Fei was so handsome. Everyone thought they made the perfect pair."

Jiang Liu had suspected this, but he still didn't like to have his guesses confirmed. "So what happened? Why did they break up?"

"That is a long story." Chang Tian clinked glasses with Jiang Liu. "If you're not busy tonight, I'll tell you everything."

7 | Reconciliation

Jiang Liu was immediately interested. "Tell me everything! I always have time for a good story."

Chang Tian cut his steak carefully. "Although I know everything that happened, I can't always tell you *why* something happened. Anyway, I'll just focus on the parts that I know. I can't remember how the two of them first became a couple—oh, I think it was when Yun Fan was a first-year in junior high, and Qi Fei was a first-year in senior high. Since Qi Fei was no longer going to the same school as us, it wasn't expected that all of us would walk home together after school. Nonetheless, Qi Fei went to the entrance of our school every day to wait for Yun Fan, and so everyone knew they were together. They would hold hands, share a popsicle, do homework together—you know, your basic school couple. They were so good to each other; I can't remember ever seeing them fight."

Chang Tian took a drink, then he laced his hands behind his head and looked up at the galaxy. "Do you know why I ended up majoring in psychology? I wanted to find out if all joy was fleeting and fragile. Whenever you felt happy, maybe it was a kind of projection, a sort of idealization of reality, doomed to disappointment. Anyway, remembering them now, I think they were happy together."

"So how did they split up?" Jiang Liu prompted.

"Fate," Change Tian said. "I've never been able to find any explanation other than fate."

"Would you stop with the mystical nonsense?"

Chang Tian chewed a bite of steak. "Mmm. All right. The immediate cause could be traced back to their parents. You've never met Yun Fan's mother—she looked just like Yun Fan, but even more striking. Her father, on the other hand, was a plain man, and Yun Fan should thank the heavens that she got her looks from her mom. Back then, Mrs. Yun always had her hair done in a glamorous style, and her makeup was like a model's. Everyone from our apartment complex knew who she was and admired her. Even when Yun Fan was in junior high, Mrs. Yun looked like she was only in her thirties. So I don't think anyone was surprised when they found out that Qi Fei's father ended up falling for her—"

"Woah! Hold up!" Jiang Liu sat up straight, his eyes wide. "Are you telling me that Qi Fei's dad and Yun Fan's mom had an affair?"

"I am indeed." Chang Tian shrugged. "What else could have broken up those two lovebirds? As I said, Mr. Qi and Mrs. Yun worked at the same company, and they knew each other. Since Yun Fan and Qi Fei were so close, the two families often got together. And then, as Yun Fan was about to start senior high school, her father suffered a big setback."

Jiang Liu finally made the connection. "Oh, was that when he was fired by the university for his claims about aliens?"

"That's right. Long before things developed to that point, there was tension in the Yun household. Mrs. Yun told Mr. Yun repeatedly not to focus his research on matters that couldn't be proved. I suspect that she had married him because she admired his intellect when they were in college, and she expected that he would end up very successful. Reality turned out to be a major disappointment. When we used to visit Yun Fan in her home, we'd hear Mrs. Yun reproach Mr. Yun. She would go on and on about how she had to work so hard to bring in most of the money, and then she had to make the extra effort to cultivate social connections with the spouses of Mr. Yun's bosses and colleagues, all in the hopes of furthering his career. She wanted him to focus on tangible successes, to get a full professorship, to climb up the administrative ladder, to do what the family needed him to do instead of pursuing empty dreams. She would sometimes start crying because she felt so wronged, even while we kids were there. Oh my goodness, Yun Fan looked so embarrassed during those times. Later, when Mr. Yun began to argue with his critics on the web, Mrs. Yun told him over and over to stop it. Finally, by the time he was fired from the university, Mrs. Yun was about to have a breakdown."

Jiang Liu could see where this was going. "So she went to Mr. Qi for comfort?"

"Yeah. I don't know the details, of course, but during that time—when Yun Fan was a third year in junior high and Qi Fei a third year in senior high—everything was a mess. There was nonstop fighting in Yun Fan's family, and then Mr. Qi and Mrs. Yun both disappeared at the same time. Three days later, the two were found together in the wreckage of a car that had been bombed. While Mr. Qi died, Mrs. Yun survived. Later, Mrs. Yun never returned to our complex; we have no idea where she went. Mrs. Qi, Qi Fei's mom, almost went crazy. Think about it: You think you have the perfect family, and then one day your husband is found dead in a car with another woman. How would you react? She made Qi Fei kneel in front of all the neighbors and swear that he would never ever have anything to do with Yun Fan. A huge crowd watched the scene. After that . . . can you imagine the two of them staying a couple? Qi Fei did poorly on his college entrance examination too. He had the grades to make it to a top college in Beijing, but his exam scores only qualified him for a local school, his safety. After that, I think Yun Fan and Qi Fei lost touch."

Jiang Liu listened to the story without any commentary.

"A whole decade," Chang Tian said, sighing. "A whole decade has passed. Time waits for no one."

"We're not always in control of our own lives," Jiang Liu said, raising his glass and inviting Chang Tian to drink.

Chang Tian clinked his glass with Jiang Liu's. "That's why I mentioned fate. In college, I tried to analyze every relationship, hoping I could sort out the causes and effects. But I gave up later. You can't analyze everything."

Jiang Liu poured out some dried fruits and nuts for Chang Tian. "If you were a psych major, how did you end up as a military pilot?"

Chang Tian laughed. "Wasn't exactly planned. During college, because the war was escalating, the air force went to all the schools to recruit pilots. They first tested the candidates for concentration and psychological stability. Since I practiced meditation for years, I passed their tests with the highest possible score. Later, even though my physical scores were only average, they picked me as a top recruit. I became a combat pilot and served for five years."

"It sounds like you were a really good pilot," Jiang Liu said. "You had a great career in front of you. Why did you retire? Did you suffer trauma?"

"Nothing like that." Chang Tian shook his head. "I just couldn't deal with it . . . All right, at the risk of sounding a bit woo-woo, I couldn't find myself. Every day, as I flew my missions, I didn't feel it was *me* doing those things. I could carry out my assigned tasks, but as time went on, I felt I was splitting in two. There was the me that piloted the fighter, but there was another me that floated in the sky, looking down on pilot-me. I didn't think it was safe to keep on going like that. I don't expect you to understand, but I *felt* it; it was real."

"I completely understand." Jiang Liu grabbed a handful of dried fruits and nuts for himself. "For a long time I felt similarly. It was like . . . nothing stimulated my nerves directly. Everything I did, my body just reacted on its own, while my nerves felt nothing. I was split in two: one acted and said the lines; the other watched the first from the audience. To make myself feel again, I threw myself into stimulation: more alcohol, louder music, but nothing worked for long. I got used to the stimulation; after a while, I inevitably felt numb again. I didn't care about anything that happened."

Chang Tian refilled Jiang Liu's glass. "So how did you get yourself out of that state?"

"Get out?" Jiang Liu laughed. "I never fully got out. I still feel like that sometimes. But later, I had to deal with so many other serious issues that my own mental state didn't feel so important anymore."

"Other serious issues?" Chang Tian probed carefully.

"Haha! Very serious questions I had to find the answers to. How many teeth does a squirrel have? Do dolphins dream? What sex positions do groundhogs favor? You know, that sort of thing."

Chang Tian knew he didn't want to give a real answer. Looking Jiang Liu up and down, he asked, "You are one of those people whose lives seem perfect. Your family is wealthy; your parents aren't divorced; you are handsome and talented. What could possibly trouble you?"

"You think I'm talented?" Jiang Liu laughed again. "Do you know how much my father donated to Harvard for me to get in? Once I got into Harvard, I felt like an idiot. Everybody who made it in by their own grades and test scores despised development cases like me."

"Seems like you're doing fine for yourself now."

"I suppose I'm good at putting up a successful front in front of strangers. In college, I realized that I would never be as smart as the top students, the real geniuses, in my class. To have them not look down on me, I invented a set of tricks to disguise my lack of talent. Later on, it turned out that much of life is no different from college: most people only look at credentials, and artificial tests can be beaten with tricks. I've gone as far as I have largely on account of my ability to *appear* smart."

Chang Tian laughed. "I wouldn't have taken you to be such a straight shooter."

Jiang Liu put on a serious face. "Ahem. This is just between you and me. Don't tell Qi Fei. I'm still competing with him."

Chang Tian doubled over with mirth. "All right, all right! I won't tell him a thing. You two are actually very similar; you should have a competition to see who's more vain."

Jiang Liu clinked glasses with Chang Tian. "Drink up! Go to bed after this. Thanks for the good talk."

"I could tell that you are a good guy." Chang Tian drained his glass. "That's why I wanted to have a real conversation with you. You should get some sleep too."

Later, both spent a long time in their cabins watching the stars before falling asleep, unaware that others on the ship were also suffering from insomnia.

+ + + + +

The next day—by ship's time, as they weren't subject to the cycle of day and night on Earth anymore—Qi Fei was the first to get up.

Actually, it would be more accurate to say he was *roused* by his alert system. Every night, Qi Fei set Qiankun to monitor all emission bands for signatures from the Atlantic Alliance. This was a trick that Qi Fei developed after years of espionage and counterespionage work. The Atlantic Alliance tended to have specific spectrum signatures, like fingerprints, for all their electromagnetic emissions. By homing in on these signatures, it was possible to respond quickly to incipient attacks. For instance, Qiankun was capable of activating rapid-scanning radars within a minute of detecting the signatures of a missile launch, and then deploying active anti-missile systems to neutralize the threat. The AI alert system had saved the Northwestern Military District from multiple potentially lethal strikes.

Qi Fei rolled out of bed with Qiankun blaring in his ear.

Still in his standard-issue one-piece space pajamas, he ran into the cockpit, where he confirmed that there was indeed something approaching the ship rapidly from behind. He sat down and directed the radar and cameras to home in on the object for an analysis: a self-guided shell, essentially a miniature missile. Although the missile was still too far to be identified, it was only about four thousand kilometers away, and it exceeded their own velocity by about four thousand kilometers per hour. They had less than an hour before interception.

Qi Fei slammed his fist down on every alarm button in the cockpit. Klaxons shrieked throughout the ship.

"If this is some sort of joke, I'm going to strangle you," mumbled a bleary-eyed Jiang Liu as he stumbled into the cockpit.

"You won't have time for that," Qi Fei said. "In fifty minutes we'll be stardust once that missile catches up to us."

"Oh?" Jiang Liu excitedly scanned the sensor panels. "This is interesting."

Yun Fan and Chang Tian joined them. Except for Yun Fan, who managed to put on a tracksuit, the rest were all in one-piece pajamas—but there was no time to worry about everyone's vaguely ridiculous appearance. Four faces pressed close together, staring at the blinking dot on the monitor closing in on their position.

"Are you sure it's a missile?" Jiang Liu asked. "Maybe it's a satellite or some kind of communications probe?"

"Use your brain, please!" Qi Fei rolled his eyes. "Can a satellite move this fast? Your family spaceship is no slouch: Our velocity is around 36,000 kph. But that thing is moving at 40,000 kph! The only possibility is a missile launched from some base on the moon."

"Then it must be the Atlantic Alliance." Jiang Liu pondered this. "Maybe when we were in our transfer orbit we stumbled into their no-fly zone?"

"I think it's more likely that bastard Chris Zhao reported us to the AIA," Qi Fei said. "But we don't have time to figure out what happened. We must evade or shoot down that missile before we turn into space debris."

Yun Fan's brows were knotted. "There's no air in space. How can missiles explode?"

"Space missiles are designed with their own supply of oxygen," Qi Fei said. "The lack of air just means that shrapnel will have even higher velocity; they'll slice us apart like a million blades."

"So what can we do?" Yun Fan asked.

"Does our ship have any countermeasures or missiles?" Chang Tian asked.

"Uh, this is a pleasure yacht for the rich and famous," Jiang Liu said, "not a warship. Usually, its itinerary consists of a few orbits at the edge of space, or maybe a few turns in a geosynchronous orbit. Shooting down an incoming missile is not something the designers ever planned for this ship."

"All right, then our only choice is to evade," Chang Tian said.

"Do you think you can dodge the missile?" Jiang Liu asked.

Qi Fei broke in before Chang Tian could answer. "No way. The missile has already adjusted its course at least four times. The guidance AI on that thing is obviously advanced. There's no way we can shake it off just by some fancy flying."

Jiang Liu pondered this. "How about the two of us work together?"

"What do you have in mind?" Qi Fei asked, locking eyes with Jiang Liu.

"I can interfere with their communications channel and try to breach the defenses; you can then send over Qiankun to disarm their targeting AI. Hopefully, the anti-interference system on that thing isn't too much for me."

"It's worth a try."

The two busied themselves at their consoles. Jiang Liu linked his bracelets to the ship's systems so that he could tap the ship's communications relays and antennas to amplify the interference waveforms. The tattoos on his arms glowed blue again. The interference signals he generated depended on direct neural links to his brain. This was because hacking through a system required rapid adjustments based on the target system's responses; no matter how advanced the equipment or the AI, he found a direct link to his own mind, drawing on his intuition and instincts, to be far more effective. By now, after three years of training, the equipment felt like an extension of his own nervous system.

Qi Fei, on the other hand, used the time to modify the onboard system to accommodate Qiankun. Each AI system relied on fundamentally different base algorithms, and it was not always possible for different systems to work together harmoniously. In an emergency, it was sometimes possible to push the host system aside entirely, route around the base logic, and take over the reins with a new system.

By the time Qi Fei and Jiang Liu were finished with their preparations, the monitor showed the missile to be only forty-six minutes away. They agreed that they couldn't wait any longer and began the hacking attempt. Qi Fei sent out Qiankun on a carrier signal directed by Jiang Liu, hoping to find a way through the missile's defenses. However, as soon as the signal connected with the missile, Qi Fei felt resistance. Jiang Liu jumped from band to band, probing for a weakness, but Qi Fei sensed that the resistance had been purposefully designed to thwart AI intrusions, always ready with the perfect countermeasure.

"We need to change our plan," Qi Fei said in a low voice. "This won't work and we're running out of time."

"That is one impressive anti-interference shield," Jiang Liu said. "What sort of missile is this? I've never seen anything like it."

"It must be a new secret weapon. I have no record of it either."

"I'm not sure what else we can try."

"How much more time do we have?"

Jiang Liu glanced at the monitor. "Thirty-one minutes."

Qi Fei and Jiang Liu had never looked so serious before as they thought about the problem. Suddenly, Qi Fei looked up. "Digital doppelgänger!"

Jiang Liu understood immediately. "Ah, you think we can create a signal phantom."

"That's right," Qi Fei said. "I can direct Qiankun to create a phantom copy of us; you can project the phantom in front of the missile's sensors. It needs to be stronger than even our real signal. Can you do it?"

Jiang Liu rolled up his sleeves and licked his lips. He hadn't felt so stimulated in ages. "Let's go!"

Qi Fei started to wave his baton like a wizard casting a spell. He guided Qiankun to create a perfect replica of the EM signature of their spaceship as seen from the missile's perspective, taking into account the distance, relative velocities, size, shape, angle, and other factors. Jiang Liu projected the digital doppelgänger out and bombarded the missile's sensors with the new signal. At first, he made the phantom occupy the position of the real spaceship; gradually, he moved the phantom away from the real ship, until it was more than ten degrees apart. This was no easy task. He had to make sure that the digital doppelgänger overwhelmed the real signal in all EM bands, not just visible light, or else the missile's AI wouldn't be fooled.

Chang Tian had to help by diverting power from other subsystems on the ship to boost the strength of the phantom signal as Jiang Liu struggled to maintain the integrity of the signal. Finally, after about ten minutes during which everyone held their breath, the missile changed its heading, altering its course to chase after the digital doppelgänger rather than the real spaceship.

With only one minute to go, the missile brushed past the spaceship and exploded. They had only about three degrees to spare. They could feel the spaceship tremble as fragments of the missile struck it.

Jiang Liu and Qi Fei let out a long-held breath and collapsed against the instrument panels.

"Oh no!" Chang Tian shouted.

"What is it now?" an exhausted Qi Fei asked.

Chang Tian was pointing at a large asteroid on-screen: about ten meters across and sitting right in their path. At their velocity, a direct hit would pulverize them, the same as a direct missile strike. Chang Tian pulled the joystick hard to the right and tapped a bunch of buttons. Then he pushed the joystick forward and directed the spaceship into a long, curving course that swept past the asteroid.

"So much mass," Chang Tian sighed. "Can't believe how hard this thing is to steer. I don't remember working this hard even in the air force. That was terrifying."

"Don't relax yet," Qi Fei said. "There will be a lot of asteroids for a while, and there may be other missiles."

Indeed, as they continued on, they had to dodge three more large asteroids and two more missiles. Qi Fei trained Qiankun to learn from them how to evade asteroids as well as how to generate digital twins to fool incoming missiles. Finally, after extensive testing and entering interplanetary space, he gave the A-OK signal to the others.

Only then did everyone realize how exhausted they were. After hours of mental and physical strain, they all needed a nap. The four returned to their cabins for some much-needed sleep, and by the time they woke up again, it was already the evening of their second day on the ship.

They were hungry.

+ + + + +

Dinner was extra special. Out of beef brisket, carrots, and ketchup, somehow Chang Tian managed to whip up a stew reminiscent of Hungarian goulash. There was also fried sea bass and steamed har gow. Given that he had only a flameless electric stove that never got very hot and all the ingredients were frozen, this was nearly miraculous. Even though sashimi and stir-fry were out of the question, Chang Tian, a master of multiple cuisines, still managed to coax mouthwatering flavors out of that cramped galley. He spent at least as much time in the galley cooking as he did at the table eating with everyone else.

A near brush with catastrophe whetted everyone's appetite. Even Yun Fan decided to stay in the common area to eat with everyone. And surprising everyone, she agreed to have a drink: to be sure, it was just a glass of red wine, but it was still unprecedented.

Jiang Liu and Qi Fei continued to discuss the missile attack during the day. As the conversation meandered, they naturally turned to technical subjects.

"When did you first start training Qiankun?" Jiang Liu asked.

"A long time ago. I was a third-year in college. During my internship with the research institute, I was given a political assignment: a super AI trial to deploy military supplies. By then, most urban infrastructure had come under AI control, including electric and transportation grids, but military supplies posed a completely different challenge. It was all about dealing with instability and learning to adjust to changing circumstances. It was difficult to train an AI to make good judgment under complex and uncertain conditions."

"Did you succeed?" Jiang Liu asked.

"Well, it was a matter of steadily improving on Bayesian learning." Qi Fei paused. "However, I can't tell you the result. Listen, if you want to know military secrets, you have to find a better way."

Jiang Liu laughed. "Fine. Fine. I'm just trying to have a theoretical discussion with you. I've always wondered: As an AI expert, do you really believe that given enough data and the right algorithms, you can calculate everything?"

"Yes," Qi Fei said. "If I have enough computing power, I can compute the entire history of the universe."

"But the world is uncertain."

"There's no such thing as true uncertainty. Even in quantum mechanics, Schrödinger's equation is deterministic."

"But we know from countless simulations that the essence of the world is chaotic, indeterminate. You cannot predict the future."

"That's only because you don't know enough about the initial conditions and the computers aren't powerful enough."

"What about . . . what's in someone's mind? Can you compute that?"

"Human behavior is also data. Given enough data, you can certainly figure out what's in someone's mind."

Jiang Liu quirked an eyebrow. But rather than giving his own opinion, he continued questioning Qi Fei. "Is your plan to calculate the operation of a whole society with AI and then allocate human beings the way AI allocates electricity and supplies now?"

"I wouldn't go so far as to use the word 'allocate,' but things certainly can be optimized. Do you not ride in autonomous cars and airplanes? Those are all examples of algorithmic optimization. You seem to enjoy the results just fine."

"How can you compare a human being to a car? In a society, every individual member has their own mind, their own desires. How do you optimize *that*? And even if you could somehow find a solution, is it ethical to subject everyone to that one solution, to control them for their own good?"

"Your choice of words evokes oppression," Qi Fei said. "But I prefer an alternative way of phrasing: out of many, one. Xunzi writes, 'The righteous path gathers orderly distinctions into harmony. Out of many individuals, one society. So united, they have strength, and so strengthened, they grow powerful, thereby overcoming all challenges. However, a mob is no society, for instead of orderly distinctions there is only competition, and competition leads to chaos, which leads to division, which leads to weakness, which leads to being overcome by external challenges.'[8] If all members of society can be united in the pursuit of one righteous path, then human potential can be maximized."

Jiang Liu smiled. "Nice quote. But let me respond with another quote: 'Why is it that those above cannot regulate those below, and those below cannot serve those above? In fact, they are at each other's throats! Because they do not share the same conception of what is right.'[9] How can you expect everyone to see the same 'path'?"

---

8 Xunzi (third century BCE) was a Warring States period Confucian philosopher known for shoring up Confucianism against Daoist and Mohist criticisms. The quote here is from *A True King's Rule*, his chapter on an ideal ruler.

9 It will not surprise the reader that Jiang Liu quotes from Mozi again. This one is from *Exalting Unity*, Mozi's chapter on a unified conception of morality as a precondition for social order.

Qi Fei nodded. "But you are quoting from *Exalting Unity*, which explicitly advocates for a unified conception of what is right."

Jiang Liu shook his head. "For Mozi, 'exalting unity' is not about an optimization algorithm, but the need for those who rule to ascertain the desires of the ruled, and to conform their will to the consent of the governed."

"So what is your method for ascertaining the will of the people?"

"The will of the people is nothing more than each individual acting according to their own will," Jiang Liu said. "In the ancient world, there was no way for everyone to communicate with everyone else, which is why the proxy of a true king was needed. But in today's world, everyone is equal on the blockchain, and all information is transparent and public. Once everyone has made their choice, consensus emerges automatically. A decentralized world has its own emergent order."

"Ha! I knew you would always come back to your blockchain. But remember, it was a democracy that put Socrates to death. Your blockchain can also produce fifty-one percent mobs."

"I don't take the same lesson as you from the fate of Socrates. Athens was a tiny city-state, closed-off, self-important. That is the root of the tragedy. Today's blockchain is free and global; there's enough space for all."

"Once we get back to Earth," Qi Fei said, "I'll have to ask you for more lessons on the superiority of your blockchain governance."

"Not at all," Jiang Liu said. "I look forward to learning more from you about the potential of super AI."

The more he talked with Jiang Liu, the more excited Qi Fei grew. His face relaxed, and he felt the pleasure of finally arguing and debating with someone who *understood* the problems that troubled him. It was so rare and joyous to converse with another mind that matched his, as pleasurable as drinking.

Jiang Liu was also surprised. He had become used to Qi Fei's cold expression and the nonstop competition between the two, but this discussion was bringing them closer. He was also feeling pleasantly buzzed, and if the conversation continued, he was afraid that he would blurt out to Qi Fei, "The only heroes left in the world are right here: you and me."[10]

---

10 This is an allusion to an episode from *Romance of the Three Kingdoms*, when Cao Cao, after an alcohol-lubricated conversation with his rival Liu Bei, made a similar comment.

Looking to the side, Jiang Liu noticed that Yun Fan was flushed and unsteady. Supporting her, he asked, "Are you all right? Why don't you go to your cabin and rest?"

Unexpectedly, Yun Fan laughed and said, "I've been listening to your debate. 'There is no righteous path outside the heart, and no search for what is right without subjectivity.' You may talk all you want about institutions and systems, but in the end, the only answer that matters resides in everyone's heart-mind."[11]

Jiang Liu chuckled. "I should have known that Fanfan is a follower of Wang Yangming."[12]

"'There is neither good nor evil in the substance of the mind; both good and evil come into being through the will,'"[13] Yun Fan, flushed and swaying, chanted. "What's in someone's heart can't even be ascertained, let alone computed."

Jiang Liu understood that she was answering Qi Fei, from earlier. Making sure she was paying attention, he said, "The heart is hard to ascertain, but easy to change. It's best to let go of what you can. Let go, and be not troubled."

Yun Fan stared at him, her bright eyes unblinking. "No. I can't let go of what I did wrong. To let go is to . . . sin again."

"You didn't do anything wrong. Don't do this to yourself."

"It *was* my fault! *My* fault!" Yun Fan raised her voice. "To deny that it was my fault is to deny my very existence."

"All right. Let's not speak of this anymore." Jiang Liu held up the swaying Yun Fan. "I think you're drunk. Let me help you back to your cabin."

Chang Tian returned to the table at that moment with dessert: soufflé with fresh fruit and jam.

"Are you leaving?" he said to Yun Fan, disappointed. "You should at least have

11   In Chinese, 心 can mean both the heart and the mind (*cf* Anglo-Saxon "breóst"). In this section of the translation, I also use the two words interchangeably.

12   Yun Fan quotes Wang Yangming (1472–1529), whose philosophy, Yangmingism, is a refinement and development of Confucianism. By fusing influences from Daoism and Buddhism and emphasizing the inevitability of subjective interpretation of external phenomena, Yangmingism became deeply influential throughout East Asia. (Developments in Confucianism during the Song-Ming era, including Wang Yangming's work, are often known in the West as "Neo-Confucianism.")

13   Another quote from Wang Yangming. These are the first two lines from his "four-line teaching," often seen as a succinct summary of his most important ideas.

a taste of this first. How about a quick trip to the observation deck? The stars there are amazing."

Yun Fan nodded. And so, with her leaning against Jiang Liu to steady herself, Chang Tian carrying the soufflés, and Qi Fei bringing a bottle of wine, they all went to the observation deck. The four squeezed into the cramped space by having Qi Fei sit on the back of the booth. Yun Fan began to sing, and for a while, no one spoke as they all listened to her. Her lovely voice seemed to be the song of the spinning stars.

It didn't take them long to finish the bottle. Jiang Liu and Chang Tian went back to the galley for more. Qi Fei and Yun Fan were left alone in the observation deck. They listened to the noises of the other two in the back of the ship.

"Ah!" It was Chang Tian's voice.

"You're bleeding." That was Jiang Liu. "Let me help you. Hmmm, where is the first aid kit?"

Apparently, it would be some time before those two returned.

"Are you all right?" Qi Fei broke the awkward silence.

"Can't you see me?" Yun Fan giggled as she spread her arms. "I'm perfectly fine."

"That's not what I meant. I wanted to know about . . . what happened to you in the last decade."

"A decade is a long time," Yun Fan said. "I can't remember everything."

"There's something I wanted to tell you, but I never got the chance. My mother, she—"

"I know. I know!" Yun Fan wouldn't let him finish. "I know what your mother wants. Don't worry about it. I'll never let her see me for the rest of this life."

The pain in her voice silenced Qi Fei. At length, he said, "I'm . . . sorry."

"Really? That's all you have to say? You're sorry?"

"No!" Qi Fei swallowed. "When I left for college, the first thing I packed was the musical wristband you gave me. Over and over, I listened to what you said to me in that recording. I did it every day in college. I . . . I . . ."

Yun Fan looked up at Qi Fei, tears flowing down her cheeks. "Forget it. I don't want to hear about your regrets. I've been just fine all these years; you don't need to worry about me. After this trip, I'll be gone from your life, and you can forget about me."

Yun Fan got up to leave. Qi Fei reached out and grabbed her hand. For a moment, the two stayed still.

Footsteps. Chang Tian and Jiang Liu were returning.

Yun Fan broke free from Qi Fei. She wiped her face and strode for the exit—just in time to meet Chang Tian and Jiang Liu, holding fresh bottles. She pushed past them into the narrow corridor, keeping her face lowered. But it was too late; Jiang Liu had seen her tears.

Yun Fan ran for her cabin. Jiang Liu pushed his bottles into Chang Tian's arms and went after her.

He caught up to her outside the sleeping quarters. They were bathed in starlight from a window in the hallway.

Holding her by the shoulders, he said, "Chang Tian told me everything: the history between Qi Fei and you, and what happened to your family."

Yun Fan said nothing.

"Why do you keep on insisting it was your fault?" demanded Jiang Liu. "It obviously wasn't your fault. You did nothing wrong. Why do you persist in this flawed attachment?"

Yun Fan said nothing.

"You don't have to say anything," Jiang Liu said. "You can talk when you're ready, when you want to. I'll be here."

Yun Fan started to cry again. "Stop it! Stop being so nice to me! I can't be nice back, do you understand?"

"I understand. It's all right. All right." Jiang Liu gently held her; she leaned into his shoulders and wept silently. As her tears seeped through his shirt, he felt the warmth.

A long time after, Yun Fan gently freed herself and wiped her eyes. "Sorry." She went into her cabin and closed the door.

Jiang Liu remained in the hallway, looking up at the stars.

+ + + + +

Qi Fei and Chang Tian were also looking at the stars in the observation deck.

"I guess you had a long talk with him last night," Qi Fei said.

"You heard?" Chang Tian wasn't surprised.

"I couldn't make out the details," Qi Fei said. "But the two of you were like a couple of twittering birds. I couldn't sleep."

Chang Tian chuckled. "I told him everything."

"You idiot," Qi Fei said. "Why did you confide in him?"

Chang Tian laughed meaningfully. "I seem to remember you having a wonderful heart-to-heart with him tonight. I can't remember the last time you talked so much."

"We were talking about . . . academics," Qi Fei said. "It's different."

"Sure. Different." Chang Tian looked at Qi Fei. "Look, you clearly enjoy research and learning for the sake of learning. Why don't you just do that? All that politics and structure and hierarchy . . . you don't like any of it. And you're no good at pleasing your superiors or building a network among your colleagues. I've seen you at parties with the generals: you are about as charming as a block of wood."

"You don't understand," Qi Fei said. "You can't just do things you like."

"Why not?"

"You don't understand," repeated Qi Fei. "I need . . . I need to feel that strength."

Chang Tian said nothing.

"I can overcome my weaknesses," Qi Fei said. "I have to conquer myself."

Neither of them said anything as they stared at the distant Earth and moon, both tiny spheres now, both bright and pure.

8 | Key

The next morning, Chang Tian was the first to awaken.

By the time the others emerged from their cabins, Chang Tian had not only set out breakfast but was also busying himself in the cockpit. Jiang Liu and Qi Fei, not bothering to eat, rushed into the cockpit as well. The spaceship was on autopilot, adjusting course to intercept the source of the VLF signal. Chang Tian was there to monitor but didn't have to intervene yet. However, instead of looking relaxed, his brows were furrowed at the screen.

Jiang Liu and Qi Fei, both nursing a hangover, looked at each other awkwardly. Qi Fei's face was once again the habitual expressionless mask.

"Did you see something?" Jiang Liu asked Chang Tian.

"I just don't get it," muttered Chang Tian. "At such a close range, we should be detecting the target in other bands as well. But all we have is just the VLF signal. Nothing's changed."

"We know they have excellent EM cloaking capabilities," Jiang Liu said.

"But this is weird," Chang Tian said. "Typically, cloaking techniques involve absorbing electromagnetic waves. That's how stealth planes evade radar. But that should leave a dip in the observed signal landscape, like a hole. There's nothing like that right now. See? Scanning the area around the object yields a perfectly smooth view in every EM band."

Jiang Liu pondered this. "Maybe they're using background radiation simulation to achieve this."

"What do you mean?"

"Okay, look at me." Jiang Liu pointed at himself. "I'm not transparent, so you can see how I stand out against the background by blocking the light from behind me. But suppose I have a camera on my back that can capture that light, and then I project that image onto my shirt in the front. If I do it exactly right, you'll think you can see right through me, and I'm not there at all."

"Sure . . ." Chang Tian said hesitantly.

"That's the principle. If the ship is able to bend light around itself or to simulate the light that it absorbs for an observer on the other side, then the ship would be invisible."

"What can we do about it, then?" Chang Tian asked. "I can't navigate us to something that we can't see. VLF signals aren't precise enough for location."

"Don't worry about it." Jiang Liu rubbed his hands. "I'll make it appear after breakfast."

Yun Fan was once again completely silent during breakfast, as though last night involved a different person or never happened. Instead of her usual stylish dress, she wore a black bodysuit that emphasized her strength and efficiency. Jiang Liu asked her why she looked so different. She said nothing.

"Do you observe some sort of law of conservation of conversation?" Jiang Liu asked. "If you talk too much one night, you're done for the week. Is that how it works?"

Yun Fan ignored him. If anything, she pressed her lips tighter together.

"I'm going to cast a magic spell in a few minutes to reveal the alien spaceship," Jiang Liu said. "Do you have a guess for what it will look like?"

Yun Fan looked at him.

"You told me that the Kunlun in classical mythology is an alien spaceship," mused Jiang Liu. "So I imagine it will be shaped like a mountain, and also be as big as a mountain."

"It's possible," Yun Fan said. "But Kunlun didn't necessarily look like a mountain. The ancients only wrote 'Kunlun.' It was only much later that people started to interpret the ancient texts to describe a mountain."

"What about the other mythological figures of that time? Xiwangmu, Fuxi, and so on . . . were they all aliens?"

"Maybe, and maybe not," Yun Fan said. "They could also be humans who contacted aliens and learned from them. Xiwangmu and Fuxi were powerful figures, and you can readily imagine that humans who gained power from alien technology would be seen by others as gods."

"Fanfan, I have to ask you to consider an alternative," Qi Fei broke in after some hesitation. "You've insisted all along those aliens helped humans in the past. But I haven't seen enough proof. I know what I'm saying annoys you, but we cannot afford to be rash. You don't know for certain whether they're friend or foe, and the only rational choice is to prepare for both possibilities."

"We won't know until we see them," Yun Fan said.

"I don't think it's wise for everyone to go over together," Qi Fei said. "We should send two people to investigate, while the other two stay behind to observe and possibly help if something goes wrong."

"There's no need for that," Yun Fan said. "I'll be the only one going over."

Everyone was startled. "That's absurd," Jiang Liu said. "How can you expect three men to stay behind while a woman takes all the risk? We're not cowards."

"I've thought this through," Yun Fan said. "I've trained for this moment extensively, going on more than five hundred simulated space walks. I know how to move in space and how to open the alien spaceship hatch. You don't know any of that. All you need to do is get me there."

Qi Fei shook his head. "We're not as useless as you seem to think. I'm going."

Yun Fan sighed. "You can't go. My black box is the key. You don't know how to use it."

The three men were dumbfounded. She never intended for them to do anything except bring her here. She was going to be the one to enter the alien spaceship. They looked at one another.

"It's too dangerous," Jiang Liu pleaded.

Yun Fan swept her eyes across the three faces. In a tone that brooked no disagreement, she said, "I never expected to return alive from this mission. All I care about is finishing what I promised to do."

"I can't let you die!" Qi Fei blurted. "If you won't back down, then we'll all go. All four of us."

"I won't allow that," Yun Fan said. "I can be crazy, but I'm not going to drag you along. Why do you think I drank last night? It was my farewell banquet. I'm glad that you drank with me. It's the best goodbye."

"No!" Jiang Liu said. "We—"

"Enough," Chang Tian said. "This sort of argument will lead nowhere. Let's not make any plans until we've seen the alien spaceship."

The argument stopped, but Chang Tian could sense the tension from both Jiang Liu and Qi Fei. They kept themselves busy with the scanners and instruments, their eyes locked on the screens, searching for the elusive alien ship.

The way to make the alien spaceship show up wasn't a simple matter of electromagnetic interference or signal processing, but a skillful combination of both techniques. First, they had to carefully sift through the observed data for "edge effects," where the border of the stealth signal couldn't quite match the real background signals perfectly. Then, they needed to use deviation to reconstruct the stealth signal and generate the interference waveform to eliminate it.

While the principle was simple, the execution was anything but. Jiang Liu and Qi Fei, working together, struggled for a long time over the problem. The source of the VLF signal was about three hundred thousand kilometers ahead—about one light-second, or seven hours at their current speed. But even at such close range, they couldn't discern any edge effects at all. It wasn't until they switched to infrared that they had a breakthrough.

As they approached, Qiankun noticed the deviations in the infrared band. Latching on to a couple of imperfections, the AI soon pulled out a whole seam of such data anomalies. Jiang Liu and Qi Fei rushed in to help, deploying different signal analysis algorithms and filters to the task. Soon, they had a long curve of the stealth signal that they could use to develop the counter-stealth waveform. Once the disguise was filtered away, one edge of the alien ship finally lay before their eyes.

It was no mountain; rather, the alien vessel seemed to be a long, sinuous band.

Jiang Liu and Qi Fei kept on working, extending their countersignal into the visible range. With this, they could eliminate the entirety of the disguise and reveal the shape of the alien ship. Jiang Liu directed the ship's communications array to its maximum output and swept the target vessel with a powerful beam of interference emissions, as though wiping glass with a cloth. Finally, they could see the true form of the alien ship, from tip to tail, including every hatch and appendage.

It was . . . a loong.

Jiang Liu and Qi Fei each sucked in a breath. The alien vessel was literally a loong from the ancient murals come to life. The head of the ship resembled the head of a massive beast with the eyes of a rabbit, the antlers of a stag, the lips and ears of an ox, the skull-shape of a horse, the barbels of a carp, and the mane of a lion. The body was a sinuous serpent, covered in fish scales. The tail was like that of a massive crocodile. The whole ship glowed a metallic blue-gray, and all the joints were formed from massive components, like a mecha. Indeed, the ship, while certainly impressive, was not at all what they expected in a high-tech spaceship.

As the four watched the vessel snaking its way gracefully through space, waving from side to side, the head always pointed toward Earth, they were shaken and felt overcome by awe. Preliminary measurements showed that the alien vessel was about 1600 meters in length, and 16 meters in height (about five stories). If the ship were coiled from head to tail, it would encircle about as much space as sixteen football pitches. The mechanical loong flying through space gave off a solemn and dignified air, a magnificent sight that felt at home among the stars. In the background could be seen the red glow of Mars, like a guiding pearl. For a moment the four felt like pilgrims staring at a distant altar. None could speak.

At length, Qi Fei asked, "Should . . . should we initiate communications?"

"It's worth a try," Jiang Liu said.

"There's no need of that," Yun Fan said from behind them. "I'm already in communication with them."

Jiang Liu and Qi Fei turned to look at her. She was holding up the octagonal black box. In that dark, seamless form, a red light was flashing.

"What happens next?" Jiang Liu asked.

"We approach the ship," Yun Fan said in a tone that was no different from describing a walk in the park, "and look for a hatch on the ship that also has a flashing red light—it should be close to the jaws. Once we find it, I'll go over with the box. I put the key in and perform a certain procedure, and the hatch will open."

"A procedure?" Qi Fei asked. "Teach me the procedure so that I can do it for you."

"Do you know anything about Hetu and Luoshu? Or how about bagua? No? Well, those are the keycodes to the hatch. Only I can open the hatch."

"Then we'll go together. We'll protect you," Qi Fei said.

"What happens after you open the hatch?" Jiang Liu asked.

"I have no idea," Yun Fan said. "My father told me that once I open the hatch, I must go in and follow my instincts. He was just passing on the instructions he received from my grandfather. Neither of them knew what the instructions really meant."

Qi Fei and Jiang Liu saw that docking with the loong-ship could lead to three broad types of outcomes. The first type involved failure to dock or the inability to open the hatch. The second type involved successful docking and meeting friendly aliens. The last type involved successful docking and meeting hostile aliens.

Ideally, everyone wanted an outcome in the second category, but they had to prepare for the first and third as well. After an hour of planning, they came up with the following plan for action.

First, they would weakly tether their own spaceship to the alien vessel before attempting to dock. The idea here was that the weak tether would serve as a safety line for the spacewalkers to return to their ship. But they couldn't make the tether too secure, which would hinder escape by the spaceship if the situation turned hazardous. In the end, they decided to use Qi Fei's spider-silk lines. Bundles of the super strong strands would be woven into a rope, with one end secured to their spaceship and the other end attached to the spacewalkers. The ship, piloted by Chang Tian, would maintain about ten meters between itself and the loong-ship, while the other three performed a space walk to open the hatch. Once they succeeded, Chang Tian would follow them. They modified Jiang Liu's booster shoes to serve as emergency thrusters on their space suits. In case of any problems during the space walk, they could use the electromagnetic thrust from the shoes to get back to the spaceship.

Also, everyone would be armed. Sure, the aliens were far more technologically advanced than humans, and the loong-ship might be full of alien warriors armed to the teeth, so there was no expectation that the small human crew would win a head-to-head confrontation. However, defensive weaponry and other equipment could be useful in an escape. For instance, they had scanners to give them advance warning of the presence of any life-forms. Also, everyone would wear armored cloaks and bring multiple decoys to frustrate pursuit. Beyond that, the party would bring daggers, nunchucks, miniature bombs (both traditional chemical explosives as well as laser-triggered)—all of which were deliberately limited in their destructive capacity. Once Yun Fan got the hatch open, they planned to have Qi Fei and Jiang Liu in the lead as scouts, Yun Fan would then be in the middle with the critical communicator box, and Chang Tian would take up the rear.

By the time they had finished the planning and rehearsed the necessary maneuvers, they were practically on top of the loong-ship. Not only was the image on the screen crystal clear, but they could also see the mythical beast with the naked eye. As the seconds ticked by and they got closer and closer to the alien vessel, everyone's heart leaped into their throats, their bodies tense like a drawn bow.

"Let me ask you one last time," Yun Fan said. "Do you really want to go? I only wanted you to bring me here. None of you should feel compelled to risk yourself for me."

"What kind of date is this?" Jiang Liu asked, grinning. "We're right at the door to the theater, and now you tell me: 'Hey, there's no need to see the movie with me. Go home!' Fanfan, come on!"

"It's not a movie, though," Yun Fan said. "This is dangerous."

"We told *you* it was dangerous! But did you listen?" Qi Fei said, mock glaring at her. "So why should we listen to you now?"

"It's different! I have a mission," Yun Fan said. "Also . . . I wrote my last will and testament three years ago. But you—you all have families or loved ones waiting for you at home. I think you should call home first. What if—"

"Hey, hey! Don't say such unlucky things!" Jiang Liu broke in. "I don't want to call anyone. No one cares if I die anyway." He turned to Qi Fei and Chang Tian. "What about you? Want to make a call?"

"Stop being so maudlin!" Qi Fei said. He pointed at the approaching alien ship. "Focus on *that*."

The loong-ship grew bigger and bigger, a slumbering mythical beast at once ancient and mysterious. The 270-degree cockpit window gave them a perfect view. The yawning mouth of the loong faced the spaceship directly, giving the occupants a good view of the internal structure. The hatch was inside the "oral cavity," where the "throat" of a real creature would be. The jaw served as a kind of stoop or porch, or maybe a loading dock.

The four of them counted down silently as they put on their oxygen masks, earpieces, and helmets.

+ + + + +

The docking maneuver began.

Using thrusters and gyros, the spaceship matched the loong's velocity. The space-ship's hatch opened, revealing the spacewalkers tethered with strands of spider silk.

Jiang Liu was the first to leap out, drifting across the ten meters of space sep-arating the two vessels in no time at all. He caught the teeth-railing on one side of the throat-hatch and turned around to help Yun Fan and Qi Fei.

All three took a minute to stabilize themselves. This was their first real space walk, and since Qi Fei and Jiang Liu hadn't trained for this the way Yun Fan had, they needed even more time to learn how to find their balance. As they adjusted, they made their way slowly toward the throat.

Right away, they noticed the octagonal depression in the hatch, in size and shape an exact match for Yun Fan's box. Jiang Liu and Qi Fei held her steady as she removed the box from her belt and gently pressed it into the depression.

The flashing red light within the box sped up, soon turning into red ripples that spread out from the center. After a while, the ripples re-formed into a twenty-by-twenty matrix of red dots.

Yun Fan counted to herself silently and performed the requisite mathemat-ical operations in her head. Quickly, she pressed-down five dots in the middle, a miniature cross. Then she pressed down nine dots above the cross, three to the left, seven to the right, and one below. More waves rippled across the top of the box, replacing the red dots with blue ones. Yun Fan continued her calculations and pressed down four dots in the upper-left corner, two in the upper-right, eight in the bottom-left, and six in the bottom-right.

The black box began to turn, the hatch around it rotating likewise. The mas-sive metal door's movement could be felt by everyone around it, the vibrations pass-ing from the railing into their bones. When the rotation stopped, the hatch irised away, revealing yet another closed hatch under it. The top of the black box cracked to reveal a second layer as well. More red and blue dots appeared on this second layer, and Yun Fan punched in yet more numbers, causing the hatch to rotate and open again, revealing a third hatch.

Jiang Liu sucked in a breath. The center of the third layer of the black box showed a yin-yang symbol. Around it were three concentric rings that could rotate independently. The rings were marked with long and short segments such that by rotating the rings, one could form eight trigrams of broken and solid lines around the yin-yang.

Qi Fei asked (through the earpiece), "I assume you have to form the correct bagua pattern here?"

Yun Fan nodded. "The previous two passcodes were based on Hetu and Luoshu."

"Interesting," Jiang Liu said. "Was it hard to memorize?"

"Not at all," Yun Fan said. "Luoshu, for instance, is basically the earliest sudoku. It's easy if you see the pattern."

"So what do you do with these trigrams?" Qi Fei asked.

"The yin-yang in the middle is a handle to rotate the hatch," Yun Fan said, observing the mechanism closely. "The rings are like the dials in a combination lock. There are two combinations of trigrams that I have to dial in: Fuxi's Earlier Heaven and King Wen's Later Heaven."

As she spoke, she began to turn the dials. At first, the rings wouldn't even budge—the rings were directly connected to the mechanism of the hatch and required quite a bit of strength. Jiang Liu and Qi Fei both had to help. Finally, the three succeeded in inputting the two sets of trigrams. Grabbing the yin-yang at the center, they turned.

The third hatch rumbled open to reveal a cylindrical space within, more than ten meters in diameter and about as long. It appeared to be an air lock since the far side showed yet another hatch.

Qi Fei floated in and examined the wall. Finding no danger, he waited for the others to enter before beckoning Chang Tian to come over. The other man untied the spider-silk bundles and then leaped through the gap between their spaceship and the loong-ship.

As the third hatch irised away, the black key-box was left floating and spinning in space. Instead of its former octagonal shape, the box, having shed three layers, now appeared to be a smooth cylinder. Yun Fan reached out to grab it. But just as her fingers were about to wrap themselves around the cylinder, the loong head began to move to the side. The cylinder slipped out of Yun Fan's hand.

Worried, she kicked the curved wall of the air lock and propelled herself after the cylinder.

The loong-head continued to move to the side, carrying the three men in the barrel-shaped air lock. Yun Fan, on the other hand, floated in the other direction and was spat out of the loong's throat.

"Yun Fan!" the three men shouted in alarm.

Jiang Liu leaped after her. But despite his speed, by the time he reached the lip of the loong, Yun Fan was already some distance away in space. Jiang Liu looked around and realized that the loong was curving around, in the process of forming a circle with the head connected to the tail. Yun Fan was outside the circle and getting farther each second.

Qi Fei and Chang Tian arrived at the lip as well.

"I'm going after her," Jiang Liu said. "Can you anchor me with the spider silk?"

"No problem," Qi Fei said.

"You better not let go," Jiang Liu said. "Both of our lives are in your hands."

"Trust me," Qi Fei said.

Jiang Liu tied one end of the spider-silk rope to himself and handed the other end to Qi Fei. He turned on the booster shoes and shot after Yun Fan. Since she was no longer accelerating, it didn't take long for Jiang Liu to catch her. However, the thrust from the shoes and the sudden grab caused the two to start spinning uncontrollably. Before long, both were completely entangled in the spider-silk line. Despite Jiang Liu's best efforts, he couldn't use the thrusters to stop the chaotic spinning. Soon, the line was stretched taut.

"This is bad," Qi Fei said. "I can't hold on to them forever, and the line is going to snap. Here, you take my place. I'll go after them."

Before Chang Tian could object, Qi Fei had handed over the safety line and jumped out himself. As Chang Tian strained to secure the line to something inside the loong mouth, he could see that the tail was getting closer and closer.

Qi Fei used his own booster shoes to approach Jiang Liu and Yun Fan. He knew that he had to be careful lest he also be entangled in the mess. Cautiously, he maneuvered to the far side of the couple and held out one hand.

Jiang Liu understood what he wanted right away. As the pair continued to spin, he wrapped one arm tightly around Yun Fan and held out his other hand, aiming at Qi Fei's extended hand.

Palm to palm, the contact lasted only a fraction of a second. It was enough to transfer some of the pair's angular momentum to Qi Fei. The other man, unentangled in the spider-silk line, could then use the booster shoes to coun-terbalance the incipient spin. Once he was stabilized, Qi Fei held out his hand again.

Three high fives later, all the angular momentum had been dissipated. Jiang Liu and Yun Fan disentangled themselves, and all three propelled themselves back toward the loong-ship.

By now the tail had almost reached the mouth, and Chang Tian frantically waved at them to hurry.

The three turned their booster shoes to the max, aiming for the narrowing gap between the tail and the mouth.

Five meters. Four. Three. Two. One.

They slammed into the loong's yawning mouth, taking Chang Tian with them. All four collapsed against the inside of the oral cavity.

The tail had reached the mouth.

The tail flared open into a set of mechanical branches, perfectly matching the teeth in the mouth. After a series of clangs and rumbles that reverberated through their suits, the loong's mouth bit into the tail, the teeth and tail spikes meshing seamlessly. The last twinkle of starlight was blocked by the sliding metal panels.

They were sealed within the loong-ship.

Everything had happened so quickly that there was no time to plan out their moves before they found themselves trapped. The four stared at one another, find-ing terror and anxiety in the eyes of each. But they all knew that there was no other choice at this point, save exploring ahead.

"Lead on," Qi Fei said to Yun Fan.

Yun Fan took out the black cylinder that had almost cost her life. "This is the final key."

They looked to the other end of the air lock, about ten meters away. Even with their lights, it was hard to make out any details. All four adjusted their booster shoes and floated toward the inner hatch.

The interior hatch was a perfectly flat surface with a single round hole. Yun Fan inserted the black cylinder. Soon, the familiar red flash appeared again inside the cylinder, and after about five flashes, the rest of the hatch began to glow with a blue light. The spreading blue light, like ripples in a pond, revealed intricate, mazy lines on the surface of the hatch, evoking the lines on a printed circuit board. But for some reason, all four were also reminded of the tight square spirals and whirls decorating classical bronze vessels. The blue "circuits" spread to the edge of the hatch, and soon the surface of the spaceship hull around them began to glow with similar circuits.

The ship rumbled, and they could sense that there was movement. The gyro sensors told them that the entire ship was starting to spin, as though the ouroboros loong were a giant wheel.

"Ah!" Chang Tian exclaimed. He was staring at the instrument panel on the arm of his space suit—as his suit was intended for maintenance and support, it was equipped with the most comprehensive suite of sensors. "There's air!" Indeed, everyone could see the needle on his pressure gauge swinging wildly.

As the ship's spin accelerated, they could feel the effects of artificial gravity although they were still drifting. The inner hatch also began to lower in the direction of the new "down." Rather than retracting into the floor, the hatch swiveled down like a drawbridge, leaving the black cylinder key poking up from the floor like a mini altar.

Qi Fei looked over to Jiang Liu. "Ready to walk?"

Jiang Liu looked at the gyro sensors. "I don't know if the spin is fast enough."

"Let's give it a try." Qi Fei adjusted the thrusters to propel himself toward the new floor.

Having landed, he tried to walk a few steps and jump a little. "Not too bad. It's almost like the moon. Better than floating for sure."

The others landed as well and tried out walking against the centrifugal force.

"It will feel better once the spin really picks up and stabilizes," Qi Fei said.

"How's the air pressure?" Jiang Liu asked.

"About half of one standard atmosphere," Chang Tian said. "But there's a higher proportion of oxygen . . . fifty percent; the rest is mostly inert gases along with a small amount of carbon dioxide."

"Perfect," Jiang Liu said. "Half of fifty percent . . . that's comparable to the oxygen content on Earth. Time to get rid of this." He pointed at his helmet.

"Wait!" Qi Fei said. "We better do some more tests first."

"Anyone got a fire starter?" Jiang Liu asked.

"I do," Chang Tian said. "I always have a mini electric fire starter with me."

"What are you waiting for, then?" Jiang Liu said. "Give it a try."

Chang Tian took out a sphere about the size of a marble and rubbed it. A flame burst into existence. Everyone cheered.

To be safe, Jiang Liu asked the others to stay put while he carefully removed one glove from his suit. He waited to be sure everything felt all right. Then he unlocked his helmet, lifted it up a fraction of an inch, and took a breath. He gave everyone the thumbs-up. "All good!"

They took off their helmets and stripped off the space suits, instantly feeling better. By now, the artificial gravity had reached about half of Earth's, allowing for natural, but nimbler, movement. Jiang Liu jumped and made several acrobatic flips, smacking his lips in satisfaction. Yun Fan looked athletic and energetic in her black bodysuit.

"I'm beginning to believe your theory," Chang Tian said to Yun Fan. "The aliens are definitely friendly if they are going to such trouble to make us comfortable."

Instead of answering him, Yun Fan strode to the black cylinder poking up from the floor. "Look at the base of this tower."

The others joined her.

The black cylinder was resting on top of a small tower that seemed to be made of smooth stone. The tower was squarish in cross-section, with convex sides and a cylindrical hole down the middle for the key. The sides were covered in dense decorative patterns reminiscent of beast heads.

"It looks familiar," Jiang Liu said. "But I can't remember exactly where I've seen it."

"It's a jade cong," Yun Fan said. "You probably remember it from exhibits of Liangzhu culture artifacts."

"What?" the others exclaimed.

"Round in the center for heaven, square on the outside for earth. The sides are covered in beast motifs." Yun Fan reached out and caressed the tower surface. "This is pure, smooth jade. Classic Liangzhu cong."

"But how could this be jade?" Qi Fei frowned.

"Maybe the loong-ship once contacted Liangzhu culture and saved some artifacts," Chang Tian said.

"No. I'm not puzzled about its connection to Liangzhu," Qi Fei said.

"I know what you're trying to figure out," Jiang Liu said. "You're wondering how could jade conduct electricity and embed circuits, right?" He crouched down to examine the cong and traced the intricate lines around the outside with one finger. "I think it has to do with the key in the middle."

Qi Fei also went down on one knee next to him. "What do you mean, exactly?"

"Jade is a monoclinic crystal with calcium and magnesium ions," Jiang Liu said. "Theoretically, it's not impossible for it to experience electrical effects. However, most ions in crystals are bound in potential wells and cannot move freely, so that's why crystals are generally nonconductive. However, given certain conditions . . ."

"You mean through quantum tunneling?" Qi Fei looked thoughtful. "The black key-cylinder is the instrument that triggers the tunneling?"

"Why not?" Jiang Liu asked. "I don't claim to know how it works. The black box is a total mystery. I examined it closely beforehand but couldn't find any mechanisms. Yet just now it showed itself to contain multiple layers of complex structure."

Yun Fan looked at the mini tower and said, "So many people have seen jade cong in the past, but none ever guessed they were receptacles for keys. I bet there are lots of other receptacles and keys throughout this ship."

"The more we see evidence of contact between ancient humans and these aliens, the more I'm confused," Qi Fei said. "Why did they show up? Why did they leave? Why did they leave behind so many artifacts among humans? Also, why aren't they out here to greet us? What's the point of all this mystery?"

"This is only an air lock, after all," Jiang Liu said. "Maybe they're waiting for us deeper inside. I can't imagine they're hostile if they went to all the trouble of giving us oxygen."

Qi Fei looked skeptical. "I'm not saying it's impossible. But . . . I can't figure out their agenda. Why should they go to so much trouble to help humans covertly? What's in it for them? The cosmos isn't populated by alien scouts trying to earn 'Assisting Strange Species' badges or seeking to emulate Comrade Lei Feng. It makes no sense."

"We can't figure out the answer by standing around here, can we?" Yun Fan said. "Let's keep going."

"You have the chemical and laser explosives on you?" Qi Fei asked Jiang Liu. "Of course."

"If this turns out to be a trap," Qi Fei said, "you'd better be ready to give us all a quick end. We must not be caught—"

He was interrupted by a shout of "Careful!" from Chang Tian, who leaped at Yun Fan, pushing her out of the way. Instinctively, both Jiang Liu and Qi Fei jumped back.

Thump!

A giant rock had fallen from overhead, landing exactly where the four had stood a moment ago. Had they been a fraction of a second slower in reacting, they'd be pancakes now.

The four sat on the ground, staring at the murderous rock, unable to speak.

What other dangers were concealed within the dark belly of the loong-ship?

9 | Secret Codes

It took them some time to recover from the shock.

"Do we really want to go on?" Yun Fan asked.

"Have you accomplished your mission?" Jiang Liu asked. "I didn't realize you just wanted to come here and take a peek at the lobby."

"I'm not finished."

"Then we need to go on. Why are you suddenly hesitant?"

Yun Fan sighed. "I used to think only about myself. But now there's the rest of you—it's hard to be fearless and determined when you have others to worry about."

"Ridiculous," Jiang Liu said. "How many times have we gone over this point? I hate it when people can't just accept that others want to help them. Let's never discuss this again."

"But . . . what if they turn out to be not as friendly . . ." Yun Fan trailed off.

"We aren't children," Jiang Liu said, laughing. "Of course you can't vouch for them. We'll make up our own minds and plan accordingly."

Qi Fei got up. "We have no choice but to go on anyway. The hatch is sealed behind us, and we can't just wait here. Let's keep exploring but be more careful."

"What's the worst that can happen?" Jiang Liu asked. "If we die, we'll all die together. You'll be pretty lucky to have me around for eternity, in my opinion."

Qi Fei rolled his eyes. "Jiang Liu, let's investigate and figure out their technology."

"Sure." Jiang Liu smacked the wall of the corridor. "This looks perfectly unremarkable, but I bet it's filled with embedded circuits."

"Can you scan it to see if there are hidden structures?"

"On it." Jiang Liu knelt down on one knee to search the pouches wrapped around his calf and retrieved a few objects that he held up in a palm. "These are perfect for scanning."

The others looked at his palm: six tiny drones shaped like beetles.

Jiang Liu leapt up and tossed out two beetles high into the air, above and ahead of himself. Then, as he landed, he tossed out the other four, ahead and behind. All six beetles buzzed in the air, slowly approaching the alien surfaces around them.

"Right now they're using X-rays," Jiang Liu said. "If that's not enough, they'll switch to something more penetrative."

As the six beetles scanned around them, Jiang Liu adjusted his bracelet to stitch all the data together and projected the result back onto the walls so that the projection showed what was beneath the wall at each point.

Indeed, the corridor walls were filled with dense swirling lines, like an integrated circuit magnified many times, but also resembling the decorative patterns on ancient Chinese bronzeware. In some spots there were other black cylinders like the one Yun Fan brought; however, the beetles' X-rays couldn't penetrate inside them to reveal internal structure.

"As we suspected," Qi Fei said.

"Do you think we can establish a link with the ship?" Jiang Liu asked.

"It's worth a try," Qi Fei said. "But we have no way of knowing if the aliens designed their computers around binary data, or if we'll even be able to decode their machine language. It won't be easy."

"Let me see if I can find us a port first." Jiang Liu pressed a hand against the wall and the tattoos on his arm glowed blue as he probed for the flow of electricity in the wall. However, everything seemed dormant. As his scanning beam reached each spot, it awakened ripples of activity that immediately subsided as the beam moved away.

"The ship's systems don't seem to be on." Jiang Liu frowned.

"That's odd," Qi Fei said. "Then what was responsible for all the activities earlier?"

"Not sure. Maybe it was just a localized reaction."

"The only way to learn more is to go forward."

Jiang Liu summoned the beetle-drones back. Before he put them away, however, Qi Fei asked, "Could we send them ahead to scan as scouts?"

"Scanning is no problem, but I have nowhere to project the images if we're moving."

"I have my contacts." Qi Fei pointed to his eyes. "You could project onto my lenses if you don't mind."

Jiang Liu knew that Qi Fei's AR contacts could display images transmitted by his cranial implant. "I don't mind at all. However, you'll have to give my computing module access to your cranial implant. Are you okay with that?"

The two men locked eyes. The suggestion posed risk for both. For Jiang Liu, it meant that all the data in his computing module would be exposed to Qi Fei; for Qi Fei, it meant that Jiang Liu could harm his nervous system through the cranial implant. Jiang Liu's computing module, a chip implanted under the skin of his right wrist, not only served as the central hub and command center for all his wearable accessories, but it also stored his most private personal data. For two master spies who had breached countless defenses and countered innumerable hacking attempts, such a connection represented an extraordinary act of trust.

"I don't mind," Qi Fei said.

"Aren't you worried that I'll hurt you?" Jiang Liu grinned.

"Will you?"

Jiang Liu held out his arm. "Let's go."

A blue dot flashed on the inside of Jiang Liu's wrist. Qi Fei gripped the other man's arm around that spot and allowed his nervous system to fall into the familiar receptive pattern he used to interface with his bike-mecha. The two cyber implants engaged in their own handshake atop the physical one between the two men. Soon, Qi Fei could see in his eyes the subsurface scan from the beetle-drones, along with the numerical data, superimposed over his regular view.

Qi Fei held up a hand to show that everything was good.

"Wait," Chang Tian said. "I think we should put on some protective clothing."

He took out from a side-pouch four tiny packets that unfolded into four extremely thin cloaks.

"These offer excellent radiation protection," Chang Tian said as he distributed the cloaks. "The collar has sensors that monitor kinetic threats. In the event of an approaching projectile or other similar threat, the cloak will electrically stiffen the fibers and turn into temporary armor. It won't save you from everything, but it is effective against shrapnel and thrown rocks—we used to wear these for protection from guerilla ambushes."

Having shed their space suits, all four were in dark-colored bodysuits that allowed free movement. Tools and weapons were strapped to their limbs for ease of access. With these cloaks as the final touch, they resembled ancient assassins, ninjas, or xiake.

The group started their exploration deeper into the loong-ship.

Although earlier scans had shown the ship's electrical systems to be inactive, the walls of the corridors came to life as they passed by, illuminating a region that extended to about ten meters ahead of where they were. After they passed, the walls subsided into darkness and inactivity again.

Everyone was amazed by the degree of automation as well as the utter lack of any other signs of life. Even after walking for more than one hundred meters, the corridors they passed through remained completely empty, their voices echoing far into the darkness.

Qi Fei, keeping an eye on the scan results from the beetle-drones, asked Jiang Liu, "Why don't you have a cranial implant? Combined with your computing module, a cranial implant would give you a lot more power."

"I don't want my brain invaded," Jiang Liu said.

"That's the wrong way to look at it," Qi Fei said. "It's augmentation. Machines are not your enemies; they're more like . . . Disney animal sidekicks."

"I think you miss your Qiankun." Jiang Liu grinned.

Qi Fei didn't deny it. "If Qiankun were here, it would have computed many solutions."

"You see, everything has benefits but also costs. Qiankun is powerful, but you can't bring with you the quantum computing center and all the servers that make Qiankun possible. My AI assistant is nowhere near as powerful, but I can carry it everywhere in my computing module. While it doesn't augment my brain, it's a tool I can always count on. I'm used to being a vagabond—better for me not to become dependent on anything I can't take with me."

"So you'd rather be weak," Qi Fei said.

"I'd rather be me," Jiang Liu said.

"I remember something my father used to say," Yun Fan said. "Social evolution isn't very different from biological evolution. The earliest life-forms on Earth were all unicellular; multicellular life emerged much later. When you look at a multicellular creature, each cell is still alive, but they've given up the ability to live independently. They gave up their individual identities to merge into a greater identity: out of many, one. They gain some things but also lose some things."

Qi Fei nodded approvingly. "They merge into a single being under the control of one central nervous system. They lose the freedom of being their own cells, but they gain more power as life."

"But living beings aren't fundamentally comparable to computers," Yun Fan said. "The components of a computer are completely controlled by the CPU. Without its instructions, the components, even if powered, can't do anything. But cells are different. Each cell retains the ability to maintain its own existence. Even in a patient whose brain has ceased to function, each organ, and each cell within each organ, continues to function on its own. In other words, cells are largely autonomous. The brain isn't like a CPU, completely controlling every aspect of every cell, but merely coordinates and regulates. I think an ideal society should strive for the balance between freedom and control in life itself. Only a living harmony between autonomy and regulation can keep society robust against the threat of collapse."

"Are there any societies that have achieved that perfect balance?" Qi Fei asked.

"I don't know; I'm still studying the problem," Yun Fan said. "I've long been interested in patterns in the evolution of civilizations. How can a civilization evolve into a more advanced civilization?"

"Do you really believe that aliens helped humanity advance both in technology and civilization?" Jiang Liu asked.

"I do," Yun Fan said. "You've now seen the evidence of alien contact with the ancients. Hetu and Luoshu, the Liangzhu jade cong . . . how can you not believe it?"

"I believe they came to Earth—we all do." Jiang Liu glanced at Qi Fei. "But I'm still skeptical that they helped humans advance. I have to agree with Qi Fei on this point. I don't see why aliens would want to help us. There's just no reason."

"Why *wouldn't* they help?" Yun Fan demanded.

Qi Fei took over. "The fundamental engine of life is the drive to sustain and replicate itself. This is true of all species. You must find a logical explanation for why aliens would devote the resources to travel across the cosmos just to help us without killing us or taking our resources."

"Why do you insist on applying 'rules' discerned from humans, all that talk about nature red in tooth and claw, to aliens?" Yun Fan grew more passionate as she talked. "We don't know anything about them; we don't know if their civilization follows different patterns and rules. Remember, humans have had civilization for barely more than five thousand years; how arrogant for us to assume that we can represent *all* civilizations in the universe."

Jiang Liu pondered this. "I think that depends on whether there is some higher principle or set of laws that all life in the universe must follow."

"What would those laws look like, then?" Yun Fan asked.

"I don't know," admitted Jiang Liu. "I haven't thought that through."

"Competition," Qi Fei said. "That's the principle you're looking for. The victor writes the history of the universe."

"But competition by itself cannot bring about advancement," Yun Fan said. "This is a subtle but important point. By studying anthropology and history, we know that competition has been a constant everywhere in the world. From the earliest days of *Homo sapiens* to the twentieth century, many parts of the world saw tribes living largely the same way as their ancestors did: hunting, fishing, gathering. There was intense competition with others around them, and sometimes such competition escalated to war. However, for thousands of years and for most people, these contests did not lead to any advanced technology or civilization."

Qi Fei shook his head. "That's because competition wasn't intense enough in those situations. Take a look at the centers of human civilization: the competition at these places was at an entirely different level. In China, thousands of tribes fought until only a few hundred states remained; they fought one another until the rise of the five hegemons of the Spring and Autumn period, and the seven powers of the Warring States period; only after that did the Qin empire emerge. This was the kind of competition that could lead to technological advancement. It was the same in Mesopotamia: from the earliest days, no empire in the cradle of civilization could ever escape the fate of coming onto the stage only to exit a few lines later. Then there was the nonstop warfare among the Greek city states, the existential threat of the Persian invasion, the rise and fall of Alexander and Rome . . . When you compare those parts of the world that didn't develop advanced civilization with these centers, it's clear that 'competition' was at totally incomparable levels."

"I don't agree with you entirely on that point," Jiang Liu said. "Even in these so-called centers of civilization, advancement occurred only sporadically. The vast majority of revolutions in agriculture and industry took place in just a few places and then spread to the rest of the world. Competition, even intense competition, provided no guarantee of major advancements. Writing was likely independently invented no more than twice, and metallurgy likely developed only a single time and then spread across Eurasia. I think major advancements follow similar patterns seen in biological evolution: there's a big component of fortuitousness. Competition doesn't inevitably lead to progress; otherwise, why would we even speak of the 're' in 'Renaissance'?"

"But the end of the Middle Ages was brought about precisely by the intensifying competition between European powers," insisted Qi Fei. "It was all about blood and iron. Without the search for treasure, the wars over trade, the race to explore, and ultimately the colonialist partitioning and exploitation of the rest of the globe, there would be no subsequent industrialization and the modern world. I think—"

Yun Fan stopped the debate by holding up a hand, her expression alarmed. "Quiet!" she whispered to the others. "I hear voices."

But it wasn't a remnant. The other three heard the voices too.

The voices of men and women came to them from afar, soft, ethereal, slow, the rhythm recalling the devoted chanting sutras or reciting prayers. A mystical air pervaded as the voices reverberated within the empty alien corridors. All four stopped, their hearts in their throats.

"Can you hear them too?" Yun Fan was astonished. "This is exactly how it sounds when I hear remnants of voices."

Carefully, they made their way toward the voices. As they got closer, they could make out more. Some of the voices sounded like they were speaking older forms of European tongues, others ancient languages of the Indian subcontinent. Suddenly, all four recognized Chinese. At first, they couldn't believe their ears, but as they concentrated, the words became clearer and clearer.

"*Dao is a vessel from which the flow never ends. Unfathomable! Like the origin of all things.*"

Yun Fan couldn't help but mutter the rest of the verse to herself: "Dulling edges, dissolving entanglements, hiding glows, fusing with terrestrial dust, it fades away . . . or does it? I know not from what it descends. Maybe it's older than the Creator."[14]

The ship seemed to hear her and to recognize her words. The space before them lit up all at once. No, not the dim light that had illuminated their passage through the ship so far, but a brightness that turned the night inside the belly of the loong to day. They could see that the compartment before them was filled with objects, and the curved ceiling overhead was studded with images of the constellations.

They stepped forward into . . . an ancient Chinese palace.

The floor was charcoal-colored with cloud-wave decorative motifs. To the sides were deep black wooden pillars atop heavy stone pedestals in the unique Qin-era style, unadorned and strong. The pillars held up the square lintels in the roof truss.[15] Between the lintels in the roof truss were carvings of fenghuang and other mythical birds. Lining the walls were palace lanterns and sculptures of mythical beasts. Some were familiar, such as the azure loong, vermillion bird, white tiger, and black tortoise; others, formed from chimeric features and draped in exotic plumage, were unrecognizable to the visitors. The color scheme of the palace favored black, and even the sculptures were mainly of dark iron, with occasional decorative touches in gold. The entire place felt imposing and solemn.

Qi Fei, frowning, shook his head ever so slightly to show that the beetle-drones revealed nothing unusual in their scans.

As they walked down the palace hall, they heard more voices. All the voices spoke in Chinese, and the four could hear that they were chanting passages from ancient classics of the pre-Qin era, when a hundred schools of philosophy vied to reveal the truth of the cosmos. The clear voices, reciting the ancient words earnestly and passionately, wove a most awe-inducing chorus. From time to time, Yun Fan muttered along with the voices.

---

14   Yun Fan and the alien voice are reciting from Laozi's *Dao De Jing*. (More specifically, verse 4 in the "standard" ordering of chapters.)

15   One of the most distinctive features of classical Chinese wooden architecture is the use of a roof truss constructed from multiple layers of post-and-lintel frames to transmit the weight of the roof to the ground through rows of pillars. In contrast, European roofs, to grossly generalize a bit, tend to use triangular trusses to transmit the weight of the roof to the walls.

"Human nature is endowed by heavenly fate; to follow human nature is to follow Dao; to cultivate Dao is the purpose of education . . . To know the course of the heavens and the doings of humanity is the limit of knowledge . . . A good king needs four things to make his name: timing, the hearts of the people, skill, and position . . ."[16]

They reached a short set of steps blocked by a giant bronze ding, which the four approached and examined closely. Nine hanzi in elaborate seal script appeared on its sides. Yun Fan, the only one in the group capable of deciphering seal script, read the hanzi one by one: "The Creator, ever benevolent, brings joy to the people."[17]

After that, the bronze ding silently slid to the side, allowing the group to reach the steps. Their confusion only increased. Their route so far had not been easy, but it hadn't been very eventful, either. The voices and the inscription seemed like tests, but what would have happened if they hadn't passed the tests? What sort of place was this that the ancient classics were on display everywhere, and why would aliens use the hundred schools of philosophy as trials? Nothing made sense!

The moment they began to ascend, the steps shook with a deep rumble. Looking up, they could see that the set of steps climbed up to a round platform, almost twenty meters in diameter. Nine sculptures of giant beasts crouched around the platform, each with a massive bronze ding in front of it. In the middle of the platform was a huge fenghuang. Farther back, beyond the platform, twelve looming figures made of metal stood facing a high dais, on top of which sat a throne.

"The twelve colossi!" Qi Fei and Jiang Liu shouted.

Once he had defeated the other six states and unified China, Qin Shi Huang was supposed to have melted down all the weapons and turned them into ceremonial bells and statues in the ancient world's earliest act of national disarmament. Among the artworks created from the metal were twelve colossal human figures, each so heavy that a thousand men were required to lift it.

---

16   These are quotes from Zisi (Confucianism), Zhuangzi (Daoism), and Hanfeizi (Legalism).

17   A quote from King Tang of Shang, founder of the Shang Dynasty (sometime in the second millennium BCE), who made a speech that began with these words to his supporters and allies after defeating King Jie of Xia, a notorious tyrant and oppressor. It is a foundational text in Chinese political philosophy.

"Where are we?" Jiang Liu asked Yun Fan.

"I don't know!" Yun Fan looked confused. "My father never told me what to expect after entering the alien ship. I doubt he knew. But . . . based on everything I've seen so far, this must be . . ."

The other three looked expectantly at her.

She swallowed and continued. "This must be Epang Palace."

"What?" Qi Fei exclaimed. "You mean this is Qin Shi Huang's palace? But I thought Xiang Yu had burned it to the ground."

Epang Palace, one of the grandest wonders of the ancient world, was a place of legendary beauty. Traditionally, it was said that Xiang Yu, the greatest warrior of the time, had destroyed it in the tumultuous rebellion that overthrew the Qin dynasty after the death of the first emperor.

"That story about Xiang Yu has long been discredited," Yun Fan said. "After archaeologists located the site of Epang Palace, we realized that there was no evidence of a massive fire. In fact, the consensus view right now is that Epang Palace was never completed, and only the foundations had been dug. But if that's true, why would there be all these records of the wonders of Epang Palace? The historical records describe the statuary in the palace and the carvings in the roof truss in great detail. It couldn't have been pure invention."

"Oh . . ." Qi Fei finally understood. "You don't mean this is a re-creation of Epang Palace. You mean that we're standing literally in Epang Palace itself. Back in the time of Qin Shi Huang, this ship was docked in Xianyang, the capital."

Yun Fan nodded. "Maybe they were building this ship. Or maybe Qin Shi Huang had constructed this interior, which was then moved onto the alien ship. This would explain many mysteries. For instance, we know that Yu the Great constructed nine bronze ding to be the symbols of legitimate rulership of China. However, by the time of the Qin empire, they had disappeared. Similarly, no one knows what happened to the twelve colossi—they vanished with no more mention. But it all makes sense if they were taken aboard this alien ship."

"But why would they be here?" Jiang Liu's frown deepened. "I don't understand."

"I know why." Yun Fan took out a black regular icosahedron from a side pouch. Pitch-black and smooth all over, it was similar in style to her necklace and the octagonal key-box from earlier. "I was asked to deliver this here."

Eyes straight ahead, carefully holding up the icosahedron in her right palm, Yun Fan ascended step-by-step toward the throne like a priestess bringing a sacred offering to an altar.

But something in this solemn scene bothered Jiang Liu. He looked from Yun Fan's intense expression to all the strange artifacts around them and felt an eeriness in every pore of his body. He shouted Yun Fan's name, but she ignored him as though she hadn't heard.

He looked around at Qi Fei and Chang Tian and realized that they also weren't themselves. Qi Fei was staring at the throne atop the dais instead of at Yun Fan, his eyes burning with yearning. After a moment, he followed Yun Fan and also began to climb to the throne. Chang Tian, on the other hand, looked lost—as though he had forgotten who or where he was. His gaze was focused on Qi Fei.

Jiang Liu didn't know what was going on, but he knew he had very little time. Yun Fan was almost at the level of the round platform guarded by the nine beasts. He raced up the steps and pulled on Yun Fan's left arm to stop her. "Wait! I think something is wrong."

"It's all right." Yun Fan smiled at him. But the smile was so eerie that it was chilling. "When I was a little girl, I read in *Shan Hai Jing* a certain passage: 'On this earth, between up and down, east and west, north and south, surrounded by the four seas, bathed by the light from the Sun and the Moon, seen by the spinning stars, tracked by the seasons, marked by the duodecimal cycles of Jupiter, all are born from the spirits of the cosmos. This is why there are countless forms, and some live long and others but briefly. As to the why and wherefore and how . . . only the wisest know.' It must be talking about this place."

"Listen to me," Jiang Liu persisted, refusing to let go of her arm, "this isn't right. Please, think about it: the whole ship is empty. Where are the aliens? This place feels like a trap."

But Yun Fan pulled away from him. Smiling that false smile, looking for all the world like Ophelia before her lasting sleep, she climbed. One step. Another. The moment she stepped onto the round platform, it began to rotate. The movement caused her to lose her balance, and she fell to the platform. Jiang Liu and Chang Tian ran up to help her, but Qi Fei, who was following right behind Yun Fan, got there before both. He also fell from the platform's spin. Jiang Liu and Chang Tian made their way over to them and crouched down. No one was on their feet.

The spinning platform slowed without coming to a complete stop. Shocking all, the nine giant beasts sitting at the rim began to move toward the center. The beasts didn't all move at the same time; rather, one would advance rapidly toward the center and then retreat, yielding to another to repeat the same maneuver. Jiang Liu jumped up and kicked at the forehead of one approaching beast. Although he didn't slow it down at all, he was able to, through the brief contact, determine that that the beast was made of solid rock, likely granite or marble. There was no chance that they could confront one directly; all that would be left would be four meat pancakes on the floor. Yun Fan and Qi Fei still weren't themselves, their eyes obsessively wandering back toward the throne. Jiang Liu and Chang Tian had no choice but to scramble and drag the two out of harm's way as the beasts pistoned in and out.

The platform sped up and then slowed down; there seemed to be no pattern to the motion at all. The beasts seemed to speed up as well, ratcheting up the pressure. Just then, however, Chang Tian blurted, "There are symbols on the bronze ding! I think they must match the beasts."

Jiang Liu looked at one of the nine ding and realized that Chang Tian was right: around each ding was a circle inscribed with a different symbol. He slapped Qi Fei and shouted his name until Qi Fei looked him in the eye, at which point he held up his right wrist so that the bright blue flashing lights would transmit the necessary stimulus signal onto Qi Fei's contact lenses.

As though waking from a dream, Qi Fei gasped. "What happened? What's going on?"

"There's no time to explain," Jiang Liu said. "I need to search for a piece of information in my general knowledge database, but there's no place for me to project the data. I must rely on your eyes and contact lenses. Can you look through what I'm about to show you and find the symbol for each beast?"

Qi Fei was still confused from his ordeal. But the urgency in Jiang Liu's voice told him that he had to press ahead. He nodded. Jiang Liu called up the world culture database that he relied on to educate himself in his travels around the world.

He looked up the entry on "The Nine Sons of Loong." The illustrations looked just like the beasts around them.

Jiang Liu and Qi Fei worked together to match the symbols on the ding to the beasts. As the platform continued to rotate, bringing a different ding before each beast, they would shout "Stop!" when there was a match. Once a match was made, that beast would no longer attack. Gradually, all the beasts stopped attacking and sat back docilely. The symbols on the ground began to glow with a golden light until they were all connected together in a circle, like a spinning lotus pedestal.

With a loud clang, some mechanism activated in the center of the platform, and the giant fenghuang took to the air. Metallic, refined, complex—it was like a much more advanced version of the fenghuang they saw in the mausoleum. The grace and elegance of the massive mechanical avian form gliding through the air was truly breathtaking, a numinous sight.

As he stared, slack-jawed, at the giant black metal bird, Jiang Liu suddenly remembered a quote from the half-forgotten *Shijing*, a book of the oldest Chinese poems: "Heaven ordered the Black Bird to descend to the mortal realm. There it became the ancestor of the Shang."

He didn't know what to think. *Who is the master of this ship? Do the ancient gods named in the myths really exist?*

But there was no time for him to get philosophical. The round platform came to a complete stop, and Yun Fan got up to continue her steady march toward the throne on the higher dais, her expression dazed. Jiang Liu chased after her.

But Yun Fan, holding up the black polyhedron with both hands, was a priestess who would not be deterred. Her ponytail had come undone, and the long draping locks added to her classical, solemn appearance. Daunted by her steadfast air, neither Jiang Liu nor Qi Fei—who was now no longer under the influence of whatever had earlier seized his mind—dared to hold her back. Instead, the two followed Yun Fan uncertainly, trying to anticipate any danger.

"What is going on with her?" Jiang Liu asked Qi Fei. "And you! You were the same way."

Qi Fei hesitated. "I felt an opening that . . . had data in it, and I plunged right in. It was like swimming in an ocean of data, and I didn't know if I'd ever have such an opportunity again, so I kept on drinking. I can't remember what happened after that, and I don't even know how I ended up here. But I can tell you that during the brief period when I had a connection with this alien ship's systems, I was able to see its structure and the route we should take."

"Really?" Jiang Liu asked excitedly. "You were able to get all that with your neural implant? Do you still remember? What should be our course?"

Qi Fei nodded. "I do remember. With the loong head swallowing the tail, the ship is now a ring, right? However, there is no direct opening from the head into the tail; instead, we have to go all the way through the loong until we're in the tail, where there is a perpendicular passage, like a spoke, that leads to the center of the circle. I don't know what's at the center; the data I saw showed a bright spot there. I do know that the spoke highlighted is the only one open; all the other spokes are sealed off."

"Then that's where we have to go," Jiang Liu said determinedly.

By then Yun Fan had reached the throne. The other three gathered around her. The throne sat alone, the highest vantage point in the palace. Behind it was a tall screen with an ink painting of mountains and rivers, majestic but also cold. Looking back down on the route they had taken, even the wide central space between the rows of pillars appeared as but a narrow path, and the giant stone beasts and metal fenghuang were reduced to mere toys.

The world lay at the foot of whoever sat in this throne, a true colossus.

In the center of the throne was a polyhedral depression. A simple glance confirmed that it would match Yun Fan's icosahedron.

But as Yun Fan approached the throne, that uneasy premonition seized Jiang Liu again. He tried to stop Yun Fan, but it was too late. Yun Fan's fingers let go, and the icosahedron rolled into the depression, stabilizing after a couple of wobbles. A perfect fit.

The icosahedron and the throne began to glow with a bright light. The throne trembled and slid back toward the screen. Before anyone could react, the throne had slid off the dais and dropped away. Yun Fan gasped and rushed up.

But the ground quaked, and wide cracks opened as the dais collapsed and fell. All four fell along with the dais. Fortunately, the abrupt descent didn't last long, only a second or two, and they found themselves on a rocky slope tumbling down.

Finally they reached the bottom of the slope, full of bruises and bumps. Before they could recover, Chang Tian shouted, "Watch out!"

A giant rock was rolling down at them from the slope. Qi Fei fell on top of Yun Fan and rolled with her out of the way. Jiang Liu and Chang Tian jumped to the side. The giant rock rumbled by, throwing up dust everywhere.

They peered ahead into the murk. Twinkling lights, will-o'-the-wisps, tempted them into the unknown. Yun Fan, now freed from her earlier dazed state, looked terrified and confused, as though she couldn't remember anything she had just experienced.

Broken stones began to rain down around them, bouncing, ricocheting, their jagged edges like razors. Jiang Liu and Qi Fei jumped up and took out their nunchucks and baton to deflect the hail of stones. Dancing, parrying, spinning, dodging, the two put on a display of their mastery of martial arts, and the sound of weapon striking stone was constant.

Yun Fan and Chang Tian held up their stiffened cloaks to protect themselves. However, as the hail of broken stones intensified, the confusion and terror in their hearts grew.

Gradually, the four were separated from one another by the accumulating piles of broken stones. As each was so focused on survival, it took some time before they realized their state. By then it was impossible for any of them to see the others, having been divided by impenetrable stone walls.

Only then did each of them begin to hear voices.

"Fanfan, is that you?"

Yun Fan shook from the shock of recognition. It was her father. Without hesitation, she stumbled into the murk, pursuing a barely glimpsed figure.

Meanwhile, apart from her, Jiang Liu was also dealing with his own shock.

"I'll wait for you right here!"

The sweet voice plunged Jiang Liu into a nightmare.

10 | Through the Looking Glass

Yun Fan felt a chill down her spine.

She strained after the voice, trying to discern if it really was her father. Step-by-step, the sensation that she was walking into familiar territory, some place she knew, grew.

The uneven terrain was difficult to navigate, and she had to pick her way carefully between the jagged rocks poking out of the sand. It reminded her of the artificial landscaping in a park from her childhood.

Once, she had become separated from her parents in that park. The place was filled with people, and she couldn't find her mom or dad no matter how hard she looked. Terrified, she stopped next to a fountain and sobbed. A crowd gathered. Some tried to comfort her with snacks; others tried to distract her with toys. But she wanted none of that; she just wanted to find her parents. She began to worry that her parents had abandoned her and that she would never see them again. Tears gushed from her eyes. The people around her changed, but her crying continued. By the time her mom finally ran up to her, her face, arms, hair, and even part of the dress were all wet from tears. Holding on to her mother, trembling, she wanted to throw a tantrum. But she was so tired that she couldn't even summon the energy.

She was five or six at the time.

Yun Fan passed through the park and found herself in the living room of her childhood home. A movie was playing on the walls, some action film with muscled men and beautiful women, but no one was watching. The ersatz explosions, projected all around, seemed so real that she could swear the room was filled with smoke. But no one was watching.

She went into the dining room. Her parents sat at the table. Mom was crying; Dad was silent.

"Are you okay, Mom?" Yun Fan went to her.

"Go watch some cartoons in the living room, all right?" her weeping mother said. "Dad and I have to talk."

"When can you come to be with me?" Yun Fan asked. "I'm scared."

"Get out of here now!" Dad had never spoken to her like that. Yun Fan started to cry, too.

"I don't want to leave. Mommy, I'm scared."

"Fanfan, it'll just be a minute. Let me finish with your father." Mom wasn't looking at her.

"Why are you fighting?" Yun Fan asked. "Is it because I got lost in the park? I'm sorry! I didn't do it on purpose."

Mom came over and hugged her. They cried together. "It's not because of you, Fanfan. It's not your fault."

For the next two hours, Yun Fan sat against the wall next to the dining room door, listening. She heard many things, but understood very few.

Her mother: "When will you actually pay attention to your family? To us? . . . I'm exhausted. I can't do everything . . . I thought I was going mad when I didn't see Fanfan . . . When have I *ever* gotten any support from you? . . . You never come home until after midnight. Do you even know what your daughter looks like? . . . I don't care if you can't get home on time so long as you bring home money. But in this family, I'm the one who earns the most! . . . Why are you so obsessed with that nonsense? When can we be like a normal family? . . ."

Yun Fan pressed her hands against her ears. Her mother's voice was so powerful that even though she wasn't shouting, Yun Fan could hear her over the movie's explosions and crashes. Yun Fan sobbed and sobbed. She knew that it was her fault. If she had been more obedient in the park and held on to Mom's hand instead of running away to check out the cotton candy cart, Mom and Dad wouldn't be fighting. She hated herself for her lack of self-control. What was so interesting about cotton candy? She should have squeezed her mother's hand tight.

Her father said almost nothing in response to the barrage from his wife. Once in a while, his tired voice came through. "What can I do to make you happy? . . . I make all the meals and do all the housework on weekends . . . I'm just waiting for one result. It's very important . . . I know. I'm trying . . ." Mixed in with the angry screams from her mother, her father's exhausted protestations made Yun Fan feel powerless. She wanted to run away, but there was nowhere to run to. She wanted to build a wall around herself, to keep the intolerable pain at bay.

Her head ached. The world seemed to spin, dizzying her, so she closed her eyes and felt herself spin with it. Squeezing her teddy bear tight, she wanted to scream but nothing would come out.

She spun and spun.

By the time she opened her eyes again, she was panting.

In front of her, Dad lay dying in a hospital bed. The thin blanket failed to conceal the sharp angles of his gaunt body. Although he was only forty-nine, he looked to be thirty years older. *Why? When did he lose so much weight? Was it because of all the antidepressants he was taking? Or maybe it was the alcohol?*

She approached the bed. He was asleep. But even in slumber, his brows were knitted, as though he couldn't find peace even in dreams.

Slowly, she knelt down, grabbing hold of his hands. She shook all over, and her heart convulsed. The dam holding back her memories broke. She had been back home only once or twice since senior high graduation, and even on those visits, she surely had not held his hands. That meant that she had not touched him for more than seven hundred days. She couldn't understand how his hands had become like this: skin wrapped around bones. Though he had not played with her much as a little girl, on the few occasions he had taken her out, the strength in his arms had impressed her. Back when she had moved out of home, in senior high, he had looked healthy. But now . . . he was clearly on the verge of death.

Tears spilled uncontrollably from her eyes onto his hands. She saw them spasm and rushed to wipe the tears from those hands, but her own hands shook so much that it was impossible. She thought of the harsh words she had thrown in her parents' faces: *You've ruined my life! You're so selfish! Do you ever think about me?* She could clearly remember that resolve to cut off all contact with her family, but now, seeing her father, she felt as though her heart were being shredded with scissors. In college, she had heard that her father had been diagnosed with bipolar disorder, and she had instinctively refused to accept it. She wanted to have nothing to do with any of it. For seven hundred days she had tried to deny reality.

"Dad." She pressed her face into his arm. "I'm sorry."

His eyes opened then. Slowly, he turned his face, and in a voice hoarse from disuse, he said, "Fanfan, I won't live much longer." He broke into a fit of violent coughs. When he finally recovered, he continued, "I don't want you to tell me you're sorry. Please . . . I hope you can help me."

+ + + + +

Jiang Liu's first reaction upon hearing the little girl's voice was to turn and run. But after a few steps, he stopped, turned around, and walked back toward the voice. Even he couldn't quite explain why.

He was once again in that war-torn land.

Around him, everything was on fire. The latest Super-I Silver Eagle miniature tactical nuke had turned the neighborhood into a sea of flames. Although the official announcement claimed that the attack, directed by advanced AI, was extremely targeted and intended to strike only military installations, this region was so poor that the penniless refugees had built their huts and shacks right next to the military base. Even a few sparks from exploding munitions was enough to start a fire that soon engulfed the whole camp. Many were already dead, and more would die soon. The rest would lose all their possessions.

None of this would appear in the news reports celebrating yet another great victory in the contest between the great powers.

But why had the refugees built their homes next to the military base? It was simple, really. One, they believed—quite erroneously, as it turned out—that the base would offer them protection. Two, the officers and soldiers were the only ones with money. If the refugees wanted to make a living, where else would they find customers?

The world never changed.

Jiang Liu walked on, struggling not to gag at the smell of charred human flesh. He wasn't ready for any of this. He had come here during a school break to do his "community immersion." The choice of this region of the world had been intended to allow him to show off his courage to his classmates. *Oh, me?* he had imagined himself saying in the most casual of tones. *I went where there was the most conflict—best way to get real-life experience, right? Yeah, I went through no-man's-land. I did. Riding an autonomous combat motorcycle while giving a live report streamed to millions—oh boy, that was something.* A pause and a shift in tone. *Yes, I helped some refugees.* A modest glance away. *I wish I did more.*

That would have looked so good on his résumé. Later, during on-campus recruiting, he would have the best stories to share with his interviewers, stories that demonstrated his ability to endure hardships and his generosity of spirit. *In the desert, I helped those poor people find water, protected them from danger.* He would make such an impression! Imagining all that, he felt his eyes almost moistening at his own display of social responsibility.

But that was just imagination. He wasn't ready for reality, wasn't ready for the utter sense of powerlessness.

He was like a helpless, lonesome grasshopper. Alarms blared, warning of on-coming bombing raids; he hopped about, unsure where to find safety. Everyone around him, face caked in mud, clothes torn to shreds, numbed by the sight of death, calmly went about their business. They packed their few possessions into a single bundle and went on the road to the next refuge. No one paid any attention to him. He could find neither food nor water. Desperate, he had to beg the refugees for a drink of water. Instead of a hero, he was the pitiable creature that everyone else tried to save.

"Friend!"

The childish voice came from between piles of burning rocks. Trembling, Jiang Liu looked around for the speaker. Finally, he found a girl of about five or six behind a few large rocks, a shack burning not too far beyond. She was alone, her face dirty and hair matted, mud all over her clothes—in the style of the natives but barely better than rags at that point.

"Can you understand me?" The girl held a translator next to her mouth.

"Yes! I can," Jiang Liu said. The translator, a small, sleek box, seemed pretty advanced. Maybe she had found it in the rubble, or maybe some soldier had given it to her.

"I'm hungry, friend," the girl said. "Do you have any bread?"

Jiang Liu felt so ashamed. "I'm so sorry," he said. "I . . . I don't have bread. But I have money. Can I give you money?"

The girl nodded.

Jiang Liu looked through every pocket and managed to find a few coins for the girl. Having always lived in places that functioned on retinal scans and digital currency, he wasn't in the habit of carrying cash. In fact, this trip was the first time he had ever seen physical currency. Inexperienced, he had taken very little cash when he was offered the chance to get some. He wanted to ask her if she had a BitPay account—but he swallowed the question as he took in her muddy, terrified face.

He gave her all his coins.

"Thank you," the girl said. She counted the money. "Can you spare more? My mother is very hungry. She's going to die."

Jiang Liu had never felt so awful. "I . . . I don't have anymore, but I can get more from the next town. Can you meet me here tomorrow?"

The girl nodded. Jiang Liu wrote down his local number and handed it to her. "If you can't find me tomorrow, just call."

"I'll wait for you right here," the little girl said. "Thank you, friend!"

Near dusk, Jiang Liu finally found a ground-effect motorcycle to take him to the "next town," which was, in reality, 200 kilometers away. After much effort, he found a financial kiosk willing to allow him to withdraw cash. After spending the night in the town, he rushed back to the village first thing in the morning. But the little girl wasn't at those rocks. He looked for her all over the place but couldn't find her.

That afternoon, he got a call.

"Friend, can you come to where I am?" The girl gave the address of a warehouse. "Can you bring seven thousand Urals? My mother is very sick."

Jiang Liu felt uneasy. That warehouse was supposed to be the territory of a local gang. He wondered if the little girl had already been taken by the gang and was now luring him in so that he could be kidnapped and ransomed. Maybe the girl's encounter with him the previous day had been part of the trap. There was no sick and hungry mother; he was the target of a scam.

It was the worst few hours of his life. He paced back and forth in the dust storm, kicking at pebbles on the ground, his hands balled into fists in his pockets. The girl's small, dirty face kept on floating into his view, her large eyes pleading.

But he thought he could also see the chain of profit and greed behind her. He couldn't possibly defeat a gang of thieves and robbers; he had no weapon, and he was alone. He had to go back to school in a few days. A Nobel laureate was supposed to visit his lab soon, and he had already made plans to go skiing with friends over Christmas break. And he was going to travel the world after graduation. He couldn't allow himself to die in a place like this, could he?

He almost made it to the warehouse by dusk. But he turned away and left before he could see anything.

A few days later, his "community immersion" at an end, he was on his way to the airport when he passed the village again. In a trail branching off the main road, he saw a few corpses abandoned in the desolate landscape. One of the bodies was a little girl, and as he passed by at a distance, he thought it was the same girl—the same pose, the same profile, the same slight tilt to the head, looking up. But Jiang Liu didn't go over to confirm it. His feet were rooted to the spot, and he couldn't make them move.

He left as though running from pursuing Furies. He never returned to that country again.

"I'll wait for you right here!"

Once again, Jiang Liu was in that burning village. To the left were two empty huts with earthen walls, the thatched roofs in flames. To the right was a market, all the carts and kiosks abandoned, the vendors dead or gone. Like a lonely ghost, Jiang Liu wandered through, terrified. The girl's voice echoed all around him. He wanted to run but there was no escape.

That day . . . if I had gone to see her.

That day . . . if I hadn't been such a coward.

He couldn't escape the thoughts. He began to run, searching for the source of the voice, but he couldn't. He dashed about aimlessly as though he had gone mad, but he found no one, and he couldn't escape the burning, the smell, the voice.

He ran and ran. He ran.

+ + + + +

Qi Fei found himself in a familiar training ground, one he hadn't been to in a long time.

Someone called his name. He went over and saw that it was Zhao, his second drill instructor. Zhao had given him hell, but he had also seen the most potential in Qi Fei.

"I want you to work with these barbells," Zhao said to him. "Three sets of twenty each. Then go work on your abs over there. After that, come back and give me three more sets."

Qi Fei looked at the barbells. They were heavier than the heaviest he had ever used. His face fell.

Zhao slapped a meaty palm on his shoulder. "You lack upper body strength, so I must keep on pushing. Until you've gained muscles here, here, and here, I can't go easy on you."

Qi Fei bent to grip the weights, but he didn't look convinced.

"Ah, I see now." Zhao chuckled. "You think this is nonsense. You think I'm outdated. Let me tell you: I don't care how smart you are and how much science you know, a human body follows the same pattern it's always followed. I don't give a fuck about robots or artificial muscles or any of that shit. There's nothing that will give you strength except hard work. I'm not just training your body, but also your heart and mind. I want you to have muscles of steel as well as nerves of steel. Don't think I'll go easy on you just because you have a goddamned big brain. Even if the king of heaven came here for training, I'd tell him to lift these barbells."

Qi Fei took a deep breath, held it, and drawing on every ounce of strength, managed to lift the barbell to his chest. Instructor Zhao nodded, indicating the height was sufficient, and that he should put it down and lift again. After five or six lifts, he could feel his arms trembling. Zhao clapped his hands to encourage him but wouldn't let him stop. By the time Qi Fei had done twelve lifts he was feeling the effects of the lack of oxygen, which actually made the last few lifts easier, despite the feeling of numbness. After the final lift he felt everything go dark and stumbled, almost falling to the ground.

Zhao held him up. Giving him a thumbs-up, he said, "Good work." But without any break, Zhao pushed him to the next station. "Rest for one minute and take a drink of water. Then give me three sets of crunches. Come on!"

Qi Fei had never suffered so much pain as that afternoon. Several times he thought he was going to black out, but somehow, he managed to get through it.

Twice he was so exhausted that he fell while jogging, skinning his hands and knees against the gravel track.

"Very good," Zhao said. "The more scars on a man, the better." He kicked Qi Fei in the ass. "Get up. Don't slack off."

"I need you to do two sets of calisthenics before I'll let you stop for today," Zhao said. "Without good coordination, you won't be much of a fighter."

It was Qi Fei's first experience of military training. Though he wasn't part of the military proper, what he had been put through was exactly like bootcamp for fresh recruits and gave him a taste of the new life that awaited him. Through it all, Qi Fei never complained but simply did as he was told. Instructor Zhao would always tell others that Qi Fei left him with a good impression after that first session. *He's like a wolf.*

Once again, Qi Fei saw the finishing line of the track. His chest heaved, as though weighed down by a ton of rocks; the taste of blood was in his throat. He had to get to the finish line. Had to. As he burst through, the world went dark and vanished.

In the darkness, he saw Dad's face: bloated, terrified, sad.

His eyes snapped open, and he sat up, panting.

After three years as a graduate student undergoing military training, he had learned to enjoy a feeling that he couldn't describe in words: the pleasure of mastering his body with his mind.

After that first day of hellish training, he felt like he was floating, his body no longer entirely his. But his will felt sharp and clear, the very core of his being. He couldn't remember the last time he was so *aware*. In subsequent training, he was determined to explore this sensation further, and for each drill, he consciously focused his mind to wield his body, even to abuse it. He discovered the power of directed will.

If I want you to do it, you will *do it.*

If I don't want you do it, you won't *do it.*

Thus did his mind dictate to his body.

Over time, he found his body submitting to the mind. His agility and endurance increased, as did his tolerance for pain; his desires and cravings, however, diminished. No matter what kind of hardship faced him, as long as his mind insisted to his body, "You *will* endure it," his body would continue to bear it without complaint.

He passed through trial after trial. He became more disciplined—sometimes even abusive to himself. Since his body no longer asserted itself against his will, he could even control his own hunger and need for sleep. He began to seek out new challenges, ways to torture himself, trying to find the limit of his mind's dominion over his body. He trained hard every day, ran further, lifted more weights, denied himself food and sleep while pushing his body to do *more*. Every time, as his body pushed through yet another record and reached a new level of submission, he experienced pleasure through the pain. It was the pleasure of conquest. He learned that the greatest pleasure in the world was the pleasure of conquering the self, which was far more enjoyable than anyone else's obedience. In the process of conquering himself, he was also conquering the world.

For years he had not allowed his emotions to sway his will; the same denial applied to his body.

Dad, why can't you be like me? Why can't you control yourself?

Again and again, as Qi Fei did push-ups in the dark, he spoke to Dad in his mind. Even five years after his death, the old man's postmortem swollen visage didn't fade in his memories. All he had to do was close his eyes and he would see Dad lying in the coffin, the face that had been wrecked by shrapnel resting among plastic flowers like some unfinished wax figure. As a boy, he had seen Dad standing tall against the setting sun, nose firm and jaw square, thick hair perfectly combed, like a statue of some god. Where had that man gone? Staring at Dad's corpse, Qi Fei felt powerless, unable to find a trace of the father in his memories.

Did his memory paint too perfect a picture of reality? Or did reality corrupt a perfect memory?

He remembered weeping as he knelt next to the coffin. Mixed in with the grief and sorrow was a trace of rage as well. *Dad, why did you give in to desire? Why weren't you stronger?*

Night after night, he awakened from the same nightmare. It was the summer of his third year in senior high. Mom's screams reverberated in his ears, and his performance on the gaokao examination was execrable. He couldn't concentrate at all while the robot proctors asked him questions emotionlessly. Even after he was done with the examination, he didn't want to go home. Mom had spent a large sum of money to turn a scan of Dad's brain into a digital persona with whom she conversed daily. He couldn't stand the sight of her talking to the simulation on the wall.

To tire himself out, he went jogging for long hours late at night. That was how he first met General Yuan.

"Someday you'll understand that everything you go through is a trial," the old general had said to him.

For some reason, the general cared about Qi Fei and took him under his wing. At first, Qi Fei wasn't sure why.

"Nothing is ever wasted in this world," the general, a cigarette between his fingers, said to him in a low, gravelly voice. "What you went through was a way for the universe to send you a message: it's a sin to be weak. What matters always is whether something is right, not whether it's beautiful or good. Compassion is a form of hypocrisy, do you understand? In the name of kindness, they do the wrong thing—that is weakness, which in the end leads to suffering for everyone around them. It's better to harden your heart, to be cruel. Remember: always do the right thing. Even if it seems heartless, it will lead ultimately to the greatest kindness."

Qi Fei listened to the general in the dark and said nothing. Being next to the old general made him feel safe.

"Don't be compassionate; pursue only victory," the general said. "A soldier's duty is to obey; weakness is a sin."

Fog rose in the darkness. It was impossible to see beyond a few steps. Qi Fei was running through the night again, unable to find his way. There was no way. The mist enveloped him like the panting breath of some universal lung, and his heart strained against the surging currents. Where does this pain come from? How could he have conquered the world but still be defeated by this pain? The dark night, like a black hole, threatened to suck him in. There was no path, and the fog thickened.

Confused night.

Intoxicated night.

Cold night.

Enraged night.

A soldier's duty is to obey; weakness is a sin.

A soldier's duty is to obey; weakness is a sin.

+ + + + +

Chang Tian escaped from the fog, but he couldn't escape the sensation of being stabbed by those sharp rebukes.

"Deserter!"

"Coward!"

"Traitor!"

"What is he hiding?"

When he chose to leave the military, those words, whispered or not, began to follow him like inescapable shadows. Sometimes he wanted to run far away from everyone so that he could be alone, so that he could read for a while. But the words followed him and buzzed around his head even when no one was around, refusing to give him any peace.

The war was heating up, and it was supposed to be sweet and fitting to die for country and glory. But Chang Tian chose a different path. No one believed that he just wanted to run a bistro. Some questioned his courage; others thought he had been corrupted by the enemy. The more this went on, the more Chang Tian realized he had made the right choice. He knew who he was, what he wanted; he knew his own weaknesses and his own strengths. Let them call him a coward—better to be a coward this one time so that he could bravely live the rest of his life the way he wanted.

But he couldn't get rid of the voices in his head. No matter how much he tried, he couldn't outrun them. He begged them to leave him alone, but they just got louder.

"Coward!"

"Deserter!"

Chang Tian ran without a destination in mind. The fog around him thickened and thinned. He seemed to be free of the mist one moment only to be plunged back into it the next. He was without direction, driven only by the need to *escape*.

A clear and familiar voice rang out.

"Chang Tian! Is that you? It's me: Yun Fan. Can you answer me?"

Even though he heard her, Chang Tian continued to press his hands over his ears, spinning in place. It was only when Yun Fan grabbed him by the shoulders that Chang Tian slowly put down his hands and focused his dazed eyes on her.

"What . . . happened?" Chang Tian asked.

"I don't know," Yun Fan said. "I think I was in a . . . hallucination."

Chang Tian squinted, thinking over what she said. "What did you see?"

Yun Fan took a deep breath. "I was a little girl again, and I saw my parents. What about you?"

"I got to reexperience the time around my discharge." Just the mention of the time made his temples throb with pain. He put his hands over them as Yun Fan helped him sit down.

They sat on the ground, shoulder to shoulder, taking deep, slow breaths to calm down. They looked at each other, and at the alien ship around them. The mist was gone, along with all traces of their hallucinations. Gazing around at the featureless, cold alien corridor, Epang Palace seemed very far away. They estimated that they had made it about a quarter of the way around the loong-circle. Still some ways to go.

The deserted corridor, slate-black, was illuminated only by some blue lights on the ground.

"Have you seen Qi Fei and Jiang Liu?" Chang Tian asked.

Yun Fan shook her head.

"Should we keep on going or wait longer?"

"Let's wait," Yun Fan said. "We need the rest."

"All right. Why don't you tell me what you saw?"

After a slight hesitation, Yun Fan told him everything. She spoke of the time she got lost in the park, of the subsequent argument between her parents, of seeing her father's decline on his deathbed, of regret and pain, flashing back to her departure from home during senior high school, when she lived in the tenant hives clustered under the maglev highway ramps, refusing to go home, and finally, of the last weeks of her father's life, when she had strained to memorize everything he whispered to her, all the signals and codes, until she watched him die in her arms.

Yun Fan sobbed silently. Chang Tian offered her his shoulder and gently patted her back. He had not known this part of her story.

"I noticed something." Chang Tian's tone was gentle. "You don't seem to have many memories of your mother after your childhood. What happened to her?"

"I don't know," Yun Fan said. "She left. She never told me where."

"She never came back to see you?"

"Only once. Right before my father died. I don't know how she knew—maybe he sent her a message. She was there for the funeral."

"But you didn't see that in your hallucinatory episode just now, did you?"

"I didn't. I don't know why."

Chang Tian looked thoughtful. "When did you move out from home?"

"As a first-year in senior high."

"So it was not long after your mother and Qi Fei's father . . ."

Yun Fan nodded. "It happened right before the senior high entrance examination. I moved out at the end of that summer."

"And then your mother left and never returned." Chang Tian worked through the timeline in his mind. "In other words, your father was alone at home during those years, and his mental illness worsened. Is that why you feel such guilt? You think your leaving triggered his condition, and that is why you insist that everything was your fault." In fact, Chang Tian suspected that Yun Fan in some sense viewed herself and her mother as a joint entity. Since she couldn't forgive her mother, she also couldn't forgive herself. But he kept the speculation to himself.

Yun Fan looked into the distance. "I just . . . want to remember my father. I have to remember that it was my fault, in order not to forget the mission he passed to me upon death. If I forgave myself, then my memories would fade, and I would forget the task he asked me to finish. In that case, my father's death would be meaningless, and his whole life would be meaningless. That is why I must not ever forget my own fault; it is the only reason I can keep going."

"I understand." Chang Tian's voice was soft and comforting. "Completing your father's mission isn't just a matter of legacy; it's also atonement."

Yun Fan started to cry again. "It really was my fault. Everyone had abandoned him by that point. If I had stayed . . . A single person who stood by him would have . . ."

"Let it go." Chang Tian patted her back as she cried and cried.

At length, when she felt calmer, Chang Tian tried to cheer her up by saying, "See, talking about your troubles makes you feel better. Although Jiang Liu and Qi Fei are both in love with you, neither can match me as a shoulder to cry on."

Yun Fan blushed and chuckled. Wiping the tears from her eyes, she said, "You're indeed better at this. But you're wrong about them. They aren't in love with me."

"What are you talking about?" Chang Tian also chuckled. "Every day, they are at each other's throats over you."

"Oh please." Yun Fan shook her head. "Men may claim to fight over a woman, but they're really fighting for themselves. They are both so competitive that they can't help it; it's nothing to do with me. Haven't you noticed? Jiang Liu keeps everyone at arm's length."

Chang Tian was taken aback. He had indeed felt this way, but he was surprised that Yun Fan noticed it as well.

"Jiang Liu is always telling people what they want to hear," Yun Fan said. "He's basically picking out phrases and responses to optimize the situation—not terribly different from an advanced AI. That shows he doesn't care at all about what he's saying. But how can a flesh-and-blood human not care about anything? It's a sign that he keeps his real heart sealed away somewhere untouchable. He doesn't want anyone close enough to know his heart, and he keeps all at bay with that disguise of witty banter and bad pickup lines."

"That's very insightful," Chang Tian said.

"I remember my third year in college, when I took a bunch of STEM classes so that I could make sense of all the material about aliens my father had passed on to me. I was always more of a Literature-and-Arts kind of student, and those classes bored me. My mind wandered. I have this memory of a physics class, when the professor was discussing the model of the atom. She said the nucleus was very small, and all around it was a vast vacuum through which the electrons whizzed and whirled, like a rarified mist. Jiang Liu reminds me of that atom. His heart, his real heart, is like the nucleus, and all his words and deflections are the cloud of electrons."

"I don't know him well," Chang Tian said. "But I share your impression. He's very guarded."

"As for Qi Fei . . ." Yun Fan bit her bottom lip. "He had long closed the door on the past."

Chang Tian felt as though there were needles in his throat. With effort, he said nothing. He knew that Yun Fan wasn't entirely wrong, but it still hurt to have his friend spoken of this way. "Qi Fei's situation is . . . well, in college, he did seem to change his personality completely. But that's because there are deeper, unresolved issues."

"You've stayed in touch with him all this time?" Yun Fan asked. "I thought you didn't even go to the same college."

"I always worried about him," Chang Tian said. "Even during periods when we weren't in touch, I kept up with news about him."

"Why?"

"Guess." Chang Tian smiled.

"Oh." Yun Fan seemed to finally figure out a mystery. She combed through her memories again, and then nodded. "So that's why back then you—oh, now I get it. Now everything makes sense."

Chang Tian nodded. "Don't worry about me. After majoring in psychology, I got much better at channeling my feelings."

Yun Fan gently patted Chang Tian's shoulder, as though returning the comfort he had given her earlier. "When I saw you earlier, you said you were forced to relive the time around your discharge, when you were called a coward. With so many against you, why did you persist in your decision?"

"I had a feeling," Chang Tian said. "My life—there's a purpose meant for me, and it's not to be a military pilot."

"I don't think it's to run a bistro, either."

Chang Tian nodded. "I can't tell what I'm supposed to do yet, but I trust my feelings. My intuition is good. I connect best with the most vulnerable, sensitive parts of others."

"I know," Yun Fan said. "Thank you."

"Thank *you*, too."

They looked back the way they came, and then ahead. There was nothing but murky darkness behind them, but before them, in the distance, there was a faint light, as though enticing them with the promise of an exit. Chang Tian looked at the ground and realized that the blue lights were actually fine lines pointing forward.

"Look!" Chang Tian said to Yun Fan, pointing down.

Yun Fan peered closely. "Arrows."

"Maybe the other two are already up ahead," Chang Tian said. "Maybe we need to catch up."

She nodded. Supporting each other, they made their way toward the light.

11 | Death and Life

Still a bit disoriented from their ordeal in the hallucinatory fog, Yun Fan and Chang Tian followed the blue glowing arrows on the ground.

Their progress became easier. A warm and harmonious light suffused the air—it came from all the surfaces, restorative and comforting. Soft white sand appeared underneath their feet, and a breeze caressed their faces.

After about fifty meters, the corridor turned slightly, and Yun Fan noticed images on the walls. At first, she thought she might be seeing things since the images didn't persist but vanished after a while. But gradually, more images appeared and stayed around, and the walls turned a warmer color, like the loess of her home. The images on the walls were like the petroglyphs of ancient humans more than forty thousand years ago.

Step-by-step, they walked through humanity's history as told by petroglyphs, cave paintings, murals: the drawing of the red buffalo from Sulawesi, the wildly gyrating dancers on smoky cave walls, Egyptian pilgrims and pharaohs laden with jewels in stiff poses, Zeus and the Olympians in friezes, paintings of David and Solomon, the glyph-filled niches dedicated to the maize god and to Kinich Ahau, the rigid poses of saints and angels from the Middle Ages . . .

They identified the images; they discussed them. Yun Fan sometimes told Chang Tian stories about the gods, but even she couldn't explain why these images were here. The pictures seemed to be a response to their passage, their order the same as their places in history. An ethereal music that had no discernible melody filled the air.

Finally, they estimated that they were halfway through the circle of the ouroboros-loong. The light from the ground brightened. Chang Tian and Yun Fan looked at each other, uncertain whether this was a good omen or ill. They pressed forward. The ever-growing light was like an enticing embrace, guiding them forward, gradually enveloping them.

The light, almost blinding, formed into a tunnel, and as they stepped inside, they realized that they had reached the end of the route. Chang Tian and Yun Fan had passed through the entire length of the loong and reached the tail. The light tunnel pointed up, and as they lifted their faces, they saw that a long ladder reached high above, the other end invisible in the distance. For the first time, the two understood what it meant to look up Jacob's Ladder.

"Where do you think *that* goes to?" Yun Fan wondered.

"The loong has formed into a wheel," Chang Tian said. "So this is a spoke that leads to the hub. Now we must climb up against the artificial gravity from the wheel's spin."

"We made a big circle, almost back to the point where we started, just so we could go climbing?"

"I guess so." Chang Tian looked up and then looked at Yun Fan. "Are you up for this?"

"How did Jiang Liu put it? We're right at the door to the theater; how can we go home now?"

"Sounds about right," Chang Tian said, testing the rungs. "Let's go see the movie."

With Chang Tian in the lead and Yun Fan right below him, the two made their way up the seemingly endless ladder to heaven.

+ + + + +

A *soldier's duty is to obey; weakness is a sin.*

A *soldier's duty is to obey; weakness is a sin.*

Qi Fei emerged from the thick fog with fire burning inside his soul. He needed an outlet for his nameless rage. How he wished he had the sparring robots he beat up on while practicing sanda and boxing! Padded in sandbags and foam, the robots were clumsy but durable, able to withstand his strikes and kicks for hours on end. Back then, he always knew what to do with his resentments and grievances: Just let his fists do the talking; it was all the therapy he needed.

His interest in AI, in fact, had begun with those sparring robots. The robots' programming was designed on a simple loop: Classify the trainee's attack pattern and react with statistically the best counter in the database. Each trainee also had their own profile, which allowed the sparring robots to constantly correct its own responses and optimize counters. The robots' rate of improvement was astonishing, sometimes even faster than the rate at which Qi Fei's own skills improved. He became obsessed with machine learning. For a period, he lived and breathed robots: a morning of programming was followed by an afternoon of sparring, and after a shower, he would read robotics research papers for at least three hours in the evening. He believed that he didn't need women or friends; it was more than enough to have himself and Qiankun as conversation partners.

Punch. Kick.

Kick. Punch.

He spun in place, punching and kicking at the air, trying to let out his rage in the most articulate language of them all.

He saw Jiang Liu.

The man had emerged out of the fog suddenly. Almost struck by one of Qi Fei's fists, Jiang Liu leaped back. For a moment, both stayed still, startled.

Without saying a word, Qi Fei stepped up and swung his fists at Jiang Liu.

When an opportunity arises, eliminate Jiang Liu.

General Yuan's words reverberated in Qi Fei's mind.

Instinctively, Jiang Liu raised his arms to block Qi Fei while dodging back. Once he had an opportunity to recover from the surprise attack, he gazed into Qi Fei's eyes: they were filled with a determination that couldn't be mistaken. Qi Fei was treating him as a mortal enemy, to be killed on the spot.

Jiang Liu shivered, remembering what his father had told him.

Be careful of that boy from the Pacific League. He's not your friend. If you get the chance, get rid of him.

Despair gripped Jiang Liu. He had always despised Dad's paranoia. To treat everyone as an enemy seemed to him a form of idiocy disguised as caution. Indeed, a world in which everyone was against you was a world not worth living in. But now, seeing Qi Fei's hate-filled face, all he could think of was: *My father turned out to be right.* This depressed Jiang Liu beyond words. Burning rage made him want to throw up, to destroy everything around him.

Infusing the movement with every ounce of his strength, Jiang Liu kicked at Qi Fei.

Qi Fei dodged easily. Freeing his baton from his waistband, he swept it through the air and a gleaming blade sprung from the tip, turning the baton into a long-handled dagger. Seeing this, Jiang Liu spun away and unwrapped a metal chain from around his lower leg: a whip with a barbed tip.

The two attacked and parried, dagger matching whip, both combatants seeking an opening for a fatal blow. But just then, three arrows shot out of a wall, aimed directly at them. Jiang Liu spun slightly to let the arrows pass by; they flew straight at Qi Fei's face and chest.

Qi Fei snapped back, supporting his arched back by planting his hands on the ground; the arrows brushed over his belly and plunged into the opposing wall, vanishing as though they melted into the hull.

Pausing their fight, the two looked around warily before turning their mistrustful gazes on each other. Since Qi Fei didn't see where the arrows had emerged, he suspected that Jiang Liu had launched them as a sneak attack. Thus, he looked upon Jiang Liu with even more animosity. In response, Jiang Liu's face became stiff and cold, without a trace of his habitual grin, as though he had put on a killing mask.

"Don't underestimate me," Jiang Liu said. "Do you think I've never killed?"

"I wouldn't put anything beyond you," Qi Fei said. "For all I know, your hands are stained with the blood of countless victims. But you don't scare me."

Before they could lunge at each other, two spears dropped out of the ceiling directly over their heads. The pair had no choice but to spin out of the way. Before they could recover, the floor cracked and a row of spiked clubs sprung out, forcing them back.

Cold weapons, launched by hidden mechanisms, came at them from every direction. As they fought each other, the two combatants also had to dodge these projectiles while trying to maneuver the opponent into harm's way. Although the weapons were ancient, they were launched with such force that a single strike would have been fatal.

The knives, spears, clubs, and arrows came at them faster and denser, and both felt this was the most difficult and dangerous fight they had been in in their lives. Not only did they have to fight the other combatant, but they also had to react instantly to the deadly traps. More than once a sharp blade shaved by one or the other, missing by fractions of a millimeter, leaving a cold chill on the skin.

Jiang Liu parried a long-handled mace, but there was so much force behind the strike that he was forced to stumble backward, his arm numb from the force. As he massaged that arm with the other, Qi Fei seized the opportunity and kicked at his face. Unable to block, Jiang Liu ducked and spun, counterattacking with an elbow. Since Qi Fei's kick had thrown him off-balance, he couldn't dodge Jiang Liu's elbow strike, aimed at his rib cage. Realizing this, Qi Fei decided that he would take the hit but simultaneously aimed his dagger at the crouching Jiang Liu's back. Jiang Liu, unwilling to trade blows in such a disadvantageous exchange, rolled to the side. Qi Fei's dagger stabbed into the ground, and Jiang Liu knelt up on one knee.

"Why?" he demanded of Qi Fei.

"There's no why," Qi Fei said. "We're enemies; that's all."

"What is a friend? What is an enemy?" Jiang Liu jumped back, out of Qi Fei's reach.

"Those on my side are friends; those who aren't are enemies."

Qi Fei lunged at Jiang Liu, who struck back with the whip. Qi Fei blocked with the dagger, entangling the whip chain around the dagger. Both pulled hard, trying to disarm the other. Their stalemate was broken as a large rock fell from the ceiling directly overhead. Both let go of their weapons and jumped back. The rock fell between them, making a deafening din.

Both were slightly dazed. As Jiang Liu looked at Qi Fei, standing on the other side of the rock, a phantom scene seemed to take the place of reality. Qi Fei looked just like the armored guard he had seen in front of that armory.

Jiang Liu was observing from concealment behind a tree. Several teams of Tianshang's fighters were converging from different directions. The lone guard before the armory patrolled back and forth, machine gun in hand. As the guard hadn't activated the visor on his helmet, Jiang Liu could see the man's face clearly.

Tianshang's fighters were within range of the surveillance cameras. A swarm of bee-like security drones flew out of the warehouse and went after them. The Tianshang fighters were ready for this response and scattered into the woods, leading the security drones away. Two more fighters emerged to take on the lone guard.

The guard activated his armor; the visor dropped down, plates slid over his chest and back, and even his hands and arms were enclosed in mechanical appendages that ended in powerful guns, which instantly began to spit bullets at his attackers.

The fighters, as planned, retreated before the approaching guard. Slowly, the armor-encased guard was lured away from his post, giving Jiang Liu the opening he had been waiting for. A few seconds was all it took for Jiang Liu to turn the scan of the guard's face into a digital mask that he projected onto his own face, to run up to the armory door, and to show the disguise to the facial recognition scanner. The armory door rumbled open.

The guard, realizing his error, ran back. But it was too late. The other Tian-shang fighters launched their bombs into the armory.

As the armory burned and exploded, turning into an orange conflagration, Jiang Liu guided all the Tianshang members to safety. As he gazed up at the smoky sky, lit up like a sunset, he experienced a rare pleasure. Even in the late twenty-first century, the world was full of these armories that showed up in no army ledger, filled with miniaturized weapons of mass destruction whose principles of opera-tion were not comprehended by their guards or users. They were usually owned by groups dedicated to various causes (or no cause at all): gangs, terrorists, gue-rillas, mercenaries, rebels, hired killers maintained by drug lords, warmongering profiteers—weapons were no different from shampoo, also part of international trade, also optimized by professional managers with MBAs. Behind the warmon-gers was capital, capital invested in the research and development of the technol-ogy of killing. But conventional warfare among the great powers was never going to be enough to consume the excess capacity of the weapons industry, and so in-dustrial capital gave its silent consent for weapons to flow into the darker veins of international trade, which in turn boosted the research and development of even more advanced weapons for the booming market. That was how experimental min-iaturized weapons flooded the globe, and professional management demanded that production meet the needs of customers: No matter how complicated the principle of operation of the weapon, all the complicated physical equations had to be re-duced to a simple trigger. All weapons had to be operable by anyone without even a single day of schooling. Only such weapons could satisfy the biggest market.

The people doing the killing and the people who needed to defend them-selves alike wanted the weapons to be as simple to use as toys, and so all weapons became, in some sense, toys. You didn't need to understand the quantum Hall effect to press the trigger on a weapon that utilized the effect to kill anyone you wanted to kill. It was an absurd world.

That was why Jiang Liu experienced such pleasure every time he destroyed an armory: not only because he helped civilians who otherwise would die from those weapons, but also because he was disrupting the bacchanalia that was the global arms trade. Grandfather had been a link in this dark web of commerce, while Dad had laundered the family money by inventing a hedging instrument that stabilized the global value of cryptocurrency. Although superficially, Dad's financial innovation had nothing to do with harm, it had promoted the arms trade by allowing sellers and buyers to feel secure in the value of their various currencies. Dad had turned the family from being mere players to casino owners; everyone knew that the house always won.

The elder Jiang was smart to maintain good relations with the leaders of all the great powers. He spent a lot of money on this effort, which might seem useless. But in reality, it was a good investment. The great powers' continuing arms race was the source that supplied the demands of the bloodthirsty cravings in the secret armories. Only by controlling the source could they be sure of always having the code to the vault.

After each Tianshang operation, it was Jiang Liu's habit to go to a Tianshang family and share a homecooked meal. He always insisted on paying for his meal— with an amount that far exceeded the value of the meal itself. He never let his hosts knew his true identity; he didn't want them to know that he was trying to atone.

And now, as Jiang Liu looked at Qi Fei, he seemed to see that armory guard again. He was trying to protect something dangerous, something he didn't even understand, and yet he was willing to die for it. There had been moments on this trip when Jiang Liu thought he could connect with Qi Fei; he saw in Qi Fei a dedication to pure technology, a sharp mind that matched his own, that got him. But now, Qi Fei was a stranger in another world, an unfeeling rock.

"Let's finish this," Jiang Liu said. "We are not on the same path; there's no need to pretend we can work together."

As Qi Fei looked back at Jiang Liu, he seemed to see again the face of that pilot on the day his father died.

He remembered that day well: the beginning of summer, hot and humid, the air pregnant with rain, the heavy weight of what was to come thickening the air. When he returned home from the first simulation test for gaokao, he heard Mom's screams as soon as entered the apartment building. Mom had always had a piercing voice; all the neighbors could hear everything when she fought with Dad. But her screams this time were different; she'd put so much power into it, as though she wanted to howl until she vomited her guts out. The very sound made listeners shudder and want to run as far away as possible.

Qi Fei ran up the stairs, his head churning through every terrifying scenario. When he found out that there had been a car accident involving Dad, he actually felt relieved: Surely that wasn't the worst thing possible. Mom's screams had prepared him for far worse.

But his apparent calmness set her off again. She cried and shrieked as though she had gone mad. She wanted to get plane tickets immediately to where the accident happened—"I must see him before he dies . . . and *that woman* . . ."

As Mom shrieked and cried and cursed and raged, Qi Fei retreated into a shell. For a long time he felt nothing but numbness. He sat, dazed, dimly sensing that his life had been shifted onto a different track, but he had lost the power to think, to understand why and how the future would be different. Only when he saw the unlaundered shirts in Dad's room did he finally realize that he would never see him again. Pain pierced his heart in that moment.

Later, as the nightly news report came on, the name of a bridge drew his attention. It was the same bridge where Dad had his accident. The bridge had been bombed.

He ran into the living room to gaze at the projection wall. Mom was already gone, and the only movement and sound in the apartment came from the super-hires images and rumbling sounds emerging from that wall. The ruins of the bombed bridge burned, and row upon row of wrecked cars rested precariously on the ruin or had tumbled into the water below. It was like watching some action movie from his childhood.

The newscaster explained what had happened. The bridge was a key link in the military supply network because it connected an industrial city—with many armament factories—to a port. The wall showed the footage of a formation of Atlantic Alliance bombers departing triumphantly. Based on radar signatures, analysts were able to identity the squadron responsible: a single pilot leading ten drones.

The pilot's image appeared on the wall. Qi Fei stared into an arrogant smirk. Though it was only a file photo, not taken on the day of the raid, Qi Fei felt that the pilot was celebrating his own victory, mocking everyone who had died on the bridge that day.

In that moment, Qi Fei finally found a release for his pent-up emotions. All the grief and anger that he had not been able to feel surged out of his heart in that moment. He squeezed his fists tight and imagined doing his worst to the pilot, the man responsible. But he had always been such an obedient child and good student, he couldn't even think of good curses. His rage and frustration burned even hotter. He hated the bomber; he hated himself.

Just as Mom would focus all her rage on "that woman" and Yun Fan, Qi Fei would focus all his rage on the Atlantic Alliance.

As he gazed at Jiang Liu now, the faint trace of a smile on Jiang Liu reminded him of the pilot. *I'm going to plunge your pride into the abyss,* he thought.

"Let's finish this," he returned. "You've finally met your match."

Simultaneously, they jumped over the rock to attack each other. Since they had both been disarmed, they had to resort to fists and palms. Qi Fei activated the mecha-gloves hidden in his sleeves, and instantly, both hands were enclosed in metal gauntlets each tipped with five blades, and as he blocked and attacked, the gauntlets, reacting to the nervous impulses in his hands, transformed into different shapes to enhance his strikes. Jiang Liu, for his part, also activated the weapons mode on his bracelet so that numerous sharp spikes emerged, making each of his punches to the opponent's throat deadly. Both men relied on weapons that leveraged wearable technology to become extensions of their bodies.

This close-up fight was, in some ways, even more terrifying than the earlier phase. Often, blades and spikes missed throats and hearts by mere millimeters. Qi Fei's fighting techniques were based on military sanda boxing, but he had improved on the basics with his own invention. Jiang Liu, on the other hand, had studied Muay Thai for years, and then added to the repertoire additional techniques he picked up in his travels around the world. The two were evenly matched, and neither had met such a skilled opponent in many years.

Neither noticed this: During the time when they were facing off across the rock, the ship had stopped attacking them. But as soon as they started fighting again, cold weapons of every description launched at them from the walls. Blades, spears, axes, clubs, arrows, darts, hammers, maces—they seemed to fly at the two at the most inopportune moments. Gradually, the combatants had to devote most of their attention to dodging and blocking the ship's weapons, only occasionally managing a punch or kick at each other. Again and again, deadly weapons missed them only by the barest of margins.

Jiang Liu feinted at Qi Fei, and as Qi Fei pulled back, he seized the opportunity to slide out of his range. Getting up, he began to run with loping strides.

After a moment of hesitation, Qi Fei chased after him.

Weapons continued to fly at them from the walls. Jumping, weaving, Jiang Liu averted death again and again. He leapt over a row of spikes that abruptly erupted out of the floor and then rolled to the side, out of the way of a series of falling spears. Qi Fei wasn't having an easy time, either. He had to keep after Jiang Liu while also watching for traps with every step.

"Director Qi! Why are you so unrelenting?" Jiang Liu called to Qi Fei as he leapt over another deadly spike. "Even if we aren't allies, is it necessary to kill me?"

"If an error must be committed, it's better to kill the innocent than to free the guilty."

"Spoken like a true Legalist. But why seek the path of hegemony instead of the path of the true king? The just and merciful have no enemies."

"Mohist sophistry!" Qi Fei deflected several shurikens. "Look at all the golden ages experienced by civilizations around the world. Not a single one was based on the so-called 'path of the true king,' of mercy and justice. Those in power never yielded it willingly to another. Every peace lasting ten generations required the sacrifice of a generation to blood and iron."

"Look at you!" Jiang Liu jumped onto a rock that had just fallen from the ceiling. "Quoting the classics while putting on a martial arts show! But the more you show off your talents, the more I pity you. I lament that a talented individual has been reduced to a mere tool of war."

Qi Fei launched into a flying kick after him. "It's not your place to pity me."

"You would really slaughter millions in the name of peace?"

"The only path to true peace lies through victory."

Even as he conversed with Qi Fei, Jiang Liu didn't stop running. Just then, the floor suddenly cracked open, revealing two rows of interlocking sharp metal "teeth." It was as though they had run onto the face of some giant monster, whose jaws snapped open and shut, again and again, devouring all that stood in the way. Each time the jaws snapped together, sparks flew from the gnashing teeth.

Jiang Liu tried to stop himself, but it was too late. His momentum was carrying him into that metal maw, and with the next snap, he would be no more.

In despair, he windmilled his arms, hoping to slow his fall. Qi Fei had reached the lip of the maw by then and instinctively reached out, grabbing one of Jiang Liu's arms.

They froze in that pose. Qi Fei had not intended to save Jiang Liu; he had simply reacted. The teetering Jiang Liu had lost his balance completely. If Qi Fei let go, there was no doubt that he would fall to his death.

Jiang Liu looked up at Qi Fei, saying nothing. He had no desire to plea for his life or to entice Qi Fei with an offer. He could see into the other man's heart: nothing, not pretty words, not looks of terror, could sway the other man. They both had utter contempt for hypocrisy, for begging. If he was to live, he would live. If he was to die, he would die.

Jiang Liu had never been so close to death, and he felt the chill of absolute terror. He thought of all the secrets on the Tianshang chain that would be gone with his death, and the thought made him sad. He thought of the sunsets seen from the ruins of Keck Observatory in Hawaii, revelations of a lonely, mysterious beauty. He had always loved to go there drinking by himself when he felt he couldn't go on anymore. And now, he never would go there again.

He watched Qi Fei without speaking, without any expression. His heart was falling, falling into a bottomless abyss.

Qi Fei looked at Jiang Liu. In the other man's eyes he saw no artful cunning, no entreaty for mercy; there was only a peaceful sorrow. The eyes reminded him of a deer he had shot once, when he went hunting in the Changbai Mountains. As the injured deer looked at him, its eyes looked just like this: black, deep, full of sadness.

A prick of pain, a tiny pebble dropped into his heart, sending forth spreading ripples. He recalled the night on the spaceship when he and Jiang Liu had drunk together. Jiang Liu had told him how it had been a long time since he'd enjoyed conversing with someone so much. He remembered the grin on Jiang Liu's face when he'd tried to cheer them up. He remembered how they had fought together, side by side, against Chris Zhao to save Yun Fan. He thought about how they had risked everything to leap across the void of space, to board the loong-ship. They had not always been enemies.

Jiang Liu's eyes. The deer's eyes.

Qi Fei had not killed that deer. He had let it go.

Qi Fei told himself to be hard-hearted, to finish the mission General Yuan had given him. But he couldn't do it. The more anxiously he tried to force himself to let go, the more he couldn't let go. He seemed to see multiple visions of Jiang Liu's face floating about him: grinning, smirking, laughing, talking . . . and in the middle was Jiang Liu's face right now, that peaceful look of sorrow. Qi Fei's heart was a mess.

He didn't hesitate any longer. He pulled hard and dragged Jiang Liu out of the yawning metal maw.

Jiang Liu steadied himself and let out a long sigh. Abruptly, he jumped and pushed Qi Fei down. A massive hammer flew right through the spot where Qi Fei had been standing but a moment earlier.

Both lay on the ground, feeling weak. A day of fighting, of constantly walking on the knife's edge between life and death, would do that to you.

"We're even now," Qi Fei said. "So I'm not going to say thank you."

Jiang Liu chuckled. "We are even. But I still want to say thank you."

"Forget it."

"What sort of place is this?" Jiang Liu looked around at the featureless walls. "How could there be so many deadly traps?"

"I have no idea," Qi Fei sighed. "I can't imagine how Chang Tian and Yun Fan got through this."

"Ah, so you remember them," Jiang Liu teased. "After all that time you spent fighting me, I figured you'd forgotten about them entirely. We should have long since stopped to go help them."

Qi Fei was silent for a few seconds. "I don't know what was wrong with me. I . . . wasn't myself."

"Let's worry about that later," Jiang Liu said. "We need to go." He stood and pulled Qi Fei up. As their hands gripped together, they both knew that peace would hold between them.

They proceeded through the loong-ship, alert for more traps and projectiles. But oddly, from that point on, nothing shot out of the walls, rocks didn't fall from the ceiling, the ground didn't crack open. They proceeded through the empty, silent ship, enveloped in an endless, mysterious darkness.

"Was that the last test?" Jiang Liu asked, still suspicious.

"No idea. We should still be careful."

"This place is too strange," Jiang Liu said. "Earlier, I saw . . . visions."

"Visions? You too? What did you see?" Qi Fei asked.

Jiang Liu told him about the little girl in that war-torn country, about the missed appointment, about the final glance at the dead body. He had never told anyone about this, not friends, not family. He wasn't sure he could do it, but he finished telling the story even though he choked up near the end.

"I don't think you did anything wrong," Qi Fei said. "Places like that are dominated by local gangsters and warlords. You had no hope of taking them on by yourself. It's common for criminals in places with no social order to kidnap children and force them to become the bait in their scams. It was a terrible situation, but there was nothing you could have done."

"But I can't forgive myself," Jiang Liu said. "I'll always wonder: if only I had gone . . . maybe everything would have turned out differently."

"You couldn't have gone." Qi Fei kept his tone analytical. "If you had, you would have been kidnapped, but nothing else would have changed."

"Have you read Le Guin's 'The Ones Who Walk Away from Omelas'?" Jiang Liu asked. "There's a beautiful city, a perfect utopia. But the happiness of all its inhabitants is based on a secret: a child locked in a lightless room. Parents take their children to visit this prisoner and explain that the city's happiness is based on the child's suffering. And then they return to their lives. No matter how much the child pleads, they won't release the child. The city remains happy and joyful, but there are also some who can't stand living in such a place. They leave and do not return."

Qi Fei was silent for a long time. "I can't stand stories like that."

"When I first read it, I felt so horrible that I wanted to throw up. I kept asking myself: If I lived in Omelas, would I have the courage to save that child? I used to think: yes, I would be brave enough. But after that incident I told you about, I realized I was wrong. The girl was the child locked in the dark room. She begged me to help her. But I ran away because I wanted to go on with my happy life. I was no different from all the other selfish men and women in Omelas."

Qi Fei shook his head. "You can't think that way. Things wouldn't have been any better if you had run in there like Rambo. She couldn't be saved. This was not on you."

Jiang Liu continued, his voice echoing in the empty corridor. "The incident completely changed the way I thought about myself. When I was young, I thought my parents' dinner parties were packed with hypocrites. When my mother saw her friends, they would shower one another in lavish compliments: 'Oh my god! You're getting younger every day!' 'You're so beautiful and graceful; I can never be like you.' 'Wow! What a lovely dress! You're a model!' But in reality, they had nothing but contempt for one another. They loved to keep score and gossip about every minor slight, yet they would tell their children that nothing mattered more than love. I found the whole thing suffocating and wanted nothing to do with them.

"I always wanted to find something authentic, a solid reality that I could grasp with my hands and feel. I wanted to . . . do something meaningful, something with value. I'd always gotten what I wanted; everything was too easy. But the only things you treasure are things that don't come to you easily. So I went around the world searching for meaning, for reality. I thought I was different from the others. I went on adventures by myself in the wilderness, climbed mountains, crossed deserts, visited war zones to help refugees. I thought myself wonderful, almost a saint or a bodhisattva.

"But after that time . . . I tore an opening in my own sense of self, a rip that I could never patch. I couldn't give up my life, my world. I could see how so many suffered, but I could never truly leave my life behind to suffer with them. I was no different from my mother's friends: a hypocrite."

Qi Fei listened to Jiang Liu without interruption. Even after Jiang Liu stopped, he waited a little longer before saying, "I understand you. But if you can think like this, then you're not a hypocrite."

"Enough about me," Jiang Liu said. "What visions did you see?"

Qi Fei hesitated. But in the end, he decided to be truthful. "I reexperienced my military training."

He told Jiang Liu about the regimented life he led as a student associated with the military. He had to take a heavy load of courses, but he also had to undergo military training like the recruits. From six in the morning to midnight, he was either studying or training. It was like a life from another time.

"Why did you work so hard to be with the military?" Jiang Liu asked.

Qi Fei sighed. He explained his father's death and how that triggered his deep hatred of the Atlantic Alliance. He spoke of his own contempt for weakness, of his hope to overcome his weak body with his strong mind, to become indomitable in will.

"Can I be honest?" Jiang Liu paused before continuing. "I think the real target of your hatred is your father. But you feel guilty about hating him, and so you torture yourself as a way to seek release or atonement."

Qi Fei was silent. At length, he said, "I've wondered the same thing. But eventually, I realized that I didn't want to hate him."

"Why?"

Qi Fei said nothing.

"Because of Yun Fan's mom?" Jiang Liu probed. "Oh, I think I understand. You . . . you sympathize with your father because you know how he felt."

Qi Fei said nothing. But he didn't deny Jiang Liu's guess either.

Both remained silent as they retreated into their thoughts. Shoulder to shoulder, they sat in the empty, dark, seemingly endless corridor. They had never passed through such a mysterious place, but they also had never felt on such solid ground.

12 | Message

Jiang Liu and Qi Fei reached the corridor of murals and saw the same historical images that had greeted Chang Tian and Yun Fan.

"Do you know the stories in these pictures?" Qi Fei asked.

"I recognize some. But not all."

"Why are they here?" Qi Fei looked around in puzzlement. "Do you think this is proof that aliens really interfered in our history?"

"I can't say either way." Jiang Liu also looked uncertain. "The ship is just getting stranger and stranger. We shouldn't jump to any conclusions. Let's keep going."

As they progressed, they examined the murals carefully. Neither was an expert on Egypt, but both picked out the Hanging Gardens of Babylon. When they passed through the Greek section, they recognized Zeus and Apollo, Prometheus and Hercules. Then, in the stories of the ancient Hebrews, they recognized Eden and the Flood. As for the Chinese myths, they recognized Nüwa and the monsters of *Shan Hai Jing*. To see the myths and gods of all these different cultures mixed together was both chaotic and strangely harmonious.

The images were replicas of originals, and their colors and techniques showed off the unique artistic styles of each culture. The latest images were from the Maya, around five hundred CE. It appeared that someone had scanned the originals and then projected them onto the walls of the corridor using some advanced technique.

"I noticed something," Qi Fei said. "Of all these civilizations, only the ancient Hebrews and the ancient Chinese could claim to have continued to the present."

"I think that's a matter of definition," Jiang Liu said. "Certainly Greece and Egypt remain."

"But they're not the same as the ancient civilizations depicted here. The Mediterranean cultures all became dominated by religion. Greece and Rome were Christianized, and Egypt and Greece were then Islamized. If you evaluate the situation comprehensively, taking into account language, culture, faith, and political system, the modern civilizations in these places are not the same as the ancient ones."

"But we're still arguing over definitions," Jiang Liu said. "I'm not necessarily disagreeing with you, but we need to be precise with our terms. What is meant by continuity of civilization? If we go by culture and faith alone, in some sense, isn't the globe today swept by ideas derived from the beliefs of the ancient Hebrews? On the other hand, if we go by political system, then no ancient civilization has survived at all."

"I understand your point," Qi Fei said. "But for other ancient civilizations, various elements have dissipated. Some no longer have their state or political system; some maintained statehood but lost culture or faith. Chinese civilization, on the other hand, can be seen as having persisted throughout: mythology, language, script, culture, tradition, even statehood."

"I'm not sure I agree with you," Jiang Liu said. "The modern Chinese state is nothing like past iterations. Confucianism, as a foundational aspect of Chinese political philosophy, is gone; the most that can be said is that today's people still remember it."

"I think you're too focused on superficial elements," Qi Fei said. "There are many aspects of Chinese culture that have persisted beyond the superficial. First, there's the people's deep-seated identification with the idea of China, long preceding the European notion of the nation-state. Moreover, even the modern Chinese state retains the ancient tradition of a hierarchical civil administration, with central authority over local authority, and skilled officials being promoted through the system's layers. This remains a basic framework for the state's stability. We also can't forget about national values that remain at the core of our culture: Confucian virtues such as ren, yi, li, zhi, xin, and the rooting of patriotism in an emotional extension of familial love."

"You're talking about the feelings of a vanishing few, such as yourself." Jiang Liu tilted his head and glanced at Qi Fei. "But how many really feel that sense of connectedness with the past? The vast majority of regular people have long since broken with tradition."

"But such has always been the case," Qi Fei said. "Ouyang Xiu took up the mantel from Han Yu and Liu Zongyuan, and he, in turn, passed the classical tradition on to Su Shi and other later masters. This is how the core of Chinese high culture has been sustained from generation to generation—by the few, the dedicated, the set-apart. But it has also always been they who determined the foundation of our culture."

"I'm curious," Jiang Liu said. "Do you really view yourself as following in the footsteps of our ancestors? You clearly think and act based on contemporary institutional values."

"I do view myself as following the traditions. We certainly have more advanced technologies and institutions. But the problems addressed by the classics are eternal."

"Even Confucianism? You mentioned Ouyang Xiu and the tradition based on the classics promoted by the Eight Masters of the Tang and Song. But all of them were ultimately working within the tradition of Confucianism. You, on the other hand, don't strike me as much of a Confucian."

"I reject aspects of Confucianism that emphasize hierarchy in relations, obedience to authority, and all the rites and restrictive rules of propriety," Qi Fei said. "But there are also aspects of Confucianism that deserve consideration. For example, the belief that one should do what is right even if they know failure is certain, or the notion that the virtuous should be especially scrupulous when there's no one around to observe their actions. These ideas are very much worth preserving."

"I can understand that," Jiang Liu said, nodding.

"What about you?" Qi Fei asked. "Are you solely interested in the teachings of Mozi?"

"I believe in universal love and renunciation of aggression," Jiang Liu said. "But I can't claim to be a Mohist in everything. Look at me. Do you think I can bear a life of poverty? A life that's devoid of luxuries? I am, however, inspired by the notion of a wandering youxia who follows the order of no authority, who has no ambition for power, who roams around the land to help those who suffer and carry out heaven's will."

After a moment of silence, Qi Fei asked, "Do you really think you can know and carry out heaven's will?"

Jiang Liu smiled. "Perhaps not. But who can? You? A government?"

As the two slowly wended their way down the corridor, the fact that they were conversing so peacefully after surviving many deadly traps as well as a brutal fight between themselves gave rise to a sense of unreality. Only a few moments ago, they had come within a hairbreadth of killing each other; but now, they were discussing their deepest faiths and ideals. It felt like another life, an attempt at irony by the universe. Now that they weren't living on the edge of death, the alien ship no longer seemed so terrifying. The ancient murals around them glowed with a steady yellow light, warming their progress through history.

Abruptly, they found their route blocked by a barrier. In the middle of the barrier was a huge yin-yang symbol, surrounded by the eight bagua trigrams. They tried pushing against the barrier. Nothing. They tried to find some hidden mechanism. Nothing.

"We don't have Fanfan with us anymore," Jiang Liu said. "How do we get past this?"

"Are we sure that Yun Fan and Chang Tian got through?"

Jiang Liu nodded. "I'm sure. Before you stopped me, I was chasing after Yun Fan and saw her heading this way. We didn't see her after our fight. So I'm sure she went past this point."

"Do you remember if she punched in a passcode?"

"I didn't see. But I don't think this door is expecting a code. We don't have her black box anyway. Let's keep looking for a mechanism."

Jiang Liu tried to press on the trigrams, but they refused to move. He felt around the yin-yang symbol but found no seam or switch. He pushed harder against the door; it didn't budge. He adjusted his wristbands to ping the door with EM waves, but there was no discernible response.

Qi Fei joined him in the investigation. For the briefest of moments, both felt the door move slightly. They concentrated on the area Qi Fei had touched but could detect nothing out of place. There was still no seam, no movable part. The trigrams seemed to be projected onto the smooth surface, not reacting at all no matter how they pressed them.

As they continued their search, the pair's hands fortuitously touched the yin and yang sides simultaneously. The symbol turned. Surprised, they let go, and the turning stopped. They looked into each other's eyes, understanding dawning.

Together, they placed their hands on the yin-yang symbol, one man on each side. As they spun the symbol, a hole irised open in the middle. The more they spun, the bigger the hole grew. After they rotated the symbol 180 degrees, the two needed to change places, so Jiang Liu ducked under Qi Fei's arms. They kept on going. As there was very little space to maneuver, they had to coordinate their movements carefully as they jointly turned the yin-yang disk. After three or four rotations, the hole in the middle was big enough for a person to pass through.

They stopped and reassured themselves that the opening wouldn't snap shut. Then they stepped through, one after the other.

"What sort of strange test is this?" Jiang Liu complained.

Qi Fei shrugged. "Which test so far hasn't been strange?"

Only then did they pay attention to the white light. In contrast to the dark corridor most of the way here, the light here was soft and warm, neither too bright nor too dim. It was the light of an early spring morning, a warm embrace that assured them, that encouraged them to go on.

They saw then the same ladder to heaven that Chang Tian and Yun Fan had seen: enveloped entirely in white light, the top hidden in the haze far above. After a brief glance at each other, they made the same decision to go up and see what awaited them.

+ + + + +

The climb took longer than Qi Fei and Jiang Liu anticipated.

Based on measurements they had taken of the loong-ship, the distance from the circle's rim to the center was approximately only five hundred meters. Moreover, the closer they climbed to the center, the less artificial gravity there would be. Given these conditions, the two thought they could finish the climb in no more than half an hour. However, the actual climb was nothing like how they imagined it. As the artificial gravity diminished, the distance between the rungs also increased. They had to float from rung to rung, taking care to maintain their balance with each step. Although it wasn't a strenuous climb, it was slow going.

Still, in the end, they reached the center. As they entered a spherical cabin, the sight that awaited them shocked them to the core.

The cabin was about fifty meters in diameter, comparable to the length of a swimming pool. The entire space was filled with a bright white light, naturally evoking a sense of sacredness. What shocked them, however, wasn't the cabin itself, but the eight metal "trees" rooted in the spherical wall and growing toward the center. The trees seemed to serve a stabilizing function for the spinning cabin as the eight trees connected at the center like the spokes of a wheel. Coming out of each spoke-tree trunk were multiple curving branches with leaves, as well as metal spheres of various sizes. They truly resembled eight metal trees dangling fruits. Qi Fei and Jiang Liu both felt a sense of familiarity, but they couldn't pin down where they had seen such trees before.

Using the curved branches as rungs, they hop-floated toward the center of the cabin. By chance, Jiang Liu looked back down at the door through which they had entered the cabin and saw two humanoid metal figures on either side of the door: long faces, thick brows, giant noses, nearly vertical eyes . . .

"Look!" He pulled at Qi Fei to get his attention. "Don't those look like the bronze heads from Sanxingdui?"

Qi Fei looked and was likewise amazed. Now they realized why the metal "trees" in the cabin had seemed so familiar: they were enlarged versions of the bronze sacred trees excavated from Sanxingdui.

How could an alien ship contain artifacts from the twelfth century BCE?

They reached the center of the spherical cabin, where the eight trees came together. It was an annular space about three or four meters across, and the white light was the brightest here.

Yun Fan and Chang Tian, floating like two angels, greeted them.

"Took you long enough." Chang Tian's smile was welcoming.

"You've been waiting for us all this time?" Jiang Liu was astonished. "But . . . how did you get through all those traps?"

"What traps?" Yun Fan asked. "We saw some phantom visions. But that was it."

"Visions . . . like memories?" Qi Fei asked. "We also encountered them. But after that there was a long part of the loong where all kinds of deadly weapons swung and smashed and stabbed and dropped. We had to fight really hard to get through. Did you not have to deal with them?"

Yun Fan and Chang Tian shook their heads. They glanced at each other thoughtfully.

"Do you think they went through another trial of the first emperor?" Chang Tian said to Yun Fan.

"Maybe," Yun Fan said. "But all the previous trials had involved the four of us. Why did this particular trial only involve these two?"

"You have the black box, Qin Shi Huang's token," Chang Tian speculated. "Maybe that's why they let you pass through without challenge."

But before Yun Fan could answer, an impatient Jiang Liu broke in. "Slow down! What are you talking about? What 'trials of the first emperor'? What 'token'?"

"Sorry," Yun Fan said. "I really should explain from the beginning. Chang Tian and I have been here a while, and we've been given a lot of new information. The first few doors we passed through in the loong-ship were all trials set up by the ship working in collaboration with Qin Shi Huang himself."

Jiang Liu, heart pounding, interrupted again. "Wait. *Who* gave you this new information?"

Yun Fan pointed up. "You'll hear their voice soon. Whatever question you pose, they'll answer."

"*Who* will answer?" Qi Fei looked up, his brows knit together in alarm.

Both Qi Fei and Jiang Liu thought of "God." But as inveterate atheists, neither could bring himself to say the word aloud.

"We don't know who," Chang Tian said. "But they are very open and have given us extensive answers to all our questions—Why don't we let Yun Fan finish recounting everything before interjecting?"

Qi Fei and Jiang Liu nodded.

Yun Fan continued her explanation. "We were just as confused as you when we first got here. But then a voice suddenly appeared out of thin air, and we were terrified. However, the voice was kind and friendly and explained to us many things on its own. They told us that the first door at the entrance required passcodes and tokens because the ship had to be sure that the visitors had inherited a specific mission and were here to fulfill an old promise, instead of explorers who accidentally stumbled upon the loong. In fact, any power that accidentally stumbled upon the ship were mostly likely destructive. Once the door had been opened, the next few trials were designed to assess who the visitors were. Do you remember how at the very beginning we heard multiple human languages? That was a way for the ship to discern which language the visitors spoke. Since we reacted to the Chinese words, the trials after that were designed for Chinese-speaking visitors."

"Wow," Qi Fei broke in. "So if we hadn't reacted to the Chinese, we would have seen totally different sights on the ship?"

"That's right," Chang Tian said. "At least that was how the voice explained it to us."

Yun Fan went on. "After the ship ascertained that we could understand Chinese and read ancient hanzi, the ship concluded that we were, with very high probability, messengers here to carry out Qin Shi Huang's mission. However, the ship still needed more trials to make sure this was the case. It was, after all, still possible that we could have obtained the tokens in some other way and weren't here to carry out the mission. That was why we faced the trial of Epang Palace. In fact, that trial had been added at the insistence of Qin Shi Huang himself. He wanted to be sure that the messengers from the future were entrusted with his mission, not evildoers intent on ruin."

"What was in that trial?" Jiang Liu tried to remember. "There was the chanting of the classics . . . and the names of the Nine Sons of Loong . . . Oh, I got it! The throne."

"That's right," Yun Fan said. "Epang Palace was just an illusion—don't ask me to explain; I don't understand how it works either. The throne was meant to test the visitors' intent. Only if the visitors brought the icosahedron token left by Qin Shi Huang and then truly, wholeheartedly gave it up into the receptable, would the visitors be considered to have passed. The trials that came after that were designed to assess the character of each individual visitor."

"Are you saying that the illusions we saw were trials designed for us individually?" Qi Fei asked.

"Yes. Only individuals who possess certain characteristics are allowed to come to this central spherical cabin. I'm not entirely clear on what characteristics the trials were testing for. I had just asked the voice the question, but they didn't get a chance to answer before you showed up."

"I'm still not sure I really understand," Jiang Liu said. "Please walk me through it, step-by-step. You just told me that everything we've seen in the loongship so far is part of some trial, but what is the goal of these trials? Are they designed to select the best individuals for some task? Or are they testing our loyalty to Qin Shi Huang? Actually, what mission or task did Qin Shi Huang leave behind? What does that task have to do with the memories each of us was forced to relive? I don't understand the logic behind any of it."

"I know the task left by Qin Shi Huang better than anyone," Yun Fan said. "I'll explain it all to you in a bit. But I also have many questions about the memories we relived. When you showed up, I was in the middle of getting some answers. Why don't you let me finish that line of questioning with the voice, and then I'll tell you about Qin Shi Huang's task?"

Qi Fei and Jiang Liu nodded. Yun Fan lifted her face and shouted into the air: "Hellooooooo! Are you still there?"

A harmonious, kind voice answered out of nowhere. *"I'm here!"*

"Can we ask you more questions?"

"Of course."

"I'd like to know more about those memories and illusions we went through," Yun Fan said. "Was everything we saw in the ship just a vision in our heads? But I *felt* those visions. I really held my father's hands, and my tears fell on his hands. I suppose I can accept reliving my memories through illusions, like a dream, but I don't understand how those sights all four of us saw—the bronze ding and mythical beasts—were also only illusions."

"'Illusion' isn't quite the right way to think about it," the voice from the air said. *"Maybe a better word would be 'projection.'"*

"I don't understand."

"In the language of your species, 'illusion' refers to seeing something that isn't there, usually an error in the processing of vision. But a projection is the result of actual EM signals entering your eyes, such as a mirage in the desert or a movie. Although the things shown in a movie aren't there, the light signals are real, and so everyone can see a movie."

The four exchanged looks at the phrase "the language of your species." It seemed to suggest that the speaker didn't view themself as God, but as another species, a nonhuman species.

Yun Fan asked another question. "You're saying that everything we saw was like a movie? But how were we able to climb up those steps? A mirage in the desert can be seen by everyone, but it can't be touched."

"*Your understanding is too narrow,*" the voice said. "*All sensations begin as EM signals. The sensation of touch . . . the sense of gravity acting on your body . . . fundamentally all your senses are reducible to electromagnetic interactions, and easy to simulate.*"

"Sort of like a holographic movie?" Qi Fei asked.

"*You can think of it that way,*" the voice said. "*But current human holographic cinema is much too primitive.*"

"Are you telling me that the falling rocks, the swinging blades, the arrows that almost killed me—those were all *projections*? But a sword cut me right here in the arm, and I still have the wound."

"*As long as the simulated signals are accurate, the strength of the electromagnetic interaction will also be accurate. So long as the electromagnetic interaction accurately simulates the sharpness of the blade, the strength of the material, the velocity of the strike, and so on, the consequence of the simulation will be the same as the real thing.*"

"I think a 'movie' is not the best metaphor," Jiang Liu said. "I believe I'm getting what they're saying. It's more like a virtual reality game. So long as all the stimuli to the senses are accurately simulated, then all real-world consequences will follow as a matter of course. Even a simulated death blow can kill."

"So you made a whole simulation game just to test us?" Qi Fei asked, frowning deeper.

"No," the voice said. "*If you want to compare it to a game, you were the game's programmers.*"

"What do you mean?"

"*Everything up to Epang Palace was part of the preprogrammed test sequence in the system. Ying Zheng, your first emperor, insisted on those trials. But after that, the trials were based on what was in your heads.*"

"What's in our heads? How could you access that?" Qi Fei asked.

"*From gryons,*" the voice said. "*The thoughts in your head, the emotions you feel—the entirety of your inner life is carried by gryons. The ship has programs for capturing and translating the information content of gryons; that's how it was able to create the projections based on your thoughts and feelings.*"

"What is this 'gryon'?" Jiang Liu asked.

The voice hesitated for a moment before continuing. "*I created this word based on my understanding of human languages. Human science, as of now, is not yet aware of the existence of this fundamental carrier of information. 'Gry,' from classical Greek, means 'a bit,' like the bit in information theory. A gryon is not quite like the fundamental particles of matter; it has no form or substance but exists purely in the realm of information, including structural and dynamic information. Though it's an abstract entity, it's also the foundation of matter."*

"Let me see if I'm getting this," Jiang Liu said. "To carry on the earlier metaphor: Are gryons in the real world similar to the instructions written by programmers in a game world? A program is an abstract language of information, reducible to digital signals, but a program can generate everything in the world of a game. Looking at it another way, any change in the world of the game must correspond to some change in the digital signals of the underlying program. Am I on the right track?"

"That's a good analogy," the voice said in an approving tone.

"So . . . the real world is also generated by a program of sorts," Jiang Liu said. "If you look beyond matter, you'll find gryons as the carrier of the 'digital' instructions?"

"Correct. That's a good way to understand it."

"Who is the programmer for the world, then?" Jiang Liu asked. "Do we really live in a universe programmed by someone?"

"No one writes the program for any universe," the voice said firmly. *"Every universe consists of self-organizing information. The evolution of each universe is the history of the evolution of that universe's self-organizing information. There are an infinite number of universes with an infinite number of evolutionary histories, none with any author. However, the more advanced a civilization, the more capacity it has to access and modify gryons. To use your earlier analogy: advanced civilizations, though they start out as only characters in a game, can deduce the programming instructions for the game and rewrite them."*

"That's amazing." Jiang Liu's eyes glowed with excitement. "Back when I was searching for meaning in life, I used to think: Maybe the world isn't real and doesn't exist. It's just a program, a simulation written by someone. As mere NPCs in a game world, our sufferings and joys are all preprogrammed by a programmer in a higher plane of existence. But now you're telling me that life can rewrite the programming instructions of their universe! Incredible!"

"There are many degrees of influencing the information underlying a universe,"

the voice said. *"The minimum level is simply being able to detect gryons, which means that the civilization is not merely observing matter, but the information underlying matter—being able to read the source code, to continue the analogy. More advanced civilizations can capture gryons, decipher the information they carry, and then manifest that information as matter. This is akin to recompiling and re-running the source code. Even more advanced civilizations can collect and store gryons, and then, through certain modifications to the gryons, release energy or transform matter. Beyond that, civilizations can use entangled gryons to travel between universes. In the next level, civilizations gain the power to directly manipulate and alter the gryons of their own universe or other universes, thereby essentially gaining the capacity to reprogram universes. Finally, the most advanced civilizations can merge themselves into the universe's information, thus erasing the line between characters and programmers in a game; such civilizations are capable of creating entirely new universes."*

"Wow." Jiang Liu was speechless for a few seconds. "I can't even imagine that."

"This is not making any sense to me," Yun Fan said. "If you understand what they're talking about, can you explain?"

"I'll do my best to explain later," Jiang Liu said. "Let me try to clarify a few things first." Lifting his face again, he asked the voice above, "Let's focus on humanity right now. We have equations that explain the fundamental nature of matter and energy. Does this mean we've detected the gryons behind matter?"

"Not at all," the voice said. *"The equations are a good step in the right direction, but you're nowhere near detecting gryons, much less manipulating them."*

"Wait." Jiang Liu's mind churned. "If we're talking about what we haven't yet detected . . . do you mean dark matter and dark energy?"

"I suppose those words, at your level of development, can cover what I'm talking about." The voice hesitated before continuing. *"It's not easy to map your words to our words. Some concepts can be mapped directly, but many cannot. I'm trying to use your words to convey reality, but it's not always possible. For example, 'dark energy' and 'dark matter' are very generic words; they cover many things beyond humanity's ken right now. In reality, they describe many completely distinct phenomena."*

"Hold on for a second," Jiang Liu said. "Let me sort through everything. You're talking about rewriting all of cosmology and particle physics. My mind is a mess right now."

Jiang Liu was beyond excited. Fundamental physics has been stuck for decades, making little progress. Much of humanity's energy has been absorbed in the development of the solar system. The moon, Mars, and the asteroid belt have all been claimed, and space has become the main arena for military contest between the great powers. Thus, more than 90 percent of the scientific research budget is devoted to the exploitation of the solar system and space weapons, with a miniscule amount diverted to cosmology and fundamental physics. The last major results came in 2065, involving gravitational waves. Nothing had been accomplished in other areas.

Jiang Liu had majored in cosmology precisely because it was unpopular (although he also found the topic deeply engaging). He wanted to pick something so esoteric and obscure that he would be free from interference from Mom and Dad. Moreover, cosmology gave him the excuse to travel around the world, be as far away from his family as possible, and take in the sights of remote valleys and picturesque peaks. His older brother and sister, both dutiful and practical, had been given coveted internships at his parents' friends' companies for their summer breaks. They were proud of those opportunities, but Jiang Liu wanted nothing of the sort for himself.

Over time, Jiang Liu grew used to roaming about by himself. Like most ambitious young people in cosmology, he had tried to develop his own theory of everything, something that would encompass all of particle physics, string theory, quantum mechanics, general relativity . . . He had failed. The observation of dark matter and dark energy had been a hot topic at the beginning of the century, but over time, as concrete results failed to materialize, funding had dried up. Jiang Liu had tried at one point to get Dad to allocate some money to advance research in this area, but Dad had given him such a scolding about wasting money that he had never tried again.

Now he was like Ali Baba standing before a cave full of knowledge-treasure; he was so excited that he didn't know where to start.

Qi Fei, silent until now, broke in to ask the voice in the air. "I'd like to understand a little more about how you were able to create visions, or projections, from the thoughts in our heads."

The voice, speaking neither fast nor slow, answered, "*An intelligent creature's organ of cognition—your brain, for instance, and similar organs in other species—is fundamentally an organ of interaction with gryons. You already know that your thoughts manifest as electromagnetic radiation, but these signals are but a minuscule part of the interaction between the brain and the environment; the vast majority of the interaction takes place through gryons. All your cognitive activities— reasoning, memory, emotion—will generate information, and thus leave gryon-interaction traces."*

"Please slow down." Qi Fei's tone was cautious, as he was obviously straining to be as rational as possible. "A little while back, you explained that gryons are akin to programming instructions that generate the world of matter. But you also said that it is possible for cognitive activities in the brain to interact with and alter gry-ons. By that logic, it is also possible, through thinking alone, to alter the universe. That's basically philosophical idealism, isn't it? As a materialist, I can't accept that."

"It's not easy to explain this point," the voice above said. *"But let me start with this: the world you can observe is, fundamentally, a world that exists in your mind."*

"I don't agree." Qi Fei shook his head. "Let's put philosophy aside for now and focus just on what happened on this ship. Tell me, how did the ship generate those visions?"

"It's very simple," the voice said. *"The ship has equipment for detecting gryons and manifesting them. As you think, you generate new information, which the ship reads from the gryons. Then the ship manifests the gryons into projections. Do you remember also experiencing more intense emotions and having normally repressed emotions surface? That was because the ship also has instruments for amplifying emotional responses and enhancing information. But overall, the scenes you saw and interacted with were the products of your own minds."*

"So earlier . . ." Qi Fei paused. "The deadly weapons coming at us from every-where . . ."

"Yes, they were just projections of your enmity for each other."

The voice's calm tone set off a tumultuous reaction inside Qi Fei. He had thought he was on the verge of death, dodging those swinging swords and dropping stones. *Just a projection of my mind?* It was intolerable. "Why? Why did you do that?"

"It was a trial," the voice said. *"You're one of the few species capable of getting through the trial of illusions. This ship has, so far, been visited by creatures from three planets. You're the first to make it all the way here."*

"If we had failed the trial, we would have died."

"You would have died in your own hatred and enmity," the voice said, easily deflecting Qi Fei's accusation.

"Why? Who are you?" Qi Fei shouted, each question louder than the previous. "How dare you play with us so?"

"I wasn't playing with you," the voice said. *"I wanted to give you a taste of the consequences of a civilizational upgrade. Your civilization is still in the early stages, purely material. But as you upgrade, you'll enter the stage when mind communicates directly with mind. And beyond that, you'll advance to the stage where hostile thoughts manifest directly to injury and harm. My trial is a preview of that. Species that cannot survive the trial will find themselves in hell after the upgrade."*

"What is this civilizational upgrade you keep on talking about?" demanded Qi Fei.

"Qi Fei, listen to me," Chang Tian kicked off the metal leaf he was perched on and floated toward his friend. Gently, he clasped his shoulders. "You should be proud that we, as representatives of humanity, survived the trial of illusions and didn't die in our mutual enmity. We ought to celebrate our success. Don't be too anxious; don't let your emotions mislead you. Tell me, what exactly did you and Jiang Liu experience just now?"

Qi Fei looked over at Jiang Liu and the two locked eyes. Neither had any intention of repeating in detail what they had gone through, but both now understood the nature of the deadly fight between them. The fight had meaning far beyond the two of them—they had not expected such a thing at all, but in that glance, they both saw a new shared understanding.

If we hadn't felt that moment of compassion, where would we be now?

They could not suppress the churning, chaotic thoughts.

Yun Fan broke in. "Please tell us more about civilizational upgrade. You mentioned trials based on what was in our heads, but you've never explained the purpose of the trials or who designed the trials. I think, based on everything you've said so far, that the trials are really tests to see if we qualify for a civilizational upgrade. Am I right? Is the idea that if we pass, you'll help us complete a civilizational upgrade? Did you help humanity through previous civilizational upgrades? Now that we've survived the trial of illusions, does that mean we qualify for another civilizational upgrade from you?"

The voice overhead was silent for a moment. *"You ask such complicated questions. No one is here today except me. I think I should come down to talk with you directly."*

The four looked up, their hearts in their throats. What did the voice mean by "come down"? And who was really behind that voice? What would happen once they came down? Without blinking, all eight eyes focused on the gentle, warm light at the center of the spherical cabin.

But the voice spoke up from behind them.

13 | Civilization

The hair on the necks of all four stood up at the voice.

Jiang Liu was the first to turn around, and immediately he gasped. The others snapped around to see what he saw, and they fired out as well.

One of the Sanxingdui-style humanoid metal figures that had guarded the root of the bronze sacred tree-ladder was floating up toward them, its nearly vertical eyes under a thick brow glaring menacingly at them.

They all felt the uncontrollable impulse to back away. But in the nearly weightless environment, there was nowhere for them to brace themselves and push off. So even though they strained their bodies, they stayed exactly where they were.

The bronze figure, however, floated steadily at them like an immortal with magical powers.

They stared as the figure drifted closer and closer, stopping only a couple of meters away. The body remained stiff, and the eyes empty. The voice boomed from it. "It may be easier if I speak with you this way."

The sight was so terrifying that they had to suppress the urge to strike out or turn and run.

Yun Fan was the first to recover. "Hello. May I ask your name?"

"My name is Hudiluladiyadeluoteqilusaidiasiqiqixiluonidafanao•Li•Aluosi-kong."

"Uh . . . Hudi . . . um . . ." Yun Fan gave up. "Would it be all right if I gave you a nickname? How about Huhu?"

"That's fine," the metal figure said.

Yun Fan pointed to the bright light at the center of the cabin. "How did you come here from *there*?"

"That's a long story."

"Are you the master of this ship?" Qi Fei asked.

"No, no! I'm just here to do my job. I'll be honest. I don't know the answers to many of your questions. Unfortunately, I'm the only one on duty, and neither the captain nor our best explainer is here to help. You humans have so many questions! I've never met any species so chatty or curious. I can only have a casual conversation with you. If you want to talk to a real expert, I'll have to take you to my captain another time."

The four were stupefied by this speech. At length, Yun Fan tentatively asked, "Just now, when we were talking with the voice in the air . . . was that you?"

"Indeed," Huhu said. "It was hard playing the part of a god. I had to sound so serious all the time! If I could keep that up all the time, they would have made me a captain. Enough was enough. I got tired of it."

"So what do *you* do?" Jiang Liu asked.

"I'm just a common inspector, responsible for the six civilizations in your universe. Two of them are in your galaxy, and the other four are farther away."

"What exactly is an inspector?" Qi Fei asked, frowning again.

"You know, someone who . . . inspects." Huhu seemed baffled by the humans' confusion. "I go from civilization to civilization and inspect them."

"What are you inspecting?"

"Your progress as a developing civilization."

"And then what? What do you do with the data from your inspection?"

"Oh, nothing special," Huhu said. "You know, just the typical stuff. If you are lagging in development, we try to help. If you're developing well, we continue to observe."

"Why?" Qi Fei looked tense. "Why do you do this? What is the purpose?"

"It's all very routine," Huhu said. "The Union is always in need of new members, and inspectors are responsible for evaluating potential candidates to see if they're ready to join."

"What 'Union' are you talking about?" Qi Fei asked.

"The Union of Cooperating Civilizations," Huhu said. "You know, the union formed to resist devouring civilizations."

"What are cooperating civilizations? What are devouring civilizations?"

"Oh my. You're so exasperating!" Huhu waved a hand impatiently. "Please, let me try to explain everything bit by bit. Afterward, you can ask questions to clarify any points that you don't understand. It'll be much better than throwing random questions at me while you have no context for anything."

Huhu waved their hands in a circle, and the spherical cabin instantly turned into deep space. No, not the darkness of a typical view from the Earth, but a bright, dazzling, crowded universe full of lights. All around them—above, below, everywhere—lights glowed and burned and blazed. Moreover, a closer examination revealed countless gauzy films separating the bright points of light. The films, barely discernible, folded, bent, flexed, curled, and contorted into all kinds of wondrous shapes. Both films and lights were in constant, mesmerizing motion.

"Is this a map of the entire universe?" Jiang Liu asked. "Each light . . . must represent a whole galaxy. Am I right?"

"No," Huhu said. "Each point of light is a single universe."

"What?" Jiang Liu couldn't believe his ears. "What do you mean by a 'universe'?"

"You know, a universe." Huhu seemed to think the question rather foolish. "A topologically independent four-dimensional space-time."

"But . . . how can there be so many universes?"

"That's easy to explain," Huhu said. "There are four mechanisms for creating multiple universes, each capable of generating an infinite number of universes. Put all of them together, and you get the multiverse you see here. Of course, universes are being annihilated every moment as well. The rate at which universes vanish is even faster than the rate at which matter is annihilated in your experience."

"I . . ." Jiang Liu was at a loss for words. "What about our universe?"

"It's right here," Huhu said, pointing at one remote corner, their metal finger glowing blue. "Of course, this is only a topological map, not a full representation. The dimensions you see in this map are abstract, topological dimensions, meant to show connections and disjunctions. Your universe is represented by a single point, with no hint of its internal structure. Also, your universe is relatively isolated, as you can see from the map; there are very few tunnels leading to or from it."

"Tunnels? What kind of tunnels?" Jiang Liu asked.

"Like the one I made to visit you," Huhu said. "All universes are situated within a highly convoluted high-dimensional space, so it's almost always possible to connect two universes once you find an appropriate spot to entangle them. Listen, please don't constantly interrupt me with questions. Let me finish my lecture first. I'm no scholar, so I must be very careful and lay out the truth before you methodically. If you interrupt me all the time, I'll lose my place and mess up the explanation."

The humans fell silent.

Huhu waved their hands, stirring all the lights and films into even more fervent motion. They seemed to be searching for the right word, but the silent pause went on. Finally, they said, "I wanted to start with the origin of universes, but I can't find a word in your languages to describe the material from which all universes are made."

"Could you call it the 'metaverse'?" Jiang Liu offered.

"Sort of?" Huhu looked frustrated. "But it's not a 'verse' at all, not a universe, not a multiverse, not a quasiverse . . . it's an abstract concept. Oh, the captain, back when they were talking with your ancestors, called it . . . oh what was the word they used—"

"Chaos? Hundun?" Yun Fan fired off a series of guesses. "Taichu? Dao?"

"Dao! That's it!" Huhu looked relieved. "Yes, the word from the Daoists. Anyway, Dao gave birth to an infinite number of universes—I'm not clear on the exact mechanism; you'll have to ask the captain. Once the multiverse came into being, each universe developed on its own. Some evolved complex structures, followed by intelligent life and civilizations. These sentient beings, over time, also evolved to influence the universes and the multiverse, even Dao itself. This is the fundamental pattern of the multiverse.

"Now, it should be obvious that the civilization that evolved the earliest also had the most time to develop and the most opportunities to advance. They discovered the secret of perceiving and manipulating gryons, and then evolved to use gryons to control matter and energy, and finally transformed into beings of pure information, such that their minds no longer required physical bodies, but merged with the cosmos itself. This is the origin of the first and earliest devouring civilization.

"We don't know exactly what happened. But it was likely that the first devouring civilization expanded too quickly. As a result, it abruptly exploded into countless new, small universes. This event was called the multiverse big bang, and your own universe was born from it. Later, countless civilizations tried to repeat the feat of that first devouring civilization, but none managed to advance to that all-encompassing stage. This was because these later civilizations faced a much grander multiverse, which was much harder to devour. In addition, the universes were full of intelligent beings with their own civilizations that banded together into alliances and leagues and unions to resist being devoured.

"Forming a union requires the member civilizations to agree to entangle gryons and allow an exchange of minds. This is why inspectors are necessary. If a prospective member is too aggressive in its makeup, then a union with that civilization means suicide for all the other members. No civilization wants to be swallowed up. Thus, every cooperating civilization faces a pair of conflicting desires: the craving for new allies to join with and the fear that it would be devoured by those allies."

Jiang Liu and Qi Fei finally got some answers to their questions. Hoping to find new allies in the grand struggle against "devouring civilizations," Huhu's civilization sent out "inspectors" to survey alien life in other universes. The inspectors helped these nascent civilizations along the road to advancement, but they were leery of these new civilizations turning out to be overaggressive and dangerous. They wanted to raise up all the cuddly baby civilizations, but they were also scared that one of them would end up as a tiger or a wolf. That finally explained why, despite Huhu's people being so much more technologically advanced than humans, they behaved with such caution toward humans.

"But why do you have to go to so much trouble?" a puzzled Qi Fei asked. "Rationally, an advanced civilization should simply focus on its own development. Why should you devote energy to helping less-developed civilizations? You might as well conquer and destroy them—as has happened countless times in human history. I'm afraid that I can't trust what you say unless I have a reasonable explanation."

"Ah, you're confused because you don't understand how civilizations advance and develop," Huhu said. "We should sit down and have a long chat."

Huhu waved their hands again, and the dazzling multiverse disappeared from view. The spherical cabin began to spin, and a powerful magnetic field seemed to be produced. Everyone felt the pull of the nearby bronze sacred trees, like iron filings being drawn to a magnet. The four were pulled onto one tree, where they found places to sit on four curving leaves surrounding an empty space. The space soon filled with what appeared to be solid ground, and Huhu floated over to "stand" on that surface. And so, in the middle of an alien ship drifting in weightless space, the four experienced the illusion of sitting in a theater with a lecturer down on the stage in the middle.

Huhu swept an arm in a semicircle in front of themself. The arc turned into a screen made of light, like a long blackboard curving around Huhu, the teacher.

"What do you think are the prime causes for civilizational advancement?" Huhu asked.

The four looked at one another. The alien metal-person acting all serious while playing the role of a college professor—or even a primary school teacher—was too absurd (but also adorable).

"Are you . . . testing us?" Yun Fan asked.

"I am," Huhu said.

"Why don't you just tell us the answers? We have no interest in playing school-children again."

Huhu wouldn't yield. "I want to hear *your* answer."

Jiang Liu pondered the question for some time before venturing a few guesses. "Scientific discoveries? The drive to explore the world? The more a civilization probes into the inner mysteries of the cosmos, the more it advances."

Huhu pointed to Qi Fei. "How about you? What do you think?"

Qi Fei chuckled. "Do you really have to act like a kindergarten teacher?"

Huhu refused to give up the act.

Qi Fei turned serious. "I have to go back to competition. Historically, many human civilizations didn't start out as advanced scientifically or technologically. They had done nothing to discover the mysteries of the cosmos. But they desired conquest, victory, war, to triumph over other peoples around them. In that process, the sense of crisis and intense competition led to scientific advances, with the secrets of the universe being discovered as a side effect."

Instead of responding to these answers, Huhu, continuing in their role as a grade-school teacher, followed up with another question. "How many times has human civilization taken major steps forward?"

Yun Fan gave a serious answer. "The first major leap was the transition from hunting-gathering to agriculture. The next major leap was the emergence of cities and states. A more recent major leap is the industrial revolution based on scientific and technological advances."

As Yun Fan talked, the light-screen showed images corresponding to those stages of human history.

"Not bad," Huhu said approvingly. "But you missed one more: About seventy-thousand years ago, *Homo sapiens* displaced all other hominin species and became the only survivor of your family branch, the only intelligent beings on Earth. So, based on these examples, what do you think are the reasons behind major civilizational advances?"

"But it's different every time," Yun Fan said. "We don't know the underlying causes for *Homo sapiens* displacing other hominins. Was it the invention of language? We can't be sure. In the case of the agricultural revolution, it was very likely the result of improvements in farming technology. The birth of farming, however, seemed to be fortuitous, and to date very few places in the world are verified to have independently discovered farming. The birth of states and cities is even more controversial. Some say the causes were military necessity, others religion. However, it's clear that states and cities accompanied a massive increase in the human capacity for organization to pursue collective goals. Finally, the industrial and technological revolution of modern times also had multiple, complicated causes: the philosophical underpinning of humanism, the rise of early capitalism and global commerce, the wealth generated by the age of colonial exploration and exploitation, and so on."

"These are all mere superficial phenomena," Huhu said dismissively.

Qi Fei grew annoyed. "Then why don't you just tell us what you want to say? I hate this game. We shouldn't be treated like schoolchildren."

Huhu stared at Qi Fei with their empty, lifeless metal eyes. "How can you be so slow? The underlying pattern is so obvious. The only thing that matters is the capacity for information exchange."

"What are you talking about?" None of the humans knew what Huhu meant.

"The victory of *Homo sapiens* over other hominin species was indeed traceable to language," Huhu said. The curved light-screen before them glowed with illustrations. "In the absence of language, individuals must resort to gestures and hormones for information exchange. But speech is a far faster, denser, content-rich medium for information exchange. If you properly quantify the underlying differences based on gryons, speech offers six orders of magnitude improvement over body language and chemical signals. Armed with such an advantage, of course *Homo sapiens* would win.

"Now, let's look at the agricultural revolution. The key here has nothing to do with farming, but settlement. A settlement means a massive increase in population and more opportunities for information exchange. Hunter-gatherers spend most of their time alone or in small bands, with relatively few others to converse with. But a settlement is different. There are many more people to talk with in daily life, and more things to talk about. The information exchange in a settlement is about two orders of magnitude greater. Again, this advantage easily led to the victory of the earliest agricultural societies over their nonagricultural neighbors.

"The birth of states will require more elaboration later. But for now, focus on just one point: written language. Without writing, there can be no fixed laws and elaborate administrative regulations, which means no stable state. Writing adds multiple new dimensions to mere speech. Since the written word can reach farther and more people than speech, you've gained two spatial dimensions. Writing is also able to survive time, which adds a new historical dimension to information. This roughly translates to an improvement of three orders of magnitude. Using the standard civilization grading scale, only at this point did human civilization reach the zeroth rank.

"Let's move on to the industrial revolution. You're too focused on superficial indicators such as philosophical humanism, wealth accumulation, global trade, and so on. These elements were present earlier in your history as well. Just look at the Roman Empire: it lacked none of these things. The real underlying cause of the industrial revolution was simple: the language of advanced mathematics. Based on the work of a few other predecessors, Newton wrote *Philosophiæ Naturalis Principia Mathematica*. This is the true foundation of your modernity. A mathematical language is capable of far more abstraction and can overcome differences in diverse regional human languages and the limits of everyday vocabulary. Finally, all humanity could communicate in a single, universal language, and a language relatively close to the informational content of the cosmos itself at that. Mathematics alone elevated your information exchange capacity by about another three orders of magnitude."

"Hold on for a second," Jiang Liu broke in. "I don't disagree with the importance you attribute to mathematics. But the language of math has always been mastered by a relatively small percentage of the population. Even now, I think no more than one percent of the world's population can truly understand advanced mathematics. This is completely different from the situation of natural human languages.

I don't see how math, the preferred language of a select few, can improve the global information exchange capacity a thousandfold."

Huhu waved their hands dismissively. "You've misunderstood me. I'm talking about effective information exchange, or exchanges that carry important information and new information. Let me give you an example. You have two computers in communication with each other. Every nanosecond, one computer sends a one to the other, and the other computer responds with a zero. That means each second, two billion bits of information are being exchanged. Isn't that impressive? But in reality, the effective information exchange rate is zero, because there's no new information, no useful content. In any civilization, it's not necessary for every individual member to produce meaningful information. It's perfectly normal for a tiny percentage of individuals to generate more than ninety-five percent of the effective information exchange. Many of your human civilizations functioned this way. Moreover, you can multiply such information exchange using machines such as computers."

"I want to know what the next major advance in civilization looks like," Yun Fan said. "What's the next upgrade?"

"I shouldn't tell you," Huhu said. "This is like being told the ending after you've seen only the first episode. Oh, you have a word for this . . . what is that word . . ."

"Spoilers," Yun Fan said.

"That's right! I shouldn't be giving you any spoilers. Every civilization should develop on its own and seek out the path to the next stage of advancement. But I am a big softie, and I can't keep secrets! Back when your little emperor, Ying Zheng, asked me, I gave in and told him. I guess I can tell you as well if you really want to be spoiled."

I think it's more accurate to say that you enjoy the feeling of teaching others secret knowledge entirely too much. But instead of saying out loud what she was thinking, Yun Fan just nodded solemnly at Huhu.

"It's not hard to figure out once you understand the principle behind gryons," Huhu said. "The next stage of information exchange involves direct connections between the information networks in all your brains. Your species is quite lucky in that your organ of cognition has a sound fundamental structure and the algorithms in your neural information network are well developed. But you're still a long way from direct brain-to-brain information exchange.

"Your current communicative model is like this: The information obtained from the gryon-processing network in your brain via massive parallelism must be serialized for transmission through the vibrating vocal cord, one bit at a time. This is incredibly inefficient. For some people, the brain-to-lips apparatus is incapable of transmitting even one percent of the information generated in the neural network. It's even worse for information contained in writing or mathematics. However, if you could achieve multi-modal, real-time direct exchange of neural information, your civilization's information exchange capacity will go up yet another big step.

"Once you've reached that plateau, however, with the entire civilization's cognitive organs networked together, you'll have a harder time attaining further improvements. Experience has shown that civilizations that have reached that stage of development will find it increasingly difficult to evolve through its own internal information exchange; instead, it must find other civilizations, and, through mutual entanglement, evolve together in an information union.

"Your civilization is still much too far from being able to effectively exchange information with us. Until you achieve total brain-domain information exchange, you'll be stuck at the threshold of the next major advancement."

"How do we get past that threshold?" Yun Fan asked. "What does direct brain-to-brain information exchange look like?"

"You know what that looks like," Huhu said.

"We don't!" Yun Fan frowned.

Huhu stood with their metal arms akimbo and stomped a metal foot. "Of course you know! I showed you what it's like, and you asked me so many questions about it."

"You mean . . . those vision-projections?" Yun Fan finally made the connection.

"Exactly!" Huhu looked relieved. "Why do you think I went to all that trouble? Your brains are nothing more than clumps of proteins, fats, and ions. How can you expect *that* to exchange information? I know you are exploring the potential of brain waves; that's moving in the right direction, but brain waves are too crude and can't get you the real information content. To achieve direct brain-to-brain communication requires the use of gryons. When your brain can perceive gryons, you'll experience exactly the kind of vision-projections you went through."

Jiang Liu and Qi Fei looked at each other, their minds churning with complicated feelings. If direct brain-to-brain information exchange was just like what they went through during that fight to the death, then it was indeed an incredibly dangerous development.

"Can brains really perceive gryons?" Yun Fan asked.

"Definitely," Huhu said. "Right now, your brains are interacting with gryons constantly, using them to record and manipulate information. But you don't sense them, can't feel them. This is like . . . like . . . ah! I have it. It's like how the first primitive creatures on your planet had bodies that interacted with photons, but they couldn't sense light. Later, as evolution advanced and more complex creatures evolved, they developed specific organs to perceive light: eyes. With eyes, animals could now see the world. It's the same with gryons. When you can perceive gryons, you'll be able to 'see' a whole new world."

"Does that mean we'll be living constantly surrounded by illusions?" Yun Fan muttered. "Like how it was earlier in the ship, but all the time and everywhere? That feels both marvelous and terrifying."

"'Terrifying' is right," Huhu said. "When you can perceive gryons, you'll suddenly *know* and *feel* everything about the self: thoughts you want to have as well as thoughts you don't, even memories you had buried deep within the brain. Every bit of information is recorded by gryons, so there's no escape. Before you evolve to that stage, you must accept yourself completely. In fact, you have to do the same with others as well, because whatever you think about someone, they'll perceive those thoughts."

Yun Fan lowered her head, lost in thought.

Qi Fei spoke up. "So, all the trials you mentioned were designed to test whether we're ready for a civilizational upgrade, is that right?"

"Yes," Huhu said. "We don't want a tragedy to result when you are opened up to gryons."

"Have you seen such tragedies?" Qi Fei asked.

"Too many!" Huhu said. "Many civilizations die in the hatred and enmity unleashed in the aftermath of achieving mind-to-mind communion. At this level, the information exchanged is many times greater than the information content of speech or writing. In conversation, the link is formed from sequential sound waves, easy to control and very sparse in information content. In the case of writing and images, the exchange takes place through light. Although images and writing are two dimensional containers for information, their transmission is heavily dependent on the production process, which is very slow.

"Gryon-mediated brain-to-brain communication is completely different. The brain is massively parallel, and direct linkage between brains leads to an information explosion. Insufficiently advanced civilizations can neither learn to control the link nor how to disguise their thoughts, and the result is utter disaster as members fall upon one another in violence.

"Before I came to you on this visit, another civilization in the Milky Way had destroyed itself in this manner. It developed very quickly and made several fortunate breakthroughs. That was how it reached the critical point before you, and we helped it make the upgrade. But tragedy followed. We didn't even get very far from their solar system before they were on the verge of annihilating themselves, and we had to go back and forcefully separate the minds in order to save a few individuals."

"How many more civilizations in the Milky Way are under your care?" Yun Fan asked.

"In the Milky Way, it's just the two of you," Huhu said. "There are more civilizations in other galaxies that we are watching and cultivating."

"Where is this other civilization in the Milky Way?" Jiang Liu asked.

"You can do the math yourself," Huhu said. "We'll use your years as the basic unit of measurement. I return here once every seven hundred years or so; thus, the other civilization must be about 350 light-years away. To be precise, it's about 330 light-years from here."

"Is the other civilization the reason that you could come visit us only once every seven centuries?" Yun Fan asked.

"Exactly," Huhu said.

Yun Fan grew excited. "But where is your world? Do you spend all your time on this ship just making a circuit between two civilizations in the Milky Way?"

"My own world?" Huhu sounded surprised. "Ah . . . I forgot to properly introduce myself! Oh dear, I'm such a mess when the captain isn't around to keep things in order. My planet isn't in the Milky Way. In fact, it's not in your universe at all. By our own numbering system, our universe is Universe 0, and your universe is Duocainiaolusitafadidi Special Series 706. There are many other series and groups. A typical inspection team like mine is responsible for about eight universes on average, which should yield about forty to fifty civilizations.

"Typically, civilizations within the same universe can't ever communicate with one another. This is because within the same universe, signals must go from one place to another, subject to all the universe's internal constraints and the limits of the matter field transport—in your case, the speed of light. The speed limit is far too slow! A universe is so big that two civilizations that otherwise would benefit from communication can't even find each other. To use an analogy, it's like when two tiny bugs are trying to find each other by crawling over a giant sheet of paper. They're limited by their tiny feet, and they may crawl around for a lifetime without finding the other bug.

"Civilizations that manage to make contact typically do so by tunneling between universes. To continue the analogy, suppose the two bugs are on two different sheets of paper. Instead of crawling and staying on the same sheet of paper, it's much easier to bring the two sheets close together and then make a hole to connect them together. It's easy for me to tunnel through to get to here, but it takes hundreds of years to go from one planet in this universe to another, flying at the speed of light."

"So that's why we haven't been able to find aliens!" Jiang Liu exclaimed. "Our universe is simply too big, if one is restricted to the speed of light. But on this idea of linking together universes . . . how, exactly, does one go about doing that?"

"By entanglement, of course," Huhu said. "Oh, there's a complicated principle behind it . . . it's called . . . uh . . . oh never mind, I don't understand it either. You should ask the captain. I just know how to operate the equipment and to transmit—see, didn't I just successfully transmit myself over?"

"I was about to ask you how you came to be here," Yun Fan said. "What's up there?" She pointed at the glowing center of the cabin.

"Nothing!" Huhu said, spreading their hands comically. "Strictly speaking, I'm not really here; rather, my true self is still in the inspection station. However, through the entanglement apparatus, I managed to transmit my awareness into your universe, and I'm currently controlling this metal body using object-steering techniques. I can't really transmit my body to your universe anyway. The key parameters between our universes are very different; I would mostly likely not survive if I sent my body over. But transmitting consciousness is much easier, and it's not hard to steer foreign matter if you know what you're doing."

Yun Fan pointed at the Sanxingdui-style metal body. "Where did you get such an ancient artifact?"

"Your ancestors built it for us," Huhu said. "Since we couldn't come into your universe with our true bodies, we asked them to make us telepresence vessels. We taught them the techniques needed to build suitable metal shells."

"Oh, now I understand what happened," Qi Fei said. "We helped you build steerable avatars, and you helped us advance our technology. This makes much more sense. I knew there was no way for an alien civilization to help us altruistically."

"All sustainable relationships require mutual benefit. A one-sided relationship can't last," Huhu said. "Your civilization's advancement is the result of your own continuous effort to improve. You don't make progress only because we're helping you; rather, we help you because you're making progress."

While the humans pondered the meaning behind Huhu's words, the alien suddenly beckoned at them. "I don't think you can understand everything just from my lecture; I need to bring you to see some interesting sights."

Huhu pointed at the door through which the humans had entered the spherical cabin and gave them a push. The push was neither too strong nor too gentle, but just enough to send them floating comfortably to the door. The precision behind that simple action amazed both Jiang Liu and Qi Fei.

Following the humans, Huhu also drifted to the door. With a simple gesture, the alien managed to transform the vertical Jacob's Ladder they had used to climb up here into a spiraling slide. The rungs of the ladder expanded and merged into a smooth slope, still enveloped in that gentle, comforting, bright light. The sight struck all four as slightly absurd: an arduous and dangerous journey on the way up had transformed, at a simple wave from Huhu, into a playground slide from the clouds. As the four slid down the long, winding surface, they realized that the white light—surely it wasn't mere common EM radiation?—seemed to not only provide illumination, but also to cushion and temper their speed, allowing them to reach the ground in comfort.

Upon reaching the bottom of the slide, Chang Tian and Yun Fan, the first to arrive, stood up and moved out of the way. Jiang Liu was the third, but he tarried at the bottom, as though still trying to extract every ounce of enjoyment out of the ride. Qi Fei, the last to descend, rammed into him.

"Did you learn nothing in kindergarten?" Qi Fei yelled at him. "When you get to the bottom of a slide, you have to get up right away!"

"My favorite game as a kid was to sit at the bottom of a slide and cause a big pileup of kids to be stuck behind me. It was so much fun," Jiang Liu said, wearing a nostalgic grin.

"Are you still a kid?" Qi Fei glared at him. "Should we make you take a nap and give you a juice pack?"

"I never got to go on the slide after five," Jiang Liu said. "My mom wouldn't let me since she was annoyed at how my clothes got all dirty. You wouldn't believe how envious I was whenever I rode by a playground in my parents' car and saw all those kids playing in the mud. It's been more than twenty years since I last went down a slide. Can you believe it?" He looked at Qi Fei. "I want to go again. Want to come with?"

"I don't believe it," Qi Fei said. "What sort of 'representative of humanity' are you? We're being embarrassed in front of the entire multiverse."

"So what?" Jiang Liu gave him a playful shove. "Where in the multiverse are you going to find another slide this tall and awesome? You'll regret it if you don't go down it at least one more time."

"Fine." Qi Fei got up. "But how are we going to climb all the way back up again?"

"I can help you up," Huhu said. "Stand still."

Qi Fei and Jiang Liu stood on the bottom of the slide. Huhu waved their hands again and the slide began to move like an escalator, carrying the two up. A cloud of white light remained around their feet, securing them against the sloping surface. They went up hundreds of meters into the spherical cabin and slid down again. Jiang Liu was again in the lead, and once again, he refused to get up at the bottom. Qi Fei rammed into him.

"We have to do this again so I can show you how to get off a slide properly," Qi Fei said. "Looks like there's a lot I can teach you, in addition to how to fight."

"Ha! I think someone has forgotten who was teaching whom a lesson during the last fight."

"Oh, so you want to go again?"

"Who's embarrassing humanity in front of the whole multiverse now?"

Yun Fan and Chang Tian smiled awkwardly at Huhu. "Ah . . . sorry. These two can be rather childish."

"Oh, don't worry about it," Huhu said, joyfully wobbling their head. "I love it when others play with me. You'll probably be surprised to know that Ying Zheng was even more childish and playful than these two."

"Ying Zheng! The first emperor?!" Yun Fan's chin was on the floor.

"That's right," Huhu sighed. "We first met him when he was fourteen, right after he became the king. By the time we left, he was fifty-one. I loved the time we spent with him. In our inspection team, I was the youngest; everyone was so serious all the time and bossed me around, but no one would just have fun with me. The first few times we went to Earth, all the humans we met were also super serious and not fun at all: Agamemnon, Moses, and so on. But Ying Zheng was a kid, and I was overjoyed. We had so much fun together."

"If I'm understanding this correctly," Yun Fan said, "you stayed on Earth that time for more than thirty years. Is that right?"

"That's correct. Most of this loong-ship was built by Ying Zheng's craftsmen during the time we visited him. We stayed so long because humans finally had the technology to build the ship we wanted. During the previous visits, you were so primitive technologically that we could only get a few small components made. We're very grateful to Ying Zheng for helping us build the main hull of the ship."

"Just how old are you?" Yun Fan asked. "If you had visited Earth on earlier visits as well, I'm guessing you must be at least several thousand years in age. Am I right?"

Huhu shook their head. "Uh, you can't convert time between universes in such a simplistic manner. But how do I explain this? Uh—"

Jiang Liu broke in. "Is it like in a game? As a player-character, you might experience multiple lifetimes in the game. But from the perspective of a programmer, they might observe generations of player-characters without aging more than a few days."

Huhu pondered Jiang Liu's analogy. "It's similar, but not really. Basically, different systems have their own times that cannot be compared via direct conversion. If you must use an analogy, Jiang Liu's is fine."

Just then, a square-faced teenaged boy, about fourteen or fifteen, ran into that part of the ship. He was dressed in a black silk mianfu robe embroidered with taotie motifs and wore his hair in the slanted faji bun unique to the Qin state during the Warring States period. The boy ran up to Huhu and playfully punched them in the chest. "Da Hu! Where have you been? I was looking for you."

Yun Fan and the others were stupefied. *This boy must be Ying Zheng!* They saw that even Huhu's metal face seemed especially kind and at peace and realized that they must be seeing a vision-projection from Huhu's memories.

"I . . . I went somewhere very far away," Huhu said.

"You should have taken me!" the boy complained. "I told you already. You must take me wherever you go next."

"I promise. I'll take you the next time I have to leave."

"I was worried that you'd never return," young Ying Zheng said. "I realized that I had no way to contact you. Can you show me how to send a message to you if you aren't around?"

Huhu nodded. "I will."

"Will you leave one day and never come back?"

"That won't happen," Huhu said. "We'll always return periodically."

"But by then I'll be dead," Ying Zheng said. "Mencius said that a sage emerges every five hundred years, but I won't last five hundred years. How about you never leave?"

Huhu touched Ying Zheng's head affectionately. "We aren't leaving anytime soon. When we do have to leave, we'll take you—if you still want to go with us then. But if you don't want to leave, I'll teach you the secret of extending your life so that you can wait until we return."

"Really? Really?" Ying Zheng jumped up and down excitedly. "You'll teach me to be an immortal?"

"I will!"

Joyfully, Ying Zheng ran on deeper into the ship, disappearing into the murk.

Huhu walked deeper into the ship. Their bronze body was clumsy and awkward, but their stride was steady and determined. Wherever they stepped, light appeared around them, revealing dimly glimpsed scenes and the faint voices of many.

Yun Fan and the rest knew that they should follow Huhu closely. They were witnessing Huhu's precious memories of human history. The past was gone; even though some artifacts could be recovered via excavation, living memory could never be recovered. The stories behind the artifacts, the who and what and why, no one would ever be able to know for certain. Humanity's knowledge of its own past was not nearly as vivid as what was preserved in Huhu's head. The alien inspection team had collected drops from humanity's ten-thousand-year march through civilization, and they could re-project those memories anytime. But the memory of humanity itself lasted no more than a single generation. Even events of just two or three decades ago were often completely forgotten—we were no better than goldfish with their famous seven-second memory. How could a species so prone to forgetting the past survive in the eternal river of the multiverse?

As they followed Huhu through the ship, the deadly traps and weapons Qi Fei and Jiang Liu had seen earlier were nowhere to be found. They were surrounded by vision-projections of history; the air filled with dust while laborers strained to push heavily laden wheelbarrows. Huhu's perspective was atop a tall ceremonial dais: a group of women bearing sacrificial goods and purified water solemnly climbed onto the dais. Then many metal mythical beasts appeared: some with nine tails, some with three heads and six arms—it was as though the bestiary of *Shan Hai Jing* had been unleashed into the world.

Huhu turned to explain that early on, when humans first learned metal casting, they didn't yet know how to make their own models. To facilitate learning, the aliens used air-print technology to print the beast designs from their home planet on Earth with molten metal.

Surrounded by these visions, every human felt a sense of reverential awe. This was a condensation of thousands of years of historical progress—all that effort, all that once-upon-a-time, had vanished into dust. Each life was so brief, and even the duration of a dynasty or a civilization was but a flash in the long flow of the cosmos. Yet the face of each person in those visions, in that brief glimpse, was no different from the faces of humans today: filled with hope, pain, idealism, desire.

This was how humanity passed through time.

Huhu stopped abruptly, lightly tapping their own head as though they had just remembered something. "Did you bring the object of Ying Zheng's task?"

Yun Fan nodded. "I have it."

"Then I need to bring you all to my planet; that's where you must finish your mission." Huhu looked at them. "How about it? Want to visit my world?"

Four hearts leaped wildly as Huhu's large metal eyes stared at them unblinkingly. Those wide curving lips seemed to be always smiling, adding to the eerie atmosphere of the ship. They looked at Huhu and then at one another, uncertain what awaited them in the future.

14 | Jump

"Of course we want to go!" Yun Fan said. "It's what we've been waiting for!"

"But how do we make the trip?" Qi Fei asked.

"The same way I came here," Huhu said. "You'll just be doing the reverse."

"But how can we 'transmit' our consciousnesses?" Qi Fei was amazed. "Don't we need to . . . uh . . . upgrade our brains or something?"

"You do," Huhu said. "But it's a very simple operation. I can do it—I've done it for a few humans already."

"I had no idea it would be that simple." Qi Fei was hesitant. He wanted to know exactly how the "operation" worked—it wasn't that he didn't trust Huhu, but he had trouble accepting anything that he couldn't work out fully for himself.

"There are many levels to this process." Huhu pointed to their own metal head and then pointed at the air around them. "Transmitting your consciousnesses is the most basic level. I can help you through that, but I don't know about the higher levels. Once we reach the inspection station, you should ask the captain. All right, who's coming?"

"Me!" Yun Fan said.

"Count me in," Jiang Liu said.

"I'll go as well," Qi Fei said.

"Just one second," Chang Tian said. "I have a question. What will happen to our bodies if our consciousnesses are transmitted somewhere else?"

"Your bodies will rest in deep sleep in the supply compartment of this ship. It won't be very long. As I mentioned, time cannot be directly converted, so how long you spend on my planet won't match the duration of time passing here. The only thing that matters is topological correspondence—that is, events will be in the same order—and everything will work out fine. By the time you get back, your bodies will have only aged slightly."

"Shouldn't someone stay around to watch over the deep sleep equipment and guard the bodies?" Chang Tian asked. "What if something goes wrong in the supply compartment?"

"I don't think that's necessary," Huhu said. "If something went wrong, you wouldn't know how to fix it anyway."

"What?" Now everyone was worried.

"All right. Maybe it is better to have someone guard the bodies. The equipment is programmed with multiple emergency plans: to repair the equipment, to repair the compartment, and to perform rescue services in extreme emergencies. It's not a bad idea to leave someone behind to help in cases of extreme emergency."

"Then I'll stay to guard your bodies," Chang Tian said to the other three. "Now, behave yourselves. Don't fight with each other; don't get lost; and don't argue with strangers."

The three nodded—despite the advice being no different from what one might say to kindergartners, they found it hard to argue against.

Huhu walked farther along the loong-ship until they reached a particular spot in the curving corridor. They touched a wall, and a door appeared and slid back, revealing a passage leading upward. Yun Fan and the others realized that the corridor was full of hidden doors like this one, and they all led to the center of the circle formed by the loong-ship. Structurally, once the loong-ship had swallowed its own tail, there seemed to be multiple spokes from the hub to the rim, each terminating in a hidden door. They entered the door and found themselves in a vertical passage lined with multiple deep sleep chambers.

Huhu ascended the passage with them until they were again near the hub. There, the alien opened several chambers and indicated that they should enter and lie down.

"Were these built in the Qin dynasty as well?" Yun Fan asked.

"The shells were cast by Ying Zheng's craftsmen," Huhu said, "but the internal microcircuits were laid down by us. Typically, this is how we work: On each alien planet, we ask the natives to build workshops. Then we use gryons to holographically demonstrate the production process for all components and designs, which the native workers can imitate and learn from. We also give energy assistance so that kilns and furnaces all function many times more efficiently, enhancing the quality of the metals that are produced. For large engineering projects we can also provide energy assistance so that the projects wouldn't require too many native laborers. We must be responsible for the circuits and electronics, of course, but they are not that hard. We deploy gryons to make microadjustments to magnetic fields, and then we use the precision magnetic fields to lay down circuits. Whatever can be designed can be realized this way. In fact, such gryon-matter interaction is common in the cosmos."

Jiang Liu spoke up. "I've been meaning to ask: How does your ship propel itself? How can it reach nearly the speed of light?"

"Ah, we rely on matter-antimatter annihilation," Huhu said. "It's the simplest approach, since it doesn't require the ship to carry its own fuel. As the ship flies, it's capturing and absorbing fakunpu particles—which you don't know about yet. This is an extremely massive super particle with a medium reaction cross section, one of fifteen dark matter particles you've yet to discover. I have to say that you're much too careless with the way you think about 'dark matter' and 'dark energy.' These are generic names for more than thirty completely different particles and processes—and I'm only talking about major particles—Ah! I shouldn't digress so much. Anyway, fakunpu particles are very sparse in your universe, but they are their own antiparticle, so as long as you gather enough of them and confine them in a powerful magnetic field, they'll annihilate one another and generate tremendous amounts of energy."

"Ah! So that's why you need the magnetic fields of white dwarves." Jiang Liu looked at Huhu admiringly.

"To be clear, these techniques are useful only for short-distance flights," Huhu said. "Since you and the other Milky Way civilization are only about 330 light-years apart, we can watch over both with a single ship shuttling back and forth and share the equipment on the ship with both civilizations. But this is no good for civilizations outside your galaxy. The next nearest civilization is more than two million light-years from you, and even if we could tolerate a trip that long, the material making up the ship would never last through it. In such cases, we have to rely on each galaxy or planet making their own vessels and shells for our minds."

"But why do you need avatars at all?" Jiang Liu asked. "It seems like a lot of trouble. You might as well directly communicate via gryons."

"That won't work. *We* can communicate directly using gryons, but *you* can't."

"That's not what I meant," Jiang Liu said awkwardly. "Since you can control so many things remotely using gryon-matter interaction, why don't you just do everything yourself? Why go to so much trouble to have the natives build you ships and avatar bodies?"

Huhu looked thoughtful. "Ah, I understand your confusion now. There are two primary reasons we go to so much trouble, as you put it. First, there's the matter of energy. Having you do the construction, while we project models and directions and give energy assistance, doesn't require us to expend a lot of mental energy. On the other hand, if we were to control matter in your universe remotely and conduct mega-engineering directly, it would be a huge drain on our mental resources. Second, I feel that you haven't quite grasped the reason behind our actions. We come to your universe not for your matter—what good are your resources to us? We're also not here just to teach you some technology—what good is technology on its own? Our true purpose is to help your civilization ascend the ladder of wisdom, so that eventually you can develop into a gryon-aware civilization, a civilization capable of entangling with ours and evolving together with us. To do that, you must learn and improve. This is facilitated by having physical manifestations, shells containing our minds, so that we can converse face-to-face like this. You learn better this way."

Yun Fan burst out laughing. "So you specialize in education! No wonder you're always talking like a grade-school teacher. 'I want to hear *your* answer.'"

"Pay attention," Huhu stood with arms akimbo. "I've worked hard on these explanations. If you were to talk with the captain, I'm sure they wouldn't be nearly as patient."

Qi Fei had another question. "You've mentioned your captain multiple times. But why aren't they here? Are you the only one from the inspection team on duty?"

"I am," Huhu said, sighing. "The rest are all too busy right now. Our planet is facing a crisis. In the past, a visit was very different. One time, we had almost forty members on the team! And we used twenty, thirty steerable shells and stayed on

Earth for years. But for the last couple of visits I was the only one to make it, and I couldn't get much done."

"When did the visit when you had almost forty members on the team take place?" Yun Fan asked.

"Oh, that was the eleventh century BCE by your reckoning," Huhu said. "Not only did my inspection team come, another team nearby also stopped by for the visit. It was a grand party! We took over a few mountains on Earth, and the two teams had a friendly competition and mock fight, with wagers and everything. Later, the ancient Greeks and your ancestors ended up telling stories about our deeds during that time."

"Are you talking about the Homeric epics and *Fengshen Yanyi*?" Yun Fan asked. The fantastic revelations came nonstop.

"Yes," Huhu said, their metal lips smiling. "I really enjoy reading your stories about what we did."

"So all the stories about Zeus, Prometheus, Nezha, and all the other heroes and gods were about *you*?" Jiang Liu asked.

"Yes, in a manner of speaking," Huhu said. "The way you named us . . . it's confusing."

"What about the eighteenth century BCE?" Yun Fan asked. "Do myths of the Great Flood have anything to do with you?"

"That was our fault," Huhu said. "At the time, we were thinking of constructing a semi-permanent base on the Qinghai-Tibet Plateau. We decided to build the whole thing through remote manipulation, but my shixiong made some errors in the calculations and released too much energy, which melted the glaciers on two mountains. There was massive flooding in both the Middle East and China. The captain was so mad that they put my shixiong in confinement. My shixiong, intent on atoning for this error, snuck out onto Earth in a steerable shell to try to salvage the situation. They ended up using a flawed program that caused gryons near the surface of the Earth and within a certain range to self-replicate, which led to a massive buildup of gryons that gathered matter, essentially materializing earth out of thin air in order to dam and control the flooding. But abusing gryons in this manner led to a massive, unsustainable drain of mental energy, which almost collapsed the tunnel between your universe and ours. The massive flood of chaotic mental energy even twisted the very curvature of space. The magistrate back on our home planet was so angry at this that they handed down a most severe punishment for my shixiong, so the captain had to send them back to a sealed rehabilitation space. Later, I also helped with the channeling of the floodwaters on Earth. What a terrible situation! That was why all of us from then on had to follow the rule that inspection teams aren't allowed to directly perform mega-engineering on alien planets but must collaborate with the natives."

"Ah. So your shixiong must be Gun, the hero who stole from the Yellow Emperor xirang, the magical soil that constantly grew, in order to help the people fight the flood," Yun Fan said. "Then . . . that must make you Yu the Great!"

"Your names are too confusing!" Huhu said. "I get a different name every time I visit Earth. Yes, I confess that those deeds were mine, but please stick to calling me Huhu."

Yun Fan made some mental calculations. "Let me see . . . I'm going to guess that Erlitou culture, where we found the earliest Chinese bronzeware, was also the result of your intervention. Correct?"

"Yes," Huhu said. "That was our first attempt to collaborate with you through a workshop. We never imagined the collaboration would last a few thousand years. Luckily, even as the humans in power changed, the techniques were passed on."

Yun Fan nodded thoughtfully. "Xia, Shang, and Zhou all had secret technologies and rituals. It was said that whoever learned these secrets would conquer the rest of the land. So your teachings were behind the legends of the nine ding of power. The secrets were well protected."

"You're right about that," Huhu said. "Ying Zheng's father learned the secrets and found out about us. That was how we ended up working together."

Yun Fan still had more questions. "Have you always landed in a spaceship and deployed avatars when you visited Earth?"

"Not necessarily," Huhu said.

"I want to know if you came around thirteen hundred CE," Yun Fan said. "The material evidence for your previous visits was very strong: the pyramids, Egyptian and Mayan, sudden improvements in bronzeware, the mausoleum, and so on. There was also an oral tradition in myths and historical legends that clearly reflected your presence. But after the Maya, there seemed to be no more evidence of alien visits."

"That's because I was the only one visiting that time," Huhu said. "I told you: I couldn't do much by myself."

"Did you not even bother to land?" Yun Fan asked.

"I did come down on a tiny pod," Huhu said. "I found a spot in the deserts of central Asia, and I used a metal sculpture as my shell—I think you saw it earlier. Anyway, I met a man named Marco Polo, who was on his way back to Italy from China. We had a good chat. I told him that he must work hard to bring back to Europe the books on mathematics that had scattered to the East. The Greeks had been on the verge of multiple important breakthroughs. But then the most important knowledge was lost, and the books were scattered all over Asia. Unless they gathered those books again and built on them, human civilization wasn't going to develop properly. He agreed to help me look for those books.

"I went on to Italy and met Dante, who was very interesting. We talked and talked, and I told him so many stories—even more than I told you. He didn't know as much as you, so he didn't ask nearly as many questions; however, he was so imaginative! I would tell him one thing and he'd make up ten verses on the spot."

"I had no idea!" Yun Fan sighed with the satisfaction of finally being shown the solution to puzzles that had long bothered her. "There are many competing theories on the origin of the Renaissance, and scholars can't agree on the start of the Xia dynasty. I had some guesses in both cases, but only now do I truly understand what happened."

"To be honest, I was very worried about this current visit," Huhu said. "Your civilization has moved from the Age of Worship to the Age of Expansion. This is when communication is most difficult."

"Can you explain these terms?" Yun Fan asked.

"During the Age of Worship, a civilization dreams of a greater power, a power that is in charge, a power that can come to its aid. Such civilizations find everything mysterious, including the forces of nature and the weather, and are prone to worshipping mysterious powers, such as a more advanced civilization. They are very receptive to teaching and help. But over time, as civilizations grow and learn and increase in wisdom, they begin to gain power over nature. As they become the masters of luminous matter, they enter the Age of Expansion. This is when a civilization believes it is the master of all that it surveys, when it feels itself the center of the universe and refuses to accept teachings from anyone. The real issue here isn't the level of technology, but psychology. In the Age of Expansion, civilizations are focused only on successes and achievements. They neither care about the past nor fear the future; the only thing they want is to enjoy the glory of the present. Civilizations in this stage cannot advance even when they receive technological assistance."

"If we hadn't come to meet you, what would have been your plan?" Yun Fan asked.

"I wasn't even sure if I wanted to land," Huhu said. "Your civilization has reached the point where you will no longer treat alien advice as revelations from the gods; rather, you'd very likely want me to prove my power by producing some weapons. In fact, the only things you'd want me to give you would be powerful weapons. But that isn't how a civilization advances. If I refuse to do as you ask, you'd very likely capture me and take me apart. But after that, you'd discover my body to consist of nothing more than ordinary bits of bronze put together using earthly techniques, at which point you'd discard the pieces, disgusted."

"I have to say that things would have likely turned out exactly the way you predicted," conceded Qi Fei.

"That's why it's tough to help civilizations in your position," Huhu said. "Whether you can advance beyond this point is largely out of our hands."

"It seems very inefficient to devote so much energy to cultivating allies for your union," Qi Fei said. "According to what you just told me, a large portion of the civilizations you inspect end up stuck in narcissistic admiration or die from internal enmity. It doesn't seem a profitable venture."

"Humans also engage in venture capital investment, right?" Huhu said. "The principle is the same. Although very few civilizations will advance to the point where they're capable of entangling with us, each one is a tremendous help to all of us. Currently, our union has a total of 831 civilizations from all over the multiverse, each distinct in its mode of thinking. Our combined information exchange has produced an incredible amount of mental energy. More than a few of these civilizations emerged from the efforts of inspection teams like mine."

"So many!" exclaimed Qi Fei.

"We need to go see for ourselves," Jiang Liu said. "We can ask questions all day, but we'll still learn more just by being there."

"I think so too," Yun Fan said. "Besides, I have to complete my mission."

Huhu nodded. "Go ahead and lie down in the deep sleep apparatus."

"What about the message I'm supposed to bring to the first emperor?" Yun Fan asked as she lay down.

"Don't worry," Huhu said. "The moment you placed the icosahedron inside the receptacle, the message therein was transmitted to my home world. You just need to go and help him unseal it."

Reassured, Yun Fan lay down, completely at peace. Jiang Liu and Qi Fei, though nervous about what was to happen, also lay down in their own deep sleep chambers.

"One more thing," Huhu said. "The transmission process is pretty simple, and you won't feel much. But once there, you'll have to learn to steer a body that isn't yours, with your will. It's difficult the first time, and you'll feel as though you're no longer you. But you'll adjust."

"What bodies will we be steering?" Jiang Liu asked.

"Oh, it's not too different from the one I'm wearing," Huhu said. "You'll see in a bit."

The three closed their eyes as a gas-like light enveloped them, bringing with it a deep sense of drowsiness. As they fell asleep, they seemed to feel the walls of the deep sleep chambers close in on them, soft and noiseless, like night.

+ + + + +

The time that followed passed both quickly and slowly.

They dreamed, but it was no ordinary dream. They felt their surroundings weren't real, like in a dream, but they also knew they weren't dreaming. It was a feeling they'd never had, and thus impossible to put into words.

Everything had fallen apart, including the self. There was no more "I," not even the role of an observer in a dream. All that was left were fragments of consciousness, inseparable from everything in the cosmos, drifting, churning, broken, but still aware. Nothing was connected, the self had dissolved into a million pieces, but still, a clear perception that thinking went on, indicating the existence of a continuous self-constructing mind. It was so strange. So very very strange.

They saw bits and pieces: faces they thought they'd forgotten, words that had hurt so much in childhood, arguments that they preferred to bury, terrifying nooks and crannies, things that could never be sorted through or explained, shards of time. They seemed to be drowning in a sea of memories, torn apart by waves of information.

The time seemed to last forever, but also passed in but a fraction of a moment. The three awakened.

They saw first the massive ceiling looming far above. The building they were in was cone-shaped: a circular base and a circular wall that ascended and narrowed to a single point. Eight bright beams of golden light shot up from the floor, converging in a large, indistinct ball of light near the apex of the ceiling. The building towered hundreds of meters, so high that they couldn't see the very top. It was a single grand hall as tall as a building of several hundred stories on Earth.

Awed by the sight, they lay still for a long time. Only gradually did they start to pay attention to . . . their bodies.

Jiang Liu was the first to recover. He tried to lift his arm.

His brain gave the order: *Lift the arm.* But two attempts resulted in no movement. He changed tactics. Instead of trying to do anything, he tried to *feel* for the boundaries of his own body, to sense where he ended and the rest of the universe began. After a few attempts, he suddenly *felt* his fingertips and arms. He tried to twitch his fingers; it worked! He felt the flat surface he was lying on. He tried to lift his arm again, and this time it worked.

He put a hand up in front of his eyes. He had to suppress the sudden urge to throw *it* away.

It was no hand, but an iron claw.

Terrified, he strained to sit up so he could look over himself. Following what had worked earlier, he started by trying to *feel* for every part of his body, and to move a part of the body only after he had recovered the sensation of touch there. It took much effort to recover the use of his legs, but the torso was even harder. For some reason, this body felt so much heavier than the flesh-and-blood body he had possessed back on Earth. Even after he could move all his limbs, sitting up seemed like a monumental task.

Finally, he managed to roll over onto his side, from which pose he could push against the surface with his hands—no, claws—until he was finally upright.

That was when he saw Qi Fei—or at least what he thought must be Qi Fei.

Oh my goodness. Qi Fei is now a loong!

Qi Fei was a loong made of steel (though it could be some other metal as well). Well, a quasi-loong, or some form of loong-ish creature. Certainly not a dinosaur, and also not the serpentine loong that inspired the spaceship. This creature had a loong-formed head, sharp horns, long spines pointing away from the back of the head, a body covered in scales, and a thick, crocodilian tail. The whole body glowed a deep, iridescent blue, and the scales and joints were perfectly formed and intricate beyond belief.

Jiang Liu had a pretty good idea of what he himself looked like now. He turned to look the other way. There was Yun Fan—or what he hoped was Yun Fan. She had turned into a golden fenghuang, also made of metal, with giant, graceful wings. But the face wasn't that of a bird, but more like a doe's. Even her feet resembled the fleet hooves of a deer.

Jiang Liu extended a claw to help Qi Fei and Yun Fan sit up.

They saw one another, and amazement flooded all their faces.

"What do I look like?" Jiang Liu asked, even though he had already guessed.

He realized that he could speak, and the process felt perfectly normal. There was a slight delay between hearing the voice and feeling his mouth speak, as well as slight alterations in his timbre. He figured that it must be the result of some kind of computational simulation—the metal loong avatar must be equipped with translation and speech synthesis equipment.

Qi Fei looked to Yun Fan, who said, "You and he—ahem. Excuse me. I have to get used to this voice . . . Ahem! You look similar to him. But your body is white and a bit shorter. As for the spines on your head and tail, they're a pale blue, lighter in shade than his."

"I see," Jiang Liu said. "Can you tell where we are?"

A familiar voice sounded behind them. "You're awake! How do you feel?"

They turned and saw a qilin running at them. Yes, it was a real qilin. The body was flesh and blood—or at least some sort of organic matter. Although the qilin was covered in thick scales, the body underneath was supple and agile, nothing like the metallic bodies the three of them wore. The qilin was bright fuchsia in color, but the scales on the back as well as the horns all glowed a shining golden hue, very pretty. The qilin wore steel armor on their limbs and neck. Eyes glowing with joy, they ran three loops around the three embodied humans before finally stopping.

"It's me!" The voice was Huhu's. "Don't you recognize me?"

"I didn't realize that you . . . are a qilin!" Yun Fan said.

"Ha. When I was on Earth, I showed my picture to some humans. I had no idea they would write down a description and pass it down so many generations."

Jiang Liu chuckled. "So this is why Confucius said that sages emerge when qilin return to the world. He was basing it on your photos."

"You seem to be doing great in your steerable shells!" Huhu said. "Some species can't make the adjustment after transmission."

"Have many species come here?" Yun Fan asked.

"Yes. Our planet is one of the five major bases of the Union of Cooperating Civilizations," Huhu said, "and we're also one of the oldest civilizations in the union. Many newer member civilizations gained entry through us."

"Where do we go now?" Jiang Liu asked.

"I'll take you to see the captain," Huhu said. "They love Earth. Except for the last two times, they've been on every mission to your planet. Whatever questions you still have, I'm sure the captain will have answers. The captain is amazing."

"I need to sort something out with you first," Jiang Liu said. "You told us that the bodies we'd be steering would be similar to the Sanxingdui bronze figure you were using. So how did we end up as loong and fenghuang?"

"I told you 'not too different from the one I'm wearing.' That's topologically speaking, right? As long as the body has one head, one torso, two eyes, a mouth, four limbs, and a central organ of cognition, my point applies! It's sufficient to be able to project your brain and every part controlled by your brain to a corresponding part in the new body. Now, if the new body had six arms, five light-sensing organs, and other tubes that go all the way through in addition to the gastrointestinal tract, I wouldn't be saying that, and you'd have a much harder time controlling the new body. Do you see?"

"I understand why you said what you said," Jiang Liu said, "in theory. But you . . . should have given us more details!"

As Qi Fei shuffled off his platform, he asked Huhu, "How do you pick the shells for minds from other universes? Can any random object be steered as a suitable vehicle?"

"Of course not," Huhu said. "The steerable vessels are always meticulously prepared. It must be first coated in an ultra-thin layer of carbon fiber membrane, which functions as a kind of super nervous system for the object. This is done by carefully directing gryons, which in turn control the electromagnetic field, which nudges the carbon fibers into position. This is of course what civilized minds do. Now, there is a barbarous technique for steering, which involves simply taking over another brain—"

Huhu was interrupted by the opening of a massive door at the side of the conical hall. An even larger qilin strode in, along with a gust of wind. The larger qilin was apparently older, judging by the wrinkles on their face, and the armor they wore seemed to suggest an individual with more power. This qilin also wore a helmet with long, colorful spikes on the back, perhaps some kind of weapon or communications equipment.

They strode up to Huhu, and both qilin's horns began to glow brightly. Huhu's body language immediately changed, showing that the qilin was very tense.

Huhu turned to the humans—or the loong and fenghuang—and said, "This is our captain, Teailuedidateluaisilukelaiqinaimihuoqiwusilinlinte•Miaier•Yangsiwuti, recipient of the highest Medal of Honor of Planet Liluhuoman, Commander of the Third Echelon, Preceptor at the Lintehuoyiaierlandasipututewuaiti Academy.

"Captain . . . Te!" Yun Fan extended a wing. "It's an honor."

"It's a pleasure to meet all of you," the captain rumbled. "I've heard about everything you've accomplished. Earth is one of my favorite planets, and I would have really liked to show you around. However, this isn't a good time. We're now at defense readiness level 0, and everyone is about to go into battle. If I should live beyond this catastrophe, I promise to invite you again for a proper visit."

The tension and anxiety in their voice was plain to hear, despite their attempt to remain calm. Oddly, despite the translation apparatus and their different appearances, planets, and even universes of origin, it was no trouble at all for the humans to sense the emotional content in the captain's speech. The captain's unease and apprehension floated through the air and weighed heavily on the hearts of the three humans.

"May we ask what threat is facing your world today?" Qi Fei asked. "Can we help in any way?"

Captain Te shook their head. "There's basically nothing you can do against an assault from a devouring civilization. Its civilizational rank is above even ours. Though we cannot win a head-to-head contest, we'll strive mightily and refuse to yield."

"What is a civilizational rank?" Jiang Liu asked. "If it's so advanced, why is it still intent on devouring others?"

"There's no time to explain," the captain said. "Come. Follow me." The qilin pointed to a door on the other side of the conical hall. "I'll bring Ms. Yun to complete her mission now. All of you should then return to Earth as soon as possible. Oh, but wait." The captain paused. Twisting their head around, they asked, "Could I trouble you to bring something to Earth on your return voyage?"

"It would be no trouble at all," Qi Fei said. "We'd be happy to do this for you."

"Good. Then there's still hope," the captain said. "This will not be easy. I have no words for my gratitude."

"Not at all," Qi Fei said. "I've learned that your world has aided the advancement of humanity multiple times in history. This is the least we can do."

Captain Te nodded, indicating that they should all follow. Jiang Liu, Qi Fei, and Yun Fan all scrambled off the platforms they had been resting on and tottered after the captain—they still weren't used to moving in the bodies of these mythical beasts.

With Huhu and the three humans trailing, the captain strode through a corridor, turned twice, passed through a door, until they entered a garden under a glass dome. The place, about the size of two football fields, was covered in lush grass and verdant trees. In the middle was a plot of about twenty red flowers that resembled roses, but with smaller, translucent petals, and no thorns. The flowers were all quite distant from one another.

Captain Te lifted a front paw and waved at the flowers. One floated out of the plot and hovered next to them. Flowing fluid and air bubbles could be seen within the translucent branches and leaves, while the roots, devoid of any soil, glowed a greenish blue.

"I've been cultivating this garden for ages," Captain Te said. "These pity flowers took a great deal of effort, and I can't bear to see them annihilated in the coming war. Can you take one to Earth? If we should survive the trial, I'll ask you to bring it back. But if we perish, please care for it on my behalf on Earth."

"This flower must be very special," Qi Fei said.

"Indeed. As you know, every civilization begins by drawing on the power of its own star. It's only when the civilization has advanced to voyaging through the grand cosmos that it draws on the power of other stars. One way to rank civilizations is by their efficiency in the utilization of the power of their stars. On Earth, right now you derive almost all your power from your sun, excepting a negligible amount of nuclear energy. Much of that solar power you draw only after it has been fixed via photosynthesis. For instance, your food, vegetal or animal, is all based ultimately on plant photosynthesis. The fossil fuels you burn for electricity are also converted from the products of past photosynthesis. Therefore, the efficiency of photosynthesis is the core parameter determining your overall energy efficiency.

"Currently, you're focused on exploring better utilization of wind power and hydro power. These are fine approaches, but most other civilizations have gone down a different route to upgrading their overall energy efficiency: improving the efficiency of photosynthesis. On Earth, photosynthesis is centered around chlorophyll, the result of a fortuitous mutation that has continued to influence all subsequent energy pathways. In contrast, this pity flower's photosynthesis efficiency is four orders of magnitude grander than chlorophyll's.

"I'm sure you can work out that should the key pathways in the pity flower spread and become common on Earth, most of your energy difficulties would fall away. But even more crucially, pity flowers have extremely long roots. In cultivating it, my hope was that its root system would penetrate every inch of our planet's soil. These roots have a unique ability to record information, such that even when the plant is taken away from the soil of its birth, it should be possible to replicate all aspects of its origin world through the information embedded in its roots.

"If survivors of our people must begin to rebuild on a new planet . . ." Here, the captain paused, as though something was constricting their throat. "So long as the plant survives as well, it should be possible to recreate this world and give the survivors their first taste of home."

"We understand," Qi Fei said, accepting the pity flower with great care. "We'll keep it safe and bring it back as soon as the crisis is over."

"I have a question," Jiang Liu said. "We understand jumping between universes to involve only the transmission of consciousness. How can we jump back with a physical object such as this flower?"

Huhu broke in. "When I explained jumping between universes, I was only discussing the simplest, most basic form. There are higher levels of jumping that can allow matter to travel between universes, involving the use of inter-universal wormholes."

"How?" Jiang Liu asked. He was a bit miffed. If physically jumping was possible, why did they have to become loong and fenghuang?

"That requires individuals with extremely powerful minds," Huhu said.

Captain Te nodded. "Jumping between universes is based on entanglement being equivalent to wormholes. This is something your own scientists have begun to realize."

"What? I've never heard of such a thing!" exclaimed Jiang Liu.

"The theory was first proposed back in the 2010s, by your calendar, and then in the 2030s, as a result of lack of experimental confirmation. It was largely forgotten, though you still find humans talking about it now and then."

"Oh, now I remember," Jiang Liu said. "You're talking about ER=EPR, am I right? It's about the Einstein–Podolsky–Rosen paradox entanglement being equivalent to an Einstein-Rosen bridge, if I remember correctly."

"That's it," Captain Te said. "Among your theories, that one comes closest to the truth. Entanglement is equivalent to bridging distance. However, you cannot entangle matter between two universes. Only gryons can entangle across universes and open wormholes. Ordinarily, such entanglement is limited to information, not matter. That is how your minds can come visit our universe but not your bodies. But there is a special case: when the apparatus creating the information entanglement is located close to the site of the entanglement, such that the separation between the two universes is infinitely blurred until a true wormhole appears for the briefest of moments, the entanglement apparatus can straddle the universes.

"But there is one rule that cannot be broken: any apparatus or equipment driven by mental energy cannot pass through such a wormhole. This is analogous to the principle by which perpetual motion machines are impossible. You cannot generate more electricity from a generator powered by electricity. The only source of infinite mental energy is the organ of cognition of a sentient being—that is why we call the energy of gryons mental energy, for consciousness is its greatest generator—and so, an individual of extraordinary mental strength can, by entangling universes with their own mind, jump across universes."

As the humans strained to digest this barely-comprehensible speech, Captain Te gave the final conclusion: "I'm going to send Aluosikong"—he pointed at Huhu—"and this pity flower to your universe. Please take care of them."

"What?" Huhu shouted in shock.

"We must preserve hope in the face of the apocalypse," the captain said.

15 | The Mission

"Captain, I won't go!" Huhu said. "My place is here, fighting next to you."

"I gave you an order," the captain said. "You must preserve the spark of our civilization."

Huhu hesitated for some time before relenting. "When . . . should I leave?"

"We have about eight junols before the attack begins," the captain said. "Let's help Yun Fan finish her mission, and then you'll go."

"Understood." Huhu stood up straight, their horns glowing bright red.

Captain Te turned to Yun Fan and the others. "Come with me."

They emerged from the domed garden and followed another corridor on the other side. Along the way, they saw many other Liluhuomanians—all of them qilin—busy with preparations. Most were in sturdy armor with spikes on their backs and helmets.

Liluhuoman followed a uniform architectural style, with all the buildings shaped as geometric solids: cylinders, cones, square pyramids, pentagonal pyramids, and so on. The walls were smooth and flat, decorated with motifs reminiscent of ancient Chinese bronzeware. One side of each building was studded with spikes similar to those on the inhabitants' armor—the humans weren't sure if these were decorative or functional. The buildings were also connected by long corridors that reminded the humans of the loong-ship.

Qi Fei quickened his steps to move up next to Captain Te. "I'm very interested in gryons and mental energy. A question: Can artificial intelligence also produce mental energy?"

"You mean computers?" the captain answered. "Yes, of course."

"Is it possible to make computers the main producers of mental energy in a civilization then?"

"No, that isn't possible."

"Why not?"

"Because the intelligence of computers is derivative," Captain Te said. "I'll use an analogy. Earlier, we discussed how solar power is converted to bio power in animals and plants, which then become fossil fuels, which you dig up as fuel for your power plants to generate electricity. With each step you lose some power, and the final electrical energy you generate cannot exceed the original solar power input. The principle is the same when it comes to information. You take the thoughts generated by human brains and convert them to algorithms implemented in computers. Then you input into the computer human-derived data as raw material, which, after processing, becomes the output. But no matter how much computation happens in the middle, the final output cannot exceed the information in the brain in the first place."

Qi Fei shook his head. "That's not right. We've already seen many novel ideas generated by AI that weren't input by humans."

"Think about this carefully," Captain Te said. "You had to input all the algorithms and data for the AI to do their work, correct? These algorithms and data are the products of human cognition. The computer simply took them and gave you a result that you hadn't seen before, but the total amount of intelligence cannot exceed your input. All algorithms, image banks, linguistic corpora, voice recordings . . . everything the computer draws on are the products of human mental energy." Captain Te sighed. "Watching you obsessively attempting to create a more powerful intelligence through algorithms born from your own mind is like watching the fools who doggedly pursued the fantasy of perpetual motion machines."

"But how can brains generate an infinite amount of new information and mental energy?" Qi Fei asked, utterly at a loss. "What is the difference between a brain and a computer?"

"A brain is the product of the natural evolution of the cosmos itself, an instance of self-organization," Captain Te said. "I'm sorry, but there's simply not enough time today for me to delve into this complex topic. If I should survive today's battle, I'll be sure to explain everything to you in detail."

They stopped before a massive metal door. Captain Te's horns shifted through a range of hues, and the door, at least a meter thick, swung open slowly and silently. The metal surface was covered by square spirals that again reminded the humans of ancient bronzeware.

They found themselves staring into a vast and empty hall, bell-shaped, the floor decorated in radially symmetric patterns. The wall, painted an inky blue, seemed to show a night sky full of stars. The bright lights were connected by lines, not unlike paintings of the constellations on Earth. However, Jiang Liu and Qi Fei both remembered the hologram of the multiverse Huhu had shown them and realized that each light must represent a universe, and the lines must show links between universes.

The group walked into the hall, where the solemn air felt cold and weighty. Gazing up, they could see that hundreds of meters up, the ceiling let in a few beams of light that dimly illuminated the deep, inky, circular wall. They shivered involuntarily, overawed.

"This is Union Hall," the captain said. "All 831 member civilizations may be found on the wall."

Jiang Liu, Qi Fei, Yun Fan looked around; no one said anything.

"A ceremony is held here whenever a new civilization joins the union. A light representing that civilization is added to the wall on that occasion, which light is extinguished when that civilization withdraws from the union. Normally, civilizations communicate with one another through information entanglement, but this hall is still used to announce important decisions and to hold commemorative ceremonies."

Captain Te stood in the center of the hall, where they gently tapped a spot—the spot where all the swirling decorative lines on the floor converged—with a front paw. A small tower rose from the spot, about half the height of an adult human and half a meter in diameter. Lines similar to those on the floor spiraled up and down its surface.

"Come," Captain Te said to Yun Fan. "This is it."

Yun Fan went up to the tower. "What about . . . the information?"

"It's already inside," the captain said. "But you must open the seal. Ying Zheng himself wanted it to be this way."

Yun Fan nodded. She walked up and covered the tower with her magnificent wings. The graceful fenghuang form contrasted nicely with the metallic material of the body, giving her an august, sacred strength that drew wonder and admiration. Only then did Jiang Liu and Qi Fei realize that the fenghuang avatar was the perfect form for Yun Fan to complete her mission.

Yun Fan solemnly intoned, "Upon my death, let my body be taken by the spirit of loong, so that I may defend and protect the land of Huaxia for eternity."

Her voice was soft, but as she enunciated and paused between the syllables of the final pronouncement of the first emperor, her voice seemed a pure, ethereal instrument, sending forth a transcendent call that soared and echoed throughout the silent hall.

In response, the top of the small tower she was guarding began to glow. Circle by circle, ripples of light emanated from the luminous tip and rose up to form into a shining base suspended midair. A human figure appeared above it, rising and expanding, until he stood some forty meters tall, like a gigantic Buddhist statue.

It was unmistakably Qin Shi Huang.

To be sure, none of the humans present had ever seen the historical first emperor. The figure in the light didn't wear a robe embroidered with imperial loong motifs, nor did he wear a crown atop his head. However, the three were all seized with an unshakable conviction of the identity of the man looming above them. He wore a simple black robe edged in golden wave patterns. His hair was pulled into a tall bun, and a dark mustache sat above his upper lip. The slender face, angular and sharp, seemed chiseled out of rock, and those slender eyes, devoid of the upper eyelid crease, held a penetrating gaze.

Captain Te took a few steps and stopped just outside the circle at the center of the floor. A beam slanted down from the ceiling, spotlighting them. Instantly, a holographic projection of Captain Te appeared above, opposite the towering image of Qin Shi Huang. The qilin projection, also about forty meters in height, locked eyes with the emperor.

"Good to see you again, Ying Zheng," the captain said.

"Teacher, I'm sorry it's taken so long," the emperor said, holding up his cupped hands in a gongshou greeting.

"You should thank this woman, who carried you here." Captain Te nodded at Yun Fan. "She is wearing a shell right now, so she doesn't appear to be human. But it was she who cared for you and brought you all the way from your tomb to our universe."

"My gratitude knows no bounds," Ying Zheng said, bowing his head to Yun Fan. "Is your family name 'Yun'?"

"It is."

"Ah. Then Yun Da must be your father, or grandfather, correct?"

"You speak of my grandfather," Yun Fan said. "Fifty-seven years have passed since your encounter with him."

"That's longer than I expected," the emperor said, sighing. "Is Master Yun still well?"

"No. He's not well at all." Yun Fan's voice cracked with emotion. "My grandfather died at the age of fifty-five, before I was even born."

"What terrible news," the emperor said. "How did he die?"

"From cancer. I suspect that it had to do with proximity to a source of radiation." Yun Fan paused to get her own emotions under control. "My grandfather forced my father to swear, as a child, to dedicate his life to carrying out the task you assigned, no matter the difficulty or effort. Do you know what that meant? My father spent a lifetime searching for clues. You gave him almost nothing to go on, and more than two thousand years had passed. How was he supposed to find out exactly when and where aliens would return? My father carried out his promise to his father and to you faithfully: he studied archaeology, history, folklore and mythology, history of science, geography, anthropology, astronomy—he gained enough academic credentials for five or six PhD degrees! He lived in the library more than at home, combing through the maddeningly unclear historical record, trying to figure out the patterns in alien visitations.

"I can still recall, as a little girl, how terrified I was to see the walls of my home covered in strips of paper filled with dense print: history, mythology, archaeology, long ago events that mattered more to my father than the here and now . . . . You have no idea what you put my family through, do you? Because my father was captivated by something that no one else could see or understand, my mother went through hell. Her income had to support the entire family, and she had to run all the errands and take care of me all by herself. Later, when my father became the laughingstock of the world because of you and was fired from his job, it was the last straw for my poor mother. Do you understand any of this? A single word from you, a favor you wanted, ruined an entire family's life. You know nothing!"

Yun Fan was too choked up to go on.

Ying Zheng listened quietly. "I'm very sorry," he said at length. "I truly didn't understand how difficult the task would turn out to be."

"That's all I wanted," Yun Fan said. "Your apology. I cannot live up to the standards of my grandfather and father. They were men of faith, dedicated to the classical virtues, whose word was their bond. I saw my father die alone and disgraced, and I couldn't take it. I regretted not helping him earlier. Agreeing to help him, to carry out his unfinished task, was my way to atone, to give him peace in his last moments—but I also took up their task because I wanted to face you one day and tell you what you did to my family. I want you to understand what the people I loved went through to fulfill a promise to you. The classics admonish us to treasure a promise more than a vault full of gold—my father lived that ideal. You should apologize to *him*."

"I do," Ying Zheng said, not even attempting to argue or defend himself. "I am sincerely sorry for the sorrow I caused your family."

"Ah Zheng," Captain Te said, "you've changed."

Ying Zheng inclined his head in acknowledgment. "More than two thousand years have passed on Earth. If I were still the same man I was back then, I'd have wasted the gift of extra time."

Now that Yun Fan had finished her speech, she felt calmer. "First Emperor, I have one more question: What did you show my grandfather when you brought him inside the mausoleum? After that, he was utterly devoted to the task you gave him, and he would never agree to any plan to excavate the underground palace. Why?"

The emperor's voice was low and steady. "I showed him shadows of the debates between philosophers of the hundred schools of thought."

"What do you mean? I don't understand."

"Before construction on the mausoleum was completed, I invited the leading scholars of the hundred schools of thought to come into the underground palace and hold discussions and debates. It was an amazing sight: so much learning, so many new ideas! Everything was recorded by gryons. When I brought Master Yun into the palace, I showed him projections of the gryon recordings. The passing millennia had done nothing to diminish the power of that magnificent scene of intellectual blossoming. That was how I convinced him that I was telling the truth."

"So you didn't burn the books or bury the scholars alive, as so many have claimed," Yun Fan asked in wonder, "but actually encouraged the flourishing of different ideas by inviting all schools of thought to hold a grand debate?"

"Burning books? Burying scholars?" Ying Zheng repeated in amazement. "Where did you read such lies about me?"

"It is so written in *Records of the Grand Historian*," Yun Fan said. "Every schoolchild knows you did these things."

"Every historian has their own agenda," the emperor said with a scoff. "But even Sima Qian, whom you quote with so much admiration, never once wrote that I buried scholars.[18] It seems to me that in subsequent ages, people misread what was written in the histories, and rumor, passing from mouth to ear, mutated into unrecognizable lies and displaced the truth."

"So what happened to all those scholars you gathered to grow the foundation of philosophy and learning?"

"About half lived out the rest of their natural lives near my tomb, and the other half accompanied my son, Fusu, to the base of the Great Wall to establish a second foundation. For those who chose to live near my tomb, I arranged their final resting places in my mausoleum as well."

"Why?" Yun Fan asked. "What was the point of these efforts?"

"My teacher"—Ying Zheng indicated the captain—"taught me that the foundation of civilization is the exchange of ideas. Only the constant flow of fresh ideas can turn into an infinite source of mental energy. My goal was to encourage the exchange of ideas to build up a large store of mental energy, a treasure trove that can be drawn on for thousands of generations to power the civilization of my people."

Yun Fan nodded, but she was still puzzled. "To increase the exchange of ideas is a wonderful policy, but why did you have to conduct such a thing in secret in the underground palace? Why not do so in the plazas and grand public halls of the

---

18   The disagreement between Yun Fan and Ying Zheng is over how to read one particular passage in Sima Qian's biography of the first emperor. The first emperor is correct that the Grand Historian himself never directly accused the emperor of burying scholars alive, and the passage that has been read to support this accusation has, in the views of many, been misinterpreted.

capital, where the crowds can be the largest? Wouldn't you have generated even more mental energy with that approach?"

"The people of my time wouldn't have understood my project," Ying Zheng said sorrowfully. "I had no choice but to stockpile the energy, waiting for the day when the store could be tapped."

Captain Te broke in. "Ah Zheng, I think you should explain your plan and the true purpose of the Terracotta Army. It will make them understand better."

"Oh, I've long given up on my old plan," the emperor said. "So much time has passed."

"You must try to make them understand."

"My old plan . . ." The first emperor sighed. "How arrogant I was back then! How foolish."

"That is too harsh," the captain said. "You were faced with a difficult choice balanced on a knife's edge. Experience has taught you to judge your younger self critically, but you wouldn't have had this experience without that earlier choice. You must tell the whole story. As the descendants of your subjects, they have a right to know the truth."

Ying Zheng nodded. "As you wish."

Lowering his head, the towering projection of the emperor turned to Yun Fan and the others. "Let me start with a question. Do you know why I designed all these trials along the way from Earth to here, even unto the last step, when the messenger must recite my final words to unseal the lock?"

"We don't," Yun Fan said. "Please enlighten us."

"I planned for a grand future for the people and civilization of Huaxia." Ying Zheng sighed again. "Thus, I had to be sure that the messenger was a descendant of my people, that they would know the words I left behind. Only then could I entrust my plan to them, a plan that I had devised and honed more than two millennia ago."

In a soft voice, Yun Fan asked, "What is this plan you wished to entrust to your messenger?"

"To draw upon the vast store of mental energy and drive the Terracotta Army to pacify and unify all humanity." Ying Zheng's tone was placid, as though speaking of a stroll through the park.

A burst of laughter. Jiang Liu couldn't help it. "Uh . . . oh my goodness. Did you give up on that plan when you finally realized how fragile terracotta bodies are?"

"You know nothing!" Ying Zheng looked down contemptuously at the loong-man. "You've never glimpsed the art of object-steering. Even a body of clay, when infused with mental energy, can become an indestructible warrior of fantastical powers."

"That's a joke!" Jiang Liu laughed out loud. "Just look at me! I know plenty about the art of object-steering. Suppose I return to the Earth now in my present form. What good would it do me? There are weapons on Earth right now that would turn me to scrap metal in a fraction of a second. I won't be indestructible, much less in possession of any 'fantastical' powers."

"That is because your mental energy is weak, not because the object you're steering is weak. The strength of the underlying material has nothing to do with the power I allude to."

"I'm sorry," Huhu broke in. "But the two of you will never get anywhere arguing this way. Fortunately, I was a participant during all the crucial episodes of this history, and I can offer an objective account. If I leave anything out, Ying Zheng or the captain can help fill in."

"Thank you, Da Hu," Ying Zheng said. "You do understand me best."

Huhu began to tell a story. "When we arrived on Earth during Ying Zheng's time, he had just ascended to the throne of the Qin state and was still years from be-coming the first emperor. We told him the principles of civilizational advancement, which struck him deeply. Thus, from the moment he pacified the other six warring states and unified the land, he began to plan for a civilizational advancement for all humanity so that your species can become part of the cosmic Union of Cooperating Civilizations.

"However, back then, he had control only of the Qin Empire. Still, it was a good start. He unified the scripts of the warring states into one script, promulgated a uniform system of weights and measures, and put in place a single standard for roads and carts. These were all efforts to mold a single Huaxia out of many disparate identities, thereby creating a lasting civilization that will continue to generate more ideas and mental energy.

"What about the rest of humanity though? He asked us to extend his life so that he could pacify and unify the rest of humanity into an even grander, planet-wide civilization. We offered him the choice of jumping to our universe with his consciousness and then staying here on Liluhuoman, from where he could continue to observe the developments on Earth over the years. He refused. Rather than becoming a member of the audience, he preferred to remain on the stage, to play an active role in human civilization. He wanted to wait until he had enough strength to pacify the world. Thus, we developed a material called 'stone wood,' which, when used to replace Ying Zheng's human body, allowed his life to persist for thousands of years at an extremely slow rate of metabolism.

"Ying Zheng's original plan was to build many shell-soldiers and wait for the right opportunity. Once he believed he was strong enough, he would then infuse these shell-soldiers with mental energy and lead an invincible army to war. Other than the Terracotta Soldiers and chariots you've excavated, there are many more soldiers and horses buried under the tumulus of the mausoleum. Moreover, the underground palace conceals numerous mechanical beasts, not unlike the ones you're wearing now. Ying Zheng has a quick and agile mind. Although we were the ones to teach him the techniques for making bronze beasts, he directed his artisans to study and develop the art on their own, until they created many fierce and clever mechanical beasts of entirely original designs. Earlier, he was right to note that the power of objects being steered by mental energy depends not on the technological advances within the shells, but on the strength of the mind doing the steering. For instance, the loong-ship that took you here was constructed in the Qin dynasty, but it still functions perfectly well today. The key here is that gryons can manipulate magnetic fields and photons with a precision and directness that you can scarcely imagine, and the resulting nanocircuitry is indeed capable of wonders.

"Ying Zheng then made a pact with us. In time, he would awaken and find a reliable messenger to deliver us a message. If he decided to go to war, he would send over a token in the shape of an arrowhead. But if he gave up on that plan, he would send over the icosahedron that contained his consciousness. In the event that his messenger brought an arrow, he wanted us to help him unlock all the consciousnesses of his elite troops, and, in addition, he wanted the captain to aid his cause as a supremely skilled object-steerer—"

"Wait a minute," Qi Fei interrupted. "What do you mean: 'Unlock the consciousnesses of his elite troops'?"

"Every soldier who had his portrait taken in clay also had his mind stored," Huhu said. "Have you not noticed that each soldier in the Terracotta Army is an individual, different from everyone else? We taught Ying Zheng how to make a degradable material that can be adhered to the human body to form a model, how to use clay to make a mold around the model, and how to then dissolve the degradable model, leaving an empty mold behind. Though analogous to the lost wax method, this degradable material is much better for use on humans. All the soldiers also had their brains scanned, and the resulting brain snapshots were stored by us. When awakened, they each can steer the terracotta copy of their own bodies, forming an invincible army."

"Let me just be sure I'm understanding this correctly," Qi Fei said. "The first emperor's original plan was to wake up after two thousand years, draw on the support of the captain here, and then command the Qin army to unify all humanity?"

"That was plan A," Huhu said. "But as the emperor explained, he changed his mind, and you carried out plan B."

"Why did he give up on plan A?" Qi Fei asked.

Huhu turned to Ying Zheng. "I'm afraid you'll have to explain this part yourself."

Ying Zheng nodded. But instead of answering right away, he turned to the captain. "Teacher, I have a question for you first. Please answer me truthfully."

The captain nodded.

"Even if I had asked you to carry out plan A, you wouldn't have agreed, correct?" the emperor asked. "You never would have supported me in a war of conquest."

"Why do you ask this?"

"I've seen so much in two thousand years," the first emperor said. "For you, the history of Earth is but the blink of an eye; not so for me. For more than two millennia, my consciousness drifted above the East Sea, the whole land spread out beneath my gaze. I've seen prosperity; I've seen starvation and plague; I've seen the atrocities of war; I've seen the courage of unyielding spirits who resist evil to the last; I've seen nations return from the verge of extinction; I've seen states overexpand and fall from their own arrogance. After all that, I no longer think the way I did in my youth. I recalled the conversations between us, and many things you said, which I ignored at the time, began to feel like true wisdom to me."

"Which of my words do you think hold wisdom?" the captain asked.

"You told me that the pursuit of eternal glory, to be the greatest and most powerful, is a dangerous path. As a young man, those words seemed to me nonsense. I thought you were doubting me, didn't believe I could succeed in my plan."

"And how do you understand my warning now?" the captain asked.

"The danger that you were cautioning me against wasn't the danger of failure, but success—a success that leaves you only one path. The pursuit of glory, of being the strongest, greatest, best, is without end. Once you've started the climb, there's no stopping. Ultimately, you'll be an arrow at the apex of its flight, a lonely ghost trapped at the peak of ephemeral glory, deprived of all worth." Ying Zheng paused before going on. "Now, given my youthful fire at that time, the more you told me it couldn't be done, the more I wanted to do it to prove to you that I was special. Until that point, I had never failed to accomplish what I set out to do. Thus, after you left, I devoted myself to thoughts of strategy and tactics, conquest and victory. I wanted to use the long days ahead of me to come up with the greatest plan, and I imagined that when I presented it to you upon your return, you'd be so amazed that you'd help me without any more doubt.

"But I never expected that the result of my meditating for so long on my goal was to realize that it was the wrong path, a road not worth following. Only then did I remember the devouring civilizations you spoke of."

Captain Te nodded. "The cosmos has numerous devouring civilizations. They all pursued the path of becoming the greatest, strongest, best. Once they launched themselves on that trajectory, they couldn't stop."

"What fate awaits them?" Ying Zheng asked.

"For a civilization to climb up the stages of development, it must periodically upgrade its entire intellectual power, its capacity for information exchange." The captain's voice was steady and strong. "There are two ways to achieve this upgrade in intellectual power. One relies on increasing connections between individual minds within a civilization, forming ever more complex information networks that augment the overall creation of new information by orders of magnitude. In contrast, the other way depends on ever-escalating competition within a civilization, until some individual finally gains the power to devour the mental energy of other individuals by dominating and controlling them, thereby expanding the boundary of that individual's consciousness. The result is the psychic analog of a nuclear chain reaction: the more mental energy that individual devours, the stronger it becomes. In the end, a single individual mind can devour the mental energy of a whole planet, and one mind controls all bodies. Such a singular civilization-mind is so powerful that it can, by itself, open wormholes and invade other universes, where it then continues its path of conquest and assimilation. In the first few stages of civilizational development, such conquest can feel incredibly satisfying and seem 'efficient.' But the cosmos is so grand that there are an infinite number of universes. The longer this path of expansion continues, the harder it becomes. Moreover, a devouring civilization is a single mind, which means it lacks the ability to generate new ideas. The inevitable consequence of continuous expansion is the drying up of new information. That is why devouring civilizations cannot develop beyond Stage Five."

"Can these civilizations not realize their own looming crisis?" Ying Zheng asked.

"The temptation to be the greatest, strongest, best is incredibly enticing," Captain Te said. "Every individual within a civilization must be sober to resist such temptation, which is no easy task. The fate of your own civilization is also dependent on your choices. Moreover, there is a legend in the cosmos that the very first civilization to reach the apex of development was a devouring civilization. That ancient devourer had developed to the point where it was one with its own universe and could swallow other universes. Although the cosmological devourer ended itself in the multiverse Big Bang, such legends nonetheless can make the path seem tempting to many worlds."

"Is the legend true?" Ying Zheng asked.

"There's no way to know," Captain Te said. "Whether the legend is real is unimportant; what's important is the choice made by each civilization over the treatment of individuals. Sometimes, a devouring civilization can develop faster than any cooperating civilization and become a great threat. But if a cooperating civilization understands the source of its own faith and why it made the choice to go a different path, then it wouldn't waver because of temporary setbacks in the development process."

Ying Zheng pondered this. "Then . . . is the key to emphasize the boundaries between individuals? To define with more clarity the space around every individual will?"

"No! The very opposite," the captain said. "Borders and boundaries lead to territoriality, to the competition for aggrandizement, to the desire for expansion. The core faith of cooperating civilizations is not drawing lines between individuals but building relationships *between* individuals."

"Relationships?"

"Relationships. The bond between two individual minds is the best guard against the temptation to devour. The distinction between a relationship and a border is this: the first makes both stronger, but the second requires the gain of one to come at the expense of the other."

Deep in thought, Ying Zheng's brows knitted together.

"What are you thinking?" Captain Te asked.

"I'm thinking of a word that I never much approved of in the past."

"Which word?"

"Ren."

The others pondered this exchange. "Ren" is at the core of Confucianism, naming a concept that has no exact translation into other human languages. It's a type of love that doesn't fall within the typology of philia, eros, storge, and agape, a love that emphasizes mutual respect, exchange, and the abiding humaneness that drives true altruism. In pronunciation, it is a homonym for the word for "human." As a hanzi, it is written as a compound formed from the hanzi for "person" and "two." A less elegant but more digestible way to express the ideas within "ren" might be: you and I, being human together.

Just then, everyone teetered as the ground at their feet quaked. Even the tower projecting the image of Ying Zheng shook, causing the projection to waver.

"They're attacking early!" the captain exclaimed. "Ah Zheng, we must stop here. If I should come out of this alive, you and I shall converse for three days without interruption."

Captain Te dissolved their own projection. With a gentle sweep, they dissolved the projection of Ying Zheng as well, and the small tower retreated into the ground. Then, the qilin led the humans out of the hall, rushing back along the same route they had taken to get here. However, unlike the journey earlier, everything along the road now was slanted to the side, as though the very ground had tilted.

"There's very little time left," the captain said. "I must take you to the jump immediately."

Jiang Liu was confused. "Is the enemy very powerful?"

"Very," the captain said. "It's a civilization at Stage Eight, the most powerful adversary we've ever encountered."

"I don't understand these stages you keep on referring to," Jiang Liu asked as he ran to keep up. "Do they describe the degree of information exchange within a civilization?"

"No," Captain Te said. "These numbered stages describe the amount of power that a civilization can command.

"Stage Zero is pre-civilization, when individuals can only control their bodies in the search for food and shelter.

"Stage One civilizations can use tools, which augment the body's power with mechanical advantage.

"Stage Two civilizations have entered the realm of chemical power, where they release stored energy with combustion and gain control over luminous matter.

"Stage Three civilizations have entered the realm of electromagnetic power, where they can control electric and magnetic fields as well as radiation.

"Stage Four civilizations have entered the realm of fundamental particle energy, where they can obtain power by controlling subatomic particles.

"Stave Five civilizations have entered the realm of geometric particle energy, where they can obtain energy from dark matter.

"Stage Six civilizations have entered the realm of mental energy, where they can control gryons and obtain energy by manipulating them.

"Stage Seven civilizations have entered the realm of entanglement energy, where they can obtain power by direct transmission across vast distances via entanglement.

"Stage Eight civilizations have entered the realm of gravitational energy, where they can control gravity fields and alter the distribution of matter in their universe.

"Stage Nine civilizations have entered the realm of dimensional energy, where they can manipulate the topology of their universe and alter its shape.

"Stage Ten civilizations have entered the realm of Dao energy, where intelligence has become indistinguishable from the cosmos itself, and they can step across universes as easily as you step over stones in a pond.

"It's possible that there are still more stages beyond these, the only ones we've been able to confirm. Earth has just entered Stage Three, and your control over electromagnetic fields is still short of true mastery. You're still some distance from

Stage Four, which requires control and mastery over quarks. As for us . . . we should be counted among Stage Seven civilizations, if I'm being completely objective. But the civilization attacking us right now is in Stage Eight, and we believe they'll be attacking with gravitational field manipulation, which are virtually impossible to defend against."

The captain didn't slow down at all as they rattled off this string of new ideas. The humans tried to remember as much as they could, but it was overwhelming. Although some of the keywords in the captain's speech seemed to make sense, the vast majority sounded like gibberish, signposts beyond their ken, legendary land-marks in the terra incognita of human knowledge. However, the fact that humans were only in Stage Three while the enemy was in Stage Eight instantly explained why the captain seemed so anxious.

"What is it like to be subjected to a gravitational field attack?" Jiang Liu asked.

"It involves altering the fundamental parameters in the gravitational field of our system, such that there is resonance in the orbits of our planets, leading to severe vibrations that can tear planets apart. Moreover, an increase in our star's gravity would cause our planet to fall toward the star, razing all the artifacts of our civilization in one giant conflagration."

"How terrible!" Jiang Liu pondered this for a moment. "Captain Te, have you ever regretted choosing the path of collaboration, which may have led to slower development for you than devouring civilizations?"

"We made our choice not because the path of collaboration is invincible, but because we believe every individual consciousness has the right to exist. This is a matter of faith, not a prize to be won."

"Even if such faith leads to your annihilation?" Jiang Liu asked.

"Even unto death, I have no doubt of our chosen path."

They had just reached the entrance to the hall where they jumped through when the ground quaked again, and a slender obelisk to the side fell, striking the ground between them and the hall entrance. Everyone jumped back in alarm.

Qi Fei had been clutching the red pity flower carefully all this time. The sudden movement caused it to fly out of his claw. Qi Fei tried to grab for it, but the metal loong-claw was not agile enough to catch the flower tumbling through the air. A sudden gust of wind carried it even farther, leaving Qi Fei no choice but to jump after it. However, as Qi Fei finally caught the pity flower, a piece of the roof of a nearby building fell and separated him from the others. Qi Fei leaped again, hoping to jump off the fallen roof piece to reunite with the others.

The moment his feet touched the roof fragment, the ground underneath cracked open. In but a few seconds, the seam had expanded to four or five meters wide and nearly fifty meters deep, and it was still widening and deepening. The fragment of roof that Qi Fei was on was now tumbling into the yawning gap. Drawing on his instincts and training, Qi Fei pushed off the fragment with all his strength, but despite his quick reaction, it was too late; he missed landing on solid ground by inches and slid back into the still-widening crevasse.

Jiang Liu leaped over to try to catch Qi Fei. Both loong-humans extended their arms and Jiang Liu managed to clutch Qi Fei's claw tightly. However, Qi Fei's momentum was such that Jiang Liu couldn't stop his slide; instead, both loong fell into the crack.

"You have wings!" Huhu shouted from above. "Fly!"

Jiang Liu and Qi Fei tried to follow Huhu's directions. But they had never had the experience of using their back muscles to manipulate wings—this was a bit of a topological miscalculation on Huhu's part—and their feeble efforts were in vain. The crevasse had now turned into a valley several hundred meters deep, and the two loong continued to tumble into its depths.

But then they both felt a force lifting them by the waist; their fall slowed, and then reversed course. Looking up, they realized that it was the captain who had flown down to rescue them. None had noticed the wings on the back of the qilin—studded with shiny spikes and not very large, but the appendages were evidently extremely powerful. Soon, the qilin rose out of the seam and deposited the two loong gently on solid ground.

"There's no time to return to the jump terminal," the captain said. "We'll have to try something more risky." He turned to Huhu. "Can you carry Ms. Yun? We'll go together."

The captain took off for the apex of the tall cone that was the jump terminal, carrying Qi Fei and Jiang Liu in their claws. Huhu, with Yun Fan riding on them, followed. Seen from the inside, the ceiling had appeared to the humans to be only a few hundred meters tall, but now that they were outside, they realized that the building was at least a kilometer in height. In fact, the cone's tip extended much higher into the sky, long beyond the interior ceiling.

They landed around a circular opening at the top, about three or four meters in diameter. Peering inside, they could see tiny objects on the floor, far below them. Everyone carefully squeezed around the opening, standing on a narrow ledge.

Captain Te turned to Huhu. "Aluosikong, you must memorize the directions I'm about to give you and carry them out exactly. You mustn't hesitate or shrink back. Not only your life, but the lives of your three human friends, depend on you. Don't be afraid. You're powerful. Believe in yourself."

As the captain gave Huhu their orders, both qilin's horns began to glow with different colors. Huhu closed their eyes, listening intently, but abruptly their eyes snapped open, looking stunned.

While the qilin were deep in conversation, the humans took advantage of those few seconds to take in their panoramic view of the surrounding landscape. They were shocked to discover that the planet Liluhuoman was surrounded by thirty or forty moons. The moons were at different heights, forming three concentric rings, and all the moons were connected to the surface of the planet by giant metal ladders. Additional ring-shaped corridors connected the moons within each ring. It appeared that all the moons had been tidal-locked, lending more stability to the structure.

The entire structure—the moons, the ladders, the connecting rings—resembled the ouroboros loong-ship. Thus did the humans finally discover the inspiration for the loong-ship's design.

From their high perch, they saw that the brightly lit metropolis around them was falling apart in the planet-shattering quakes. Building after building collapsed, sending bitter pangs through their hearts.

Captain Te was finished giving their orders. They urged Huhu to hurry.

"Captain, let's go!" Huhu said.

"Let's," the captain said.

Huhu stood in front of the captain and closed their eyes. The horns on both qilin glowed in various bright hues. Soon, the group felt strong winds swirling around them even though there was no visible sign of any air currents.

A transparent barrier of energy rose around them, separating the group from the outside world. Huhu continued to squeeze their eyes shut as their horns glowed ever brighter. Abruptly, Captain Te's eyes snapped open, and, as they pushed Yun Far, Jiang Liu, and Qi Fei to be closer to Huhu, they jumped back and up in the air, leaving the protection of the transparent barrier. Huhu, deep in concentration, didn't notice this at all. As the captain left the area, the barrier rose and closed up overhead, sealing everyone inside a bubble. The conical building under their feet suddenly erupted with a bright white beam of light that shot out of the opening at the top, carrying the bubble slowly into the sky.

Time sped up. Just before everything faded to black, they saw the conical building collapse outside the bubble, and the ladders between the planet and the moons shatter and fall. The white light winked out as everything around them vanished.

Eternity in a moment.

16 | The Return

Vision returned.

They were back inside the familiar loong-ship: gentle white light, oversized sacred tree-ladders, tiny doors leading out of the large spherical cabin.

Joy. Unspeakable joy.

As they jumped across universes once more, they felt not the dissolution of the individual, but an absolute emptiness. They didn't experience fragmentary memories, confusing emotions, or a shattered sense of self. The *I* was whole, complete, but also absent, empty, without, devoid of sensation, experiencing neither time nor space.

It was a good thing that the gap lasted only a short duration. From the void of nothingness to the recovery of vision, their subjective sense of time measured but a minute. However, no one could say how much time *actually* passed, for time had also vanished during the jump, and measurement was impossible.

When they looked at one another, they received yet another shock: they had jumped back inside their avatars. Qi Fei and Jiang Liu were still metal loong, and Yun Fan was still a chimera of fenghuang and deer. In contrast, Huhu was in their real body: a qilin. The transparent bubble remained around them, and Huhu continued to strain, their eyes shut tight, an expression of pain on their face. Jiang Liu remembered that Huhu had said that the parameters of their own universe was different from the parameters of this one, and it was impossible for their body to jump across. From the strenuous effort Huhu was making, Jiang Liu guessed that Captain

Te had taught them some technique for adjusting their body to accommodate the parameters of this universe.

They waited patiently until the look of pain had faded from Huhu's face, the glow in their horns dimmed, and the faint spasms in their taut body smoothed away. Huhu opened their eyes.

The qilin looked around: Jiang Liu, Qi Fei, Yun Fan . . . a look of shock.

"Where's the captain?"

"Captain Te didn't come," explained Qi Fei.

"That's impossible!" Huhu shook their head vigorously. "Without the captain, who opened the tunnel?"

"You did," Qi Fei said. "You were the one who took us through that."

"Captain Te said to believe in yourself," Jiang Liu said.

"But I had never . . ." Huhu's voice faded.

"There's always a first time," Jiang Liu said. "Congratulations!"

Instead of celebrating, Huhu sobbed loudly. "Captain!" The humans had not known that it was possible for qilin to cry—the noise was no different from the cries of a baby.

Yun Fan approached Huhu and tried to comfort them with a wing. Gradually, Huhu stopped. The qilin gently stomped their feet and the transparent barrier around them thinned and then vanished. Only now did they truly return to their home universe.

Jiang Liu and Qi Fei could see their own metal bodies expand and twist, the material apparently also adjusting to the parameters of this universe. Fortunately, the carbon fiber membrane that served as their nervous system didn't transmit pain the same way as their own nerves, and they were spared the excruciating agony that Huhu must have gone through.

"What are we doing to do about this?" Jiang Liu asked Huhu, holding up a claw. "I have no wish to live as a loong for the rest of my life!"

"As soon as we return to the deep sleep chambers, you can switch back to your original bodies. It's very easy to achieve entanglement at such close distances."

"When you say 'entanglement,'" Jiang Liu asked, "are you talking about quantum entanglement?"

"In a manner of speaking," Huhu said. "The quantum entanglement you know is but one form of general entanglement. The cosmos itself is abstract, and its foundational quality is entanglement. In fact, mathematical decomposability is the most common condition."

"I don't understand!" exclaimed Jiang Liu. "There are so many things I don't understand! When can we ever know everything?"

"There's no rush," Huhu said. "Now that I'm in your universe, you can always come to me for more lessons. Aha! Why don't I open an academy? Ying Zheng was once the captain's pupil, so you should be *my* pupils. It's my job to inspect your universe anyway, so I can get my work done even better with some disciples. What do you think, eh? How about you start calling me teacher, master, sensei, shifu? Eh, eh?"

Yun Fan, Jiang Liu, and Qi Fei looked rather stunned.

"Uh . . ." Jiang Liu was the first to recover. "Why don't you focus on getting us back into our own bodies first? If you can't get that done, I think we'll have to call you something else. Not shifu, for sure."

"Ah, that's easy! Very very easy!" Huhu's mouth cracked into a huge grin. "Actually, maybe I should change into a different shell as well. Should I remain as a qilin, as you call me, or become a bronze person again?"

"You sound like Zhuangzi," Yun Fan said. "Now I wonder if he had jumped across universes as well . . . maybe that was why he wondered if he was truly a butterfly dreaming of being a person, or a person dreaming of being a butterfly."

"What do you plan on doing next?" Qi Fei asked. "If you intend to go back to Earth with us, you'd better switch to the bronze person again. I can't even imagine the circus if we brought a live qilin back with us. But if you stay on the spaceship, I think you might as well remain in your own body. Oh, how do you obtain sustenance? You know, food and water?"

"Let me think about what I should do," Huhu said. "Why don't I take care of your situation first?"

And so the three, following Huhu, drifted toward the door leading to the deep sleep chambers. As soon as they were in the hallway, they saw Chang Tian napping in front of the chambers.

Chang Tian was in uneasy slumber, and the movement of the approaching party awakened him. His first instinct was to check the deep sleep chambers; upon finding them undisturbed, he sighed in relief. But then, as he turned around, he was confronted by the most terrifying sight in his life: a giant qilin, two loong, a fenghuang—all floating in air and staring at him.

"Ahhhhh!" Chang Tian scrambled back. However, remembering his friends still trapped inside the deep sleep chambers, he returned to his post and held out his arms to defend the chamber entrances.

The qilin took a step toward him.

Chang Tian remembered his training as a military pilot. Calmly, he searched through his utility belt and pockets for an appropriate weapon with his left hand, while he continued to hold up his right arm to keep the fearsome beasts at bay. Finally, he managed to retrieve a set of nunchucks. Though he was not skilled with it, he tried his best to put on a threatening pose, forcing Huhu to retreat.

Jiang Liu, Qi Fei, and Yun Fan were deeply moved. Their friend was ready to give his life to defend theirs.

"I'm Huhu!" the qilin said.

"What?" Chang Tian was amazed.

"This is my real form," insisted the qilin.

Chang Tian recognized the voice and relaxed slightly. "Are you really Huhu?"

"Of course! Otherwise, how could I have known about this? We jumped over to my home planet, but then my planet came under attack, and we couldn't use the jumping equipment. That forced the captain and me to use our minds to open up a direct inter-universal tunnel to return us here physically. This body you see now is my true body."

"But what about the rest of them? Why aren't my friends back with you?"

"They're right here!" Huhu pointed to the three mythical beasts.

"Um—" Chang Tian's chin was on the floor.

Jiang Liu, Qi Fei, and Yun Fan came up and spoke with Chang Tian in turn, proving through their voices that they were who they claimed they were. They gave a short summary of everything that had happened on their journey. Chang Tian asked several questions about specific details before finally believing them.

Next came the process of returning the minds of the three humans to their true bodies. But just before the three climbed into the deep sleep chambers, Huhu stopped them. "I almost forgot! Would you like to try to link your minds together? Since you've passed the trials, I'm authorized to upgrade you. Might as well get it done now so that you don't have to go through this process twice."

The humans were stunned. They had not expected the "upgrade" to come so early.

"Are you sure this is possible right now?" Qi Fei asked.

"Sure I'm sure. This is much easier than jumping between universes. The brain is in constant contact with gryons, so if two minds can be entangled at the gryon level, each would instantly be able to access the other's emotions and thoughts."

"Is it like invading the other person's brain?" Jiang Liu asked.

"No. The link I establish will only allow you to sense what the other is feeling and thinking at that moment. To dig into memories and deeper information requires a lot more precision and advancement."

"Can we still keep secrets from each other?" Qi Fei asked.

"You will need to be more honest than before. It's not that you can't lie anymore, not exactly. For instance, you can still intentionally direct your thoughts to untruths. However, the other minds connected with yours will sense not only your silent words, but also the images and memories that concurrently surface in your mind, emotions and free associations—a thought-packet, if you will, with all aspects of your cognition in that moment wrapped up together. The gryons will carry all of that between you, and it's much harder to lie through a thought-packet than language alone."

"Will the link be constant?" Yun Fan asked. "But we all need privacy in . . . certain moments."

"The link won't always be on," Huhu said. "At first, I'll give you each a mental switch, which allows you to control whether to entangle your gryons or not. It's . . . like your phones. When you turn on the link, your phone is connected to the network; when you turn it off, nothing goes through. I'm giving you a gryon-entanglement switch."

"How can entanglement be so easy?" Jiang Liu was incredulous. "In our laboratories, we have to struggle mightily to get even a pair of photons to be entangled. And once the entanglement is lost, it can't be recovered."

"You don't understand the nature of the cosmos," Huhu said. "It's all information! Gryons are abstract, but photons are concrete. For gryons, all you need is to change the sign . . . ah, forget it. You can't understand this given your current state of knowledge. But if you agreed to be my disciple . . . hehe."

Jiang Liu said nothing.

Chang Tian asked, "There are people on Earth who claim that they have telepathic powers or the ability to communicate with spirits. Do you think they might have developed the capacity to sense gryons ahead of the rest of us?"

Huhu shook their head. "I don't think so. Your brains have not activated that system. However, I can't rule out the possibility that some humans are extremely sensitive and may, upon the barest hint of a touch from gryons, react by generating dreamlike images and associations."

"So how will you actually give us the ability to sense gryons?" Chang Tian asked. "Are you going to add something to our brains?"

"It's more than just sensing—it's about *understanding* what you sense. Your brain is constantly interacting with gryons, but you don't know that. So making you *know* is the key here. To use another analogy: even without eyes, your body is constantly interacting with photons, but your brain has no knowledge of this interaction. Gryons are the same. You're literally immersed in them and interacting with them nonstop. But you have no idea. The important thing here is to develop some kind of receptor, like the light-sensing cells in your eyes, that will interpret the gryons for the brain. Now, these receptors don't require any fancy new material; we just need to restructure your neurons a bit—the new power emerges from complexity. Don't worry; it's very safe!"

"Can you give us some time to talk it over?" Chang Tian asked.

"No problem. Discuss as long as you need." Huhu left the hallway.

The four humans looked at one another, and for a long time, no one said anything. Chang Tian, who was still not used to seeing his friends as mythical creatures, had to turn his face away to calm himself down. It was hard to hold a thoughtful discussion under such circumstances. But what alternative did they have? They couldn't have imagined that a transformative choice for humanity would be forced on them like this, almost casually, almost carelessly.

"Are we making this decision on behalf of all humans?" Yun Fan finally asked.

"I was thinking of the same question," Qi Fei said. "Is Huhu just asking about the four of us, or the desire of all people on Earth?"

"Do you think that humanity wants this, right now?" Jiang Liu asked.

"Yes," Yun Fan said.

"No," Qi Fei said.

Chang Tian was silent.

"Why not?" Yun Fan asked Qi Fei. "This is an opportunity to upgrade our entire civilization! Who knows when such an opportunity would come again?"

Qi Fei didn't know how to make her understand. Should he tell her that he and Jiang Liu had almost killed each other earlier? Should he tell her that based on his experience with human nature, the only predictable consequence of direct brain-to-brain communication would be rivers of blood? Should he just stick to the truism that humans liked their privacy and secrets? Or maybe he should claim that humans didn't care about rankings and stages of civilization?

All he knew was that he felt an instinctive terror and anxiety at the prospect.

"I just think . . ." Qi Fei paused before continuing. "I just think that if humans aren't even capable of maintaining peace when our communication is linear and limited, who knows what will happen when we are subjected to the complexities of thought-packets? It's too risky."

"How about this," Jiang Liu said, "why don't the four of us, as representatives of humanity, try a little experiment? Let's be guinea pigs and experience brain link firsthand. Are you willing to try that?"

"Yes," Chang Tian said.

"No," Qi Fei said.

Yun Fan said nothing.

Chang Tian glanced at Qi Fei but didn't ask why not. He knew very well why Qi Fei was afraid. "We must be unanimous to try this experiment," he said to everyone.

"So why don't you want to try the experiment?" Jiang Liu asked Qi Fei.

It was impossible to know Qi Fei's emotional state based on his metal shell. The loong's mechanical features didn't show how he felt. Instead of answering Jiang Liu's question, Qi Fei asked, "Why should you be the only one asking questions? What about you? Are you willing to represent humanity and volunteer for this experiment?"

"I am," Jiang Liu said. He stared into Qi Fei's eyes. "I most certainly am."

Qi Fei said nothing.

"I wasn't even afraid when you beat me in our fight," Jiang Liu said. "So what do you have to be afraid of?"

"Are you sure that you don't mind the rest of us knowing everything you're thinking?" demanded Qi Fei.

"I don't mind," Jiang Liu said. "I have nothing except this bit of courage. I'm afraid of nothing."

Qi Fei was silent for a few seconds. "I don't think you're brave; I think you're crazy."

"So what?" Jiang Liu asked.

"Well, I'm not that brave," Qi Fei said.

Jiang Liu turned to Yun Fan.

Yun Fan looked away, turning her doe-like head to the side. "I . . . I'm not sure."

Jiang Liu looked at her steadily. "Just now, you said that humanity wants this. But why do you hesitate when it's yourself?"

"I . . . I'm suddenly worried."

"You were ready to die! What could make you falter now?"

Yun Fan said nothing.

"Why don't I tell you a little bit about my own experience?" Jiang Liu said. "Even as a child, I knew that I was rich. I had many more possessions and a powerful family. But that wasn't all. I was also gifted, capable of mastering many subjects that others struggled with. I asked myself: Why should I be born so fortunate? Why should there be men who must wander the streets with no place to sleep while I lived inside a giant mansion?

"Later, I realized that all my gifts and possessions and good fortune meant that I had to judge myself accordingly. Whenever I saw something terrible in the world, something wrong, I asked myself: Can you do anything to make it better? If I thought, 'No, I can't,' then I had to ask myself: If you can't even make this better, who can? If you, with all your talents and resources, can't make the world better, who do you hope will come and save you? I felt that I couldn't run away, couldn't hide. If I tried to shirk my duty, then who was left to do the work? Should we expect those beggars wandering the streets to take up the burden?

"Listen to me, all of you. The four of us are among the 1% of the 1%; we have more talent and resources than most of the world. Every single one of us is extraordinary, blessed beyond reason. If the four of us can't even make brain-to-brain communication work, who else can we count on to make it work?"

"You've convinced me," Qi Fei said. "You've pointed out, correctly, that this is a matter of duty; I can't walk away from that. I volunteer."

Yun Fan nodded. "Me too."

"That's agreed, then," Jiang Liu said. "In the worst case, if we can't bear it, we'll just all agree to switch the gryon-sensing off."

They told Huhu their decision. The alien didn't seem surprised at all. They asked the humans, three of them still in their metal avatars, to squeeze into the same deep sleep chambers as their real bodies, and then to go to sleep. Huhu initiated the upgrade process.

They lost consciousness.

+ + + + +

After a seemingly endless slumber, they returned to the world of the living.

There were no words for the overflowing joy as Jiang Liu, Qi Fei, and Yun Fan wiggled their fingers, realizing that they were back in their real bodies. Not until they had lost it did they realize what a treasure the human body was.

Huhu indicated that they should remain in their beds as they ran through another set of diagnostics and made final adjustments. They asked the humans to practice thinking the unique keywords they had each chosen to initiate and terminate entanglement. Finally, all four emerged from their deep sleep chambers and looked at one another. Everything seemed back to normal after a long dream.

Their brains didn't feel any different.

"All done," Huhu said. "You can initiate entanglement whenever you're ready."

"What about you?" Jiang Liu asked. "Have you decided where you want to go?"

"I have," Huhu said. "I think it's best for me not to return with you to Earth. I have to take care of the pity flower, and that task is much harder on Earth, with all the people around. I found a good place in the solar system: it's in the asteroid belt, with plenty of water. As long as there's enough water, pity flowers will do fine, no matter the temperature. I'm going to stay there for a while."

"All right, then," Qi Fei said. "But be careful. Whenever you need us, don't hesitate to—wait, since our brains aren't entangled, how can we talk to you?"

"Ah, you don't need to worry about that," Huhu said. "Now that you can sense gryons, everything is so much easier. If I need you, I'll send a message to Yun Fan's necklace, and then she'll know."

"But what if we need to get hold of you?" demanded Qi Fei.

"We can still use Yun Fan's necklace. When she's wearing the necklace and concentrating on 'Huhu,' I'll receive the message. Oh, you should take that bronze person with you. If necessary, I can pop into the shell to join you."

Huhu took them to the mouth of the loong-ship. They waited until the humans put on their space suits and got ready. As they stood in the jaw of the loong, Huhu's horns glowed, and the loong opened its mouth and spat out its tail. The humans found themselves staring at Jiang Liu's family spaceship, drifting just a few meters away. Using spider-silk lines for safety, they easily spacewalked back to their old spaceship.

Once aboard, the four turned around to bid farewell to Huhu, but the alien had already disappeared inside the loong-ship.

+ + + + +

A glance at the clock aboard the ship informed them that they had been gone for twenty-eight hours—even though they felt they had been away for months. Physically, they were exhausted and starving, as the entire time they had been away they had eaten nothing.

"Chang Tian! I beg you to feed us!" Jiang Liu said. "Anything will do—don't be such a gourmet and take hours to prepare something fancy. I'm about to die of hunger here."

He lay on the sofa and spread out his flopping limbs to illustrate his condition. Grinning, Chang Tian walked into the galley to cook. Yun Fan went back to her cabin to shower and change. Qi Fei sat down next to Jiang Liu.

"You know . . . What you said earlier about responsibility . . . that really got to me."

Jiang Liu looked at him. "I'm curious: Why are you so worried about the rest of us knowing what you're thinking? To me, you are the very definition of wholesomeness."

"Eh . . . everyone has a dark side, a shadowy corner of the psyche."

"Shadows are like asses," Jiang Liu said. "Who can live without an ass? Once you accept that, it's no big deal to have someone see your backside."

"Now I'm curious," Qi Fei said. "How are you so open and fearless about this?

Chang Tian, Yun Fan, and I have known each other for decades, and still we hesitate. You've known us for only days, and you show no reservation at all."

"That's because I can see something in Yun Fan and in you that I don't have," Jiang Liu said. He was now leaning against the back of the sofa, cushioning his head on an arm and looking up at the ceiling. "Both of you are dedicated to something, anchored to an unshakable conviction. In Yun Fan's case, it's her mission. In your case, it's love of country. Your conviction is so pure that I can't help but be envious. When someone has found an ideal that is worth their faith, a task worth dying for, that person's soul glows, like a keen edge. I've been searching for something that can awaken in me that kind of conviction, but I've never found it. Everything feels to me empty, meaningless. Did you know that I used to think seriously about becoming a Buddhist monk?"

"You?" The expression on Qi Fei's face was indescribable. "No way."

Jiang Liu chuckled. "I thought about it all the time. In college I traveled around extensively, and every time I visited a temple, I wanted to shave my head and undergo pabbajjā, leaving the secular world behind forever. Back then, I found worldly life meaningless, utterly meaningless."

"This must have been before you founded Tianshang, right?"

"Yes, that's right. Later, after I graduated from college—so after that incident I told you about—I started Tianshang. At first, I wanted atonement, and so the initial threshold I imposed for becoming a member of Tianshang was having lost a loved one in war. But later, more and more people wanted to join, and I had to open it up."

"You did a good thing there," Qi Fei said. "You made a difference."

"When we went to Huhu's world, do you know what made the biggest impression on me?"

"Qin Shi Huang?"

"No." Jiang Liu shook his head. "It was when Captain Te said, 'Even unto death, I have no doubt of our chosen path.' I was so moved. I can picture you saying that as well."

Qi Fei nodded, a little surprised by Jiang Liu's insight. "I . . . think so. You know, my favorite books are about Chinese history. In China's long history, every era has honored individuals willing to die for their deeply held convictions and ideals. Remember Cui Zhu of Qi during the Spring and Autumn period? Cui Zhu, the most powerful official in the Qi court, killed his lord, the Duke of Qi. Cui Zhu didn't want people to speak the truth of his crime, yet the court historian wrote down on bamboo strips: 'Cui Zhu killed his lord.' When Cui Zhu had the historian executed, the next historian wrote the same thing. And when that historian was also executed, his successor still would not alter the truth. In fact, there were others lined up with bamboo strips, ready to follow if Cui Zhu continued his campaign of terror. Historian after historian gave up their lives to defend the integrity of their charge, the truth that must be recorded for posterity.

"Why did they do that? They didn't do it out of loyalty to the dead duke—he was already dead! They didn't do it for honor and glory—what good is praise when you're not around to hear it? They didn't do it for religion—Chinese intellectuals have long had little use for religion, even in ancient times. Then why? I thought and thought, and realized that those historians did it because they believed it was the right thing to do. They believed that the truth, the incorruptible integrity of their own spirit, was worth committing to, and even unto death, they had no doubt of their chosen path."

"Too bad that in subsequent ages, their conviction was not always the popular choice," Jiang Liu said.

"Even a few sparks are enough to preserve the flame," Qi Fei said. "Their ideals never died, and you can find the spiritual successors of those historians in every age."

Yun Fan, having showered and changed, had returned to the common area during the latter part of this conversation. She had been listening quietly to the discussion between the two, but now she broke in.

"Speaking of the virtues of the ancients, there's something I've been pondering," she said. "Do you remember the final exchange between Qin Shi Huang and Captain Te?"

Jiang Liu thought about it. "I believe . . . they were discussing Confucius."

"Not Confucius," Yun Fan said. "They were discussing 'ren.'"

"Oh, that's right." Jiang Liu chuckled. "They were talking about 'ren.' But I always think of Confucius when 'ren' is brought up."

Yun Fan nodded. "I don't blame you. Confucius was indeed the most well-known promoter of 'ren.' However, Confucius himself always made it clear that he didn't claim credit for the concept. Rather, he was trying to revive and popularize an idea he learned from the ancients. When Captain Te spoke of building relationships between individuals and Qi Shi Huang brought up 'ren,' a lightbulb went on in my head."

"Enlighten us, please," Qi Fei said.

"Tell me: What does 'ren' mean to you?" Yun Fan asked.

Qi Fei pondered for a moment. "Well, 'ren' is a type of love: compassion and empathy for others."

"That's a gloss from later ages," Yun Fan said. "However, I remember reading another explanation, which now I think is far more relevant. Remember, 'ren' is written as the hanzi for 'person' combined with the hanzi for 'two.' And whenever you have two persons, you also have a relationship. The hanzi 'ren' was created to represent the concept of an ideal relationship. 'Ren' is to be contrasted with 'li,' the other core concept of Confucianism, which we often understand as ritual and order. If 'li' is about one's place in society, 'ren' is about one's relationships in society.

"Until recently, my understanding of 'ren' was largely limited to philology. However, when Captain Te explained that the Union of Cooperating Civilizations was founded on the concept of good relationships, I saw a new connection! I think Captain Te had spoken with our ancient sages, before the time of Confucius, and told them the importance of good relationships. These teachings persisted through other teachers such as Laozi until the time of Confucius, who then systemized the teachings into a new philosophy based on 'ren.' We can see this intellectual strand when Fan Chi, the Master's disciple, asked about the meaning of 'ren,' and the Master replied, 'Love humanity.'"

"I see what you mean now," Qi Fei said. "I recall from *Liji* this passage: 'The meaning of ren is humanity, and the heart of ren is relations.' In the past, 'relations' was understood as kinship, but I think it should be understood much more broadly, as an exhortation to focus on good relationships in general."

"I'm not sure I agree with this reading," Jiang Liu said. "I recall uses of that quotation that say otherwise. I have to confess that I've never enjoyed reading Confucian texts and can't say definitively whether you're right."

"Well, I'm just telling you my instinct here," Yun Fan said. "When we go back to Earth, I'll have to spend a lot of time in the library to sort through the evidence."

"Hey, who's talking about good relationships?" Chang Tian asked as he emerged from the galley. "You have to include me in the discussion if you want to talk about healthy relationships. Anyway, you all should fill your bellies first before brandishing writing brushes and showing off your erudition."

Chang Tian was carrying four plates of fried rice with black pepper, mushroom, and beef. Even before the chef had set the plates down, the enticing aroma already made the other three ready to sign away their souls for a taste. After twenty-eight hours of fasting, hunger was the most amazing spice for these three, who had never felt its pangs in their comfortable lives. There was no talking as everyone buried their faces in the delicious food and vacuumed everything down. All they could think of was that they had never tasted such a wonderful dish.

The three men, having cleaned their plates, leaned back and let out satisfied sighs. Only Yun Fan continued to eat slowly, savoring the flavors.

Chang Tian chuckled. "When I was in the kitchen, I heard the three of you debate 'good relationships.' My goodness, you're all theory with no practical knowledge at all. What do you know about healthy relationships?"

"All right, expert, why don't you enlighten us?" Jiang Liu asked.

"A good relationship must first allow each party to face their own faults and defects, and in that clarity, they can strive to heal and become complete. Moreover, both parties must ultimately accept the other as they are—in that process the two will repeatedly approach, resist, re-approach, re-resist; they must learn to open up and reveal their core selves and learn that it's okay to be vulnerable without being hurt, being abandoned, or hurting and abandoning. And after acceptance, there comes the challenge of long-term trust—"

"Oh, sure, so we're the theoreticians here," Jiang Liu said, poking at Chang Tian and laughing. "You, on the other hand, are all about practical advice—except the advice requires a psych degree to implement, uh-huh."

"Hey, I at least can put my own theories into practice," Chang Tian said. "The three of you . . . heh, you can't do as you preach."

"I won't tolerate such libel!" declared Qi Fei. "My actions have always conformed to my words. I'm a man of honor."

"Look, I'm being serious here," Chang Tian said. "I can see my own faults, but the three of you cannot. I know exactly what my weakness is: low self-acceptance. This has been an issue since my childhood. Because of it, I try too hard to please others—of course this can't be separated from my family situation . . . Anyway, let me ask you: If someone around you doesn't like you, how do you feel?"

"That's his problem," Jiang Liu said.

"Who cares what others think about me?" Qi Fei said.

"I don't mind if they don't like me," Yun Fan said. "That means they'll stay away from me. I hate it when I have to deal with people who 'like' me."

"See?" Chang Tian said. "The three of you are so self-confident, so comfortable with your superiority, that you can't be negatively affected by how others view you. This is because you're indeed talented and extraordinary, and also because you were securely attached as children. I wasn't like that. If someone around me didn't like me, my first reaction was: 'I must be doing something wrong.' And then I would spend hours obsessing over exactly what I did wrong, and how I should change to be more likable. And once I did make such a change, I would then worry about whether others noticed the change and liked me better. Over time, the result was an extreme lack of self-confidence, and a tendency to be driven by others' opinions of me. After I learned to diagnose myself and to intervene, my situation improved a great deal. Because I know my issues, I can learn to deal with them and build healthier relationships. The rest of you, however, still don't know your own issues."

The other three looked at him blankly, apparently unconvinced.

"Let me ask you a question," Chang Tian said. "What is your vision of an ideal life?"

"Why don't you start?" Qi Fei said to Jiang Liu.

"Why should I go first?" queried Jiang Liu. "I think *you* should start."

"How about *I* start?" Yun Fan said. "To be honest, for the last few years, I haven't been able to imagine my life beyond completing my father's mission. I was prepared to die in the process of carrying out my task, and so I never bothered to plan beyond this moment.

"In fact, just now, when I actually finished what I set out to do, I felt . . . empty inside; it didn't feel nearly as good as I hoped. At that point, I didn't know what to do with myself. However, later, when Captain Te brought up relationships, I made the connection with 'ren,' and suddenly became excited that I had another academic puzzle to pursue. I want to spend a few years to sort out my theory on 'ren' and write some popular explanations for the public. That's my ideal life."

"Oh, Fanfan, I meant to ask you," Jiang Liu said, "how are you going to support yourself? Your father is gone, and your mother is nowhere to be found. You don't have a steady source of income. Do you need money?"

"See, that question shows how little you know about the lives of ordinary people," Yun Fan said. Her expression was mocking, but not unkind. "Do you even know how much money you need to support yourself? I don't know how you're going to make it if your family cut you off.

"Anyway, I've been supporting myself since sixteen as a freelance writer. I'm pretty sure that if both of us had to rely on our own resources, I'd make more in a month than you."

"Impressive," Jiang Liu said. "I had no idea."

Yun Fan laughed. "If your family kicked you out and you had no way to fill your belly, come to me; I'll feed you."

"Would I be right to say that your ideal life involves being by yourself to pursue whatever subjects aroused your curiosity and write essays you enjoy?" Chang Tian asked.

"Sounds about right," Yun Fan said.

"Now, you two." Chang Tian turned to Qi Fei and Jiang Liu.

"My ideal life is to be able to drink by myself at Keck Observatory every night, toasting the setting sun and listening to my favorite music," Jiang Liu said. "The layered strings are the best accompaniment to the layered glowing clouds—there's nothing more wonderful."

"So your ideal life is to be alone in the company of the stars?" Chang Tian asked.

"I think so. Oh . . . also I want to be able to travel around and look at everything."

"Your turn." Chang Tian turned to Qi Fei.

"Me? I used to want to see a major breakthrough in AI research. But after talking with Captain Te, I think I'm going to change my research focus to cognitive neuroscience. I want to make some substantive contributions to our understanding of intelligence."

"I'm asking about your ideal life, not ideal work," Chang Tian said.

"Honestly, I would love to live in the lab. I want anything outside of research to take up as little of my time as possible. The research topics I'm interested in are so complex and deep that a lifetime of work won't even guarantee results. Life is too short; I want to devote it all to my work."

Chang Tian nodded. "Exactly as I thought. Have you noticed that there's a common feature in all of your ideal lives: you're alone! There's no place for even one single other person. I would guess that you think being alone is much better than being in the company of others."

"Of course," Qi Fei said.

"Without any doubt," Jiang Liu said.

"I agree," Yun Fan said.

Chang Tian clasped his hands behind his head and leaned back, smiling. "The three of you know nothing about how to be with others; you prefer your own company to the exclusion of society. Isn't it silly for you then to philosophize on the nature of good relationships? You don't have any healthy relationships in your own lives! You can't build good relations with other earthlings, and you aren't even willing to try. How can you possibly hope to give anyone else advice?"

The three others looked at one another awkwardly. This was indeed a perspective on their own lives that they'd never taken, and they had never questioned their own choices. Chang Tian was forcing them to look at an aspect of their own existence that they had so far hidden behind a decorative painting. But they knew Chang Tian was right: they had to face their own weakness before they could flip the entanglement switch in their heads.

But before they could ponder the problem more deeply, the spaceship shook as though struck. Jiang Liu ran into the cockpit and started pulling up camera and sensor feeds onto every available screen.

They froze at what they saw. No, nothing physical struck the spaceship, but it was under a barrage of laser cannons. The shots weren't at full power—they had been intended to intimidate rather than kill, at least for now.

At the edge of sensor range was a whole line of military space fighters, proudly escorting a massive carrier in the middle. Every fighter was painted in pale silver and wore the insignia of the Atlantic Alliance.

Chris Zhao's grinning face appeared on the monitor. "Hello! Hello! What a pleasure it is to see old friends again."

17 | Protection

The sight of an Atlantic Alliance space carrier battle group told Jiang Liu and Qi Fei all they needed to know as to how much things had escalated in their absence.

Chris Zhao, grinning like a cat that had just swallowed the canary and dangling an electronic cigar from his fingers, dragged his syllables out mockingly. "Oh my dear friends, Qi Fei and Jiang Liu, though we parted ways only a few days ago, you look *soooo* tired. May I inquire as to where you went?"

Jiang Liu and Qi Fei looked at each other. Qi Fei tapped his temple with two fingers. Jiang Liu nodded.

Jiang Liu concentrated on the keyword in his mind, and then tried to call into the void with his thoughts.

[Qi Fei! Are you there?]

[I'm here.]

Both were stunned. It was so strange to hear another voice in one's own head.

The exchange of information sped up. They didn't always resort to language, but directly plunged into each other's information stream. When Qi Fei was observing the formation taken up by the fighters and the carrier, Jiang Liu could *feel* the other man's focus—right between the third and fourth fighters on the right side. Jiang Liu could also sense that Qi Fei, based on his years of experience analyzing combat footage, had concluded that the two fighters would, once in action, pull apart, leaving a small gap sufficient for their spaceship to pass through. Though risky, it was their best chance to escape.

Qi Fei also sensed what Jiang Liu was thinking: Jiang Liu wanted to draw Chris Zhao into conversation, giving Qi Fei a chance to deploy AI analysis on the signal stream and find an opening to hack in. Thereafter, Jiang Liu would be able to implant a virus. Even if the virus only managed to paralyze the carrier's systems for three minutes, it would massively boost their chances of a successful escape. Qi Fei agreed to the plan.

All of this occurred wordlessly within a second.

"Mr. Zhao," Jiang Liu said, a warm smile on his face. "We've missed you! You're looking so handsome and energetic. May I ask where you went to restore yourself since we parted ways?"

Chris laughed. "I look so happy because I finally found the two of you! After our last friendly exchange, I felt so inspired and wished, more than anything else, to have another opportunity to continue learning from you. When I couldn't find you, I felt so lost. But now, haha, I am very, very pleased."

"Mr. Zhao is far too polite!" Jiang Liu said. "Is it necessary to bring out a whole aircraft carrier and its complement of fighters to be our honor guard? That is the protocol reserved for welcoming heads of state! There's no need to be so formal when you just want to spar with us. Too much ceremony isn't appropriate among good friends, am I right?"

Qi Fei's voice broke into Jiang Liu's consciousness.

[My AI agents haven't been able to find a way to hack into their signal yet. However, I found something else interesting: Chris Zhao is on a reconnaissance spacecraft, the second one in the formation on the right. Strangely, the transmitter on this spacecraft is known to us; sixty-four hours ago, the very same transmitter signature established contact with our ship.]

[Sixty-four hours ago?] Jiang Liu tried to do the math in his head as he continued to banter with Chris.

Qi Fei and Jiang Liu layered their memories together and, with two minds recalling and processing, sorted through the events of the last few days in a flash. Tracing back from their time in the loong-ship, they realized that sixty-four hours ago, they were dodging the missiles from the Atlantic Alliance. Instantly, both grasped that those missiles, likely launched by Chris, had not been meant to blow them out of the sky; on the contrary, their purpose was to electronically bug their spaceship so that they could be tracked and followed.

That meant Chris Zhao most likely already knew exactly where they had been during the last sixty-four hours, and there was no point in lying.

[Red alert!] [Red alert!]

Both thought the same thing at the same time. The Atlantic Alliance's Quantum Fog was notoriously stealthy *and* powerful. Very few knew exactly how it worked, but the best guess was that the intelligence-gathering system amplified the uncertainty of quantum wave functions in such a manner as to permit a viruslike probe program to be implanted in the target vessel's control systems. The probe then expanded and collapsed randomly, not unlike the wave function itself, so that subsequent observations of the results could be used to compute probabilistically the location of data that the Quantum Fog operator was interested in. The intrusion of this fog-like, unpredictable system was difficult for targets to even detect, much less defend against. Very often the system succeeded in stealing information before the target was even aware that it had been breached.

If Quantum Fog had intruded into their system as early as sixty-four hours ago, then Chris Zhao had likely seen everything that was in their vessel's computer systems, including their scans of the loong-ship, the recorded communications, and even the process of docking with the loong-ship. Chris had likely spent a day mobilizing the carrier battle group, hoping to catch Yun Fan and the others while they were still on the alien ship. However, since they had spent just a little over one day on the alien ship, the carrier battle group caught them on their way back to Earth.

[Their real target must be the loong-ship,] Jiang Liu thought.

[Then we can't try to escape. If we do, we'll be leaving the loong-ship at their mercy,] Qi Fei thought.

[Can we draw them away?]

[Why don't you try to locate the loong-ship while I distract Chris for a bit longer?]

As they were thinking at each other instead of talking, everything happened a hundred times faster. As soon as Jiang Liu thought of *the loong-ship*, Qi Fei thought of *protection*. The two men couldn't imagine how they would have reached consensus and coordinated their actions so efficiently in the absence of direct brain-to-brain communications.

"Mr. Zhao," Qi Fei said to the screen, "we'll never get anywhere if we keep on beating around the bush. Tell me: Why have you trapped us here with your fighters?"

"I like Director Qi's forthrightness!" Chris replied. "Fine, I'll get right to it. I know that the two of you met some guests yesterday. I just want to know who these guests were, and what you talked about."

"I see," Qi Fei said. "Would you answer a question from us as well? Why do you want to know about our private meeting? Even if you were the police investigating us, you would still need to produce a warrant. Where is your warrant?"

"I think it's a bit preposterous to claim your meeting was private. Do you really go to space to meet with friends?"

An old man next to Chris interrupted the conversation at this point. The old man—energetic, stocky, with a bit of a beer belly—wore an Atlantic Alliance space force uniform with no rank insignia. His chestnut hair was peppered white. However, based on his air and attitude, he was obviously the leader of the carrier battle group.

"Stop wasting time. Just tell them the options." The old man spoke in English.

[Can you find out who that is?] Qi Fei thought.

Jiang Liu nodded. But first, he shared the results of his earlier search for the location of the loong-ship. The alien vessel was incredibly fast. After departing from it four hours ago, they had traveled about a hundred thousand kilometers; meanwhile, the loong-ship had sped more than seven million kilometers. In fact, it was still accelerating, and Jiang Liu estimated that within a day, it would pass outside the orbit of Mars and be in the environs of the asteroid belt. The loong-ship had also recloaked itself; Jiang Liu had been able to locate it only because he knew how to apply the appropriate signal filters.

Although this should be considered good news, Chris Zhao's next words through the screen made both men very anxious.

"They're not going to tell us," Chris said to the old man, again in English. "Why don't we launch from Mars right now?"

The two of them openly discussed their plans right in front of Qi Fei and Jiang Liu, obviously unconcerned with them and their friends. Such arrogance was likely a sign that they had prepared for this mission extensively and thought they had all contingencies covered.

[Damn! If they have additional resources they can launch from Mars, then they must be following the loong-ship and know where it's heading,] Jiang Liu thought to Qi Fei.

[Maybe Huhu has already made preparations,] Qi Fei thought. [They should be able to detect such a large battle group, don't you think?]

[I'm not sure,] Jiang Liu thought. [Huhu is not nearly as experienced or meticulous as Captain Te. Moreover, the loong-ship isn't a warship, so Huhu may not have the necessary sensors or weapons.]

[I think we should have Yun Fan get in touch with Huhu,] Qi Fei thought.

The thought-conversation took place in a fraction of a second. Qi Fei snuck out of the cockpit and quickly summarized the situation for Yun Fan. He asked Yun Fan to contact Huhu, and suggested that instead of entering the cockpit with the answer from Huhu, she instead try to *think* the answer at the men.

To get her ready, he practiced thought-entanglement with her.

[Can you hear me?]

[Yes!]

[How does this feel?]

[Very . . . very weird.]

[You'll get used to it. It's so efficient.]

Qi Fei and Yun Fan didn't yet realize the full implications of this form of communication.

When Qi Fei returned to the cockpit, he caught Jiang Liu asking the old man on the screen in English, "Let's get on with it. What are our options?"

"You have three paths in front of you," Chris said. "Number one: take us to where you met your 'friends' and introduce us. Number two: leave Yun Fan behind with us, and the rest of you may go back to Earth. Number three: we'll go look for your friends by ourselves—if you don't like it, you're welcome to complain to our lasers."

Jiang Liu and Qi Fei exchanged looks. None of the choices, as anticipated, was appealing. The first path required them to betray Huhu; the second, Yun Fan. The last choice was a fight they had no chance of winning. Jiang Liu and Qi Fei rapidly exchanged thought-packets as they worked through the possibilities.

[I got in touch with Huhu,] Yun Fan thought in their minds. [They can't jump with their real body right now because they're mentally exhausted.]

Jiang Liu's and Qi Fei's hearts fell at this.

[Can the loong-ship fight?] Qi Fei asked.

[They said they'll never fire on humans. First of all, inspection teams don't have the authorization to engage with native life-forms. Any use of force must be approved by headquarters. But Huhu can't get in touch with headquarters right now. Moreover, Huhu doesn't think fighting will do any good. The loong-ship was built during the Qin dynasty and is no match for modern weapons.]

Qi Fei and Jiang Liu felt even worse.

[Maybe they should accelerate and leave the solar system altogether,] Jiang Liu thought.

[That won't be necessary,] Yun Fan replied. [Huhu said not to worry about them. They are going to take the pity flower and get into a small escape pod, which can also be cloaked. Due to the size of the probe, it will be nearly impossible to discover.]

Jiang Liu and Qi Fei were overjoyed. [That solves the problem, then. We can reestablish communications with Huhu after the crisis and pick them up,] Qi Fei thought.

[We still have to shake this carrier battle group off our tail, though,] Jiang Liu thought.

[Just hand me over to them,] Yun Fan thought. [Door number two.]

[Unacceptable!] Jiang Liu and Qi Fei both protested. Yun Fan felt the surge of anger in the men directed at the Atlantic Alliance. She also sensed their humiliation and resistance to the idea of selling out their friend for their own safety.

She tried to reason with them by playing out their current predicament in her head. If they tried to escape without leaving her behind, then the entire carrier battle group would be after them, and not only would they all be captured, but they'd be leaving Huhu without any support. If they tried to take on the space fighters in a direct confrontation, they were sure to lose. If they pretended to accept the first proffered choice and took the Atlantic Alliance to the loong-ship, then they would surely be subjected to strict surveillance along the way, leaving no opportunity to help Huhu. The only solution was to give her up and win themselves a temporary reprieve, so that they could then find Huhu and help them. She was in no personal danger because she knew many secrets about the aliens. Surely her captors would keep her safe for the journey back to Earth in order to interrogate her further. Once they were back on Earth, her friends would have plenty of chances to rescue her.

[Your reasoning is sound, but I can't accept it,] Qi Fei thought.

Yun Fan and Jiang Liu both felt the strong sense of guilt in Qi Fei's mind, despite his efforts to suppress it.

[Don't let your emotions get in the way,] Yun Fan thought. [You know I'm right.]

[It's still too risky,] Jiang Liu thought. [Let's keep on thinking about it. I bet we can come up with a better solution.]

[You need to let me take more risks,] Yun Fan thought.

[What are you talking about?] Jiang Liu and Qi Fei both thought.

[When I set out to find the loong-ship, I was ready to die,] Yun Fan thought. Jiang Liu and Qi Fei felt the coldness—right on the edge of irrationality—in her mind. It chilled them to the bone. Yun Fan continued, [But I didn't die. Now I feel I don't know what my purpose in life is. I feel so empty inside, as though my life hasn't fully returned to me. Let me take risks; let me do something. Maybe the experience will reawaken my desire for life again.]

[It makes no sense to look for reasons to live by deliberately putting your life at risk,] Qi Fei thought.

[Don't worry, this is a calculated risk,] Yun Fan thought. [I know Chris Zhao. He's a calculating person who takes pride in his cleverness. I'm sure he won't try to grill me using barbaric "enhanced interrogation" techniques; rather, he'll try to trick me. I know how to deal with him.]

[Have you considered the fact that Chris is no fool, and if we give you up, he'll suspect a trick and be extra vigilant?] Jiang Liu thought. [Maybe he'll send fighters to tail us.]

[Surely you can shake a couple of space fighters?] Yun Fan thought. [I'll do my best to make sure Chris and his boss and the rest of the Atlantic Alliance head to Earth. As long as Chris isn't following you personally, you should be able to get away.]

[I still don't like it,] Jiang Liu thought. [I have a proposal. Let's try to flee in the opposite direction from the loong-ship's heading. They'll be forced to split their forces—and I bet they'll send most of the fighters after the loong-ship, which will give us a chance.]

Qi Fei was in agreement. [Putting Fanfan at risk should be our last resort.]

Yun Fan acquiesced. [Fine. But remember that I'm happy to play my part and take risks. Don't let your concern for me become a weakness.]

Again, all this "discussion" took place in the blink of an eye. Emotions, thoughts, feelings, memories, images—the thought-packets were so efficient and direct that their communications transcended what was possible with language alone. They were amazed at how easily they grasped one another's ideas. It was a qualitative leap up from primitive speech.

It was time to put their plan into action.

Qi Fei conferred with Chang Tian and explained the plan to him. They turned the spaceship abruptly to a heading opposite the direction of the loong-ship, and accelerated to the max. Soon the ship was flying in excess of 30,000 kph. At the same time, Qi Fei scoured their system until he found the invasive electromagnetic signature. Although he couldn't be sure he had found the viral implants from Quantum Fog, at least he could be sure he got the signature of Chris Zhao's sensor spectrum. Jiang Liu took the signature and used it to make more than a dozen "digital twins" that filled Chris Zhao's screen with phantoms. At the same time, he cut off the actual signal connecting Chris's reconnaissance craft and their own spaceship. So while the real cicada was speeding away, exuviated shells littered the path of their pursuer.

The Atlantic Alliance battle group went into hot pursuit. Two reconnaissance spacecraft—including one with Chris Zhao as the commander—took the lead. Behind them, the main squadron behaved exactly as Qi Fei had predicted: a gap appeared between the third and fourth fighters in the formation. The lumbering space carrier followed behind. In essence a giant space station, the carrier was a mobile base for space fighters, but also had its own complement of heavy cannons. However, it lacked maneuverability.

Chang Tian was prepared to take advantage of the carrier's weakness. As soon as he confirmed Chris Zhao was distracted by the phantom digital twins and lost track of the real target, he pulled hard on the control stick and spun the spaceship around in a tight arc. Now facing their pursuer rather than running away, the spaceship accelerated to the max, heading straight for the underbelly of the carrier.

During their flight, they had pulled only about five thousand kilometers ahead of the battle group. They could cover that distance now in no more than eight or nine minutes. The diving trajectory they were pursuing was meant to take them skimming "under"—there was no absolute up or down in space—the carrier, which would make it especially difficult for the fighters to engage them, as the bulk of the carrier "above" their ship would form a natural shield. The opportunity to pull off such a maneuver was fleeting, as it would take but a few minutes for Chris to realize that he had lost the real signal in a sea of phantoms and then to relocate them. Once they were found again, their proximity to the battle group would make redeployment of the fighters to intercept even easier.

They were betting on speed: if Chris Zhao took more than six minutes to realize his error and redeploy the fighters, they would be hidden by the underside of the carrier and be secure.

The plan went well at first. For the first three minutes after they whipsawed around, there was no change in the heading or formation of the carrier battle group. The pursuers had apparently been fooled by the digital phantoms and failed to notice where the prey really was.

At five minutes and ten seconds, the two reconnaissance spacecraft began to close in on Chang Tian's true flight vector, apparently realizing that they had been tricked.

At five minutes and forty-five seconds, the fighters finally were close enough to fire on the fleeing spaceship. They were, at that point, no more than a hundred kilometers from the calculated point of safety under the carrier.

Chang Tian pulled hard on the control stick to dodge the first wave of laser fire. Without pausing, he pushed the stick and sent the spaceship into a steep dive, heading straight for the underbelly of the carrier.

Fifty kilometers.

Twenty kilometers.

They let out held breaths and resumed speaking.

"Why do you think we're safe now?" a puzzled Yun Fan asked. "We're still some distance from the carrier. It's not much of a shield."

Qi Fei chuckled. "You don't know how the Atlantic Alliance works. The fighter wings assigned to their carriers are heavily automated. See all those fighters out there? At most three have real pilots; the rest are all drones piloted by AI. The Atlantic Alliance has a safety switch designed into their AI: the drones will not fire if they're within a certain distance of Atlantic Alliance vessels to prevent friendly fire. We're within that range."

"Oh, that's what you were counting on!"

"So, in a sense," Jiang Liu said to Qi Fei, "you used self-attachment to defeat the machines' obsession with law, their own version of dharma-attachment. Crazy!"

"I'd rather be crazy than dead," Qi Fei said, laughing. "I *am* pretty attached to this living self."

Just as they were about to sweep under the carrier, the reconnaissance craft carrying Chris Zhao began to fire on them—that ship was presumably piloted by real humans, not AI. Two other space fighters approached and fired on them as well. There was very little room for them to maneuver, with the carrier and the web of laser fire cutting off most escape vectors.

"Launch the escape pod in the stern!" Jiang Liu shouted.

Chang Tian immediately grasped what Jiang Liu had in mind and pressed the "Escape Pod" button on the console. Not only did ejecting the pod add more momentum to their spaceship, but it also created a diversion as the escape pod drew fire from the fighters.

There was no sound as they plunged into the looming shadow of the carrier, but everyone seemed to feel a psychic *whoosh* and the oppressive presence of the carrier pressed down on their hearts. No one said anything as the ship sped forward under the belly of the mechanical monster. Even their minds seemed to go blank under its brutal shade.

Shoop! A psychic explosion of joy in the silence of space. They emerged from the other side. Cheers filled the tiny cockpit.

But their celebratory mood didn't last. Instead of abandoning them to pursue the loong-ship, the entire battle group decelerated, turned around, and began to pursue and flank the fleeing tourist spaceship. Contrary to their expectation, Chris Zhao would rather catch them than go after the aliens.

"He's crazy . . ." Jiang Liu tapped the instrument panel helplessly.

"Uh, we have a problem," Chang Tian said. "We're running out of power. If we want to survive reentry, we're going to have to decelerate."

"How can we be out of power?" Jiang Liu tried to do the math in his head. "My family should have filled this thing with enough juice for a trip of thirty days. Maybe your daredevil flying has used up far more energy than planned. How fast *can* you go?"

"To be safe, we should really decelerate to under 20,000 kph. If we hold at 25,000 kph, I can't guarantee we'll make it," Chang Tian said.

"Then let's decelerate to under 20,000 kph," Jiang Liu said. "We need to be safe so we can go pick up Huhu later."

"But if we go that slow, we can't get away from the fighters," Qi Fei said, frowning.

"Even if we stay at 30,000 kph, we still won't be able to shake them," Jiang Liu said. "Our bet was that they'd give up on us and go after the loong-ship. Since they didn't do as we'd planned, they'll catch us sooner or later."

"So what do you want—ah."

Qi Fei felt the thought-packet flashing through Jiang Liu's mind and realized that the two of them had converged on the same idea.

"You don't have to do it," Jiang Liu said, putting on his habitual silly grin. "You're welcome to go home and let me and Fanfan try this plan on our own. If we end up dead, just bury the two of us in the same grave. Deal?"

"No deal." Qi Fei also had on his habitually serious mien—though there was a trace of a smile in it. "You should be worried. I may decide to bury you in the same grave with Chris Zhao."

"Haha! Director Qi is mad!" Jiang Liu laughed. "Excellent. Now the enraged director is going to get rid of Chris Zhao, and all the rest of us can live happily ever after."

"Don't you ever shut up?" Qi Fei said.

Jiang Liu punched in a bunch of directions for the ship's computer and brought Chang Tian over. He made sure that the mind-to-mind communication with Chang Tian was working smoothly before showing him an encrypted data port within which could be found many secret communication lines to various resources under Jiang Liu's control. He told Chang Tian that once he was back on Earth, he could get whatever help he needed by contacting these people—all he had to do was to show them the secret key.

"What is all this about?" Chang Tian was confused. "Why are you telling me all this?"

"In a few minutes we're going to go over to the carrier," Jiang Liu said. "I've programmed this ship to wait a bit before locking the doors and launching off on its own—with you locked inside. At that time, I want you to dash back to Earth at maximum speed without any hesitation."

"Wait, wait! What? You're going to be on the carrier?"

"We already know we can't outrun them," Qi Fei said. "There's no point in prolonging the inevitable. Better for us to go over and distract and trick them. Meanwhile, you can escape and help Huhu."

"This is a dangerous plan," muttered Chang Tian. "Both of you are surely on the Atlantic Alliance's most wanted list."

Jiang Liu smiled. "Well, if we don't go, then Yun Fan has to go by herself. Don't you think that's even worse?"

"Hey! I can go by myself," Yun Fan said.

"Not going to happen," Qi Fei said. "I forbid you from taking such risks."

Chang Tian and Yun Fan acquiesced to the plan. While Chang Tian prepared to pilot the ship back to Earth all by himself, Yun Fan took off her necklace and put it on Chang Tian so that he could get in touch with Huhu. She taught him how to sense the information passed over the necklace and how to concentrate his mind to reach out to Huhu. It didn't take the former psychology major long to get the hang of it.

"Huhu and I were chatting just now," Yun Fan said. "They've already left the loong-ship in a cloaked escape pod. Right now the pod is drifting perpendicular to the original heading of the loong-ship, and there's no sign that the carrier battle group has discovered it. Huhu is going to give you constant updates on their position, and you can work out with them where and how to meet up. Huhu said they already took care of the loong-ship, and there's no need for us to worry."

With everything ready, they decelerated the spaceship. Soon, the Atlantic Alliance fighters surrounded them in a sphere, and the carrier also stopped some distance away.

Chang Tian manually guided the ship to dock with the carrier. The carrier was equipped with multiple arms extending out from the hull for fighters to dock, and it wasn't hard to adapt one of these to accept a small commercial passenger spaceship. Once Chang Tian completed the docking procedure, the air lock opened automatically.

Before they could enter the carrier, the image of Chris Zhao popped onto the screen inside the air lock.

"Welcome!" Chris smiled, showing all his expensive, white teeth. "I'm so glad that you are all so reasonable. Now, what was that old quote from the history of the Three Kingdoms period? 'Those who adapt their actions to changing circumstance are true heroes.' Am I right? Sorry if my Chinese is inadequate. I really didn't want to mar your beautiful faces with bullets, so I'm grateful that you saved me the trouble by surrendering."

"You have no idea the real meaning of the quote you just used, do you?" Jiang Liu said. "Anyway, we aren't interested in talking to you. Where's Colonel Lorenzo?"

"No problem," Chris said from the screen, sweeping his hand in an inviting gesture. "Please, come inside."

Jiang Liu was in the lead while Qi Fei took up the rear, sandwiching Yun Fan between them. As soon as Qi Fei entered the carrier proper, Jiang Liu gently waved his hand behind him. With a loud hiss, the spaceship snapped shut its air lock and freed itself from the carrier's docking arm. Cold flames and radiation shot out of the engines, sending the ship away.

Caught off guard, the fighters around the carrier took some time to react, and Chang Tian almost got away before the fighters formed a tightening three-dimensional web around the escaping spaceship. Despite Chang Tian's attempt to dart around unpredictably, it seemed only a matter of time before he would be caught.

As Qi Fei, Jiang Liu, and Yun Fan gazed anxiously on this scene through a window, the fighters abruptly pulled out of the web formation and retreated— apparently the pilots and the drones all received the order to cease pursuit. Chang Tian seized the opportunity and accelerated away toward Earth at maximum thrust, vanishing from view in seconds.

The three sighed with relief, though they were baffled why the carrier battle group had suddenly decided to let Chang Tian go.

"Come! I suspect you'll be *very* interested in our discovery."

The three turned around to find an excited Chris Zhao greeting them from the screen at the end of the corridor.

[Do you think they've found Huhu?]

[What should we do if they have?]

[We'll have to wait and see. Even if they captured Huhu, we could still find ways to protect them.]

Following bright glowing blue arrows on the floor, they entered the interior of the carrier. Four space marines, heavily armed, escorted them the rest of the way. Instead of spinning like the loong-ship or using a combination of magnetized surfaces and metal shoes, as was done on Jiang Liu's spaceship, the carrier simulated gravity with electromagnetic field alone. It was difficult for the three to make progress in the weak artificial gravity, drift-walking awkwardly. Chris Zhao made their journey even more unpleasant by showing up on every screen they passed, grinning idiotically.

"Don't you want to ask me about what we've found?" Chris winked.

They ignored him. Chris Zhao was one of those people who craved an audience to perform to, and they weren't going to give him the satisfaction.

As they reached the next door, Chris decided that he couldn't wait any longer. "We found a huge spaceship! It's very crude and looks ancient. I imagine that's where you met your friends, no?"

[So their "big discovery" is just the loong-ship,] Yun Fan thought.

They were relieved. There was little the Atlantic Alliance could learn by studying the empty shell of the loong-ship. So long as they didn't capture Huhu, there was no need to worry.

[I would love to be there when Chris Zhao goes through the hall of illusions,] Jiang Liu thought, laughing in his mind. [What sort of monsters do you think that fool will conjure into being?]

[Don't celebrate too early,] Qi Fei thought. [After Yun Fan completed her mission, who knows if the interior of the loong-ship would still be set up the same way. Also, without Yun Fan's key, I doubt they could get inside. Once they realize that, they'll be sure to come harass us.]

[That's nothing to worry about,] Jiang Liu thought. [You also interrogated me once. Did you get far?]

They were brought to the carrier's bubble-shaped control center, with a 270-degree view of the surrounding space.

Chris Zhao's gigantic visage loomed over them from the curved screen. Colonel Lorenzo, the old man standing next to him, was looking in another direction instead of at them. According to the information collected by Jiang Liu and Qi Fei, Lorenzo was one of the leading thinkers among the hawks in the Atlantic Alliance.

"What a magnificent setting for you to meet your friends the last few days!" Chris said, still grinning ridiculously. "Why don't you tell us what's inside?"

A view of the loong-ship replaced Chris on the giant, curved screen. Once again, the ship had become an ouroboros-wheel, about a kilometer in diameter, with multiple spokes leading from the rim to the center. The wheel was "standing" perpendicular to the approaching trajectory of the carrier, like a sun wheel.

Qi Fei, Jiang Liu, and Yun Fan felt an overwhelming sense of awe. They weren't able to see the ship in this form earlier, when they were exploring the inside; in fact, they had worked out the shape of the ship purely by deduction. Moreover, now that they were linked telepathically, they could feel the admiration and amazement bouncing back and forth between their minds, becoming more amplified with each wave. It was an unprecedented experience of collective emotion.

The loong-ship was no more than a hundred thousand kilometers from the carrier. Somehow, the loong-ship had traveled some seven or eight million kilometers in a short amount of time and returned to the location where they had first found it—or maybe even closer. It meant that the loong-ship had, instead of running away from the Atlantic Alliance battle group, approached it on its own.

On the screen, they could see Chris's reconnaissance craft flying toward the loong-ship. It reminded them somehow of a moth flying toward the blazing sun.

[We probably looked like that earlier.]

[How much changed in a single day!]

Chris's ship circled around the ouroboros, looking for an opening but finding none.

"How did you get inside?" Chris's face reappeared on the screen.

"Oh no! Are you having difficulties?" Jiang Liu asked, his face mock helpful.

"Since you were able to get in and get out, the inside must be safe," reasoned Chris. "Tell me how to get in now, or else!"

"We pick 'else'! That's our choice!" Jiang Liu said, as though he were picking prizes.

"Don't push your luck," Chris said, a trace of anger in his voice for the first time. "We have plenty of time, and I'm sure I can persuade you to cooperate." He ordered the other space fighters to approach the loong-ship and secure it with thick cables. "We'll start by dragging this thing back to the moon."

Pulled by dozens of cables, the loong-ship began its long journey toward the moon. The carrier flew behind the formation. The three companions had no idea what fate awaited them there.

[I have something I want to say.] Yun Fan's thoughts broke their reverie.

[Don't say thank you, and don't say sorry, either,] Jiang Liu thought.

[I want to say,] thought Yun Fan, [in a few hours, if I start to say things that are hurtful to you—whether with my lips or in my mind—try to remember that I'll be lying. The best trip of my life is this one, right now, with the two of you.]

[We know,] Jiang Liu thought.

18 | Separation

Because the loong-ship was so massive, it took three full days for the Atlantic Alliance battle group to drag it back to the moon. Qi Fei, Jiang Liu, and Yun Fan were given individual cabins, and marines brought them all their meals. Although the food wasn't as good as Chang Tian's cooking, it was by no means inedible. The three weren't allowed entrance to the more sensitive parts of the carrier, but within a designated area, they were free to roam about as they pleased. While they talked, visited, read, Chris Zhao never showed up to harass them, and there were no attempts at interrogation. Indeed, they didn't even see any obvious signs of surveillance. It was very odd.

[What is Chris up to?] Jiang Liu thought.

[Maybe they're just saving the bad-cop routine for after we land?] Qi Fei guessed.

[So our plan is to escape after we land?]

[It's the best plan we have.]

The three spent some time planning strategies for getting away after landing on the moon.

As the carrier group landed at the Atlantic Alliance's moon base, the ground staff looked up in amazement—not because of the carrier, but what was being towed behind the carrier.

The carrier was about three hundred meters in length, but the ouroboros loong-ship, with a diameter nearly three times that, simply dwarfed the buildings on the moon base. The slow descent of the massive wheel was like the arrival of some god. In the vacuum of the moon, the noiseless, elegant fall of the titanic alien vessel shook every observer to the core.

Jiang Liu, Qi Fei, and Yun Fan stood at a window in the carrier, gazing down at the approaching moon base. Abruptly, a door leading into the restricted area they were confined in was flung open.

A column of people strode in, led by a thin man dressed in a crisp suit. He stopped in front of the three and spoke in English to Jiang Liu, his tone commanding. "Mr. Jiang. I'm a representative of the WTO. I'm ordered to take you back to Earth."

"I have no connection with the WTO," Jiang Liu said.

"Your father does," the man said. "If you prefer, he can come personally."

Jiang Liu was about to argue some more when another man strode in. Wearing the dress uniform of the Pacific League, this man was covered in medals, epaulettes, and starburst buckles—as though ready for a military parade. Jiang Liu identified the man from his personal database: General Yuan.

A stunned Qi Fei took a step back before saluting. "I . . . How did you get here, General?"

"I'm here to take you back," the general said.

"You traveled all the way to the moon just to . . ." Qi Fei was at a loss for words.

"That's right. I flew all the way here just to take you home," the general said.

"I'm sorry for all the trouble," Qi Fei muttered.

"Bringing you back is the League's top priority," the general said. He paused before taking another step forward, his face stony. "This is an order, not a topic for discussion."

The step helped Qi Fei make up his mind. He nodded and saluted again. "I understand."

Qi Fei followed General Yuan out the door. Just before exiting, he turned and gave Yun Fan and Jiang Liu a complicated look. In it, there was more concern than the joy of homecoming one might expect. The other two could sense little from his thoughts; it was as though Qi Fei was deliberately trying to keep his mind blank.

[Get in touch when you can.] That was the last thought Qi Fei left them.

Jiang Liu and Yun Fan balled their fists. Jiang Liu knew that his own rebellion was about to come to an end. Even if he said no to the WTO representative, his parents would show up eventually and put an end to all resistance.

"I'd like to bring my friend," Jiang Liu said to the WTO man, indicating Yun Fan.

"I only have permission to take you," the man said.

"What if I don't go with you?" Jiang Liu asked.

The man held up a hand, and instantly eight soldiers in space armor rushed into the room. Every single one of them outweighed Jiang Liu by at least a hundred pounds, and they were all armed to the teeth. Jiang Liu sighed.

"Why?" he asked.

"Your father wanted it this way," the man said. "He is the Director-General of the WTO. If you don't like these arrangements, you must speak to him directly. There's nothing I can do."

He waved his hand again, and four soldiers came up to surround Jiang Liu, guns at the ready. Yun Fan was pushed away.

"I thought the WTO had no need for force," Jiang Liu said, holding up his hands to placate the threatening soldiers. "When did it get an army for itself?"

"The WTO has no soldiers, of course," the man said, shrugging. "But the Atlantic Alliance has decided to support your father this time. These men are theirs."

Finally, Jiang Liu understood Chris Zhao's plot. He had not bothered them on the carrier because he had been busy negotiating with the senior Jiang and General Yuan. And now that he had succeeded in getting rid of both Jiang Liu and Qi Fei, he would be alone with Yun Fan.

[What a crafty fox!] Jiang Liu thought.

[Just go. Don't make more trouble,] Yun Fan thought.

[But you'll have to deal with—]

[Don't worry. I can take care of myself.]

Qi Fei's thoughts broke into their minds. [Chris is smarter than we gave him credit for. Even though he didn't see what we saw in the loong-ship, he figured out a lot. He's already shared his findings with the others. Just now, General Yuan asked me for clarification on several points.]

Jiang Liu continued to hesitate. Yun Fan locked eyes with him. [Listen, I'll keep this channel open so you'll know everything that happens to me. If I really think there's danger, I'll ask for help. You'll have a lot more resources to draw on if you get back to Earth.]

Jiang Liu nodded. Yun Fan was right. He had to get back to Earth to help his friends. He turned to the man from the WTO and indicated he was ready to go.

Alone in the restricted zone, Yun Fan meditated and did her breathing exercises, readying herself for the confrontation with Chris Zhao.

+ + + + +

Yun Fan woke up from a nap.

The first thing she saw was Chris Zhao in a chair by her bed, staring at her intently. She almost screamed and jumped out of bed.

"Don't mind me," Chris said, smiling as though what he was doing was perfectly socially acceptable. "Sleep some more if you like. You need the rest."

"What do you want?" Yun Fan asked in a low voice.

"Oh, I just wanted to ask you to have some coffee," Chris said. "You know, so we can get to know each other better."

"I don't drink coffee."

"We can drink tea instead. Let's see . . . we have Anji white tea, Wuyi rock tea, and Yunnan Pu'er. All excellent brews. We also have some osmanthus tea, very fragrant, which I think would suit you perfectly. Whatever you want."

"You shipped all these to the moon?" Yun Fan was incredulous.

"Wherever we are, we can't neglect the good life, right?" Chris got up and bowed. "In particular, we must take care of our special guests."

"Why don't you just tell me what you want?" Yun Fan said. "There's no need to drag it out with all this nonsense."

"I'm afraid I can't tell you here," Chris said. "Tea is important, of course, but I also must show you something."

Realizing that arguing with Chris was a waste of time, Yun Fan got up to follow him out the door. She was curious exactly what he had to show her.

In the corridor, she tried to call out to Jiang Liu and Qi Fei.

[Are you there? Can you hear me?]

She waited a long time, but there was no answer. Her heart sank. She didn't know if the moon was too far for their mental link to bridge the gap, or if the other two had suffered some unforeseen setback. She only knew that she was now truly alone.

Once again, Yun Fan found herself in the control center at the bow of the carrier. She was overwhelmed by its grandeur, with its fifty-meter diameter and floor-to-ceiling hemispherical glass wall, it was more spacious than some opera houses she had been to. Two rows of concentric consoles lined up under the hemispherical wall, full of complicated instruments and monitors and buttons and levers. The austere beauty of the moon filled the view.

Yun Fan looked closer: the ring-shaped loong-ship, resting on the lunar surface, dominated the scene. It was as though a new crater had formed on the moon, one worthy of the name of Kunlun.

"What did you want to show me?" Yun Fan probed.

"Take a look at this." Chris brought her to a small monitor.

A single glance told Yun Fan all she needed to know. The screen showed the three avatars they had embodied on Planet Liluhuoman and then returned with—the loong and fenghuang were each about two to three meters in height. Next to them sat a series of smaller metal beasts: centaurs; nine-tailed foxes; chimeras with the head of a bird, the body of a tortoise, and the tail of a serpent; and many others. She realized that they must be the avatars the other members of the inspection team had worn on ancient Earth.

"What am I looking at?" Yun Fan asked.

"You tell me."

"I've never seen these things before. Where did you find them?"

Chris searched Yun Fan's face for clues. "We found them inside the loong-ship."

"How did you get in?"

Chris hesitated, apparently unsure how best to entice Yun Fan to reveal more. "We didn't enter the ship proper. However, the 'spokes' in the wheel are weaker, and we found seams where they connect to the rim. With a laser cutter, we managed to remove one of the spokes and found these inside.

Yun Fan's heart beat wildly. Forcing her face to remain blank, she said, "Oh, if you could remove a spoke, surely you could follow the opening into the ship itself."

Chris narrowed his eyes. "Are you telling me that you've entered the ship before from one of the spokes?"

Yun Fan almost blurted out, "How else do you think those spokes work?" However, she caught herself in time. "I haven't. But I'm curious why you couldn't just slice your way into the main hull with your laser cutter."

"How did you get into the ship before?" Chris demanded.

"How do you know I've been inside?" Yun Fan shot back.

"You vanished for twenty-eight hours. Where did you go during that time, if not inside the alien ship?"

"Vanished?"

"I put a tracking device on one of you. You couldn't get rid of it by changing clothes or showering." A smug smile appeared on his face. "Even now, I know exactly where he is. Hmmm, he's back on Earth, and I see him . . . wouldn't you like to know where he is?"

Yun Fan didn't react.

Chris went on, a bit disappointed. "The period during which he was invisible to my surveillance equipment coincided with your rendezvous with this ship. I know for certain that you've been inside."

"You are despicable," Yun Fan said. She was worried about Qi Fei and Jiang Liu's safety.

"I'll be totally honest with you." Chris leaned against a console. "We couldn't get in. There was an unknown substance that blocked the opening from the main hull into the spoke. No matter how hard we tried, we couldn't break through. I'm admitting our failure to you as a gesture of goodwill. Now, can you tell me how you got in?"

Yun Fan gazed at him steadily. "Why should I tell you?"

"What do you want in exchange?" Chris asked. "Name your price."

Yun Fan snorted. "What if I don't want anything?"

"Everyone has a price. How about this? What if I collect all of your father's papers and translate the volume into every language in the world, announce the publication project at the biggest press conference ever organized, and demand that UNESCO celebrate your father's accomplishments and rehabilitate his reputation as a hero of humanity? Are you telling me you won't be tempted?"

Yun Fan's eyes widened, not because she was amazed by the offer, but because she was shocked at how much Chris knew about her. It was terrifying to have someone dangle your innermost desires and secrets in front of you.

"Mr. Zhao, I'm afraid you've made a terrible mistake," she said, her tone icy. "My father died a long time ago. He has no more use for fame or honor. What you offer is useless."

"Really? Is that so?" Chris didn't seem surprised that she refused. "How about something going the other way? What if the secret tunnels your family had dug into the underground palace of the mausoleum were revealed to the authorities? What if it were known that you had broken your country's laws regarding the protection of antiquities? Are you going to remain so steadfast when you're about to go to jail, your name and reputation dragged through the mud?"

Yun Fan was disgusted. Chris Zhao was a maggot who had burrowed into her and her friends and wouldn't let go.

"What do you really want?" Yun Fan asked.

"I want to know the alien ship's secrets," Chris said.

"What's the point of knowing these secrets?" demanded Yun Fan. "Why do you care so much?"

"I'm interested in technical matters," Chris said, smiling. "I just want to know what technologies are hidden in this ship, and how you learned these technological secrets."

"And then what? I guess then you'll be promoted as a hero of the Atlantic Alliance? You'll get more money and power?"

Chris didn't bother refuting her. "Think what you want. I just want to know if you want to make this deal that benefits us both. You get what you want, and I get what I want. Those other two idiots don't understand you, and they'll never be able to help you the way I can."

"Why don't you ask those inside the ship?"

"Ha! If anyone remained inside the ship, how could we have so easily hauled it all the way back here? And why would they have allowed us to slice off a spoke? We were very cautious in our probes and tests, and never once did we see any sign of resistance. Given the technology we've already seen, the aliens are far more advanced and wouldn't be afraid of us. That proves the ship is deserted."

Yun Fan appeared to ponder the situation for a long time before speaking again. "We can make a deal: You keep to yourself what you know about my improper excavation of the mausoleum, and I'll keep to myself your illegal attempts at conducting surveillance against your president and the Atlantic Alliance's secretary-general."

"What?" Chris's expression turned severe.

"You know exactly what I'm talking about."

Chris's eyes narrowed. He sifted through Yun Fan's words carefully, uncertain just how much she knew (and *how* did she know?). Instinctively, he wanted to trick her into revealing more about the extent of her knowledge so that he could negotiate with her, but he realized that was the wrong approach. His top priority right now was to form a temporary alliance with Yun Fan based on unity of interests, not to turn her into a negotiating partner across the table. He was shocked by Yun Fan's blackmail attempt; he never could have predicted that.

Chris modulated his tone to be much more friendly. "We should cooperate and help each other. You don't really know those two boys as well as you think."

"I bet now you're going to impress me with how well you know them. So predictable."

Chris laughed. "Do you know how many listening devices Jiang Liu implanted in and near your office back at the mausoleum? All my knowledge of your activities comes from the intelligence Jiang Liu gathered. He's been secretly watching you all this time. Have you thought about why he's collecting information on you? Maybe he wants to sell the knowledge on Tianshang. He may flirt with you and tell you what you want to hear, but deep down, he's using you." He could see that his words were having an effect based on Yun Fan's expression. Pleased, he went on. "Now, as for Qi Fei. Surely you know that he accompanied you in order to obtain alien technology and get on the fast track for promotion? He was hoping to succeed so well on this mission that he could return and marry General Yuan's daughter. Qi Fei is the biggest brownnose of them all. All his seriousness and dedication are an act, a performance for the general. You were risking your life to give Qi Fei and his future wife a wedding gift."

Chris was sure that no matter how calm Yun Fan appeared, these words would sting her. Everything he said was a fact, but facts needed to be interpreted to have meaning. He believed he knew exactly how best to interpret the facts to wound Yun Fan, giving him an opening to get her to help him.

"Why are you telling me all this?" Yun Fan demanded.

"You don't have to listen," Chris said. "But do be careful that you aren't taken advantage of. Think about it, why did those two try to get close to you? Why should they help you? There's nothing as dark as the human heart, and only when you understand someone's true motive do you know them. You can't trust your eyes. No one can remain unmoved when tempted by sufficient profit. Let me tell you, before too long, you'll see your sweet Jiang Liu out there with his family, making money hand over fist. Also before too long, you'll see your Qi Fei being celebrated as a hero of the republic, a savior of the Pacific League. You? You were no more than a pawn in their game of self-aggrandizement. I've seen this same story repeated all too many times. At least I'm telling you upfront what's in this for me, as I have no interest in playing with your feelings. This is why collaborating with me is the only wise choice."

Chris watched Yun Fan carefully, waiting for that anticipated flash of pain.

+ + + + +

Jiang Liu was brought to a vacation home his parents owned at the foot of the Alps. As soon as he entered, he knew something wasn't right. The house was too perfect, too perfectly suited to him.

Neither of his parents were there, but two chefs busied themselves in the open-plan kitchen. Festive streamers and other decorations hung all over the living room. He remembered coming to this house in high school, and indeed, there in the living room, he found a framed photograph of the whole family taken when they were on vacation here. In the looping picture, he and his brother were horsing around, chasing each other around the rest of the family, Jiang Liu throwing water on his brother. Only near the end of the loop did the two of them finally stop to stand next to Mom and his big sister, both in pearl dresses, for the camera. Again and again, Jiang Liu watched the loop, watched himself and his brother aimlessly circle the frame, while Dad stood in the middle of it all, expressionless. He felt dizzy.

He wanted to go upstairs to his bedroom to nap, but one of the chefs stopped him, asking whether he wanted meat or fish for lunch, to pick his sides and wine. Although Jiang Liu usually loved to obsess over such details to act the part of the gourmet, he wasn't in the mood today. He wanted to figure out a plan to rescue Yun Fan, but no good idea came to mind, and the lack of progress only added to his anxiety.

He lay on his bed, tossing and turning. He tried to reach out to Qi Fei and Yun Fan in his mind; there was no answer.

On the way back to Earth from the moon, he had switched off the gryon channel in his brain because the thin man was trying to engage him in conversation, telling him what his father wanted. As it turned out, before joining the WTO, the man had worked for Jiang Lang Trading. Jiang Liu shut off the switch in his brain because he couldn't anticipate what ridiculous things the man would bring up, nor how he would respond. He couldn't bear having Yun Fan and Qi Fei listen in on such a conversation.

In the end, the man simply repeated the "deal" Jiang Liu and his father had agreed to before his departure into space: as part of the recent reforms at the United Nations, Jiang Ruoqin had managed to insert blockchain as one of the democratic decision-making mechanisms, a replacement for polls. It would play a weighty role in the final reformed institution. He needed Jiang Liu's help to make it happen, and he had some specific directions he wanted the man to pass on.

Jiang Liu found the whole situation ridiculous. His father needed an agent, a middleman, just to talk with his own son. The old man couldn't face him.

However, now that he wanted to reactivate the inter-brain connection, Jiang Liu found that he couldn't do it. He was worried. *What's happening to them?*

Jiang Liu tried to work through every possible rescue plan, yet they all ended with him feeling helpless, unable to do anything. He could try to negotiate with Chris—except he didn't have enough chips to get Chris to the table. He had no leverage with the military, so there was no way for him to send in the cavalry or space marines and act out an action movie. He did have Tianshang, but the members were the poorest of the poor, the victims of war and civil strife, whose top priority was survival. Although they could be counted on to join a raid to rob the rich, they had no resources to get to the moon. He even thought of hiring one of the space mining gangs to go on a secret hostage rescue mission—until he realized that he had no way to access the necessary funds. All his money was in family trust accounts. The second he tried to withdraw over a certain amount, the request would be rerouted to his parents for approval. He envied his big brother and sister, who each had taken over a subsidiary that they ran as their own empire, and regretted his own intransigence in this regard as a teen. Many things in the world required large sums of money, and only those who commanded capital got to allocate money wherever they wanted.

While he was despairing over the lack of options, his mother entered the room. She wore an expensive but simple dress, real silk, the kind of subtle luxury that she wielded in the endless competition for status between her and her friends. She carried a tray with coffee and cheesecake.

"Don't get up!" Mom said. "You're tired."

"I'm not tired." Jiang Liu got up and took the armchair by the window.

Mom sat down on the chaise lounge next to the bed. Solicitously, she asked, "You must be exhausted after such a long journey?"

"I'm all right."

"I heard that you saw an alien spaceship!"

"Mm-hmm."

"Was it amazing? Did you take pictures?"

"My bodycam took some shots, and we collected a lot of data on the trip." Jiang Liu thought back to when he directed the beetle-drones to scan the interior of the loong-ship and projected the images onto Qi Fei's contacts; it felt like another life.

"Oh, I want to see!" Mom sounded excited. "Can you process the data for VR?"

Jiang Liu nodded. He twisted the bangles to pull up the raw data on exterior views of the loong-ship and the shots taken during the space walks. Connecting wirelessly to the VR projector in the room, he re-created the sights for his mother, who exclaimed in admiration as she surveyed the alien ship.

"This is fantastic," Mom said. "Send me all the data. I'll edit it and post it to your VR space. This will go viral for sure!"

"Please don't. This is serious, Mom, and so it's best for all the governments of the world to handle the news together. Also, I think the focus ought to be on scientific research. I'm not even sure it should be publicized just yet."

"Oh, but the people have a right to know!" Her excitement didn't diminish at all. "Such important news should be broadcast to everyone on Earth right away. Governments? This is about all humanity, so why should any country's government be put in charge of what to do? My baby Eric, listen to Mommy, you're now a hero of all humanity. You should stand up and take your rightful place as a representative of the interests of all of us. Don't worry about governments."

Mom's speech seemed reasonable, but Jiang Liu could sense a hidden agenda. "I'm no hero. I can't represent anyone except myself."

"What do you mean? My son is so handsome, so smart, so brave. Of course you're a hero."

"Mom, I don't want to be a hero. I don't want to be in the spotlight at all. I'm used to being a free wanderer."

"Oh, Eric, my poor baby." Mom smiled meaningfully and deliberately shifted on the chaise lounge to be closer to Jiang Liu. "I think I was too hard on you in the past and didn't take the time to understand your work as I should have. Please don't blame me. Mommy just wanted all three of my children to realize their full potential, to live good lives. What mother doesn't want her child to be the best? Now that your brother and sister are both independent and in charge of their own companies, I should have more time to focus on you."

"Mom, I'm twenty-seven." Jiang Liu frowned. "I'm fine. I don't need you to take care of me."

"No matter your age, you'll always be Mommy's baby! Look at your brother. Even at thirty-six, he still asks my opinion when he wants to buy a new shirt. Now, you're used to taking life easy, maybe too easy. However, I can help you! With my help, in two years I guarantee you won't even recognize yourself. You have so many resources! In fact, I think you're even more talented than your brother, but you haven't made the most of your gifts. Let me tell you, success in life is only thirty percent native talent; the other seventy percent is execution and management. Good management is the only way not to waste natural talent, the precious talent you're throwing away by drifting through life.

"Eric, in the past, Mommy didn't understand the work you did with Tianshang. But now I *do* understand. You are a philanthropist! We need to work on properly publicizing your accomplishments. Now that you've been to space and found the alien ship, you're absolutely a hero of humanity. Young people across the globe need you as an idol."

Jiang Liu finally understood what Mom was after. She wanted to be an idol-factory, with him as the sole product. She would produce viral VR clips, turn Tianshang into a prestige brand, make him into a star. Only when her Baby Eric had become as accomplished as his brother and sister would she, the wise and proud mother, be able to beam with pride and enjoy the adulation of all the jealous parents.

Instead of directly challenging his mother, as was his habit, he simply said, "It's not a good fit with my personality."

"Don't worry." Mom's smile was unwavering. "You don't have to do a thing. I'll take care of it all for you."

"But I don't want any of that."

"I certainly don't want you to do anything you aren't comfortable with.

However, people change. You should wait until you've experienced the life of a hero before you say no. Also, let Mommy tell you something from the bottom of my heart: I hope that now that you're back home, you can spend some quality time with us. Don't run around anymore with that boy from the Pacific League and that odd girl. The war is about to escalate, and being too friendly with those people will bring you trouble. I can tell that girl is a schemer, and she's trying to attach herself to you because she has designs on our family. You have to protect yourself from women like that."

That night, as Jiang Liu had anticipated, there was a party at the house. The guest list was very selective. Several prominent merchant families in Europe came, and there were seven or eight handsome young people Jiang Liu's own age. A few had brought along their own children, who chased one another around the sofa in the living room, much like he and his brother in the looping photo. The party was supposed to celebrate Jiang Liu's space mission, but other than an over-the-top speech from Mom at the beginning, after which a few strangers asked Jiang Liu a couple of questions, the topic wasn't brought up again for the rest of the party. Beautiful men and women raised their champagne flutes and silently put a hand on a hip or back, words flowing out of their mouths like endless fountains, their eyes swimming with desire.

Dad didn't come. Jiang Liu wanted to discuss a new deal with him, but Dad didn't give him the chance.

Jiang Liu was used to parties like this. He was good at flirting and pretending to be interested, even when he hated to be where he was. However, on this evening, he chose to step away by himself so that he could sit on the balcony and gaze up at the moon, a drink in hand. Again and again, he called out in his mind, searching for a familiar reply that never came. Pain creased his smooth brow.

+ + + + +

General Yuan took Qi Fei to a small isle in the Spratly Islands, the location of the Pacific League's Central Command. All the major military districts stationed their permanent representatives and staff officers here.

Concerned about leaking military secrets, Qi Fei shut off the gryon channel on the way.

White sand, green water—the tropical island was like a land out of fantasy.

General Yuan spent about half of his time in Xi'an, and the other half here in meetings. Qi Fei, on the other hand, had come to Central Command only once in the past and didn't get a chance to see much. However, instead of taking him on a tour, General Yuan brought Qi Fei directly to his headquarters, a two-story house hidden behind a dense grove of palm trees. Unadorned and streamlined, the house was indistinguishable from all the other buildings on the island, sharing with them a design intended to maximize survivability in the event of an air strike.

Qi Fei followed the general into his office, which was furnished similarly to the general's office back in Xi'an. A giant world map dominated one wall, on which flashing lights showed the latest flashpoints and highlights from military intelligence. The general indicated that Qi Fei should make his own tea and got to the point right away. "This place is completely secure. Speak freely. What did you see?"

"Uh . . . it's a long story." Qi Fei tried to think of a good way to explain everything. "We encountered an alien civilization. At first, it was just on the ship. But later, we went to their planet, called Liluhuoman."

"How did you get to their planet?" The general looked interested.

"We jumped. Uh, how should I explain this . . . All right, this alien civilization had contacted and influenced humanity in the past, and many of our ancient legends were based on them. They visit us about once every seven or eight centuries. Oh, they explained some advanced physics to us, including the principles behind inter-universal jumps. Simplifying grossly, the brain can interact with something called gryons, and entangling gryons allows jumping. There are many details that I don't understand about the process, so more research is definitely needed."

"Based on your observations, how much more technologically advanced are these aliens compared to us?"

"Much, much more advanced. They explained to us a system for ranking civilizations. We are barely at Stage Three, while they are at Stage Seven."

"That's a big gap." The general looked thoughtful. He got up and retrieved a pack of cigarettes from the windowsill. Lighting one, he asked, "Do you think there's any possibility they'll still want to ally with us despite the difference in power?"

Qi Fei was overjoyed. "Oh, there's more than just possibility. They belong to a union of cooperating civilizations, whose central tenet is mutual aid between civilizations. They are very active in helping less advanced civilizations, and they've been helping Earth all along."

"No, that's not what I'm asking." The general pointed to himself and Qi Fei. "I meant: Are they willing to ally with *us*?"

Qi Fei's heart sank. "I . . . I'm not sure I understand."

"There may be a major battle in a few days, a decisive battle between us and the Atlantic Alliance." The general's tone was casual, as though talking about dinner plans. "We haven't settled on where, but it will most likely be in space. It's hard to fight with no reservations on the ground because we are constrained by civilian casualties and other humanitarian factors. But in space, neither side needs to hold back. It will be a pure contest of power. It's time to show them what we've got.

"We were thinking of taking them on in geosynchronous orbit, but maybe it's better to go even higher. Did you say that the Atlantic Alliance towed the alien ship to the moon?"

"Yes."

"So maybe we should set up this confrontation near the moon." General Yuan ashed his cigarette. "Then we can seize the ship from them and get your girlfriend back."

"What?" Qi Fei's heart pounded.

"Yun Fan is being held by the Atlantic Alliance. Don't you want to get her back?"

"I do."

"How do you think your mother will react when she finds out about her?" The general's tone was ominous.

"Please. Don't tell her."

But the general was already waving at the wall, summoning onto the giant screen a video call program. It showed that a call to Qi Fei's mother had been initiated. Before Qi Fei could stop it, the call had connected, and Qi Fei's mother appeared on the wall.

"Xiao Fei! Is that you?" Mom's face was twisted by anxiety. "Where are you?"

Her eyes darted around the room until she found Qi Fei. Instantly her face relaxed, and she let out a long sigh. "Xiao Fei, it's really you! I'm so happy. You have no idea how worried I've been."

Reluctantly, Qi Fei got up and walked to the wall. He smiled at his mother. "Mom, I'm fine."

She examined Qi Fei through the screen. "Where have you been? You told me that you had to leave on some mission but didn't tell me where. I heard later that you went to space. That's so dangerous! How could you just go like that when you've had no training? You scared your mother so much! You have no idea. I couldn't sleep the last few days, and every time I dozed off, I'd wake up from a nightmare where you fell into space and drifted away, never coming back. I could only lie in bed, sobbing and worrying, and wait for the sun to come up. Look at me. My hair is falling out from the worry."

She tried to hold up her sparse hair to the camera. Qi Fei tried to soothe her. "Please don't worry. Look, Ma, I'm perfectly fine. Space isn't so dangerous."

"Is everyone who went on the mission with you all right as well? A few days ago I heard someone mention Yun Fan. I was so shocked. I thought it was that same . . . woman. But General Yuan explained to me it's a different person with the same name. What a coincidence! So how many people went with you? Were they your friends?"

"Ma, really, everything is fine. Don't worry. Everyone is really nice to me, and they're all doing well. Look at me: I'm better than ever. Please get some sleep. You really need it."

Mother and son went back and forth in this vein a few more times before she finally allowed the call to end. Qi Fei felt more terrified and anxious during the call than during his adventures in space, and his skin felt clammy with a thin layer of perspiration. He couldn't imagine how she would react if she found out that he had been with Yun Fan, the daughter of the woman she loathed.

As far back as college, Qi Fei had fallen into a pattern of conversation with his mother where all his sentences were variations of: "I'm fine. I'm perfectly good. Please don't worry. Please get some sleep. You don't need to worry about me. I'm fine. I'm perfectly . . ." However, the more he said "I'm fine," the less he wanted to go home—perhaps he was unwilling to let his mother know the yawning gulf that separated his true mental state and the verbal formula "I'm fine."

Qi Fei had to sit on the sofa for some time after the call to recover his composure.

General Yuan waited.

Finally, Qi Fei broke the silence. "General, I guess you knew all along about me and Yun Fan?"

The old man nodded.

"Then why . . ."

"I knew from the start the complicated backstory between you and Yun Fan. So you're wondering: Why did I still send you to accompany her? I'll be perfectly frank: it's because I trust you to know what matters and that you can rationally weigh the difference between those worthy of your devotion for the rest of your life and those you're merely infatuated by and shouldn't associate with for the long run. It's precisely because of your history with Yun Fan that she trusted you and allowed you to know her secrets. If I hadn't sent you, we wouldn't be in such a good position now. I gambled on you, and I won."

"So everything . . . was just a game to you?"

"Qi Fei, life is just a game. Until the day you die, you're placing bet after bet, hoping to win more than the other players. The smart ones get to play at the table with the highest stakes and try to win it all. Do you know why I'm being so honest with you? I want to take you with me to the most exclusive table."

Qi Fei felt like he was being controlled by some mechanical conversation AI. "What game are we playing?"

"I'll help you rescue Yun Fan, and I promise you I won't tell your mother about her. You, on the other hand, will get in touch with your alien friends—I know you can do it—and convince them to help us in the battle. Us, do you understand?"

"The stakes really are high," Qi Fei muttered. "General Yuan, I'm truly amazed by your strategic acumen. I have so much to learn. What kind of help are you hoping for?"

General Yuan chuckled. "Well, if the battle is going to be in space, then you'll have to figure out what will guarantee our victory. I trust you to negotiate with the aliens and get us what we need. Don't worry, the League knows how to reward those who bring victory. Once we defeat the enemy, I can guarantee you'll be promoted to the rank of major general. You'll be the youngest major general in both the Atlantic Alliance and the Pacific League. Your name will forever be linked to the peak of Pacific League glory."

"What about you, General? What do you want?"

The general smiled. "Nothing. A victory is all I desire. Today's Pacific League shows many signs of corruption and weakness, and I see many cowards who would beg for peace with the enemy at any price. These maggots are willing to cut off our own flesh to feed the Atlantic Alliance. If they come into power, what do you think will happen to men like you and me? They are rotting the League from within! I want nothing more than for the League to be at the top of the world. I can give the League this, something those cowards never can. Oh, one more thing: I hope after this, you'll never see Yun Fan again and focus on building a good life with my Lulu."

Qi Fei nodded. "I understand you perfectly, General. Thank you."

"Good, good! Now you know what to do." The general smiled in satisfaction. "Qi Fei, remember, you're a soldier, a glorious soldier of the Pacific League! Don't forget who you are just because you spent a few days with that useless boy and your pretty girlfriend. The Jiang family is motivated by nothing except profit. They would serve any master that dangled money in front of them. But you're different. You serve the glorious League, and you must keep yourself away from those corrupting maggots. Have you forgotten how your father died? No? Then this battle will be your chance to finally avenge him."

Qi Fei responded like a machine. "I haven't forgotten."

"Tomorrow morning, you'll come to Geneva with me. There's going to be a meeting of the Security Council, at which the issue of what you saw will be discussed. The battle will take place right after the meeting. You have tonight to contact your alien friends and convince them to help us. I'm sure that's plenty of time."

"I understand."

Satisfied with his arrangements and instructions, the general sat back comfortably in his chair to enjoy a pipe. He failed to notice the pain that flashed across Qi Fei's face.

19 | Choice

Since he couldn't sleep, Qi Fei switched on the gryon channel to see if he could get in touch with the others. No one answered.

His heart felt heavy. While they were pitting their wits against Chris Zhao on the spaceship, they had been one mind with one purpose. But back on Earth, he had lost them, and they had lost him. He couldn't find them, hear them, see them.

He lay in the guesthouse bed, thinking over everything that had happened during the day. He felt he was weaker than he had imagined himself to be. When General Yuan had unveiled his plot for victory, his first reaction wasn't excitement at the prospect of glory; instead, he had been thinking of how to get himself out of the war. His own hesitation confused him. He had returned to Earth with the hope of finding a way to save Yun Fan, hadn't he? The battle was the perfect opportunity to rescue her. Moreover, he had trained for years with the hope of a decisive battle against the Atlantic Alliance, when he would finally avenge his father.

But he didn't want to be in battle at all, and he couldn't articulate why. Something about General Yuan's speech struck him as deeply wrong, a dangerous trap. He couldn't say exactly what; all he had was an instinctive desire to run away.

He pondered the general's directions. Tomorrow, in Geneva, there would be an emergency meeting of the Security Council to discuss the alien spaceship. The Atlantic Alliance, the Pacific League, the Red Sea Pact, and the UN Headquarters would all send delegates as Yun Fan's secret mission had become public knowledge. At the meeting, the Pacific League would declare the loong-ship an artifact of one of its member states and demand the Atlantic Alliance turn it over unconditionally. The Atlantic Alliance would refuse, giving the Pacific League the casus belli to declare war. The large-scale decisive battle in space would follow, the culmination of a thirty-year arms race, with the orbits a powder keg packed full of military satellites and space stations, carriers and fighters, just waiting for a spark.

Both sides were hoping for an excuse to pull the trigger, to see nuclear explosions fill the sky. The process by which war came about and the actual participants were, comparatively, unimportant. Nobody believed peace was possible, and the Security Council meeting was nothing more than a staged performance to be rushed through because its ending had long been written. For more than two decades, the two warring factions had yearned for this moment to launch all the missiles and shoot all the lasers. The four of them had simply walked between the arrayed warriors on the eve of the battle.

He had not imagined it would be like this.

So what had he imagined? The duty of a soldier: justice, honor, family, and country. He hadn't imagined a contest involving nuclear weapons in space over the desire for power. But what was justice? Who got to decide what it meant? Did it even exist? Was justice no more than another name for the competition for power? Could that really be true? Really?

As thousands of ships exploded and lives went up in smoke, who was going to laugh? Who was going to celebrate that sight?

As Qi Fei's mind wandered and his body grew stiff from despair, he heard Yun Fan's voice in his mind.

[Chang Tian! Chang Tian! Are you there?]

Qi Fei held his breath and listened. He wasn't ready to say anything, not yet. Just sensing her voice and emotions felt so good.

[Chang Tian, I have so much to say, but I don't know who to talk to, so I have to try to talk to you. Remember the conversation we had on the spaceship, when we talked about Jiang Liu and Qi Fei? I told you that they didn't love me. I told you that I had a feeling that we were just going to work together on that trip, and after the trip, we would go our separate ways; I don't think that anymore.]

Qi Fei tensed. He listened even more intently in his mind.

[Chang Tian, you know what Chris told me today? He said Jiang Liu collected intelligence about me so he could sell it on his blockchain. He said Qi Fei helped me so he could get medals and promotions and marry his general's daughter. I felt so hurt . . . and that surprised me. No, I wasn't surprised that maybe Chris was right, maybe the two of them really did the things he said they did. No, I was surprised at how I cared.]

After a pause, Yun Fan continued, her mind-voice even softer.

[For the last five years, after my father died, I haven't experienced any strong emotions at all. My heart has been like a still pool, and I thought nothing would disturb me again. When Qi Fei and Jiang Liu came to me, I negotiated with them just like I'd discuss any business, feeling nothing at all. But when Chris told me that they were lying to gain my trust, to further their own selfish ends, I felt such agony. I didn't even want to figure out whether they were capable of such things, I only knew that I cared. I haven't felt like that in such a long time! What I felt wasn't the possessiveness of desire, wasn't the hatred a woman might feel for an unworthy boyfriend, but something else. No, it's not romantic love, but I don't know what to call it. Maybe "trust" is the best word for it. For so long I haven't bared my heart to anyone, and when I finally do trust some people, my greatest terror is that they aren't worthy of my trust. It makes me question the whole world. I'm terrified, like that time I got lost in the park as a little girl. I'm afraid of being abandoned by the world.]

[I'm here. I'm listening.] It was the mind-voice of Chang Tian. [Don't be scared. They are worthy of your trust. They'll never abandon you.]

[I despise those who play the part of victim, who act so pitiable.] Yun Fan continued. [To put on such an act is a form of bullying, of domination. It's a way to force others to obey the false victim, to kidnap their conscience. If they don't do exactly what the false victim wants, they'll be made to feel guilty, to believe they were at fault. I absolutely despise people like that, and so that's why I never want anyone's pity. I've always told myself: everyone is free to come and go as they please; I owe them nothing, and they owe me nothing. If they really ended up living their own happy lives without me, that's totally fine. But . . . but I can't help it. I'm afraid. It's so dark on the moon; I can't see anything.]

[Don't be scared. I won't abandon you. I'm with Huhu, and we have a solution. We'll come get you tomorrow.]

[Hey!] It was Jiang Liu's mind-voice. [Who says you get to play the part of the hero coming to the aid of a lady in distress? Did you ask me first?]

[Ah, so you are here.] Chang Tian's surprised joy could be felt by all.

[When did you join the channel?] Yun Fan's mind-voice was flustered. [I tried to call you several times earlier, but no one answered.]

[I just got on. I've been here only . . . awhile. Hey, Qi Fei, come out. I know you're here.]

[Mm-hmm,] Qi Fei thought.

[So you were all here when I . . . Uh, I mean . . . I said . . .] Yun Fan was panicking.

[We heard everything. Silly girl, how could you think we would abandon you? I can't speak for Qi Fei, but I, for one, will aways be there for you.]

[Hey! I told you not to speak badly about me behind my back!]

Although they were bantering in their mind as usual, Qi Fei and Jiang Liu felt no joy, only an oppressive anxiety. Jiang Liu knew that Qi Fei could feel his own dread, just as he could sense Qi Fei's worry. Earlier, they had both been concentrating on controlling their own emotions and didn't actively reach out to anyone in their minds, yet they both felt someone else's emotions and thoughts even as they focused on their own. They realized that the mind-connection between them was strengthening over time as they learned to use it. At first, they had only been able to "hear" each other, but the longer they were immersed in the link, the more they could sense the subtler, nonverbal mental processes.

It was like . . . when first plunged into darkness, the eyes could only see the spots illuminated by flashlights. Only by shining a light directly on someone could they be seen. But over time, as the eyes adjusted to the darkness, even the parts not directly illuminated would emerge from the murk. With sufficient time, the darkness no longer seemed dark, but became a world with layers and shades and outlines and its own light.

Jiang Liu and Qi Fei could now perceive the layers and shades in each other's minds. Jiang Liu could sense the reluctance Qi Fei felt for his own assignment the next day; Qi Fei could sense Jiang Liu's resistance to his family's demands. These shadows in the mind were not the sort of feelings they ever felt comfortable talking about in the open; however, now they knew. They knew that soon, Chang Tian and Yun Fan would sense the shadows in their minds as well. The only reason they hadn't so far was because they were engaged in conversation and hadn't yet allowed their mental eyes to adjust fully to the darkness.

Only by immersing in the darkness and sensing the shadows in one another's hearts would we finally feel free.

We meet our true selves in darkness.

[Qi Fei, I thought of an idea.] Jiang Liu thought.

[Tell me.]

[My idea depends on you. My biggest realization today is this: there are many things in the world that I can't do just by myself.]

[Just tell me your idea.]

[I must explain to you first why I can't do it myself. Today, my mother suggested that I become a hero for all humanity in VR. My first instinct was to run away. Later, I tried to work out why I felt that way. I think it's not just because I despise her vanity; the bigger reason is that I can't deal with the complications. Okay, let me dig into that a bit. I don't mean dealing with the commercial and legal complexities, the give-and-take—all that external stuff I'm fine with. By "complications" I mean complications in myself; it's all internal. In my mind, there's always this idea about my "whole self." I can only exist in a state where I feel whole, where I don't have to face anything I don't want to. That is why I've been drifting alone all these years. It's only when I'm by myself that I can live according to my ideals, to feel free. The second I try to work with others, I feel constrained because I don't want to change myself. I've tried to, again and again, and have always failed. The moment I sense someone trying to change me, I take off. My mother's proposal felt the same. The very idea of becoming a VR "hero" was revolting because I could imagine the complications that would come after, the black and white and red and green and purple that would try to invade me. I wanted to run. I would rather be by myself, whole and undisturbed, than to allow other colors inside me.]

[You prefer to maintain a pure self. Nothing wrong with that.]

[But that means I can't get anything done, either. This experience has made me feel so helpless! I realized that to maintain a whole self is also to seal the self away. The price I pay is to have no power, which requires complexity, complication, and compromise. I can't rescue the person I care about. I finally understand the drive behind your desire for unity, for one strength out of many. But to achieve that I must allow myself to be changed, to be invaded. You are different from me. You can accept a self in which one half is the part you are attached to, that you uphold with all your being, and the other half consists of compromises with external demands.

You can do this, but I can't. I wondered why. Maybe it's because from childhood, I was able to do so many things well: taking tests, dancing, skiing, martial arts . . . I did everything instinctively, with little effort, and ended up with the illusion that I was omnipotent. But no one is omnipotent. Qi Fei, I confess that you have strength that I don't. Only you can carry out my idea.]

[Before you say more, I have something I must confess too.] Qi Fei interrupted. [I almost resigned today.]

[What?] Amazement from all.

[General Yuan told me today that the Atlantic Alliance and the Pacific League plan to fight a decisive battle in space tomorrow.] Qi Fei's depressive mood pervaded all his thoughts. [At one time, I might have been excited by the idea, but today, when I heard the news, my first instinct was to run away.]

The others waited. When "conversing" this way, each person sent out a whole packet of signals all at once. The words were sent along with emotional signals like a hologram of everything in the mind at that moment. It was hard to describe using words, but the immediacy and directness was unparalleled. The emotion of each reverberated in all. They *felt* Qi Fei's vacillation and anxiety, a spreading ink stain in Qi Fei's habitually restrained and steady emotional backdrop.

[I hated the Atlantic Alliance before this trip to space,] Qi Fei continued. [However, the trip made me realize that my strong emotions were really based on some things that I didn't want to face. I repressed those feelings, forced them down, and they pushed back even harder, manifesting as rage at the Atlantic Alliance. But in reality, what I couldn't face was a deep sense of resentment. The resentment was so powerful, so terrifying, that I pushed it into a well and sealed the top with a heavy pile of repression. I resented that my life had been ruined, but I didn't know who to resent. That was why I directed my anger at the Atlantic Alliance. However, the trip also made me realize . . . that my life hasn't been ruined, that I can still go on. I saw Fanfan, who was still pursuing her own life, a life true to herself. I suddenly realized that so can I. I felt a bit empty as my strong rage and hatred suddenly dissipated.]

[I know what you mean,] Jiang Liu thought. [Fanfan also affected me. I've never been so dedicated to anything as she was to her mission.]

[I feel exactly the opposite,] Yun Fan thought. [Before the trip, I knew exactly what I wanted to do. Now I know nothing.]

[Freed from the repression, my mind feels clearer,] Qi Fei thought. [Earlier this afternoon, I was thinking: I hated the pilot who bombed the bridge my father was on, but tomorrow I'm going to direct war machines to bomb the moon base. Do those inside who are about to die have sons? Will their sons hate me as well? Am I about to commit a grave error? Am I evil? Days earlier, I was one of four picked to represent all humanity in an experiment for civilizational upgrade, and now I'm going to bomb other humans. If I do this, how can humanity ever pass through the door to the next level? I wanted to get out, to run away, but I couldn't see how to save Fanfan if I left my post. I feel so useless.]

[You can't run away. You have to stand up,] Jiang Liu thought.

[How? You want me to go direct the bombing raid tomorrow?]

[Of course not! I want you to stand up and stop the battle tomorrow and become the leader of our future movement.]

[What are you talking about?! How am I going to stop the Pacific League and the Atlantic Alliance from a battle they've been planning for decades? There are so many people with so much power on both sides; they'll never listen to a nobody like me.]

[You are not a nobody,] Jiang Liu insisted. [You'll be addressing the Security Council in tomorrow's meeting.]

[My address is just a formality. You know how it goes. These meetings are all theater. Both sides will get up and make the same demands they've made countless times. Neither side will give an inch. They'll blame each other and declare war.]

[You're describing the way it is, but you can change that. You can stand up and transform the way things have always been done. I'm going to help you.]

[Even with your help, it won't work. What you demand is impossible. I can't do it.]

[Of course you can do it,] Jiang Liu persisted. [Have you forgotten the Confucian ideal you admired? "Do what is right even if you know failure is certain." Have you forgotten those court historians who dared to speak truth to power and had no doubt of their chosen path, even unto death? Even the great Confucius once was powerless and penniless, wandering about like a stray dog, trying to make anyone, anyone at all, listen to his lessons on ren. Are you going to watch the world fall into darkness and do nothing?]

[If you think it's so easy, why don't you do it?] Anger tinged Qi Fei's thoughts.

[I told you that I can't do it, but you can!] Jiang Liu's thoughts also darkened from anger.

[Stop it!] Yun Fan broke in. [This is too much. I can't breathe. Both of you are driving me crazy. I can't bear these thought-packets pressing down on me. Stop fighting! This is my problem, not yours. I don't want any of you to come rescue me. I told you I'm fine on my own. I beg you: stop trying to help me. Just stop!]

As the chaotic thought-packets buffeted everyone, and currents of emotion surged and churned, a sudden sense of peace, like a beam of sunlight, like the smell of fresh leaves, like an early spring breeze, brushed across their minds. Instantly, they all felt calmer, wanting to immerse themselves in this newfound tranquility.

[I can't leave the three of you alone for even a minute,] Chang Tian chided in their minds. [Good thing I was prepared.]

They realized that Chang Tian had somehow learned a technique for soothing their emotions over the gryon channel—maybe it was based on psychotherapy techniques he knew. They could feel their breath coming easier, their nerves relaxing, and the tension and stress from earlier dissipating. Gradually, their minds recovered their tranquility: the breath of sunlight, the fragrance of the wind, the comforting touch of waves, the heart's solace.

[Where are you, Chang Tian?] Qi Fei thought. [I've been trying to get in touch with you all day.]

[I was busy with Huhu. We're on a small islet now, somewhere in the Societies, very hidden. Huhu is so tired that they're asleep. Did you know that the qilin of Liluhuoman also sleep? I didn't. Huhu looks like a baby right now, adorable.]

[I'm glad that you're settled.] Jiang Liu thought. [Did you have a lot of trouble picking up Huhu?]

[There were certainly some adventures, but nothing too major. I'll tell you all about it some other time. Oh, we planted the pity flower. It needs a lot of water, and when given water, it grows so fast! It's beautiful. I'll show you some pictures later.]

[That's wonderful,] Yun Fan thought.

[Let's focus on what we can do tomorrow,] Chang Tian thought. [We have to turn swords into plowshares and save Fanfan. We'll have a grand reunion on this island. Huhu and I actually came up with a good idea, but Jiang Liu wouldn't let me say it earlier.]

[Fine, fine. Tell us your plan.] Jiang Liu was all sunshine now. [You tell us your idea first, and then I'll talk about my plan.]

[That's why fighting amongst ourselves is so useless. None of us can even present our good ideas!] Chang Tian's thought-packets always gave off the air of kind smiles. [But let me first digress a bit and make a few observations. First, Fanfan, you're now brave enough to express your needs. In the past, your biggest problem was acting as though you needed nothing and no one. But everyone needs other people. You just lacked the courage to admit it. Your shell was too thick. But just now, when you said you were terrified, I actually felt hope. It's a good step. Okay, now I'm going to talk about Jiang Liu.]

[What is this? Are you grading our homework?] Jiang Liu said, hoping to head Chang Tian off. [I think you've been spending too much time with Huhu. You've picked up their bad habit of always lecturing.]

[Hey, you've made a lot of progress in admitting your own weaknesses, so don't backslide now. Let me talk.] Chang Tian's thoughts were still so peaceful and calming. [I'm not lecturing you so much as trying to awaken you. Just now, you touched on a really important point, but you let it pass without seizing it. Think about it: When you say you are afraid of not being whole, of being invaded, what are you really scared of?]

[Do you actually have a plan?] Jiang Liu shot back. [If you don't want to get to the point, let me talk about my plan.]

[Fine, I'll get to my plan soon.] Chang Tian continued, unperturbed. [Let me make my observation about Qi Fei. Xiao Fei, I know you well, and I also think you need to stand up. No, it's not because I think you must be a hero. But the reason you want to run away is because you touched one of those parts of your mind you won't face. Your mind is full of these walled-off areas that you refuse to confront. General Yuan is one of them.]

Qi Fei didn't respond. Maybe he was thinking through what Chang Tian meant.

Chang Tian continued. [All right, that's enough digression. I'll leave you to think about what I said. Let me get to the plan Huhu and I came up with. Fanfan, tomorrow morning you should bring Chris Zhao into the loong-ship and lead him to one specific cabin. I'll send you a holographic map to show you exactly where you should go . . .]

+ + + + +

The next morning, Yun Fan brought Chris Zhao to the alien ship.

Chris was both excited and suspicious. "What changed your mind?"

Yun Fan smiled. "Chris, I'm curious about you. Most people in the world are selfish, but they like to pretend they aren't and justify their actions with hypocritical talk of virtues. You, on the other hand, are shameless, speaking of selfish desire with pride. What made you that way?"

Chris laughed. "I've always believed in the value of honesty. Human nature is centered around selfishness, and there's no shame in that. I prefer to be thought greedy than a hypocrite. My price is written right on my face. Yun Fan, trust me, sooner or later, the phonies who conceal their true vices in talk of virtue will hurt you."

"My fortune, good or ill, is none of your business," Yun Fan said. "But let's get down to business. I'll take you inside and tell you everything I know, and you'll take me home, remove all your surveillance equipment, and leave me alone from now on. Deal?"

"You got it," Chris said. "But I can only remove my devices. I can't make any promises about Jiang and Qi."

"Our deal only involves you and me. I'm not concerned about other people."

Yun Fan strode toward the loong-ship. Chris watched her for a few seconds before deciding to follow. They were outside the moon base and had to walk a few hundred meters over the uneven lunar terrain to reach the alien ship. Both were in space suits and talking through headsets. Chris's space suit was custom-made: form-fitting, enhanced with decorative packet, collar, and epaulettes in imitation of the uniform of the space force. The overall effect was quite pompous and ridiculous.

The two bobbed along the lunar surface, cautiously making their way around the trap-like small craters. There wasn't much talking, as each was preoccupied by their own anxious thoughts. Both glanced down at their timepieces: The Security Council meeting was going to start in less than thirty minutes.

Yun Fan approached the ship and stopped at the spot where Chris and his people had cut off one of the spokes. Abruptly, she spun around. "Do you think spirits can take over bodies?"

Even through two layers of glass, Yun Fan's expression inside her helmet still seemed very eerie to Chris. He shuddered involuntarily but forced himself to smile confidently. "I'm not superstitious."

"Do you believe that if you do something terrible and hurt others, then karma, or heaven's Dao, or something like it, will catch up to you eventually?"

Chris felt the hair on his back stand up. But he forced himself to laugh. "I've never done anything like that, so why should I be afraid?"

"Ha! Then what about the time you blackmailed the president and took the place of someone far more deserving?" Yun Fan winked at Chris.

Chris's heart thumped. Yun Fan was referring to something that had taken place within the last two days! But he was sure he hadn't given away any hints of what he had done. It was possible that Qi Fei and Jiang Liu had the intelligence-gathering capability to discover his secret, but how did they pass that information to Yun Fan?

Before he could think the matter through, he saw Yun Fan walk up to the hull, retrieve a small magnet from her space suit, and stick it onto the impenetrable door that he and his people had failed to cut through. Instantly, blue lines filled the door, and the whole circle lit up like a giant silicon chip throbbing with computation. Soon, the round door retreated into the ship and separated into two halves in the process of opening up. Chris was stunned. He couldn't have imagined a magnet would produce such results.

Yun Fan stood next to the opened door but didn't enter. Chris was about to go in when he received another huge jolt. A metallic beast was striding toward him from deep within the ship. The beast looked similar to a loong, but it wasn't a loong. He didn't know what it was called, though he recalled seeing something like it on ancient Chinese buildings. The beast stopped at the door, sat down, and lowered its giant head to look at him. The bronze body was powerful and nimble, and in the silvery light of the lunar surface, it appeared to be a god judging all it surveyed.

Chris felt terror creeping up his body as the beast glared down balefully at him.

"What . . . what's going on, Yun Fan?" Chris stammered.

"I told you: you can get all your questions answered by those inside the ship. You're welcome to enter and ask whatever you want."

Chris swallowed. "Are there . . . are there . . . uh . . . more of these . . ."

Yun Fan smiled enigmatically. "Don't tell me you're scared! I thought you wanted me to open the ship for you so that you could learn its secrets. You desire this more than anything else, don't you? Now that I've made your dream come true, why are you hesitating? Well, no matter. To go in or to run away depends entirely on you. I'll do whatever you choose."

Chris stared at the massive bronze beast, his heart thumping hard. After much hesitation, he decided to enter.

Once he followed Yun Fan inside, Chris was surprised to see the interior decorated as an ancient Chinese palace. Yun Fan was walking ahead of him, and even in her bulky space suit, she was striding with the confidence, elegance, and power of an empress of old. Chris's unease grew as they walked, because every thirty meters or so, another metal beast emerged from some concealed chamber along the corridor. Every beast looked different, but they all walked with the same powerful, solemn, arrogant air.

He was absolutely terrified.

Finally, Yun Fan stopped in front of another tunnel.

"We've arrived," she said, making a gesture of invitation.

Chris's heart was racing so fast it threatened to leap out of his chest.

+ + + + +

At that moment, delegates from all over the world were converging on the UN Headquarters in Geneva.

This new headquarters building had been completed only four years ago. The exterior was streamlined and extremely modern, with complex curves that gave viewers the impression of looking at three or four interlocking Möbius strips. Situated on the shore of Lake Geneva, the building was fronted by a smooth, broad lawn studded here and there with seating for coffee. A few medieval churches could be glimpsed farther down the shore, along with a few black swans drifting across the still blue water. The timeless, enchanting scenery seemed designed to evoke in visitors a meditative, Zen mood, in which this mortal world no longer mattered. It was no wonder that despite the chaotic international situation for the last few years, the bureaucrats of the UN seemed perfectly comfortable in their paradisal nook, their duty to maintain the international order forgotten, the colorful flags of all the nations flying out front, relics of some ancient ceremony.

Qi Fei was also on his way here from the airport as part of the staff of a diplomatic delegation consisting of the Director-General of the Pacific League, the League Secretary-General, the Commander-in-Chief, and General Yuan. In the car, the leaders sat silently, their minds preoccupied with the upcoming confrontation with the Atlantic Alliance. Qi Fei was also growing increasingly trepidatious. In his mind, he repeated words of encouragement and focus; Jiang Liu and Chang Tian tried to comfort him as well by adding their emotional strength to his.

On the flight here, Qi Fei had screwed up his courage and asked the League leaders for a chance to make a special presentation. He was scheduled to deliver a report of his space trip to the Security Council; after that, he wanted to give a speech pleading for peace. The speech might also help secure an optimal position for the Pacific League in future dealings with the aliens, he added.

"Many members of the Pacific League, including states in East Asia, South Asia, and Southeast Asia, have historically contributed to the diverse and grand traditions of Confucian philosophy. However, all the diverse strains of Confucianism are united in an emphasis on wangdao, the path of a just and equitable rule, not badao, the path of rule through hegemony and domination. Confucianism prioritizes the interest of all-under-heaven, which means the entire world, over the interests of any individual state or nation. Confucianism has always celebrated those who are concerned about the welfare of the common people, who follow the ideal of love in the form of ren, rather than those who rely on military force to uphold their temporal success. I believe the entire Pacific League can rally around these cultural commitments and ideals."

The Secretary-General and the Commander-in-Chief looked at each other, confused by Qi Fei's speech. General Yuan frowned deeply, apparently displeased by Qi Fei's unexpected boldness.

"Do you think we're in some idealized world of books?" the general muttered. "Our enemy is committed to badao, and you think we can answer their bombs and bullets with ren?"

Qi Fei bowed slightly to General Yuan. "Sun Tzu writes: 'The best path to victory lies through strategy, the next best through diplomacy, and the worst through military force.' If we can, through good strategy and diplomacy, achieve our goals *and* maintain our position of leadership, all without having to resort to any violence, would that not be preferred?"

"What exactly do you have in mind, then?" the Director-General asked. He was an old man with a kind face who seldom made his feelings explicit. He seemed to take everything patiently, always planning several steps ahead.

"I want to suggest the formation of a global team charged with charting humanity's path into the cosmic society of civilizations—and the Pacific League will lead this team."

"Do you really think the Atlantic Alliance will agree to something like that?" General Yuan asked, shaking his head. "You're too young, too idealistic."

"Lao Yuan," the Commander-in-Chief broke in, "I think we should let the young man try. In the worst case, we fall back on our original plan, and we lose nothing. You and I are both ancient, but the world belongs to the young."

The look the Commander-in-Chief gave the general was strange—almost a smile but not quite. Was a subtle power struggle going on? Qi Fei knew that the sort of politics that went on among the brass was beyond his comprehension, and he had no desire to be involved. His discretion had always protected him from factional struggles. All he needed to achieve today was to give that speech; the fewer complications he could create, the better.

After that, the delegation fell quiet. Qi Fei had no idea what the leaders were really thinking; behind those expressionless faces, minds were racing to plot out the future.

As the car passed through the streets of Geneva, he gazed at the neoclassical buildings from the nineteenth century. Time seemed to have stopped in this town.

[Where are you?] Jiang Liu was in his mind.

[About two kilometers away.]

[Are they allowing you to make the speech?]

[Yes. I got them to agree.]

[Excellent work!]

[Are you almost there too?]

[I'm already here.] Jiang Liu's grin could be sensed, even if Qi Fei couldn't see him. [I told my dad and the others to go in first. I'm having coffee by the lake.]

[All right. See you in a few.]

The car stopped. The door opened slowly, and steps gently descended to the curb. Even from a distance, Qi Fei recognized Jiang Liu right away. The other man, clad from head to toe in white, strolled leisurely across the lawn, hands in his pockets, smiling at the pigeons, completely at ease as women stopped to admire him.

Qi Fei deliberately slowed his steps so that the rest of the delegation went on ahead. Jiang Liu noticed him and walked over, smiling happily. He was wearing several new rings—probably instruments to help him with advanced signal processing. Qi Fei waited for him at the edge of the lawn. He was dressed in the black uniform of the military research institute. Though the two men hadn't planned on coordinating their dress, the black and white yin-yang effect felt very appropriate to both.

"Long time no see, Director Qi," Jiang Liu said.

"Doctor Jiang, how have you been?" Qi Fei said.

"Your humble servant stands ready. Thirty million Tianshang members are at their posts, ready to follow your orders."

"I hope I can carry out your plan and fulfill our shared vision."

Shoulder to shoulder, the two strode inside the United Nations.

20 | Reunion

The two entered the conference hall from a small door on the right. Qi Fei turned to the designated seats for the Pacific League delegation, which was on the left side of the horseshoe-shaped conference table. Jiang Liu, on the other hand, went to the middle, where UN staff members sat. For the occasion, Jiang Ruoqin made his son a staff member so that he could help the senior Jiang's plans.

Like every international diplomatic conference, the meeting was boring and slow, filled with ceremony as well as information—if one knew how to interpret it.

As far back as the 2050s, telepresence technology had made in person meetings largely obsolete. But international conferences at the UN had always demanded this most primitive format. Such important meetings, with far-ranging implications for the political, economic, and military future of the world, if conducted via telepresence, would have drawn countless hackers who thought they could change the course of the globe with deepfake A/V, forged IP addresses, even artificial participants. The risk was simply too great. That was why the Security Council held to the rule that these sessions must be in-person. Moreover, to prevent the meetings from being infiltrated by agents in high-tech disguises, participants had to be authenticated by fingerprint, retina scan, DNA sample, and other biometrics.

And thus the UN became the last place to maintain some of the world's oldest customs and ceremonies. Cutting edge companies may show off their technological prowess with new ways to hold meetings: virtual meetings in game worlds, meetings while kitesurfing, puzzle script working meetings, online smoking lounges with crypto channels . . . none of that existed in the UN: an old place with old ways, imbued with a solemnity passed down from earlier generations.

Jiang Ruoqin was betting on this place being ready for change and reform.

He was sitting in the second row, behind the rostrum, not the most prominent place, but central enough to show his importance.

After a few months as the chair of the General Council of the WTO, Jiang Ruoqin had grown dissatisfied. He had then also taken the post of Chair of the Committee of Experts on Rules of Procedure, advising the Security Council and its permanent as well as ad hoc committees. While this committee seemed rather obscure to the public, it was the organ that examined and approved all the rules of procedure governing the Security Council. Since the first Provisional Rules of Procedure, adopted in 1946, the rules had gone through more than a century of evolution, recorded in at least fifteen major revisions. However, the fundamental nature of the rules hadn't changed: Each of the fifteen members of the Security Council had one vote. In a divided world, the council could never reach consensus. Anyone who succeeded in fundamentally reforming the Security Council would instantly become a star on the international stage, a leading candidate to become the next Secretary-General of the UN.

Such was Jiang Ruoqin's political style: never stick out too much, never draw too much attention, but climb up step-by-step, slow and steady, with victory assured at the end. In the casino of life, he had never lost.

He had already spoken many times about structural reform to the current UN Secretary-General as the well as the rotating presidents of the Security Council. But progress was slow and halting. They wanted him to try out his ideas with a few small conferences, to run trials and do follow-up studies. After rounds of data collection and comparison, of phased program demonstrations, maybe one tiny, minuscule step would be taken. Even for the cautious Jiang Ruoqin, this snail's pace was intolerable. His life was too short, and his ambition too grand, to bear it.

He needed to reach his goal in one stride.

By the time it was Jiang Ruoqin's turn to make a speech, he had been observing the delegations of the Atlantic Alliance and the Pacific League for a long time. Today's meeting was, as usual, being presided over by the rotating president of the Security Council, but no one was listening while the president spoke. The arrogant delegates carried on their own conversations, and even those who seemed to be listening obviously had their minds elsewhere. Jiang Ruoqin smiled at them contemptuously.

It was his turn. He stood behind the podium and looked at the delegates from the two major alliances. Then he looked at Jiang Liu, sitting far in the back. Jiang Ruoqin's assistant sat next to Jiang Liu, helping the young man with data and procedure. Everything was ready. Jiang Ruoqin waved his hand, summoning the undulating lines of real-time data to the giant projection screen behind him.

"I'm honored to stand here today. As a simple functionary in the system, I feel incredibly fortunate and excited to deliver to you a progress report on structural reform proposals. Maybe some of you feel that my report has little to do with the main topic of today's discussion, but let me tell you: the importance of today's topic is exactly why we must explore and experiment with better decision-making mechanisms. Times are changing, and new technology is making possible what we couldn't have dreamed of before.

"Blockchain technology, as an information carrier, is unforgeable, auditable, traceable, transparent, and collectively maintained. These features allow it to solve all the problems that plagued old forms of ascertaining popular preferences such as authoritative polls and statistical projections. We believe that using blockchain to conduct opinion polls and referenda will be the best public policy decision-making mechanism going forward.

"Today, we're here to discuss a matter of grave public interest, one that will determine the fate of humanity. That makes it also the best proving ground for the public policy application of blockchain. We've already conducted several small-scale trials with excellent results. Honored delegates, please pay attention to the screen. I will now show you the real-time results of opinion polls conducted via blockchain concerning today's topic, which will inform the council's vote today. Please, don't be anxious, the referenda result on the chain today will not completely decide the issue; it will, instead, only be given a small weight in the overall decision. However, it will play a great part in showing us the will of the people and in legitimizing the decision.

"Observe, if you will, the real-time measure of popular support for various proposals on these graphs. Participants on the chain are evenly spread out all over the globe, with proportional representation from every continent, every country."

The giant world map behind him blinked with countless points of light. Jiang Liu knew that this was a private chain built by his father—yes, it was built in the name of the Security Council, but the funding and the technology infrastructure all came from Jiang Lang Trading. It was, in that sense, similar to his own Tianshang chain. Only natural persons were allowed to be on the UN chain, and there were strict authentication requirements at the time of registration. After that, however, anonymity was scrupulously maintained, and all actions of all members on the chain were completely transparent. Members were free to vote as they liked without any worry of retaliation from political parties or factions. It was the perfect way to conduct an opinion poll. Jiang Liu knew that his father had planned long and hard for this moment.

True, he had always believed in blockchain technology's potential for decentralized decision-making in public policy. Yet, he felt something wasn't quite right here. Why should a decision of the United Nations be founded on a blockchain built by the Jiang family?

Dad is no political philosopher.

But Jiang Liu had to hold back. He had to wait for an opportunity.

After Jiang Ruoqin's speech, the agenda planned for speeches by the Security Council's Ad Hoc Special Mission Committee, the Atlantic Alliance, the Pacific League, and others.

The UN committee's speech was perhaps the most predictable and useless, filled as it was with anodyne, bland diplomatese that said little with much verbiage: "Delegates from all sides exchanged their views in a frank and constructive manner, revealing many points for further elaboration."

The UN committee's views could be boiled down to one point: The alien ship is an artifact of great significance for the entire human species; therefore, it should be turned over to the UN for safekeeping, and the UN would organize an international panel of experts to study it further.

The Atlantic Alliance was prepared to shock and awe the audience. After a few brief introductory remarks, they switched to showing footage from space, accompanied by a carefully scripted narration that attempted to prove that the alien ship was their legally seized prize. The footage showed the carrier battlegroup towing the wheel-shaped alien ship back to the moon, with all signs of the Jiang family's spaceship carefully edited out.

Under the International Agreement on the Regulation of Space Mining, dating back to 2042, if space vessels belonging to any nation successfully moved any nonhuman-made object more than 100 kilometers, that was sufficient to constitute a claim that the object belonged to that nation. This was at least one of the reasons the Atlantic Alliance had deployed a full carrier battlegroup to tow the alien ship back—it gave them a legal excuse.

Confident that their argument would prevail, the Atlantic Alliance delegates ended their presentation with a live broadcast from the moon base. As the rostrum was a large, circular space, the broadcast image took up the entire area, seemingly placing all the attendees onto the moon itself.

Dark, cold sky above the moon; the magnificent loong-ship glowing silver.

The camera had been placed in such a way as to show the entirety of the loong-ship, coiled on the ground like another crater's rim. There was no one in the scene, and no voice spoke over the broadcast.

"Chris. Chris!" the Atlantic Alliance delegate said into the mike. "Are you there?"

No response.

"Chris, what's going on?"

No response.

Clearly, the Atlantic Alliance's plans for this live broadcast, whatever they were, had gone awry. But before the delegate could cut off the feed, the loong-ship began to move.

At first everyone wondered if something was wrong with their eyes. But no, the ship really was moving. Instead of lying flat and still on the lunar surface, it was lifting itself, standing up. Every pair of eyes in the conference hall focused on this incredible sight, unblinking.

Even after the wheel was standing, it continued to rise slowly. The sight filled everyone with a sense of witnessing something sanctified. A moon was rising from the moon. The solemn sight, if properly accompanied by some Hollywood soundtrack, would surely bring the audience to tears.

After the giant wheel had risen to about twenty meters off the lunar surface, the ascent stopped. At the center of the wheel, where all the spokes came together, a circular cabin began to glow. That heart of light grew brighter, bigger, as though a sun were emerging, with each spoke one of its rays.

Abruptly, a human figure appeared in the middle of that blinding light. It was a woman: long hair, flowing white dress, growing bigger by the second. Finally, the woman stood as tall as the ship's diameter, about a kilometer, and the glowing loong-ship hovering behind her was her halo. Her face resembled Yun Fan, but given her hair style, jewels, and pure white dress, she seemed like a goddess out of the ancient legends. The giant goddess-figure loomed over the moon, over the delegates in the UN conference hall, her beautiful face surveying all with tranquility.

Every chin was on the floor.

"I am Changxi, Mother of the Moon. Why have you disturbed me?" Yun Fan–goddess intoned.

Her voice was ethereal, harmonious, powerful. Everyone who heard it shivered, not daring to meet her cold gaze.

"For five thousand years, I've watched over you," Yun Fan–goddess continued. "Who are you? How dare you disturb a peace lasting a thousand years for your selfish ambitions?"

Jiang Liu and Qi Fei strained not to burst out in laughter. Yun Fan's performance was so over the top and yet so . . . "goddessy." The sight of all these generals and ambassadors staring at her in awe was too much; they had to lower their heads before they fell to the ground, convulsing.

The camera began to rotate. Soon, it had turned 180 degrees, showing everyone what had been hidden behind the camera. The sight was, if anything, even more shocking.

A metal beast, about two to three meters tall, a sort of chimera between a loong and a horse, stood in front of the camera, clutching Chris Zhao in one paw. The metal beast was forcing Chris Zhao to gaze up at the goddess in the lunar sky. Even through his space suit visor, Chris's terror was easily seen. He was trembling uncontrollably.

Finally, the dazed Atlantic Alliance delegate had recovered enough to cut off the live feed.

Qi Fei burst out with a single "ha." It was just too much to hold in.

[Get yourself under control!] Jiang Liu spoke in his mind. [It's your turn to perform now.]

[Don't forget your own role,] Qi Fei thought back.

Qi Fei strode up to the podium and bowed slightly. "I thank the Atlantic Alliance for graciously ending their presentation early. My name is Qi Fei, and I'm here to speak for the Pacific League. As the director of Research Institute 907, affiliated with the Northwestern Military District of the Pacific League, I was fortunate to take part in this first-contact mission. I'd like to give a report on what happened."

While Qi Fei was speaking, Jiang Liu turned on his personal VR space and began to stream. True to her word, Tong Yueying had turned footage of his space walk and the loong-ship into a VR clip the previous night and spent a large sum to advertise it. Overnight, the viral VR clip had been experienced 4.5 billion times, and Jiang Liu's account gained almost 9 million new followers.

He took advantage of this new resource now. Titling his live stream "Facts About the Alien Encounter," it quickly became the leading live VR stream on the globe, with five million interactors at the moment and the number going up every millisecond. Jiang Liu focused the VR lens on Qi Fei, and Qi Fei was literally now in the eyes of the world.

The delegates in the conference hall, still unaware of what was happening in virtual space, focused on Qi Fei, hanging on his every word.

"The alien civilization we encountered is highly advanced in technology. I think it's best I show you some video to convey just how advanced."

He waved his baton, which was connected to the A/V console of the conference hall, and began to play a holographic film. It was a compilation of footage taken from several episodes as well as illustrative animations: the alien ship's near–light speed flight, the perfect electromagnetic cloak that made the loong-ship virtually invisible (and his small team's successful decloaking effort), the circuits that continued to function after thousands of years in an empty ship, the ancient Chinese palace inside the alien ship, the bronze human figure inhabited by Huhu, Huhu's lecture on cosmology . . . and finally, the field of pity flowers on the hidden tropical isle. He deliberately skipped over any scenes showing what happened on Liluhuoman.

"The flower at the end here is called a pity flower, a gift from the aliens after we established contact. This flower is capable of photosynthesis at ten thousand times the efficiency of our own chlorophyll. Although we planted a single flower only three days ago, as you can see, by this morning the experimental field has already grown eighteen plants. Incredibly, the root system of the plant is highly interconnected, with high sodium and potassium conductance, similar to our own nervous system. We suspect that the flower itself can become a source of electrical power. This flower is the product of alien science. They're no longer limited to manipulating ordinary matter but have extended their art to life itself and the basis of cognition.

"I selected these scenes to give you a sense of the height the aliens have achieved in the domains of material and energy sciences. Their ship is powered by a kind of dark matter particle that we have yet to discover, and the annihilation of dark matter is what propels them across the universe at such high speeds. More incredibly, they don't even need to cross universes to accomplish this. They can cooperate with another civilization from afar, purely through manipulation of information—the vessel and other objects on the ship were constructed by ancient humans under their direction. In fact, this alien civilization had visited Earth many times already, and we've found evidence of them in the prehistory and history of many ancient human cultures. Sights similar to the goddess visiting us just now had likely occurred multiple times in our ancient past.

"Our biggest takeaway from this alien encounter is this: information exchange is critical to the advance of civilization, to humanity's upgraded future. In the past, each leap in the evolution of human civilization was the result of a massive increase in our methods of information exchange. The next civilizational upgrade likewise requires a corresponding improvement in our ability to communicate and exchange knowledge. We finally understand now that the wisdom of the aliens had already been taught to our ancestors and is recorded in our classical texts. *Liji*, for example, notes the following: 'The Grand Dao manifests in a republic of All-Under-Heaven.' Above the tribe, above the nation, above the state, there is always the grand unifying concept of all-under-heaven. For all mankind to be one brotherhood is the grand dream of every great teacher in our history, and now we know it is also the article of faith of cosmic civilization.

"Thus, I would like to propose that we form a new organization dedicated to the exploration of cosmic civilization, an organization independent of all nations, alliances, even international entities like the United Nations. This organization must belong to all humanity and follow no authority. Its mission is to explore cosmic society, to establish contact with extraterrestrial civilizations, to assist all humankind in our grand leap into the next stage of our scientific, cognitive, and civilizational advancement. I propose we call them the Jumpnauts.

"I also propose that the four explorers who established contact with aliens on this trip be named the founding Jumpnauts. Although all four of them come from the Pacific League, we pledge to give our discoveries to all humanity, with no conditions whatsoever."

After Qi Fei finished, the hall was silent. Even the constant hum of chatter among the delegates was gone. The powerful men and women seemed to have trouble digesting Qi Fei's speech, and the mood in the hall was oppressive, like the deceptive lull right before a storm.

Just then, the conference hall doors banged open to reveal an anxious assistant, who raced up to the president of the Security Council and whispered something. The president, looking worried, asked the assistant a few questions before standing up to announce. "Delegates, council members, we need to finish our discussion and put the resolution to a vote. Unexpectedly, today's meeting has become a focal point online because of a live stream of the proceedings. More than 430 million have watched the stream, and public opinion is extremely volatile and spinning out of control. There are thousands now gathered outside the doors to this conference hall, demanding to be allowed in. A riot may be imminent. For everyone's safety, we must end the discussion and get to a vote as quickly as possible."

"What does the public want?" the head of the Pacific League delegation asked.

"Their main demand is to be allowed a voice in this decision," the president of the Security Council said. "Since this matter affects every person, they don't want to be excluded. There are also agitators deliberately provoking the crowd. I'm afraid the mob will make their way in here if we delay much longer."

"Then let's get to the vote."

Traditional political leaders generally disliked giving public opinion too much influence in high-level meetings. The will of the people was good as a general reference and could be given some weight in the final decision, but the key votes, the direct power to decide, have always been held by a few, the ones closest to the core of power. Moreover, the tradition of one-country, one-vote had guided the work of the Security Council for centuries and was viewed as an unalterable principle. As the delegates rushed to vote, the scene felt chaotic, sloppy, the earlier feeling of elite wise elders confidently declaring the fate of billions long gone.

The vote didn't go the way anyone anticipated. After the 2056 reforms, the veto power of certain members of the Security Council had been eliminated. The new voting procedure involved competing proposals, and whichever proposal won at least two-thirds of the votes passed. For this vote, the competing proposals were the following: the United Nations suggested a UN agency take up the task of analyzing the loong-ship and communicating with alien civilizations; the Atlantic Alliance proposed having a research institute within the Alliance to perform these duties; the Pacific League, likewise, nominated an institute from the League. The fifteen member nations of the Security Council had fifteen votes, one for each state, and two more votes were allocated to public opinion as expressed on the United Nation's blockchain, which Jiang Ruoqin had just announced.

During the first round of voting, every country voted for its own major alliance or league, while smaller alliances and neutral states voted for the United Nations. Naturally, no proposal managed to win more than even half the votes, let along two-thirds.

At that point, the Pacific League switched tactics. The delegation suddenly announced that Qi Fei's proposal had been adopted as the League's proposal, and this new proposal soon earned the support of the vacillating neutral states. Even more dramatically, the two votes allocated to the public opinion as determined by the United Nations blockchain, which had originally supported the UN proposal, suddenly switched to supporting the Pacific League.

The bell sounded. A two-thirds majority had been reached, and Qi Fei's proposal had been adopted as the UN resolution.

Only Jiang Liu knew how this had happened. Jiang Ruoqin's blockchain, being still only an experiment, had only registered about seventy million natural persons—including thirty million Tianshang members that Jiang Liu had introduced to his father. The Tianshang members had withheld their votes early on. But in a critical moment, they voted as a bloc for the Pacific League, thereby changing the outcome of the public referendum.

The deal between the father and the son had been about this bloc vote. Jiang Liu had fulfilled the terms of the deal, except the chain had not voted the way his father wanted.

At that moment, the doors of the conference hall slammed open, and an excited crowd rushed in. The crowd was largely made up of young people in their teens and twenties, who shouted: "We love aliens!" "We want a voice!" "We get to decide!"

The elderly or middle-aged politicians in the hall were all reminded of their own youthful days. Every new generation required some social cause to rally around, to provide an outlet for their energy. For this generation, perhaps "We love aliens" would be that cause.

The experienced delegates from the Atlantic Alliance and the Pacific League got up and, under the protection of bodyguards, began to retreat from the hall.

Jiang Liu and Qi Fei were overjoyed. They had not planned a way to get out after the vote, but the present chaos was perfect for their purposes.

[Go! Go!] Jiang Liu shouted in Qi Fei's mind. Without looking back, he headed for one of the emergency exits.

"I'm afraid these children are here because of me," Qi Fei said to General Yuan and the Commander-in-Chief. "Please get to safety. I'll stay and talk to them." Once the leaders had left, he ran after Jiang Liu.

The two pushed through the emergency exit and entered the maintenance area. Deliberately avoiding other people, they wended their way through the maze-like warren of tunnels until they found a driverless truck, which they used as their escape vehicle.

Once they reached the shore of Lake Geneva, they abandoned the truck and ran. After they ran for about a kilometer, a helicopter finally descended from the clouds. Chang Tian waved at them from the door of the helicopter.

A few pedestrians recognized Qi Fei and Jiang Liu. However, by the time the news spread, the two had long since climbed into the helicopter and departed for a destination unknown.

+ + + + +

Warm breeze, palm trees, golden sandy beach. The wooden hut on this isle was crude and lacked amenities. But to the four, drinking beer and eating fresh fruit, it was heaven.

"You're lucky to come now," Chang Tian said, slicing more fruit. "The first couple of days after we got here, there was nothing. Even the roof leaked. I spent two full days doing repairs and then two more shopping. You're literally enjoying the fruit of my labors."

While gnawing on a chicken wing, Jiang Liu asked, "How did you decide on this place?"

"We had to find somewhere on Earth with easy access to a lot of water, which meant a shore somewhere. But much of the world's continental seacoast is now a battlefield, so that left the islands. But we couldn't pick anywhere in the South China Sea, the Philippine Sea, or the Indian Ocean—again, too much fighting or too much shipping traffic. In the end we had to look in the remotest parts of the Pacific for uninhabited islands. This archipelago ended up as the best choice since it's far from all the continents and has lots of wild fruit. Actually, we picked this specific isle because of this wooden hut—it was probably a shelter for workers who had once tried to build a lighthouse here, but the lighthouse was never finished, and the site abandoned. Maybe they ran out of money."

"I like it here," Jiang Liu said. "Also, it's not too far from Hawaii. I'll go back to my place and pick up a few books later."

"Is Huhu all right?" Qi Fei asked. "Why are they still sleeping?"

"They're fine." Chang Tian laughed. "I was just as scared at first. As soon as we landed, they fell asleep—you know, during the two days I was patching up the hut. They slept straight for fifty hours, and I was so terrified, thinking that they must have died because our universe is incompatible with their body. But as far as I could tell, the bio signs were all good. Only later did I find out that Huhu's species has very long sleep cycles. You have no idea what I went through. I had to worry about the three of you fighting, about the leaky hut, and about a possibly dead alien . . . anyway, I'm sure Huhu was tired after that trip to the moon. They need a long sleep to recover."

"We were worried about you too!" Yun Fan said. "How come you never contacted us over the gryon channel?"

"I don't know either," Chang Tian said. "I was using your necklace to communicate with Huhu, but then I couldn't reach you anymore. It was very odd."

"So what happened to your performance yesterday?" Jiang Liu asked. "I thought we only planned for Yun Fan to show up as a goddess, but why did you end up using the bronze beasts? Was it Huhu?"

"You got it," said Chang Tian. "Huhu was worried that if only Yun Fan performed, it wouldn't be convincing. So they used the equipment in the escape pod to jump into different metal beasts to perform with Yun Fan. It was quite an effort!"

"No kidding!" Yun Fan said. "I was so worried about Huhu. As I walked down the corridor, every thirty meters or so, a new metal beast would step out to greet me and Chris. I had to walk as slowly as possible to give Huhu more time to jump to the next beast before we arrived."

Jiang Liu laughed so hard that the beer went down the wrong pipe. "Oh my goodness! Your troupe needs a bigger budget! I can't believe you had to use one actor to pretend to be all those extras."

"Did Chris Zhao really think some spirit had come into the mortal world?" Qi Fei asked.

"I have no idea," Yun Fan replied, shaking her head and laughing. "I could see he was very scared, but he was still straining to process everything through reason. I'm sure he was confused. After they cut off the broadcast, the Atlantic Alliance sent a team from the moon base to retrieve us. They separated me from him and wouldn't let me see him. Anyway, I'm sure they're embarrassed and don't want anyone to bring up the topic again."

"I'm glad they listened to me and sent you to Australia from the moon," Qi Fei said. "If they had repatriated you back to Xi'an . . . I doubt you'd be allowed to leave the country again."

"You are a celebrity now!" Jiang Liu said to Qi Fei. "That's why they listened to you—no one wants to annoy the hero of the Pacific League, am I right?"

"But what are we going to do in the future?" Yun Fan asked. "We're sort of like fugitives. I doubt the Atlantic Alliance and the Pacific League will just let us go like that. We can't spend the rest of our lives on this island, can we?"

"Why not?" Jiang Liu asked. "I'd love to spend the rest of my life here. I'll never have to see my father again. I can imagine him taking it all out on Uncle Bo right now. Poor Uncle Bo! 'Jiang Liu! What did I do in my last life to deserve you? Wahhh! Next time I catch you, I'll teach you a lesson you'll never forget!' Well, better him than me."

Yun Fan tried not to laugh. "That's not the worst impression of your Uncle Bo, I guess."

Chang Tian turned to Jiang Liu. "Is your father really going to be okay with how things turned out? What if he investigates?"

"Let him investigate! It will make no difference. He was the one who proposed letting public opinion on his blockchain decide two votes, so he has only himself to blame for the way the vote turned out. Even if I hadn't given the signal, I'm sure the Tianshang members would have supported Qi Fei's proposal. As victims of this never-ending war, they wouldn't trust any alliance or league or the UN—they want a truly independent organization. The will of the people is like water: it's strong enough to float a steel aircraft carrier, but it can also send the ship to the bottom of the ocean. If you want to listen to the will of the people, then you have to obey it when it goes against your own desire. My father may be calculating and manipulative, but he is bound by his own rules."

"Listen to you! So well-reasoned!" Qi Fei was laughing. "Then why don't you go home and present this argument to your father?"

"Eh, even if my father accepts the result of the vote, it doesn't mean he won't make my life hell. A kid who knows he's right can still be spanked, you get me?"

"Well, we can't just carry on like this forever," Qi Fei said. "We have to go home at some point."

"Fine, you go back and negotiate with the bigwigs. The rest of us will relax here. You can stay the great hero, and we'll help you out as much as we can."

"What makes you think I'll let you have all the fun? Aha, you want to send me away so you get to spend all this time on a tropical island with Fanfan. I'm not going to let you."

Jiang Liu laughed. He picked up an apple and bit into it. "You're not going to let me? I'm not sure you've earned that. Tell you what, let's see if you can cut a piece out of this apple."

He jumped away from the table. Qi Fei grabbed a small pocketknife and ran after him. Once again, the two began to spar. While Qi Fei tried to grab Jiang Liu's hand and slice off a piece of the apple with his knife, Jiang Liu dodged and weaved, tossing the apple from hand to hand to keep it away from Qi Fei, with an occasional taunting bite of the juicy fruit. Soon, the two got into the fight and started to use their most advanced martial arts techniques. Running, leaping, spinning, flipping, parrying, deflecting, the two chased each other from the hut to the beach, and then into the surf.

Yun Fan and Chang Tian gazed at the two, mesmerized.

At length, Chang Tian shook his head. "These two . . . sometimes I wonder if they aren't really three years old."

"It's fun to watch them play," Yun Fan said. "Reminds me of when we were little. Remember how, when I first moved into your neighborhood, you and Qi Fei were always fighting too? You used to cry after, but in a few minutes, you'd forget and look for Qi Fei again. That's childhood."

"Fanfan, the best part of this trip for me is watching you change. You're remembering the past, our childhood, which tells me you're doing better. When you first showed up in my bistro, I was so worried about you. From head to toe you had the air of death. The others were too dull to feel it, but I could. I've learned to trust my intuition; it's like the sense of a shaman."

"That . . . feels like a lifetime ago."

"I went on this mission not for Qi Fei, but for you. I don't always follow Qi Fei and his sense of duty—if I cared so much about his missions, I wouldn't have left the air force. But when I saw how you were already half-dead and those two idiots didn't even realize it, I knew I had to come along."

"Thank you," Yun Fan said. Tears spilled from her eyes. "You're too good."

"That's silly," Chang Tian said. "Don't cry over that! I'm doing exactly what I wanted. I left my life as a military pilot because I knew I could help those with trauma. My intuition told me not to waste my talent."

"You really did help us. Without you, I think the three of us would have killed one another once our minds were connected."

"Hurting each other is the way most of us go through life. But it's all because we haven't reconciled with ourselves. You have to go slowly and learn to accept yourself, and so do those two."

"I don't know if I can do it."

"You have plenty of time."

Chang Tian and Yun Fan gazed at the beach. The setting sun colored the horizon orange-pink and purple-red.

"I don't know what's going to happen next," Yun Fan said, sipping her beer. "I don't know the nature of my relationship to those two, either. I don't think it's romance, but I don't know what to call it. I feel . . . it's a life-bond. I mean, I'm willing to put my life in their hands, and I won't be afraid. That's it."

"You dare to show them your shadows," Chang Tian said, handing her a piece of cake. "That takes courage. It doesn't matter what you call your relationship. The four of us are an experiment, an experiment for the benefit of all humanity. We're trying to see how human relationships can develop and grow in this next stage. The names we give to our relationships aren't important; what's important is that we continue to trust one another. We share this life-bond; we advance together."

"Do you think we can really do it?"

"No one can know the future. I don't think we've experienced truly dark moments, not yet."

"Only when we've borne darkness will we find light, right?" Yun Fan was staring at the setting sun, and her hair glowed red.

"We still have a long future ahead of us," Chang Tian said. "That's why we must eat well and laugh well. This is our most important concern of this moment."

Smiling together, the two clinked glasses.

A sound came from the hut behind them. *Thump-thump.*

They turned to find Huhu, who had just awakened, at the door.

"I heard from the captain!" Huhu was ecstatic. "The captain and the others are alive!"

"Wonderful!" Yun Fan felt so much joy. "What did the captain say?"

Chang Tian stood up to shout at the distant surf. "Hey, you two delinquents, get back here! Huhu heard from the captain!"

Qi Fei and Jiang Liu ceased their game and ran back. All four crowded around Huhu. After hungrily devouring two plates of fruit, Huhu wiped their mouth and said, "Captain Te and the other leaders of our planet fought with everything they've got and managed to repel the enemy. Most of my world lies in ruins, but our wisdom hoard remains intact, and half of our population has survived. Taking advantage of this temporary reprieve, they're busy rebuilding. The captain told me that during the most desperate part of the fight, they suddenly realized how to control and manipulate gravitational fields. This means that we would soon be upgrading our civilization to the next stage!"

"Marvelous!" Jiang Liu exclaimed.

"Is there any way I can learn the secrets about gravity manipulation as well?" Qi Fei asked.

"Now I think you have something to do!" Jiang Liu laughed. "I think the road ahead is still very long."

"Ah, but knowledge is infinite, while life is finite . . ." Qi Fei said.

"To pursue the infinite with the finite, that is courage!" Jiang Liu said.[19]

Everyone smiled and raised their glasses together. Foam spilled from the glasses and seeped between the fingers of dusk. They began to feast on coconuts and chicken soup, to drink and tell stories. Night descended over the island, and a brilliant Milky Way shone overhead in the crystal-clear sky. This spot of earth, lit by a bare bulb in a tiny wooden hut, was the warmest corner of the universe.

After dinner, there remained one more task.

Jiang Liu carved the hanzi into a wooden board; Qi Fei climbed onto a tall stool and hung the sign under the eaves.

Jumpnauts.

In the future, they'd find more official spots and more official-looking signs: maybe on the moon, maybe among the peaks of the Himalayas, maybe near the headquarters of the UN. There would be an official-looking building, what outsiders would know as the headquarters of the Jumpnauts.

But for them, this island, this hut, would always be the real headquarters.

Qi Fei was hammering the nail so hard that the beam over the door cracked. They had to look for a strip of metal to reinforce it.

"Maybe I should take over," Jiang Liu said from below. "You seem to be not very good at this."

"Stop yapping. If you want to help, go find a nut for me," Qi Fei said, standing atop the stool. "There's a bolt in place already, but I need a nut."

Jiang Liu looked around and found some random piece of hardware that he handed up. "Here. This should work."

"This is a washer. Don't you know what a nut is? Have you never fixed anything? I can't believe you were lecturing me."

"Get off!" Jiang Liu tried to pull Qi Fei from the stool. "Let me show you how it's done. I bet I can get that sign fixed in seconds."

Chang Tian had to intervene before the two started fighting again. He

---

19   The two are (deliberately) misquoting Zhuangzi here. In the original, to pursue the infinite with the finite is a recipe for disappointment and disaster.

climbed onto the stool and did his best to fix the sign in place. The carved hanzi were like chicken scratch; the sign itself was lopsided. Yet under the stars there was a beauty to it all, a sense of home.

The group stood under the sign, quietly thinking, imagining. They felt that the sign was the beginning of the curtain lifting, but they didn't yet know what drama would play out on the grand stage of the future. The road ahead was long, and they knew that they were not afraid. In the darkness of the unknown cosmos, they knew they would find light, the light in one another's hearts.

That was how the Jumpnauts came to be.

Translator's
Acknowledgments

I'm grateful to James Enge for coming up with "gryon" (based on Greek γρῦ, "a bit") as the name for the information-carrying particle in the novel.

Much gratitude to my wife, Lisa, who provided valuable feedback on the text. Thank you, as always, to Emily Jin for beta reading.

I thank my agent, Russell Galen; my editor, Joe Monti; and everyone at Simon & Schuster who, together, made this translation possible: Amara Hoshijo, Jéla Lewter, Jennifer Bergstrom, Jennifer Long, Eliza Hanson, Michelle Marchese, Sirui Huang, Lisa Litwack, Caroline Pallotta, Emily Arzeno, Ashley Cullina, Amanda Mulholland, Lauren Gomez, Zoe Kaplan, Bianca Ducasse, Kaitlyn Snowden, Alexandre Su, Paul O'Halloran, Rachel Podmajersky, and Fiona Sharp.

Finally, my heartfelt congratulations to Hao Jingfang, author and jumpnaut.